The Match maker

BOOKS BY CATHERINE WALSH

One Night Only

The Rebound

Holiday Romance

CATHERINE WALSH

The Matchmaker

bookouture

Published by Bookouture in 2023

An imprint of Storyfire Ltd.
Carmelite House
50 Victoria Embankment
London EC4Y 0DZ

www.bookouture.com

ISBN: 978-1-80314-916-5
eBook ISBN: 978-1-80314-915-8

This one's for Rachel

CONTENT NOTE

This book features parental death (in the past, off-page). If this is potentially sensitive for you, please read with care.

CHAPTER ONE

I wake at precisely three minutes past seven to the sound of the world exploding. I know the time exactly because that's what my grandmother's old alarm clock tells me when my eyes snap open. I know the world is exploding because surely there is nothing else in the history of mankind that could make such a blaring, deafening noise, especially at three minutes past seven in the goddamn morning.

For a few moments, I simply lie there, my heart racing as the beeping of a reversing vehicle joins the racket, followed by another bang, one that shudders through the house until I swear the bed vibrates with it. When another one sounds two seconds later, I know there's no way I'm getting back to sleep.

I sit up, plucking my useless earplugs out and throwing the mound of blankets off my bed. My phone clatters to the floor as I do, but I ignore it, my initial shock turning to righteous fury as I grab a sweater from my chairdrobe and pull it over my head.

"Granny!"

There's no answer as I march down the stairs, but that's not surprising. The noise is worse at the front of the house, with loud crashes and pounding drills filling the hallway until it's all

I can hear. By the front door, Plankton, my terminally lazy eight-year-old border collie, beats his tail once on the floor in acknowledgment of my presence and struggles to his feet. He's not used to me being up this early and gets no rest now he has to guard the two of us all day.

"Granny!"

I hit the last step and turn left, almost slipping in my haste as I enter the kitchen and find my grandmother sitting at the table.

Maeve Collins, my father's mother, is a tall, thin woman with a thick head of white hair, a bad hip, and a general apathy toward most things in life. She is eighty-two years old and though her body is starting to go, her mind is as sharp as ever. I love her with my whole heart, which is why I choose to ignore the slightly defensive look she gives me when I appear, as well as the distinct smell of tobacco that the open window behind her does nothing to mask.

She said she stopped smoking when I moved in with her after my parents died. Or at least she did for about three months until she caved. Now she has one in the morning and one at night and thinks I don't know about it. It doesn't bother me, though. I figure if she's made it this far in life, she might as well do what she likes.

"You're up early," is all she says when I come to a stop before her. Plankton makes it as far as the kitchen door before collapsing down again with a weary sigh.

"Only by four or five hours. Do you not hear that?"

"Of course I hear it. I'm old, not deaf."

"And you're just..." I gesture at the cup of coffee and half-filled crossword beside her. The domestic scene is so normal it's almost sickening. "*Fine* with it?"

"Why wouldn't I be?"

"Because I can barely hear myself think!" I exclaim, as what sounds like an entire army passes by the end of our lane.

She only huffs. "It's just a few trucks."

"It is not just a few trucks; it's a punishment."

"A punishment for what? And by who?"

"I don't know! The government?" I wince at another bang and swear I see the door rattle on its hinges. Granny doesn't seem to notice. "They shouldn't be allowed to get away with this," I continue, closing the window behind her. "I have rights."

"Seven a.m. is a perfectly legal and acceptable time to begin a day's work."

"Not when *I* work until one a.m." My hands go to my hips, my mood worsened by her refusal to immediately and unequivocally take my side. I'm so tired I can barely stand up straight. It's been three days of this. Three days of being woken before dawn, of being pulled from broken sleep to the commotion that surrounds me now. That will surround me for the next eight hours unless I put my foot down.

"I can't keep doing this. I can't. I'm going to go talk to them."

"What do you mean, you— *no*, Katie."

Granny's chair scrapes back as she stands, but I'm already spinning away, shoving my feet into a pair of rubber boots. Somewhere in the tiny, still clear-thinking part of my brain, I know the best thing I can do right now is go back to bed, that this is just several days of sleep deprivation talking, but the bigger, angrier part thinks this is a *great* idea.

"I'm going to find the person in charge and I'm going to talk to them," I say, my voice a good octave higher than usual. "I'm going to take a stand."

"It's not a stereo system," Granny reminds me, as she follows me down the hall. Plankton trails at her heels, giving me the stink eye. "You can't just ask them to turn it down."

No, but I can throw myself dramatically into the middle of the road and force them to stop.

Okay, maybe not that.

"You're not even dress—"

"Be right back," I call and swing the door shut behind me.

The chilly bite of late March greets me as soon as I do, and I fill my lungs with the cold air as I half purposefully stride/half awkwardly jog down the lane. It's still dark out, the sun only just beginning to rise, but the sleepy road our house is on, the one that sees maybe a handful of cars on a normal day, is lit up like a Christmas tree with orange cones and a flashing one-way traffic system. They even have a very bored, very cold-looking man standing by one of them, a walkie-talkie clutched in his hand as he buries his chin in his hi-vis jacket.

I ignore him as he ignores me and follow a passing van up the road that leads to the belly of the beast. The cause of the chaos. The bane of my existence.

The soon-to-be Ennisbawn Hotel and Golf Club.

An exclusive five-star resort featuring a spa, a stud farm, and a rumored Michelin-starred chef in the kitchens, the thing sounds more at home in some tropical utopia than rural Ireland, yet this is where they're building it.

When the church sold off the old convent that used to be here, they included most of the land that went with it, handing it all over to a large development company called Glenmill Properties. We were excited about it at the time. Sleepy towns are all well and good when you have people to fill them, but in recent years whenever anyone moved out, no one else moved in, and we were all tired of passing by the same abandoned buildings and empty fields.

All of a sudden, there was talk of jobs and tourists and getting onto an actual bus route. We got newsletters and glossy brochures through our doors promising how Glenmill weren't just going to revive the area. Oh, no. They were going to turn this place into one of the top vacation spots in Europe. They were going to put Ennisbawn on the map and change our lives for the better.

It all seemed too good to be true.

Probably because it was.

They bought two hundred acres, then three, and then five. The proposed site kept growing, eating up more and more land until, one day, the fields I'd played in as a child were off-limits, and half the routes through the forest were blocked off by a chain-link fence and a sign saying "Private." Trees were cut down, roads were cut off, and by the time we tried to push back, it was too late. Our emails went unanswered, our objections unheard, and slowly but surely, Ennisbawn began to shrink, disappearing before our eyes.

It's horrifying to watch. But we aren't going down without a fight. Protests, petitions, letters to the council. We're doing what we can, but, personally, I've always considered myself more of a lover than a fighter. Not great with the whole raising my voice thing. I mean, I marched and I signed, but I also worked full-time and looked after my granny and didn't really see how we could stop what was happening, especially once the construction work started.

But this? This right here?

This is my snapping point.

You do *not* mess with a girl's sleep cycle.

I round the bend, my steps more like stomps as I reach the entrance to the main site. Where there used to be green fields bordered by overgrown hedges now sits one giant, muddy hole. Or at least that's what it looks like. Thick wooden boards block most of it from public view, but the metal gates locked shut at night are pushed open now, letting in the steady stream of vehicles that woke me so rudely this morning. Among them, hundreds of people go about their day, moving purposefully among the chaos.

I go unnoticed.

Maybe it's because it's still dark, or maybe they can sense that I'm five seconds away from yelling at someone, but they all keep a wide berth as I approach the entry, slipping in alongside a truck whose job seems to be carrying more dirt to add to the dirt.

I have no idea who to talk to.

I hadn't really thought this far ahead. If we're being honest, I hadn't really thought at all, but I keep moving, sneaking farther inside as I search for someone who looks vaguely in charge.

Easier said than done.

There's no one walking around with a sign saying "TOP DOG" around their neck. No stern-faced overseer surveying his kingdom. Just a bunch of bleary-eyed workmen who barely give me a second glance before hurrying away with a real sense of *nope! Not paid enough to deal with that!*

"Excuse... hello? Hi." I grab the arm of the nearest person, a scruffy-looking guy who does *not* look old enough to be on a construction site and force him to stop. "Can you tell me who's the boss around here?"

The manboy frowns, his eyebrows drawing so close together they almost meet. "You mean our site manager?"

"Sure. Yes. Where are they?"

"He's..." The frown deepens as he takes me in. "Are you supposed to be here?"

"Yes."

He doesn't know what to do with that. But you say something with enough confidence, and I guess anything can happen.

"Uh, okay. I guess I could see if—"

"Justin."

The kid visibly sighs in relief as a deep voice rumbles what must be his name, and I whirl around, a rant on the tip of my tongue, only to come face to face with possibly the most gorgeous man I have ever seen.

Well, that's just unfair.

Deep-set green eyes gaze over my shoulder as I falter, falling at the first hurdle. Strong jawline covered in dark stubble, strands of jet-black hair peeking out from beneath his hard hat. I have to crane my neck to look at him, and as the resident tall girl in the village, that's saying something.

"Is there a problem?" he asks.

"There is," I say, before Justin can respond. I hear him scampering away, but I don't bother to check, not when the newcomer snaps his attention to me, pinning me with his stare. "I..."

I trail off as his gaze drops down, lingering on my legs. Or to be fair to the guy, I presume not so much my legs as the pajama bottoms that cover them. The pajama bottoms that feature a dozen yellow ducks in rain jackets that I now really wish I wasn't wearing.

I clear my throat, but it takes him a moment to look back up again. His expression blank, bordering on bored, doesn't change.

"Are you in charge?" I ask.

"No."

"Can you tell me who is?"

His walkie-talkie crackles at his hip, but he doesn't reach for it, just continues to stare at me like he didn't even hear what I said.

"You know you've got..." He lifts a hand to his cheek, and I just about want to die when I remember I'm still wearing the overnight eye masks I bought. The ones I put on to try and help my puffy, sleep-deprived face this morning.

"I know," I say, making a split-second decision to go with it. "They're meant to be there."

A pause.

"Okay."

"Look, I would like to discuss the noise levels of your site," I say in my most professional voice. "Are you someone I can talk to about that, or are you— excuse me!"

My mouth drops open as the man walks past me, not even listening. I follow him immediately, indignation fueling my steps as I hurry to keep up with his long strides.

"I'm talking to you! You can't just—"

He stops so abruptly that I almost walk into him, and I can only stand there in confusion as he grabs a spare hard hat from a pile by the Portakabin and places it on my head.

"Health and safety," he explains. The words are serious, but I'm almost certain he's making fun of me. "Have you signed in?"

"I... no, I—"

"You need to sign in to get a visitor's pass. You need a visitor's pass to walk around the site. Did you talk to Leon?"

"I didn't talk to anyone," I say, growing frustrated. "I just walked in. It's not my problem if your security is non-existent."

"No," he agrees. "It's mine."

The way he says it makes me hesitate, and I reach up to straighten the helmet. I've always had a lot of hair, frizzy brown curls that I've never managed to tame, and they're already trying to push the thing off my head.

"I don't want to get anyone in trouble," I begin.

"But you're fine with roaming around an active construction site with no protective equipment?"

"Well, I have a hat now," I mumble, and a long silence stretches between us.

"What did you say you wanted to discuss?" he asks eventually, and I try to remember the whole point of this.

"The noise levels."

He gives me a look. "The noise levels."

"Yes."

"Of a construction site."

"*Yes*, I..." I pause, not liking his tone. "Okay, look, Mr.—"

"Callum."

"Callum," I repeat. "I know, okay? I know what I look like right now. I know what I sound like right now. And that? *This?*

It's because of you. Because you have woken me up every morning for the past three mornings several hours before I'm meant to, meaning I don't get any sleep, meaning I am..." I gesture down at myself, ducks and all. "This. This is who I am now. And I'm not usually like this. I am usually normal. Like, to an embarrassing extent normal. But right now, I can't be. Instead, I have become the ranting woman in her pajamas who forgets to remove her eye masks."

"Thought you said you meant to—"

"I lied. You've also made me a liar. Happy?"

His lips twitch. Real blink-and-you'll-miss-it stuff, but, judging by how dry my eyes feel, I don't think I've blinked once since yesterday, so I see it just fine.

I'm nothing but a joke to him right now.

Which, alright, fair, I guess.

I fight to maintain my newfound bravado, feeling a headache forming. "Can you just give me the number of someone I could—"

"I'm sorry about the noise," Callum interrupts. "It sounds like hell. But there's nothing we can do about it."

"I disagree. There are lots of things you can do. For example, do you have to start work at seven in the morning?"

"Yes."

"*Yes?*"

"We need to maximize daylight and good weather. It's a tight schedule."

"Oh, you want to talk about schedules?"

"Not particularly," he says with a straight face.

"I don't finish work until *one a.m.*," I say, ignoring him. "And then it's not like I just magically fall into bed ten minutes later. I'm not even in my deep sleep stage when you guys come screaming down the road. Do you know how important deep sleep is?"

"No."

"Well, I do," I snap. "I know all about it. It's when my immune system strengthens. When my bones repair themselves. My *bones*."

"Sounds important."

"It is! It's extremely important. And I'm not getting enough of it, and you're just... you're..." I struggle to find the words, so exhausted I might cry, which would be the embarrassed cherry on top of this crappy morning, to be honest.

Around us, the world has started to lighten, gloomy blue giving way to dull gray, and the pounding in my head begins to beat in time with a nearby hammer as everyone else gets on with their lives, paying no heed to the lone dissenter in her pajamas.

I can't believe I'm still wearing my freaking eye masks.

"I'm sorry about your bones," Callum says, when I just stand there. "But I'm going to have to ask you to leave before you trip over something, and I have to fill in a lot of paperwork."

"Wouldn't want that," I mutter, but he just motions back to the gate I came through and starts walking. When I fail to come up with a brilliant new plan, I have no choice but to follow.

Maybe I just won't sleep.

I'll be the girl who doesn't sleep. That can be my thing.

Or I could get really into micro-napping. That's what tech bros do, isn't it? They record bad podcasts and they micro-nap? I could micro-nap. I could...

I lose that train of thought as what little energy is left in my brain zeroes in on a small group of people walking toward us.

Even with the hard hats adorning their heads, they immediately stand out from the rest of the workers. These people are dressed for the boardroom in expensive corporate clothing and shiny shoes. But it's not the outfits that catch my attention, not the woman with the microphone, or the camera balanced on one of the men's shoulders. It's the man they're both focused on, the one leading the pack as he comes to a halt nearby and starts to talk.

Young and handsome in that bland way all rich people are, I wouldn't have given him a second glance if not for the fact that his face has been plastered all over the leaflets that arrive through our front door every week. Leaflets that many of my neighbors have started taping to the pub dartboards to practice their aim. Sure, the guy looks different without his eyes crossed out and a dart sticking out of his mouth, but I recognize him instantly.

And I know he's the one in charge.

"Mind your step," Callum calls. "It's muddy here." He glances over his shoulder when I don't respond, stopping when he realizes I'm no longer following him. "Let's go," he prompts, a slight warning in his voice, but I don't pay any attention to it or to him, too distracted by the newcomers.

"Do you think *he* can help?" I ask, as they approach.

"No." The word is firm, and yet I take a slow sidestep, testing my guard's reflexes.

"Maybe I should ask him and check."

"Maybe you should— *hey!*"

Callum's shout draws the attention of several people around us, and I break into a short run as he lunges after me.

"You," I say, as Blondie turns at the commotion. "Leaflet guy."

"Leaflet— what?" The man steps back, as if being too close to me might give him some sort of disease. "Can I help you?"

"You can," I say, as Callum comes to a stop behind me. "How about you start by getting out of my village?"

"Your village?" He doesn't seem to have heard me, too busy staring at my pajama pants. "Callum?"

"I'm sorry, Jack," Callum says, and the man's name suddenly comes to me. *Jack Doyle.* A managing director of

Glenmill. The one who'd bought the land for them in the first place. "She was just leaving."

"No, she wasn't," I say, standing my ground despite the increasing number of people side-eyeing us as they go past. Jack notices them too, his bafflement smoothing into professionalism as he recovers like a pro.

"I'm afraid I didn't catch your name."

"Katie Collins. And I—"

"It's a pleasure to meet you, Katie." He grabs my hand and shakes it until I jerk away. "I'm going to guess you're from Ennisbawn?"

"Yes. And I—"

"You know, the community here is one of the primary reasons we chose this area," he continues, his voice rising as the cameraman angles the shot slightly, taking him in. "As well as the wealth of natural beauty, it's really the people that make it so—"

"Are you *high*?"

Callum makes a pained noise from somewhere over my shoulder, as Jack's gaze narrows on me.

"You don't care about the community," I say, jabbing a finger through the air. "You don't want anything to do with us. You don't even talk to us."

"I have to disagree. We're in constant communication with—"

"Dropping letters through our doors is not communication, it's junk mail." I step in front of him, vaguely aware of Callum trying to snatch me back as I move in view of the camera. "Glenmill doesn't answer our emails or our calls, and the only thing you're doing is taking away land until there'll be nothing left. That's all you want and that's all you care about, and I'm not putting up with it anymore. A girl needs her sleep!"

"Her what?"

"She wants to talk to someone about the noise levels," Callum explains. "Something about her bones."

Jack stares at him, but my attention has shifted to the woman with the microphone, who's watching us like a soap opera.

"I can give you an interview," I say, focusing on her and her shiny black bob. "Lots of people can. We've been trying to get ahold of the press for months. If you just let me go back and get dressed, we can—"

"I'm sorry," she interrupts, glancing back at the cameraman. "I'm not a journalist. I'm part of the Glenmill marketing department. We're making a promotional video for the website."

"A what?"

She grimaces, adding in a *yeah, yikes for you* little shrug that extinguishes a good chunk of my energy until I'm almost swaying in place.

No one says anything for a long moment, and then Jack swipes his hands in front of him as though erasing the last few minutes. "Okay," he says. "That's enough of that. Callum? Could you take our illegally trespassing friend here away from what is about to be an insurance nightmare?"

"On it," Callum mutters, crowding me until I'm forced to move or let him knock me down.

"Miss Collins? Rest assured we will take your comments on board," Jack says, as I gape at him. "And if you'd like to email in about your noise concerns, I will get back to you personally. Thanks for coming down. Please don't do it again."

"You—"

Callum steps fully into my space, blocking my view of the group. "Come on."

"But—"

"This way." His tone leaves no room for argument, and frustration chokes me as I turn, stumbling back to the entrance.

Callum's learned his lesson from last time and stays glued to my side as though to make sure I won't make a run for it again.

"He's not going to get back to me," I say, as we reach the gate. "Is he?"

"No," Callum says.

"Because I'm in my pajamas?"

"I think it was the leaflet guy comment. He's very proud of those."

I return the hard hat to him before taking an exaggerated step over the line that marks public from private land. I want to end on something devastating. Something witty and clever that will make this whole disaster worthwhile, but I've got nothing. Nothing but a brain that feels like it's wading through mud and a body that would happily curl up on a pile of leaves somewhere if it meant the chance to sit down.

"I'm not usually like this," I say again, and he nods.

"I hope you get some sleep."

"And I hope your boss falls into a very big hole."

"He'll have to crawl out of his own one first."

My eyes go wide at the joke, but Callum's back to being serious, and he does it so well that I'm almost certain I misheard him.

Almost.

"Have a nice day," he says, when I don't move and I waste another five seconds trying and failing to think of something to say, only for him to head back into the site, leaving me staring after him.

CHAPTER TWO

"You look terrible."

Twelve hours later, after one terrible nap and three cups of coffee, I glance up from the lemon I'm slicing to see my friend Anushka take a seat at the bar, her dark hair pulled up into a messy bun. Two bright red pendants dangle from her ears and, in my half-awake state, I can only gaze at them for a few seconds, hypnotized by the way they catch the light.

"*Katie.*"

"Hmm?"

Nush stares at me, the electric blue lining her eyes making them appear even wider than usual. "Did you just cross into a different dimension or something?"

"I didn't sleep."

"Again? Did you use those earplugs I gave you?"

"Yes."

"Are you sure?"

"*Yes,*" I say. "I used the earplugs, Nush. I used the earplugs, and I drank warm milk, and I put on a white noise podcast, but none of it worked because I live ten minutes down the road from a construction site and, every morning at seven a.m., they *wake me up.*"

She gives me a long look. "What about chamomile tea?"

I bite back the urge to snap at her, knowing it's just sleep deprivation making me go all rampagy. Nush doesn't like the hotel any more than I do. She moved here a few years ago because she wanted to find some peace and quiet, and so she could, and I quote, "Not have to smile so much." The development is a nightmare in her eyes, and she's still convinced we can stop it, even if she has to resort to increasingly illegal measures to do it.

Last week she asked me how I felt about arson.

I'm still not sure if she was joking or not.

She frowns at me now, pursing her lips as though the mere sight of me offends her.

"I don't look that bad," I say, when she doesn't stop.

"I disagree. Do you know that meme where someone tried to make a Disney princess cake for their kid, but they can't bake, and it ended up looking like someone sat on a zombie version of Belle?"

"No."

"Well, that's what you look like."

"Put the weapon down, Katie. She's not worth the jail time." Gemma takes a seat next to Nush, clutching a thermal flask. "You do look like crap, though."

"Can we not— you're supposed to be my friends," I say accusingly.

"Friends tell each other the truth," Gemma says. "And I'm telling you, you look like death warmed up. Still not getting any sleep?"

"Obviously not."

"Maybe if you wear your hair up," Nush begins, and I bat her hands away as she reaches for me.

"No touching my staff, please," a disgruntled voice warns,

and, a moment later, Adam emerges from the back room, a crate of freshly washed glasses in his hands. My boss is a fitness-obsessed, constantly busy redhead who was only in his late twenties when his dad died and left the pub to him. I was just a kid at the time, and he took on a kind of big brother role in my life, letting me sit at the bar and do my homework before opening each night. This routine developed into a few hours on the weekends washing dishes and became a full-time job at eighteen when I decided the college route wasn't for me. Ten years later and I'm still here. I can't imagine being anywhere else.

Kelly's is the only pub in Ennisbawn. You might think that one pub would be enough for the three-hundred-odd inhabitants of the village, but you would be wrong. There used to be two when I was growing up. And there were five of them back in the day, according to Granny. But one by one, they closed, their owners moving on with no one willing to take their place. Kelly's is the only one left, but luckily for all of us, it's also the best one.

A little set back from the main village and overlooking a small lake, it's the kind of building you see on postcards or tourist adverts. Whitewashed stone walls with bright red windowpanes, it's old, cozy, and perfectly imperfect with a limited menu of snacks, salty soups, and cheese toasties. There are dozens of nooks to sit by yourself and deep brown leather booths to sit with others, all of which are comfortable enough to sleep on (and sometimes people do). The only decorations are the photographs on the wall, which have faded with time, but Adam's never bothered to replace them. There is no television, no karaoke machine. There is just conversation, sometimes music, and always a huge sense of comfort. Of familiarity. Like you could have walked in fifty years ago or walk in fifty years from now and, bar a few changes in technology, everything would be the same. The same smells. The same sounds. The same grumpy publican, glaring at his customers from behind the bar.

"Anushka, if you're going to sit there, you need to buy something," Adam continues.

"I'm drinking water," she protests.

"Yeah, from the tap." His eyes slide to Gemma with an equally unhappy look. "And what about you? You know how I feel about outside drinks in here."

"You would deny a single mother her evening caffeine?"

"At least get something to go with it," he says, putting the crate down next to me. "I'm trying to run a business here."

"So you should encourage a beautiful woman to sit at your bar."

"And if you see one, you can let me know. Red or white?"

Nush cackles, sliding off her stool as Gemma glares at him. "Rude."

"I'm just warming up," he tells her. "Red or white?"

"Red. Small," she adds, when he plucks a bottle from the shelf. "Merlot."

"You're getting the Malbec."

"I want the cheap Merlot."

"And you're getting the mid-priced Malbec. It's a Friday night. Live a little."

Gemma continues to try and murder him with her eyes while he pours a glass with a practiced hand, but Adam's attention has turned to me.

"How long have you been slicing those?"

I take stock of the handful of intact lemons next to me, and the one-point-five I've managed to get through. "Why ask questions you won't like the answers to?"

He grimaces. "Maybe you should go home early today. It's quiet enough."

"I'm fine," I say, as Gemma slams a tenner into his outstretched palm. It's a lie, but I don't want him to worry.

Margins for the pub are tight, and I know he needs the help. I'm his only other member of staff. "I'm making lemon drop martinis."

"For who?"

"For the people who will order one once they see how good they look. Frank wants a beer," I add, nodding at one of our regulars.

"He does," Frank calls from the other end of the bar, and Adam replaces the knife in my hand with a dishcloth before going over to him.

"You should take him up on that," Gemma says, when he's gone. She takes a long sip of her apparently unwanted wine and runs a hand through her hair, shaking out the blonde curls until they frame her face. Adam really was kidding before. Even after an eight-hour shift on her feet, with mascara smudges dotted around her eyes and a slump to her shoulders, she's still the most striking person in the room. I hate her just a little bit for it. But like, in a loving friend way.

"I know." I start polishing the glasses and putting them away as the rest of our patrons gather for the weekly village meeting. "I read on the internet that if I keep going like this my collagen will start to break down."

"You don't even know what collagen is."

"I know I want it not to break down."

She's saved from responding by the urgent ringing of the village bell. It's really just Nush's bell. A small but loud brass one that she ordered online a few months ago, insisting it'd make our get-togethers more official.

No one particularly likes it, but Adam *hates* it, which is very funny to me, so I keep my mouth shut.

He glares at her now as he sets down the pint, his skin flushing until it's almost the same shade as his hair. "I told her to stop bringing the— *Anushka!*"

She gives him a *what* look, but stops ringing it as Frank joins her, his drink in one hand and a small scrap of paper in the other. Frank is the unofficial mayor of the village. Or leader. Or maybe a secretary or something. We've never really put a name to it. But he used to be a school principal and is very good at a) talking to groups and b) organizing activities for said groups, so no one really questioned when he started taking charge of our community catch-ups.

"Evening, evening. Before Anushka gets to her weekly discussion," he begins, glancing at her. "We have a few items to discuss. Bridget would like to get more people signed up for the Tidy Towns committee. Ideally, someone that's not just Katie, though thank you, Katie," he adds, and I give him a thumbs-up. "There's a storm coming next week, according to the news. Nothing too bad, but if you know someone who might need checking in on, pop them on the usual list, and we'll make sure they're looked after. We've had a letter from Glenmill advising residents not to use the back road by the lake next Thurs— *next Thursday*," he says, raising his voice to be heard over the sudden muttering. "In advance of some work they're carrying out. And finally, the library in Rossbridge are looking for a volunteer storyteller over Easter to... thank you, Katie," he says, noting my raised hand. "I'll send you the details."

"Goody two-shoes," Gemma mutters, but she's smiling as she says it.

"And unless anyone has any other items to add to the agenda..." Frank looks around, crumpling the note into his pocket. "...No? Then I pass the floor to—"

"Thank you, Frank," Anushka says, taking her position in front of the fireplace. Nush is tiny, barely reaching my shoulder when we're side by side, but whereas I tend to shrink when it comes to public speaking, she always makes herself seem ten feet taller. Gemma says it's just good posture, but I swear it's some kind of magic trick. "And thank you all for coming tonight.

I'm here this week like I'm here every week. To discuss Glenmill and their reign of terror in our home."

"I see she's going for the dramatic angle today," Gemma says, and I bite back a smile.

"They come with their promises," Nush continues, speaking like she's giving a rousing speech at the end of an action movie and not addressing a handful of people drinking in a pub. "They come with their elegant words and their expensive suits, and they take over villages like ours until there's nothing and no one left. Until we are mere shells of who we once were. We've already seen what they can do to our land, but now we're witnessing first-hand what they can do to our people. I mean, just *look* at Katie."

I stiffen as every head in the pub turns my way. Oh my God.

"Innocent, darling Katie—"

Oh my *God*. "Nush—"

"—whose only crime is living near that hellhole they call a building site."

"Make her stop talking," I mumble to Gemma, who gives a slow shake of her head.

"I will not be doing that."

"Every morning she's woken by an issue that we will all have to contend with soon. And it's that issue I want to talk about tonight. *Traffic*."

"Hah! Called it." Gemma twists back to the bar and reaches out a hand to Adam, who returns her ten-euro note with a scowl.

"Double or nothing she asks us to start chaining ourselves to trees," he says, and Gemma scoffs.

"Deal."

"We have one road coming in and out of this village," Nush continues. "One. What's it going to be like when we're suddenly adding another five hundred people to our population? We don't have footpaths. We don't even have traffic lights. It's a recipe for disaster, and I'm thinking in particular of the dangers for the younger members of our community." She places a hand over her heart. "As a mother—"

"You're not a mother," Frank interrupts.

"I have a son."

"You have a cat. Gemma has a son."

"You can have him if you want him," Gemma calls. "I'm more than happy to trade."

Nush ignores her. "Cats are expensive, Frank. Chester ate a piece of rope the other day, and I paid a hundred euros for the vet to tell me he'll just have to poop it out. A *hundred* euros."

"You shouldn't have given him the rope then."

"I didn't give him the rope! He found the rope!"

"Can we keep this meeting moving?" Adam calls, not even looking up as he wipes down the toastie machine. "Please?"

"I'm just further proving my point," Nush continues. "A hundred euros for rope poop. Think how much it will cost to fix a broken leg or an operation should Chester be knocked down. Should any of us be knocked down. You, Danny," she says, pointing to Danny O'Meara who has the misfortune of sitting closest to her. "You could be knocked down. Do you want that?"

Danny pauses with his Guinness halfway to his mouth. "No?"

"No," Nush echoes. "He does not. Which is why we need to consider the traffic that will be brought into the area as a result of the hotel. *Taxis* coming and going at all hours of the day. *Tour* buses parking where they should not be parking. *Rich* people in Land Rovers doing God knows what. Who is going to take care of the roads with the increased wear on them? Because the council certainly doesn't answer my emails. And I—"

Nush breaks off, her gaze shooting to the ceiling as a collective gasp ripples throughout the pub. Before any of us can so much as blink, the lights above us flicker before shutting off, bathing the lounge in instant darkness.

Blackout.

"See!" Nush exclaims, yelling to be heard over the ensuing groans. Adam curses behind me as Gemma raises her wine glass in a mock toast. "This is the second time this month. Coincidence?"

More than likely, but I've got to give it to her for trying to lay the blame on Glenmill.

The power cuts have been happening my whole life. Electricity is generally unreliable out here, and when outages happen, they tend to focus on getting the bigger towns back up and running first. I hate to say it, but we're almost used to them at this stage.

"You can stay here as long as you like," Adam calls over the annoyed grumbling. "So long as no one tells the insurance people. Honor code, folks."

Phone screens light up, casting small white glows around the room as a few people start to rise, muttering about houses and families and *not again*. Nush gives up trying to regain their attention and rings the bell to end the meeting. Sometimes, these things only last a few seconds, but other times they can go on for hours, and no one wants to take the risk.

"Katie?" Adam calls over, as he lights a handful of candles for the tables. "Could you grab some torches from the shed? Keys in the office," he adds, and I raise a hand in acknowledgment as I slip away, grabbing the key ring and some loose change from his desk, before heading out the back door.

It's pitch-black outside, but the sky is clear and full of stars, and I pause to gaze out at the lake as it shimmers silently. The forest that brackets the other side is dark and still and might be eerie if I didn't know it like the back of my hand.

Once the summer hits, the patio where I'm standing will be full of people enjoying the sun, but right now it's empty bar the weathered picnic bench pushed to the side and the old wishing well right in front of me. The latter has been here for so long, most people don't even notice it anymore, but I think if Kelly's is my favorite place in the world, then the well is my favorite place in Kelly's.

It's a bit of a tradition for me to come here. Though maybe addiction is a better word for it. Because just like how a few of our regulars always seem to relax after their first sip of the day, something in my chest eases every time I make a wish.

And after the day I've had, that's exactly what I need right now.

I walk slowly around it, running my hands over the stones until I feel the faint etching on the far side, the initials of two love-drunk kids who'd grow up to have me.

Ennisbawn wasn't always so tiny. It was a pretty sizeable market town back in the day, with dances and auctions and fairs. We still hold most of them, though they've shrunk in size and importance over the years. But they're an excuse to bring people together and for me to put up decorations and for Adam to roll his eyes at said decorations, and so we still host some, if only to get everyone together on a random Tuesday night.

My parents met at the matchmaking festival.

It's one of our oldest traditions, stretching back as far as the late seventeen hundreds when bachelor farmers would descend on the village, seeking a wife among the young women who holidayed with their families by the lake. Legend goes you would drop a coin down the well and wish for your true love. Granny likes to spin a romantic tale about my parents doing just that, but now that I'm older, I know that, while they did fall in love, it probably wasn't the well weaving its magic that drew them together. More than likely, it was the fact that Kelly's was the kind of place that would have turned a blind eye to two seventeen-year-olds looking to buy a beer back then and they signed up to be matched with nothing more than a good night in mind.

But it's nice to pretend.

To believe in a little bit of magic.

I trace over the familiar letters, saying a silent hello before reaching for one of the coins in my pocket and dropping it inside. I wait for the gentle plop of water that always serves as an acknowledgment and, when it comes, I take a breath, inhaling the damp smell of stone and water and earth, along with the metallic taste of God knows how many coins myself and others have dropped in over the years.

I'm so caught up in my little ritual that I don't pay any attention to the sudden pinpricks at the back of my neck, that innate sense of being watched.

I've completely let my guard down and the faint rustle of clothing a moment later is the only warning I get that I'm not alone, but before I can do anything about it, a man's voice murmurs behind me, far too close for comfort:

"What did you wish for?"

CHAPTER THREE

I scream.

Or I almost scream. It comes out like a kind of strangled yelp as I whirl around in full-on attack mode, hands flailing and ready to hit. Pain ricochets through my wrist as I connect with something, a nose, judging by the grunt from my assailant, but I barely have time to feel victorious as I lose my footing on the wet pavement slabs beneath me. My right foot slides in front as I hit the back of the well with an *oomph*, and for one stomach-dropping moment, I teeter over the edge before I'm jerked up, pulled not into the murky darkness below but straight into the broad, hard chest of a stranger.

Strong hands grip my shoulders, easing me back from where I'd faceplanted against his jacket, and I look up to see the dark-haired man from this morning peering down at me.

Callum.

His name pops into my mind at the same time I realize I'm clutching onto his coat like I'm holding on for dear life. The whole episode took about five seconds, but in those five seconds I went from weary calm to hyper-alert and my brain does not know what to do with that.

Move, I command as my body takes its sweet time connecting to my nervous system. *Move.* But I don't. I don't do anything and when a few moments pass and still nothing happens, Callum's brow creases in concern.

"You okay?"

The sound of his voice is what does it, unblocking the weird barrier in my mind so that every instruction roars through me at once. As a result, I don't so much let the man go as I do shove him away, scrambling to the side as I reach for the phone in my back pocket. Before he can so much as take a step, I switch on the torch, shining it right at him.

"Jesus," he mutters, shielding himself from the light. "Are those things supposed to be that bright?"

"What are you doing here?"

"Losing my vision, apparently. Do you mind?" He squints my way, and I reluctantly lower my weapon, angling it so it's no longer blinding him but still illuminating the space enough that I can make him out in the dark. Not to be all small-town stereotype, but it's rare to have someone not from here roaming about, especially in the middle of a power cut. Not to mention that the man is dressed for skulking. Dark jeans, dark winter coat, dark beanie pulled low over his head. Almost like he's—

"*Ow.*"

I flash the phone back in his direction as he steps forward and he immediately rears back, his palms shooting up as though to prove his innocence.

"I thought country people were supposed to be friendly."

"Not in the middle of the night to men they don't know."

"We met this morning," he says. "And I just saved you from falling down a well."

"I wouldn't have fallen down the well."

"That's sure what it looked like."

I move the phone to my other hand, registering a slight twinge before remembering what happened. "I hit your nose."

"You broke my nose."

"Really?"

"No."

When it becomes clear I'm not going to blind him again, Callum drops his hands, watching me as I do him, except he's much more obvious about it, appraising me like I'm the one who interrupted his night and not the other way around. But before he can say anything more, a shattering of glass sounds from the pub, followed by an ironic cheer, and I remember why I'm out here in the first place.

The torches.

Crap. The keys are no longer in my hand, that much I register, and I pat my empty pockets before shining the light at my feet, trying to spot them.

"What are you looking for?" Callum asks.

"I dropped my keys." And Adam will lose his shit if I can't find them. It may or may not be the third time I've lost them. Though, to be fair, I did find the last set in the inside pocket of my coat two months after we replaced them. But who checks the inside pocket? Who even regularly uses an inside pocket? Not my fault.

Okay, a little bit my fault.

I startle as a new beam of light joins mine and turn to see Callum sweeping his own phone over the patio. Right. This guy.

"You didn't answer my question," I say, abandoning my quest for the moment. "What are you doing here?"

"Looking for you." He says it like it's the most natural thing in the world. "I figured this place is small enough that it shouldn't be too hard. Didn't mean to scare you."

"You didn't," I lie. "You just have suspiciously quiet feet for someone so..." *Strong.* "Tall. And what do you mean, you were looking for me?" I stiffen as soon as I say the words, my skin heating with embarrassment at the thought of what happened this morning. Am I in trouble? Is that what this is? Are they going to try and arrest me for trespassing or something? I don't know if they can, but Nush always talks about how much money these people have and how ruthless they are, and I guess I did piss off the big boss man and—

"I wanted to apologize."

Callum's words interrupt my spiraling *I've never been in real trouble before* panic, and I swallow, grateful he can't see me too well in the dark.

"For this morning," he continues. "And the mornings before that. The team are going to sort it out."

"You're going to stop building the hotel?"

He starts to smile, his lips curving up before he realizes I'm not joking.

"No," he says after a long second. "As captivating as your case was, Glenmill Properties is not going to stop their multimillion-euro construction project. But we can stop the traffic. We'd actually planned that route to avoid too many vehicles going through the village. Unfortunately, that means they all seem to be going right by you. I talked with the team, and rerouting the entrance shouldn't be a problem. Most of the guys are coming in from the city anyway, and there's no reason they can't approach from the main road. I can't do anything about disruption from the site, but it will buy you a few hours in the mornings and maybe you could—"

"Are you serious?" I interrupt, and he pauses, taken aback by my sudden excitement.

"We'll need to trial it," he says carefully. "But yeah. We've been told not to piss off the locals and you're a local. Didn't take much sign-off."

I can't believe it. It worked.

My delirious activism worked.

"Hopefully better than nothing," he continues, when I just stare at him.

"It is," I say quickly. "It is much better than nothing. It's something. It's great. It's... thank you."

"No problem."

"And I'm sorry about this morning," I add, feeling charitable. "I was a little out of it. Probably wasn't the best way to start your day."

"You kidding me?" He laughs, a pleasant, husky sound that I instantly want him to make again. "That's the most fun I've had in weeks. I'll let you know when Jack's visiting next, and you can swing around again."

"Not likely," I mutter, wincing at the thought. "You're sure I didn't get you in trouble?"

"The surest," he says. "So, what kind of keys?"

"Oh, you don't have to— small," I say, when those green eyes swing my way. Shut *up*, Katie. "Blue key ring. Thanks."

"And they're definitely not in your pockets?"

"No." Though I check again to make sure. "I dropped the coin in with my right hand, I had the keys in my left and then I heard you and then I freaked and then..."

I catch his eye and, as one, we turn to stare at the well.

"No," I say.

"It's a possibility."

"I would have heard them fall."

"Maybe not." He rises to look into it, shining his light inside. "How deep is it?"

"I don't know. Two hundred feet? Why? Are you going to climb down it?"

"No, but you must have some rope and bucket situation going on."

"We don't use it for water. I don't think we've even had it checked." And if they're down there... I groan and spin away, heading over to the side of the pub. "Just give me a leg up."

"What?"

"The keys are for the gate," I explain, gesturing to the six-foot wooden slats blocking off the storage area. We put them up a few years ago when Adam finally got fed up with foxes burrowing in. I didn't have the heart to tell him they'd have no problem climbing over it. "The shed inside should be unlocked."

"Why isn't the shed locked?"

"Because I'm in charge of locking it and I know I definitely forgot to do it last night."

I come to a stop by our very penetrable wall and slip the phone into my pocket, plunging us into darkness once more.

"If you could just give me a boost, I'll be able to— what are you *doing*?"

Callum moves quicker than I expect, bending to grab my knees before lifting me into the air like I weigh nothing at all. I grab hold of the fence on instinct, scrambling to straddle the thing. Once I'm sure I'm not going to fall, I look down with a glare, but he's already pulling himself up to join me.

"You don't need to come too."

"Then how will you get back?" he says, and I take his point as he climbs the fence easily, his movements suspiciously nimble.

"Please tell me you haven't done this before," I say, but he only winks before dropping down neatly to the other side. I stay where I am, wondering if I'm still a little sleep-deprived, but I don't feel like I've lost any common sense. There are no alarm bells ringing, no twisting feeling in my gut telling me to run for the hills, and, knowing that Adam's going to lose a whole night of business if he doesn't get these torches, I ignore my new friend's outstretched arms and climb down myself.

Callum lets out a low whistle when I open the shed door, adding his phone's light to mine as we peer inside. "Remind me to come back here when the apocalypse happens."

"We get a lot of blackouts," I explain, pushing aside the camping gear, sandbags, and emergency supplies to find the box.

"And sometimes the river on the other side of the village floods. We've learned the hard way to be more prepared around here."

"I can see that."

"Yeah, well." I glance away from the large spider in the corner and pretend I don't see it. "Yay, climate change."

"Sure."

I frown at his tone, distracted. "What do you mean, 'sure'?"

"Nothing," he says, as I pull the heavy box toward the door. "I've just never really believed in that stuff."

I stop where I am, hunched over our prize like a little goblin. "Are you serious?"

"It's just weather," he shrugs. "Weather changes. I don't know why everyone keeps freaking out about it." He tries to take the box from me when I just stare at him, and I immediately tug it back.

"It's how it's changing that matters," I say, trying to keep my voice level. "And it's changing far too fast."

He nods, but his expression remains infuriatingly blank. "I guess."

"No, there's no guessing. There's just fact. And it's up to us to— you're messing with me."

That little lip twitch, the one I'm beginning to realize is his tell, stops me mid-rant, and he smiles at my obvious, if not furious, relief.

"Sorry."

I am this close to hitting him in the nose again. My pulse is skyrocketing with the usual sickly adrenaline I get whenever I think I'm going to have to argue with someone.

"You're mean."

"And you're cute when you panic."

"Uh-uh. No."

"Excuse me?"

"I'm too tired to flirt," I tell him, and his smile widens. "I mean it. I can't. I'll say something stupid. I'm already saying something stupid. No flirting."

"Fine," he promises. "No flirting." He grabs the box before I can stop him, but otherwise doesn't move, and the shed suddenly feels very small, and he feels very close, and I'm not even thinking about all the spiders in here because—

"You're still doing it!" I accuse, and he laughs. "You're looking at me."

"I'm not allowed to look at you now?"

"Not like that," I tell him, gesturing him through the door. "Eyes straight. Two paces between us."

"You're a very demanding person," he says, but does as he's told.

"And you're not a climate change denier," I confirm, following him out and bolting the door behind me.

"Cross my heart."

"What are you then?"

"A Libra. And an on-site project coordinator."

"Sounds official."

"It is." He puts the box next to the fence and cups his hands together. "After you."

I come to a stop beside him, hesitating. This felt a lot easier when he just grabbed me. In fact, I kind of wish he would do that again so I wouldn't have to think too much, but he just stands there patiently, waiting for me to move.

"Don't drop me," I finally warn, and he nods as I place one probably very dirty sneaker into his hands and hold on to his shoulders.

Up I go.

I catch my breath at the fluid movement, one that for a brief second makes me feel like I'm flying, and then I'm grabbing hold of the slats and hauling myself up. He passes me the box before pulling himself over to the other side and taking it from me again, and I'm just swinging my leg around when he reaches up to help me.

"Thanks," I mumble, as his hands drag briefly up my thighs before grasping my hips. Heat blooms under his touch, and I try not to react as he lowers me down, even though a ridiculous part of me wants to collapse backward and have him catch me, like some sort of Austen heroine.

Like I said, tired.

He lets go as soon as I'm back on terra firma but doesn't step away, and his undivided attention suddenly makes me a little shy.

"So you work at the pub?" he asks, when I don't say anything.

"I'm a bartender."

"That's cool. You like it?"

"Yeah. I mean, I—"

"Katie?"

I startle as Adam appears around the side of the building, shining a torch in our direction.

"I was about to send out a search party," he says.

"Sorry. I lost the keys. We think they're down the well."

"You lost the— we?" Adam stops before us, and Callum winces as he swings the light right at him.

"If I wake up with all my sight tomorrow morning, it'll be a miracle," he mutters.

"Callum works for Glenmill," I explain. "He's going to see about stopping the traffic, so I can get some sleep and not want to yell at everyone all the time."

"How nice of him." The words are as flat as Adam's expression because, apparently, being polite is just not something we do anymore.

"Adam owns the pub," I tell Callum. "Speaking of which, who's looking after it?"

"Gemma," Adam says. "Who I don't trust, so we better get

back." He says the last bit looking right at Callum, a dismissal that's impossible to ignore lacing his words.

But if Callum's surprised by his rudeness, he doesn't show it, just grabs the box and hands it to me. "Better get going myself."

"Thanks for your help," I say. "And for looking into the noise."

"I aim to please," he says. "Or at least to reroute. Can you..." He glances around, looking lost. "I parked by some recycling bins?"

A very basic *no* echoes through me at the thought of him leaving, making me want to welcome him inside and pour him a drink. But Adam is still radiating displeasure beside me, and it doesn't take a genius to know he wouldn't approve.

"That way," I say, gesturing up to the main road. "Near the east entrance to the forest. Take a left."

"Thanks." His eyes flick to Adam and, with a final nod of farewell, he disappears back around the pub. Adam waits for his footsteps to fade before taking the box in one hand and passing me the torch with the other, his face stony. But I've known the man too long to put up with it.

"What crawled up your hole?"

"What?"

I wave a hand in the direction Callum went. "You were rude to him. We're still open. You should have invited him in for a drink."

"Legally, we're not open at all and you really want to bring him inside when Nush is ready to scratch the eyes out of anyone associated with that hotel?"

"That is such an exaggeration." I hope. And it still doesn't excuse his sudden change in mood. Adam isn't the friendliest of people when you first meet him, but he's usually a little more civil than that.

"Seriously," I press. "What's up?"

"It's nothing," he says, nudging me back toward the pub. "Just help me get the place lit up and then go home to Maeve. You need to get some sleep. And to stop talking to strangers. And what do you mean, the keys are down the well?"

I wince as his tone sharpens at the last bit and follow him back inside, trying to explain.

CHAPTER FOUR

Callum keeps his word.

Within three days, all heavy traffic by my house stops. No more beeping, no more thundering, no more rumbling engines or yelling voices. It just stops. And I know it because one morning I wake up and it isn't even morning. It's sometime after twelve and I slept the deepest sleep I've had in months. By the end of the next week, I'm practically back to normal. Better than normal. Because I've never felt so alive. So energized. It's like a whole new, eight-hours'-rest-a-night world and I take full advantage of it, putting a bunch of tasks and chores into motion that I immediately regret a few hours later when I have to see them through.

"Do you want the bad news?"

"You mean first?"

"What?"

I glance at Frank, who's standing beside me with his hands on his hips. We're at the bottom of my garden, half-hidden among the weeds as both of us squint in the mid-morning sunshine. Frank's always been old to me. I guess everyone looks old when you're a kid, but I swear the man hasn't aged a bit in the last twenty years. Even now with his neat gray beard and his ruddy cheeks, reddened from broken capillaries and an apathy for sunscreen, I have no idea how long he has been on this green earth. Sixty years? Seventy? He could tell me he was thirty-eight, and I'd just have to accept it. I like that about him. His consistency. Makes me trust him more. Even if the look on his face right now isn't exactly filling me with confidence.

"You're supposed to say, do you want the bad news or the good news first," I tell him.

"There is no good news," he says bluntly. "You're going to need to cut it down."

"The branch?"

"The tree, Katie."

"The *tree*?" I stare up at my beloved hawthorn, which isn't really that beloved but is still a pretty decent tree and one that I suddenly feel incredibly attached to. "According to who?"

"Me," Frank says. "The person you asked to look at it."

"But you're meant to tell me it's okay."

He knocks on the trunk, producing a hollow thudding sound. "It's not okay; it's dead."

"It's sleeping," I protest. "Trees sleep in the winter."

"It's April, your bark is peeling, and you've got no buds."

"But—"

"Dead."

He kicks the base of it for good measure and I scowl. But I know he's right. It's why I asked him to come up here in the first place.

"So now what?" I ask.

"Now you get a professional out to take a look and get it sorted."

I make a face, not even wanting to think about the cost. "Can't you do it? Since, technically, you've already had a look?"

He shakes his head. "You're better off getting the right person, but I'll help you negotiate. You'd want to do it soon, though. Along with everything else." He glances around the garden. "You could hide a family of five out there and you'd never know it."

"That's a very specific number. Are you trying to tell me something?"

He gives me a look, one that softens when I smile at him. "If you need help, you just ask for it. You know that, right?"

"I do." And Frank isn't wrong. The place is a mess. I know it's a mess. An acre of land surrounds the house and all of it is overgrown and wild. And not in the trendy, biodiverse way. More like a passing murderer might think this is a *great* place to hide a body.

"It will get dangerous for her," Frank says, nodding toward the house. "I've almost tripped myself once or twice since I arrived."

"I know." I sigh, peering up at the tree. "I need to put a new ramp in at the front door. And then we need to get the bathroom done. Then we'll do the tree. Then the garden." And everything else. Just the thought of it all has me wincing. I feel like as soon as I tick one thing off the list, another three more expensive tasks get added to the bottom. Whatever I manage to save one month gets spent the next, and I can barely keep up with it all.

"Thanks for coming out," I say, walking him back to his car. "I appreciate it."

"I'm just glad I was able to make it. They've blocked off the entire road by Danny's farm."

"I saw."

"You know, I never really bought into Anushka's whole campaign. But it's all getting a bit too much. Like one day, I'm going to wake up and won't even recognize this place." He gives me a fatherly pat on the shoulder. "You take care of yourself now. You can't look after Maeve if you don't look after you first."

"I'll do my best," I promise, and stand in the driveway as he reverses down the lane before I turn back to my somehow still-standing house.

We live in a cottage.

When people think of cottages, they tend to picture cute, storybook places, but having lived in one all my life, I can confidently say that all they are is cramped and dark with little to no storage space. I toyed with the idea of renovating it a few years ago, figuring I'd be able to apply for a few grants to cover most of it. I spent days looking up websites before phoning a bunch of men who eventually came in their vans and spoke in loud voices while they knocked on walls, held up little sticks, and announced they were doing "readings." They all said the same thing. Tear it down, start again and pay a lot of money to do it. I gave up after that, doing my best to paint over moldy ceilings and fix cracked floor tiles as and when I had time.

It's the front step that's the biggest problem now. It's getting a little steep for Granny since she had her fall, and while we've put in a makeshift ramp, we need to get something more permanent. I make a mental note to look into it as I step inside, almost tripping over Plankton, who has chosen to lie right in front of the door.

"Helpful," I tell him, as he gives me a wounded look.

The postman must have come sometime in the last few minutes as a few letters lie scattered around him. A postcard, some bills, and another expensive-looking leaflet from Glenmill to add to our collection. Or at least to the recycling. I skim through it, eyeing the blond man I'd met last week smiling on the cover.

Jack Doyle, Managing Director.

Dickhead of the century.

"Granny?"

"Who's that?" an irritated voice calls from my right.

"Who do you think?" I toe off my sneakers, leaving them by the stairs as I crumple the brochure into a ball, but instead of finding Granny in her usual chair, I open the door to the living room to see her on her hands and knees, surrounded by boxes and scattered paper.

"What *happened*?" I ask, horrified.

"None of your business. I'm fine."

"You're not fine; you're on the ground." I kneel beside her, helping her to her feet. "Did you fall again?"

"I didn't fall; everything else fell."

I ease her onto the couch and grab a blanket for her lap before turning to scoop up the books and photographs strewn across the rug.

"What is all this crap?"

"A little respect, please, Katie. You're referring to my lifetime of memories."

"I'm referring to the crap all over the floor. What were you doing?"

"Looking for one of my books," Granny grumbles, and I know by her tone she's embarrassed that I found her like this. "*The Prince's Conquest*. There's a man on the cover."

"All your books have men on the covers." Usually in some state of undress. "Your friend Nancy sent you a postcard," I add, handing her the letter from the hall.

"Nancy died three years ago."

"No, Mary died three years ago. Nancy lives in Vancouver. And she sent you a postcard. You should stay in touch with your friends."

"Why?" She gives it a cursory glance before putting it on the table beside her. "It's not like they'll be alive for much longer. Pass me those."

I hand over a couple of books and settle beside her to sort through the photographs. We've got mountains of them around the house, mostly in boxes that neither of us can bear to get rid of. I'm familiar with most, but these ones are older and seem to span a few decades, judging by their faded colors.

"I don't think I've seen these before," I say, examining them.

"You have. But not for a few years. I used to give them to you when you were younger when I wanted you to be quiet."

"You did?"

She nods, flipping through one of the books. "I told you there was a ghost in one of them. You'd spend hours looking at them."

Ah, yes, my ghost phase.

I sit back on my heels, looking through the box with renewed interest.

"Is this you?" I ask, holding up a black and white picture of a grinning young woman.

"Should be," Granny says, peering at it. "Ugly little thing, wasn't I?"

"Would you stop!" I laugh. "You're beautiful."

"And you're a liar. But that's alright. It didn't stop your grandfather from falling in love with me. I had other attributes."

"Your charming personality?"

"That," she says. "And I was very loose."

I pretend not to hear her, pausing on the next picture in the pile. It's one of the newer ones, a snap of my mother sitting draped over my father's lap. They're both wearing Santa hats and looking more than a little tipsy as they stare into each other's eyes, sharing a smile.

My parents died in a car accident when I was five. They were returning from visiting friends in Dublin when a speeding driver hit them on the wrong side of the motorway.

My mother's grandparents lived in Wales and offered to take me in, but everyone agreed not to uproot me any further, so I went to Granny, moving into her small cottage in a village no one had heard of.

Despite all the odds, it kind of worked.

Granny is stubborn and blunt, with a gallows humor that most people don't know whether to smile or take offense at, but she was fiercely protective of me and raised me to be proud of who I was and where I came from. It was Granny who first helped me paint a picture of my parents in my mind, who made me believe that I was connected to them even though they were no longer here, filling me in on every detail she could think of, no matter how trivial.

I know, for example, that my dad was an accountant and that he played hurling and would eat dessert before dinner. I know that Mam liked sunflowers and buying expensive stationery that she rarely used. White wine gave her a headache. Her favorite color was blue. And I look just like her.

It wasn't obvious as a child, but we could have passed as twins once puberty hit. The same wild brown hair, the same button nose. A high forehead, hazel eyes and sturdy hips that would have made me very popular back when my ancestors needed to populate the earth but are not so great now when trying to find jeans that actually fit me. But I love that I resemble her. That I get to have that part of her. Like something private we share just between us.

"Frank says we have to cut down the tree," I say, placing the box back on the bookshelf. "It's dead."

"It's not dead; it's winter."

"That's what I told him," I say, as she tsks. "He also says we need to clear out the garden before you fall over and die."

She scoffs at that. "I'm not going to die in the garden. I'll die warm in bed with my granddaughter by my side."

"I hope I'm not also dying in this scenario."

"Oh no, the apocalypse floods will get you."

"If you just let me take care of it," I try again, but she waves a hand, cutting me off.

"I'll do it," she says. "I said I would, didn't I?"

"Yeah, last September."

"Everyone always wants to cut back and clear out. You know this earth survived thousands of years without anyone touching it? If you ask me, we were all the better for it." She pauses, fixing a beady eye on me. "Which tree?"

"The dead one? It's the hawthorn around the back."

"No."

I frown at her. "What do you mean, *no*?"

"You can't cut down the hawthorn tree. It's a fairy tree."

"Oh my God." I climb to my feet, my legs stiff and uncooperative. "That might have worked when I was five, but not now. Frank's going to get us the name of someone to deal with it."

"And disturb the fairies? That's what you want? I raised you better than that."

"You also raised me to believe that the pylon down the road was the Eiffel Tower."

"Hah." Granny smiles, looking pleased with herself. "I did, yes."

"We're cutting down the tree," I say. "But luckily for you and your fairy friends—"

"Not friends. Respected beings."

"—it will probably be a few months until we can afford to do it." I turn on the television, flicking through the channels until I land on a documentary about sharks. Granny likes documentaries about sharks. "But you're in charge of getting someone to clear the garden, okay?"

"So we can destroy more of their habitat?"

"Granny—"

"Just don't come crying to me if they steal you from your bed in the middle of the night."

I kiss her on the cheek, catching a whiff of lavender hand cream when she reaches up to tuck a strand of hair behind my ear. "Please get someone to clear out the garden."

"Fine. But only because you asked nicely." She pulls back to look at me, nodding at whatever she sees. "You look better."

"That's because I'm sleeping like a normal person."

"How is it?" she asks. "Up there." She gestures at the

window, and I know she means the site. She told me a few weeks ago that she couldn't bring herself to go and see it. That she was too old for so much change.

"It's weird," I admit. "Different. I can't imagine what it's going to be like when the hotel is finished. I don't think I'll ever get used to it."

"People can get used to anything," she says, growing solemn as Plankton comes in to curl up at her feet. "That's what people like them rely on."

————

An hour before lunch, I get a text from Gemma asking if I'm free, so I heat up some soup for Granny, grab my bike, and head into the village. I mean it when I say Ennisbawn is small. One lone gently curving street with farmland on either side doesn't look like much at first sight, but it has everything we need.

Kelly's is down by the lake and some campsites by the forest are on the other side, but on the street itself are mostly terraced houses and small shops. There's the general store with a converted phone box, now used as a library, and the pharmacy where the GP operates from one day a week. Nush's hairdressing salon is next to that, beside a small restaurant/coffee shop/whatever else Bridget and her wife feel like operating as. These days, there is also more than one empty building, but I've grown so used to them being vacant that I barely notice them anymore.

Gemma lives on the far side of the village in a small two-bedroom house in which I spend almost as much time as I do my own. She greets me at the door when I arrive, pulling on a pair of loafers.

"You're a lifesaver, you know that? I owe you big time."

"You're grand. I was free." I follow her in, stepping over

some discarded shoes as I peer into the empty living room. "Where's Noah?"

"I sent him to the shops. He's in a mood."

"Oh, goody."

"No backing out," she calls from the kitchen. "You know where everything is, yeah? Just don't give him any chocolate and don't steal my jewelry."

"I make no promises."

I follow her voice down the narrow hallway, spying the same Glenmill brochure Granny and I got this morning tacked to her noticeboard. Only with theirs, someone—Noah, I presume—has added a half dozen or so shapes that can only be described as male genitalia pointing at Jack's head.

"It's only for a couple of hours," Gemma says, as she flies around the kitchen, closing drawers and dumping dirty dishes into the sink. Gemma works at a frequently short-staffed nursing home a forty-minute drive away, meaning myself and a few of her neighbors often act as babysitters on call. "And if Patrick comes to the house, Noah's not allowed out with him. He's half-grounded."

"What's half-grounded?"

"It's when I still need him to leave sometimes because I want peace and quiet. What's this I hear about you sorting out that traffic issue?"

"It's because I'm such a capable adult? I managed to talk to someone who rerouted their main entrance so no one's right outside the house anymore. With the earplugs, I'm fine."

"That's great news. Who did you talk to?"

"Just some guy." I pour myself a glass of water, secretly hoping she'll push me a little more so I can tell her all about it. I haven't seen hide nor hair of Callum since. The last few nights I kept expecting him to waltz through the doors of the pub, even though none of the workers on the site have worked up the courage to do so yet. Not that Adam would mind the business, but he's right in that some of the locals might have something to say about it. Callum didn't seem too bad, though, and surely, once everyone gets talking, they'll realize most people down there are just doing their job. Then he could come all the time. Then he could—

"Are you working today?" Gemma asks, interrupting my little daydream. "I might swing by with Noah later. I have nothing in for dinner."

As though summoned from off-stage, the front door opens, and Noah appears. Gemma's son is an angelic-looking, increasingly moody pre-teen who I've known since he was five when Gemma moved them back to Ennisbawn after her divorce. She'd been brought up here but is closer to Adam's age than mine, so we never really interacted until she returned. We quickly grew close once she did, and she's now one of my best friends, meaning Noah is practically a godchild to me. I have a huge soft spot for the kid, something he exploits the hell out of.

"Hi, Katie," he says now, placing a loaf of bread on the kitchen table. He's the spitting image of Gemma, with the same blonde curls and hazel eyes. Right down to the smattering of freckles over his nose. In the last year or so, he's also got her resting bitchface down to a tee, to the point where I swear, she must have taught it to him.

"Hey," I greet in what I hope is a very cool way. It must be because he gives me a nod as Gemma holds out a palm.

"Change."

"They didn't have any."

She raises a brow. "They didn't have any change from a five-euro note for one loaf of bread?"

Noah shakes his head, his face solemn. "Because of the economy."

I choke on my water. I can't help it. And when Gemma glances my way at the sound, Noah uses the distraction to slip his headphones back over his ears, tuning us out as he starts making a sandwich.

I don't miss the flicker of concern that crosses my friend's face. Last week, Noah got suspended from school for fighting in the playground. It isn't the first time something like that has happened and Gemma was furious, but he insisted he'd been sticking up for another kid and no one could get their story straight.

"Are you going to tell Darren?" I ask, dropping my voice even though Noah's listening to music. "About the school?"

"Absolutely not," she says, like the very mention of him leaves a bad taste in her mouth.

Gemma's ex-husband moved back to Manchester a few years ago and started a new family. Now he doesn't even send his own son a Christmas card.

We do not like him.

"One of his teachers suggested sending him to a therapist."

"Noah?" I frown, considering it. "It might help."

"Yeah, and who's going to drive him the two hours it will take to get there? Who's going to pay for it?" She plucks her phone from the charger and drops it in her purse. "Remember when I thought moving back here was the thing that would change my life?" she asks. "And now I'm turning forty-three as an overworked single mother with a precarious rental situation?" She gives me a tight smile. "That's fun."

"It will be okay," I say automatically, but she's not listening, her attention back on her son. When he was younger, the two of them were best friends, but, like most parent/child relationships, it's gotten more difficult the older he gets. I know she worries about him. They bicker all the time, but, much like Granny and me, it comes from a place of love. Everything Gemma does is for Noah, which wouldn't be a problem if she didn't often forget about herself in the process.

"Okay," she says, clapping me on the shoulder as she grabs

her coat. "I'm going and I'm gone. Noah? No—" She tugs his headphones off his head, earning herself a scowl. "Hi. It's me. Your beloved mother. We're short-staffed at the home. I'm going in for three hours max and then I'll be back. Katie's going to mind you until then."

A horrified look comes over his face at the word *mind*. "I'm eleven," he says like he means twenty-two.

"Exactly," Gemma says. "Eleven. A child. A tiny little child who needs protecting and guarding and—"

"Mam—"

"—dinner and baths and an hour of television if you're good."

"Are you going or not?"

She grabs him by the cheeks, kissing him soundly on his forehead before he can stop her.

Lifesaver, she mouths to me again, and then she rushes out the door, leaving us alone.

There was a time when my looking after Noah caused great excitement in this house. When we'd get into our pajamas and eat pizza and play board games no matter the time of day. Now he just looks like he's being punished.

"Do you want to play *Fortnite*?" he asks, after a good thirty seconds of him probably thinking of ways to get rid of me.

"Do you want to play *The Sims*?" I counter, and he rolls his eyes before disappearing into the living room.

"Is that a no?" I call after him.

"You can just watch me play," he yells back, which is probably the best I'm going to get, so I do as he says, curling up on the couch next to him as he destroys some bad guys.

CHAPTER FIVE

I leave Gemma's a few hours later and, seeing no reason to go home and wait around until my shift, head straight to Kelly's. I've been meaning to try out a new cocktail recipe I've been working on in the hopes Adam will let me put it on the menu. Not a big fan of cocktails, Adam. But I got obsessed with making them a few years ago, and there are only so many boring pints I can post on our social media before people start to scroll past. (We have a healthy seventy-eight followers on Instagram. Though one of them is me and another an account I set up for Plankton. But they still count.)

The door is unlocked when I arrive, and when I let myself in, it's to see our great leader himself sitting at one of the tables, wearing a stiff white button-up and a *tie* as he bends over his laptop, lost to the world.

"Nice outfit," I greet. "You going to a funeral?"

Adam frowns as I make my way to the bar, a not-unusual expression for him. "What are you doing here?"

"Oh, I work here. Nice to meet you."

"You're early."

"Yeah, you're welcome." I grab my apron and start scanning

the shelves for the grenadine I made him buy. "I was minding Noah. Or rather, Noah allowed me to be in the same room as him if I stayed very quiet. Also, Gemma asked if you could swing by before we open. Her washing machine is leaking."

"I don't— you weren't supposed to—" He glances between the laptop and the door. "You need to come back later."

I raise my brow at his tone, a little curt for my liking. "Why?"

"Because I said so and I'm your boss."

I snort at that. "I'm going to make you try my new cocktail and then see how many of those Christmas napkins we still need to use."

"Katie, I'm serious."

"About what? If it's spreadsheet time, I'll be quiet. You won't even know I'm here."

"Would you just—"

He breaks off at the sound of a car pulling up outside, and I pause at how nervous he looks.

"Are you expecting someone? Oh my God, do you have a date? You have a date, don't you? That's why you're in a tie. Is it that woman from Rossbridge? The one with the nice coat?"

"It's not—"

"She seemed nice. She laughed at my joke."

The door to the pub swings open, and we both turn to face it, me grinning stupidly, but it's not the pretty teacher who he'd been seeing on and off before Christmas.

It's Callum.

His broad frame fills the doorway, and I straighten in surprise. He's dressed like he's come straight from the construction site, all rugged and capable and *I can carry that for you*, and the way his eyes immediately find mine makes me go all fluttery inside. Do I have a crush? I feel like I'm getting a crush.

I tie my hair back, offering him a smile, but before I can say hello and welcome and would you like to try a bespoke cocktail, he drops his gaze and steps to the side, letting in the one man I would have been happy to never see again.

Jack Doyle enters the pub, and if Callum's attention was on me, Jack's goes solely to Adam, who he smiles wildly at as he strides inside like his face isn't plastered to two dartboards by the fireplace.

"Sorry we're late," he says. "I got held up at the office. This is Callum Dempsey, my right-hand man, and I'd like you to meet Peter from our legal department. Peter, Adam. Adam, Peter."

Another man, shorter and rounder and dressed just as nicely, follows on Jack's heels to shake Adam's hand. I watch all of it with my hair half up and falling out of the clip.

"Is there somewhere we could get set up?" Jack asks, and Adam nods, clearing his throat. His movements are stiff and unnatural, like he doesn't know how to act.

"My office is in the back," he says, gesturing around the bar.

"Perfect," Jack says. "And maybe some water?" Only now does he acknowledge my presence.

"My shift hasn't started yet," I say, with a little more bite to my words than I intended. Jack doesn't seem to notice, but Adam hears it at once.

"No problem," he says, shooting me a warning glare. "I'll bring something in."

There are a few words of thanks, more small talk about the weather and the traffic, and then the three men file past, disappearing into the back room, into Adam's *office*, like that's a normal thing.

"What's going on?" I ask, but Adam shakes his head.

"I'll tell you later."

I am instantly petulant. "No, tell me now."

"Katie—"

"No, tell me what's happening right now. What is that man doing here? I'm pretty sure Nush banned him."

"Keep your voice down. And Nush doesn't work here. She can't ban anyone."

"Then I will!"

"Voice *down*." He looks over his shoulder at the office door and takes my elbow, drawing me to the side. "You weren't supposed to be here," he says, and I stand my ground, waiting for him to break.

It takes two seconds.

"They're here to go over the deeds for the pub," he says, and I swear I stop breathing as an icy feeling of betrayal slithers over my skin. What the hell?

"You *sold* the—"

"No."

Oh. "Okay, I'm confused."

"Seriously, Katie. You weren't supposed to—"

"Confused, not dumb," I interrupt. "Explain it to me before I march in there and get them to."

Adam braces his arms against the bar, looking for once in his life like he'd rather be anywhere else. "How much do you know about property law in this country?"

"Take a wild guess."

"Probably about as much as me then. Or at least as much as me up until a few weeks ago." Another glance at the door and then he lowers his voice even more. "Apparently, Grandad Pat liked to gamble," he says, and I frown.

"Bow tie man? With the majestic eyebrows?"

Adam nods. "He got into some bad debt before Dad was born and his younger brother, my grand-uncle, had to bail him out."

"Alright. And I'm going to guess by the expression on your face you don't mean with a bag of spuds and two goats."

"All his savings," Adam confirms. "And then some. Our family had a fair bit of land back then, right the way around the lake, and they transferred all of it into his brother's name to keep it secure. Everything except Kelly's, so Grandad could still earn a living from running it. The only thing was Grandad kept gambling. So, while he was allowed to keep the pub, they put in an option clause so he couldn't sell it to pay off any future debts. Basically, saving him from himself. And it worked."

"Okay," I say slowly. "I've never been happier to be an only child, but it still doesn't explain why Jack Doyle is sitting in your office."

"The option clause said that Grandad's brother, as the adjoining landowner, had the right to buy the pub and take it from him if he wanted to. One month's notice and it was his. They put it into a contract, they signed it, and then Grandad met my grandmother, pulled himself together, and the whole thing was forgotten about. It's been collecting dust in some solicitor's office ever since."

"But why would that..." I trail off as I put the pieces together. "Glenmill bought the land." All the signs. All the fences. "They own the forest next to us."

"My grand-uncle left everything to the church when he died."

And the church sold everything off.

Adam nods as though reading my thoughts. "As the new adjoining landowner, Glenmill have the right to buy this place if they want to. And they want to. It's as good as theirs."

Theirs. I make a face, imagining them turning us into some sort of franchise. One with flashy advertising and terrible uniforms.

"So what? They're just going to buy Kelly's? Just like that? Why would they even want us?"

"They don't," Adam says, and that icy feeling returns.

"Okay," I say abruptly. "You're right. I shouldn't be here. I'll come back when I'm supposed to."

"Katie—"

"Remember that Gemma needs you to fix her machine. I'll see you later."

"They're going to close us down."

I stare at him, crossing and uncrossing my arms as I try and process his words. "I don't understand."

"They're going to close us down," he repeats. "Tear us down, actually. They want to build a new clubhouse for the golf course here."

The... I scoff, the noise coming out like a snort. That's just... that's... "That's bullshit," I say eventually, and he sighs. "No, they could be lying. Did you talk about this with someone who actually knows these things?"

"Of course I did. Don't you think I went to my solicitor the second they called? I've had three different people look over the papers. There's nothing we can do."

"For how much then?" My left leg is shaking. Why is my left leg shaking? "You said they can buy the pub, but for how much? You can just ask for something ridiculous and make them go away. Tell them five million euros or something. They're rich, but they're not that rich."

"It doesn't work like that. Option clause was two hundred pounds back then."

"Two *hundred*?" It's hard to wrap my head around. "So, they're leaving you with nothing?"

"Not nothing," Jack says, striding out from the back room. I whip around to glare at him, wondering how much he heard. "Adam will be more than welcome to work at the hotel. As will you be. He tells me you're a fine bartender."

He makes the compliment sound like an insult, patronizing and placating like he's dealing with a child.

"I don't want to work at the hotel," I tell him, as Callum appears alongside the lawyer. "I want to work here. Why do you have to knock it down at all?"

"Because the last time anything of note was done to this

place was fifty years ago and even that was shoddy work at best. You haven't even seen the plans," he adds, looking genuinely confused by my attitude. "We're going to build a terrace all the way out to the lake. The view will be stunning."

"But what's everyone going to do?" I ask, turning back to Adam. "The clubhouse will be private, and people rely on this place. Where are they going to go?"

"To the hotel," Jack says as though it's obvious, and the last of my patience snaps.

"I wasn't *asking* you," I say, and his smile drops as the door to the pub swings open. The woman I saw at the construction site enters with the same guy lugging his camera with him.

Jack brightens immediately. "Ah good, you're early." He waves them in as he turns back to Adam, ignoring me once more. "We're putting together some behind-the-scenes footage to show our progress over the next few months. I thought getting some shots of the lake might be good. In fact, why don't we take our little tête-à-tête outside? You should join us. Be good to get your knowledge on a few things."

"Sure," Adam says, his eyes on me as the others file out the back door. Callum's the last to go. "I'll be with you in a minute."

"I can't believe you're letting them get away with this," I whisper as soon as they're gone.

He scowls. "I'm not letting them get away with anything."

"But you're allowing them to roam around like it's already set in stone."

"What am I supposed to do?" he asks, exasperated. "Kick them out? Bar the doors?"

"You could fight it!" I hiss. "You could act like you care."

"You don't think I've tried?" He's snapping now, or as much as he can, with our voices still lowered. "I've been looking for a way out of this for weeks. But I don't have the kind of money to deal with what they've got. Or the connections. Of course I don't want to let this place go. Of course I care. This is my life, Katie. How could you say that?"

The hurt in his tone stops me in my tracks. I've never heard him sound so wounded before, so defeated. And I suddenly realize how tired he looks.

Adam's given his life to this pub, to this village. He doesn't have a family of his own, but he always seemed content with what he had. He might complain about it, he might grumble and side-eye me whenever I announce a quiz night. But he lets anyone who wants to host everything from birthdays to book clubs to bingo. He lets me decorate every holiday, lets us all treat this place like a second home as opposed to a professional establishment. Our population skews older here and not everyone has family nearby. Sometimes, an hour or two at Kelly's is the only time they might speak with another human in days.

There would be no Ennisbawn without Kelly's. And there would be no Kelly's without Adam.

"I'm sorry," I say.

"I know." He runs a hand down his face, glancing at the back door. "Take the day off, okay? I'm sorry too. I didn't mean to snap at you, and this isn't how I wanted you to find out."

"I don't want to go home." I have the sudden irrational feeling that if I do, this place won't be here when I return. "Does anyone else know?"

He shakes his head. "I hadn't gotten that far yet."

Jack Doyle's booming laugh sounds from outside, drawing our attention.

"I'd better go out," Adam says eventually. "They want to discuss timelines."

Timelines. It all sounds so official. So formal. So not what this is.

When I don't respond, he pours some glasses of water, and joins the others, leaving me alone.

At least this explains why he was so rude to Callum the other night. Adam often took on a paternal role in my life and I thought it was just his usual protectiveness, but no. It was actually because he'd caught his lone employee skulking around in the dark with a man who was about to make her unemployed. I feel a sudden burst of anger at the thought, and as though my swinging emotions called him, Callum himself opens the door, pausing when he sees me.

"Thought I should..." He holds up three empty water glasses, and when I just stare at him, he leaves them on the bar.

"Did you know this was going to happen?" I ask, when he starts to head outside again.

He turns back to face me, his expression guarded. "Not until a few hours ago, no."

"And I'm sure you're devastated for us." I reach for a packet of Christmas napkins and tear it open.

"I'm just doing my job," he says evenly.

"Yeah, well, your job is costing me mine." There's a lump in my throat as soon as I say it, as though the idea only hits me there and then. They're going to knock down the pub. They're going to knock it down and then what?

I've never considered my life without this pub. My parents met here. They had their wedding party here. I won't pretend it's not the reason I gravitated toward this place when I was younger or why I've always felt so at home. Kelly's is more than just four walls and a roof. It's one of my last connections to my parents, and I cherish it. I always have.

"You okay?"

I shake my head, refocusing on the napkins, but something is tugging at the corner of my mind, pulling and prodding and begging me to listen.

"Katie?"

The way he says my name makes me scowl. He says it like he knows me. Like he's concerned about me. Though, how concerned can the man be if he's ripping my home apart brick by brick? If he's just going to step aside and let his boss bulldoze over the pub and the garden and the well and...

"Look," Callum starts. "I swear I didn't know this was going to—"

I drop the napkins, ignoring how they scatter to the ground as I rush to the back door, and burst outside. Adam is sitting at the picnic bench with the lawyer and the marketing team while Jack stands at the edge of the patio, his hand shielding his eyes as he peers at the lake.

Callum comes barreling out a second later, obviously not expecting me to still be there. I know this because he bumps straight into me, grabbing my apron strings before I can go sprawling. The commotion draws the group's attention and I shake him off, striding forward into the sunlight.

Adam takes one look at my expression and rises. "Katie—"

"You can't tear down the pub," I say, and this time Jack can barely hide his irritation.

"And why is that?" he asks.

"Because." The word flies out of me, confident and purposeful and followed by nothing else.

Jack raises a brow, and I swallow, almost hearing Nush's voice in my ear as I straighten my shoulders. *Chin up, Katie. Chin up, gaze straight, boobs out.*

"Because of the wishing well."

"The..." He falters in a way that tells me he definitely wasn't expecting me to come out with *that*, and glances at his team. "What?"

I gesture to the structure beside him, the one so small, so unimportant that none of them seem to realize it's there until I point it out to them.

"The well?" he repeats.

"*Wishing* well. You make wishes."

"I'm familiar with the concept." His eyes flick over my head and, a second later, Callum moves past me to stand by him.

"That well has been there since before this village was even founded," I continue. "It's a historic structure. A *famed* structure. My parents met at that well."

"How nice for them."

"They're dead now."

Adam gives me a *you did not* look as Jack's eyes narrow.

"Did you know we hold a matchmaking festival here?" I continue as my boss sighs. "Every summer. People come, and they make a wish—"

"Katie—"

"And they find their match," I finish. "Their soulmates. They find them here. In Kelly's."

"How magical," Jack says flatly, and I pin him with a stare.

"You don't believe in magic, Mr. Doyle?"

"Do you?" he counters. He's getting annoyed now. A vein has appeared on his forehead, like a little blue worm. It gives me all the confidence I need.

"You try and tear down this pub, and I will make sure everyone in the country knows exactly what you're doing. They might not care about some fields in the middle of nowhere, but they'll care about their heritage. About their folklore. I know people who still avoid fairy bushes," I add, thinking of Granny. "Do you think they'll be happy once they hear what you want to do? Destroy a part of our culture just so you can have a nice view of the lake? A few dozen people protesting might not bother you, but what about a few thousand? How's that going to look in every Google search of your company?"

"I..." He turns to his lawyer, who gives him a blank look before scrambling for his phone. "Look, Kerry—"

"Katie," I correct. "Katie Collins."

"Miss Collins," he begins. "I understand that this has come as a surprise, but as your boss here has no doubt explained, this land is as good as ours. So, unless you have another card up your sleeve, which I must admit, I'd be fascinated to hear, none of this is exactly going to hold up in court."

"Not a legal one, but what about the court of public opinion? This pub is of huge cultural significance to this town and to tear it down would mean trouble. You think we don't know how to spin a story around here? You think we won't try?"

"I think you'll find we..." He trails off as he looks over my shoulder and I turn to see the marketing people filming our every word. "What are you doing?"

The woman shrugs. "B-roll."

"I'm sure you have enough."

"Sunlight's better now."

"The sunlight's—" He breaks off with a little laugh, like we're all testing him.

I grow nervous when he doesn't say anything more, but the fact that Jack hasn't immediately dismissed me keeps me standing there until Peter clears his throat, his gaze darting between his boss and his phone.

"They moved a road."

"What?"

"They moved a road around a fairy bush," he continues, his thumb scrolling down his phone. "In 1999. And in the 1960s too. Preservation of local culture. Pretty big protests, actually. They even—"

"Yes, thank you, Peter," Jack snaps, eyeing me like I'm a stone caught in his shoe, and I open my mouth, about to argue again, when his expression suddenly wipes clean.

Uh-oh.

The back of my knees start to feel a little funny. Like I'm standing at a great height, looking down at my doom. I think I prefer it when he glares at me. At least then I know what to expect.

I start to lose my nerve, hyperaware of everyone looking at me. Time to beg. "Look, you can't just—"

"You make an important point," he interrupts, and Adam and I share a shocked glance. We're not the only ones.

"She does?" Callum asks, sounding wary as hell.

"Yes," Jack says. "And that's twice she's accused me of not caring about the community here. It sounds like I have a bit of work to do to earn back some trust. I think I'll start by giving her the chance to prove herself."

"*Prove* myself?" That does not sound good. Why does that not sound good? "What do you mean?"

"You can't just expect me to take your word for it," he says, looking surprised. "Especially seeing as how I've never heard of this festival before. But if it's the cultural event you say it is, of course we'll have to ask the Board to reconsider their plans."

"The festival?"

He latches onto the doubt in my voice. "That's what you said, isn't it? You hold it every summer."

"I... yes, but—" The triumphant look on his face stops me dead. "Yes," I say again, though the word comes out a little scratchy.

"Then I look forward to seeing it myself."

Bluff called. That's what he's really saying. That's what he's telling me with that smirky little smirk.

"Okay," Adam begins. "Let's just—"

"And we look forward to having you," I say over him, ignoring the pained look on his face. "You're not taking this pub without a fight."

I actually thought the last bit sounded pretty good, but Jack looks bored now, like he's already won.

"Uh-huh." He gestures for the camera people to resume filming the lake, clearly finished with the conversation. In fact, the only people still paying any attention to me are Callum, who keeps trying to catch my eye, and Adam, who looks like he wants to have a strong word with me.

I decide a tactical retreat is best, and so I make my way stiffly back inside, trying to ignore the sickly feeling in the pit of my stomach as I wonder just what the hell I've gotten myself into.

CHAPTER SIX

There's a reason I never did drama at school. A reason I never tried out for debate or learned an instrument or did anything that meant I'd be inviting people's eyes. I don't do well under pressure. I get nervous. I get tongue-tied. I second-guess myself and my palms get clammy. I say things without thinking and regret them as soon as I do. This is why I'm pleasantly surprised when I sit in Gemma's kitchen an hour later, feeling completely serene about what just happened, even while everyone else around me clearly does not.

"This is my fault," Adam says, as he paces up and down the small room. "I should have said something. I should have stopped you and said something."

"But you didn't," I point out.

He doesn't seem to hear me. "We can call their office. We can explain that you were upset and didn't mean it."

"That's just the adrenaline talking."

"It's damage control," he says sharply. "How are you not seeing this? Is it because you're not sleeping? Is that it?"

"I've been sleeping fine all week," I say, peering at Gemma's laptop as I bookmark an article. "I'm extremely well rested."

"Well, you're not acting like it!"

"So we're just yelling in my house now?" Gemma enters the room with an armful of Noah's sports clothes and a stern glare. "That's a thing we're doing?"

"I wasn't yelling," Adam mutters, even though he kind of was. "But you shouldn't have gotten into his face like that," he says to me. "You realize he's going to use this to rush the process?"

"That's not what he said. He said he would give us a chance to prove ourselves."

"That doesn't mean anything. The guy could send a team down there tomorrow if he wanted to, and he probably will because you pissed him off. I figured I had another year at least to get everything in order, but now..." He shakes his head, looking ill.

"We could key his car," Nush says from her seat beside me. "Or slash his tires. Or..." She pauses as the three of us turn to look at her. "Too far?"

Adam swings back to me. "Why did you have to do that?"

"Um, because it worked? I'm saving your business and you're welcome?"

He looks like he wants to yell at me some more, but a throat clear from Gemma stops him. "I've got to get back to the pub," he announces instead.

"The pub I just saved?"

"Katie—"

Noah appears in the kitchen doorway, cutting him off from whatever rant he was about to go on. "You're being too loud. I can't do my homework." He looks to his mother. "Can I watch TV until they go?"

"Nice try," Gemma says. "And no."

"But I can't concentrate."

"Then go with Adam and do your work at Kelly's."

Adam shoots her a look, but Noah seems excited about the

suggested change in scenery and runs out of the room before she can change her mind.

"Don't want to be the guy that disappoints my child," Gemma warns, when Adam goes to argue.

"I'm not minding him," he says. "I've got enough to do."

"He'll be grand. Just don't give him any hard liquor before five. He likes you."

The last bit shuts Adam up, just as Gemma knew it would, but unfortunately, all that means is he returns his attention to me.

"I'll see you later," he says, back to boss mode. "You're on wash-up tonight."

"I was on wash-up yesterday," I protest, but he ignores me, grabbing his jacket as he calls for Noah. A second later, I hear the kid's footsteps on the stairs and the door slams shut.

"He seems tense," Nush says, as Gemma programs the machine. The sound of running water fills the room, and she sits with a groan at the table, drawing her mug toward her.

"At least we know why he's been in a mood for the last few weeks," she says.

"He was in a mood?"

"He was mood*ier*," she corrects. "And now it's only going to get worse. What the hell are we going to do?"

I frown. "What do you mean?"

"With the pub."

Nush leans forward. "I still think targeting their cars sends a real message about the traffic issue."

"I already told you what we're going to do," I say, confused. Adam and I had come straight here once Jack and his team left. I'd just spent the last twenty minutes explaining what happened while Adam fixed Gemma's washing machine and grew more and more panicked.

"I mean seriously, Katie," Gemma says now.

"I am being serious." I spin the laptop around to show them

what I've been looking at. "We're going to revive the Ennisbawn Matchmaking Festival."

Two lines slowly appear between Nush's eyebrows as she stares at the screen. Gemma just stares at me.

"What?"

"We're going to revive the Ennisbawn—"

"No, I heard the words," she interrupts slowly. "I just don't understand them."

I smile. "Your doubt just makes me stronger. It feeds me."

"Katie—"

"Like a flame."

"What's happening to Adam is awful," she says firmly. "But there's no legal reason Glenmill can't—"

"I'm so glad you brought that up," I interrupt, pointing at the screen. I did some quick googling when I got here, and all it did was confirm what the lawyer had said back in Kelly's. "There are plenty of examples of companies backing down over culturally important sites. In the 1960s, civil engineers removed a fairy fort for a new road near Ballynahinch and the locals kicked up such a fuss that it made BBC news. *And* in 1999, in County Clare, they adjusted plans for a whole bypass to incorporate a bush because enough people were talking about it."

"Yes, but fairy forts are real," Gemma says. "And the matchmaking festival was just an excuse for leery men to do some leering."

Nush looks at her in surprise. "You think fairy forts are real?"

"No," she says, shifting uncomfortably. "But they're not *not* real."

"My point is that it got publicity," I say. "They moved a bypass! For a bush! So why can't we keep Kelly's for a festival?"

"Because the festival hasn't run properly in years? We barely even had it last year. You just put up some old Valentine's Day decorations. It's hardly enough to get on the news."

"Hence why we're *reviving*," I say. "Bringing it back to its former glory. What else are we going to do? Chain ourselves to the doors?"

At this, Nush perks up, but Gemma ignores her.

"I know you're freaking out about the pub," she says. "We all are. None of us want to see this happen, but there's nothing we can do."

"We can do this," I insist. "I got them to back down, didn't I? Jack said he'd wait and see."

"Because he knows you were lying! He's playing with you. Probably so it all goes up in flames and none of us ever bother him again. Why don't we call a meeting and see about another protest? Something we can—"

"We tried protesting," I interrupt. "We protested for months. Nush made signs."

"I did," Nush says, sliding the laptop closer to her.

"None of it worked," I continue. "None of it brought us the attention we need. This will."

"You'll need money to get it off the ground," Gemma points out. "How are you going to pay for it?"

"Sponsorships."

"From whom?"

"From *people*. Oh, come on!" I add, when she groans. "It's Adam. You've known the guy your whole life. We can't just abandon him like this."

"I never said I was going to."

"But it's what you're doing," I say, and she goes quiet. "We've gone down the angry letters to the council route. We've done petitions. We've done everything short of burning the site to the ground— *no*," I add, when Nush opens her mouth. "So, let's try this. Let's prove that we can bring people back to the village without destroying it. Let's show that we can—"

"Katie."

"Really make a difference to—"

"*Katie,*" Nush presses.

"What?" I ask, turning to her. There's a look on her face that's nothing short of zealous.

"I'm in."

"What?" My tone softens by about ninety percent. "Really?"

"Yes," she says, beaming. "I love a long con."

"It's not a... well, okay, it's a bit of a con, but—"

"You're not serious," Gemma interrupts.

"I'm deadly serious," Nush says. "Katie's right; nothing else has worked. Plus, I'm really good at projects. I'm a very goal-oriented person."

Gemma mutters something under her breath, and I swing back to her.

"I can do it without you," I say. "But I don't want to."

"It's not that I'm okay with what they're doing," she says. "But it's going to be a lot harder than you think to pull off something like this."

"So help me. Help Adam. He'll get behind it if you will."

"How does that check out?"

"You have an air of authority."

She scoffs, but I can see the indecision in her eyes. Behind her, the washing machine starts spinning so rapidly it begins to shake, and Nush pouts, widening her eyes until Gemma sighs.

"This might not work," she says. "You need to be aware of that."

"Is this your way of telling me you're in?"

"I... fine. Yes. I'm in. *Don't* hug me," she adds, as I go to do just that. "Adam wouldn't know what to do with himself if he lost that pub. I'd be a shit friend if I did nothing about it."

I grin at her, placing my hand into the center of our little circle. Nush immediately places hers on top.

Gemma just looks at me. "Really?"

"Don't be lame," I moan. "Join the dream team."

"You guys are ridiculous," she mutters, but she puts her hand on top anyway, and the pact is complete.

I sit back, not realizing how nervous I'd been that she'd say no. "And that's the hard part done."

"*I'm* the hard part?" she asks, sounding insulted.

"The hardest," I shrug. "You're a natural cynic. Now that I've got you and, by extension, Adam on my side, everyone else will fall in line."

Simple.

———

"But the festival hasn't run in years."

I meet the eye of John Joe Byrne at the back of the room and force down a sigh. We've been having the same conversation in various guises for the past ten minutes, and I'm running out of ways to spin this thing.

After I convinced the girls, Nush threw out the agenda for the village's usual Friday meeting so we could discuss our latest emergency. I knew the threat to Kelly's would be the last straw for many of us, but I have to admit, I thought they'd be a little quicker to jump aboard the festival train. Even after my expla-nation and then downright pleading, I still see more than one unconvinced face in front of me.

"I know that," I say. "We're bringing it back."

"But the reason it ended was because people stopped coming," Bridget says, her forehead scrunched in confusion. "What's going to make them come this time?"

"*We* will," I say, spreading my arms wide. "With everyone's help, we're going to put on the best festival in the country. St. Patrick himself won't know what hit him."

I say the last part a little too cheerfully and Granny gestures at me from where she sits near the front, making a subtle *tone it down* motion with her hands.

"Look, we've been talking for ages about ways to bring life back to the village," I say. "This festival used to be one of the highlights of the year. If we pull this off, we might not just save the very pub we're sitting in now, but also show people what makes small communities so great. We need to remind them that we're here and that we deserve to be."

Danny's shaking his head before I'm even finished. "I just don't see how this is going to work. I mean no offense, Katie, but there's no way you'll be able to go up against Glenmill on your own. You're just a bartender."

Granny whips around faster than I've ever seen her move. "And what's wrong with being a bartender?"

Danny, understandably, looks scared. "Nothing, I—"

"Do you think it's an easy job staying on your feet all night and putting up with the likes of you?"

"I just mean—"

"When you have a better idea, I'll be glad to give you the floor, but until then, you can keep your mouth quiet and drink the beer my granddaughter so expertly poured for you."

"Granny," I warn, but she just ignores me.

"Everyone's gotten far too comfortable if you ask me," she says loudly. "Expecting everything to stay the same when you don't even fight for it. You'd all be lost with Kelly's and you know it. I thought I knew the people in this village, I thought I was proud to call them my neighbors. But all I'm seeing is a bunch of people giving up."

Frank frowns. "That's a little harsh, Maeve."

"It's the truth," she snaps, as people start to argue among themselves.

"And I don't plan to do it on my own," I say, raising my voice. "Like I said, if we all work together, we'll be able to..."

Yeah, they've stopped listening.

I look hopelessly to where Gemma and Nush sit at the bar, not knowing what to do, but they just motion for me to continue. I don't. It's useless. Even if I did know what to say, it's impossible to be heard over everyone. At least it is until Nush's bell rings sharply, cutting through the arguments. But it's not Nush who grips it this time. It's Adam.

"Alright, everyone shut up," he yells, and I fight back a wince. There's a reason he doesn't do a lot of public speaking. "Okay, good," he says, when the room quietens. "Now look, when Dad died, he... well, it's no secret he thought I'd maybe want to get rid of this place. Take the money and run. But it didn't cross my mind for a second. This was his pub. And it was my grandfather's pub and *his* father's pub, no matter what a piece of paper might say. It's as much a part of me as my memories of them are, and I don't want to let that go. But I need help. I need your help. And right now, Katie's the only one trying to keep this place alive. If she thinks we can pull this off, then I believe her. We're not going to stop them from building that hotel. But we are going to stop them from tearing down this pub. At the very least, I want to try. I have to try."

Everyone stares at him. *I* stare at him. This is the sincerest Adam's ever been, and it's kind of unnerving, if not appreciated.

When no one says anything else, he meets my gaze, nodding an apology for panicking earlier.

"Go on, Katie," he says.

One by one, every head in the room swings back to me, but what little confidence I had has vanished, and I look to my friends with a clear *help* expression, as my forehead breaks out in a sweat.

"Show of support for Katie's idea," Nush calls and raises a hand in the air. I try not to show how relieved I am as a surprising number of people join her. Gemma, Adam, Granny. Bridget does as well. As does Frank, who gives me a smile when I glance at him. But it's the more reluctant ones that I watch out for until, slowly, the fifty or so assembled people in the room all raise their palms.

"Well, there you have it," Nush says. "A legally binding agreement."

Frank frowns. "It's not—"

Nush rings the bell, cutting him off, and people get up, stretching before they head to the bar. The bar that I scurry back to, seeing as how I'm technically on the clock.

"Now what?" Gemma asks, as I join her and Nush by the counter.

"Easy," I say, grabbing a handful of glasses. "Now we just need to pull it off."

"Katie," Gemma groans, but I just smile at her, undeterred.

I mean, come on. How hard can it be?

CHAPTER SEVEN

Turns out, very hard.

"You barely have a business plan, Katie."

"But I have spirit," I protest. "And gumption."

"And I admire that, but that's not going to be enough here."

I pout at Harry as he sits back in one of the low leather armchairs dotting the café. It's a chain one in the city center and is still busy with the last of the lunchtime rush. I usually wouldn't dare pay so much for a coffee I could make at home, but his office is nearby and, though it took two bus rides to get here, I wanted to meet him in person.

Harry grew up in Ennisbawn, and we dated for a while when we were teenagers, doing all the things young couples do until he moved away for college and, in the space of a few weeks, joined a rowing club, realized he was gay, broke up with me and then met the love of his life. I don't think the rowing club had anything to do with the other stuff, but he was very excited about it at the time.

We remained friends, and last year I acted as one of the groomspeople at his wedding, an extremely fancy affair where I had too much champagne and ate nine mini quiches. Now he sits before me, dressed in a navy suit and light brown shoes, with his dirty blond hair gelled to the side in such a way that I know he spent a long time practicing how to get it just right.

I called him over the weekend but am already regretting my decision to come all this way to see him. He seemed mostly amused on the phone, but now he's acting like Gemma did, shutting me down at every turn.

"Your bank literally ran a multimillion-euro campaign about backing small businesses," I tell him, as he takes a sip of his foamy latte. "*I* am a small business."

"You are a woman with an idea."

"An exciting idea."

"You need plans," he says. "You need financial forecasts. You need mini essays about the good of the community and cost analysis."

"*You* need to tell the truth in your television adverts."

"I'll pass that along," he says diplomatically. "Look, it's not a bad start. You just need to take smaller steps first. Have you applied for an arts grant?"

"It will be too late. I won't get the money until next year and this needs to happen now. That's the whole point of it. They're going to tear down the pub, Harry. *Our* pub."

"*Your* pub. I haven't been to Kelly's in years. I don't even drink that much anymore. Only on special occasions."

"You don't have to drink to visit," I say, outraged. "We have mocktails now."

He smirks, but it fades almost immediately, and I know what he's going to say before he even opens his mouth. "If you need a job—"

"I have a job."

"I can help you with some applications," he continues as if I haven't spoken. "We have lots of entry to mid-level positions open. I can think of at least three off the top of my head that you'd be great at."

"Stop trying to change the subject."

"I'm not. If the pub closes, then you'll need work. There's work in the city. Good work. With benefits and pensions and cake on people's birthdays."

"I'm not going to commute for three hours a day."

"Then move closer."

"And leave Granny?"

"Move her with you." He leans forward, clasping his hands together as he looks me in the eye. "You need to be realistic about this."

"What I *need* is money to get this thing off the ground. And surely the whole point of knowing someone in a bank is to benefit from a little nepotism. It's like we don't even know who we are as a country anymore."

"You have no experience in running something like this. If you want to put on a show, you need to get someone who knows what they're doing. Why don't you hire a project manager? Or an events team?"

"Because I don't have any money!" I half exclaim, half moan. "That's why I'm talking to you. You're supposed to tell me what a brilliant idea this is and give me a big fat check and maybe a free pen."

"We don't really do checks anymore," he says, unaffected by my glare. "I'm sorry, Katie. But I'm telling you now, you're not going to get anything for something like this. You have to think smaller."

"We can't go smaller. No one's going to pay attention if I just put up some bunting and have a barbecue."

He gives me a helpless shrug, and I sit back, abandoning my good girl posture for a sad girl slump as my blazer stretches uncomfortably around my shoulders. Anushka let me borrow it for today, saying I needed to look the part. Fat lot of good that did me.

"Okay," I say. "Second plan. You and me. Bank heist."

He gives me a look, and we fall into silence, mine decidedly sulkier than his. "How's Maeve doing?" he asks after a while.

"Fine," I say, still a little sore he didn't just hand over a burlap sack with a dollar sign on it. "She had a fall a few weeks ago."

His brow furrows in concern, but I wave it off. "She's grand. It wasn't that bad. She just got extra grouchy afterward because she was embarrassed."

"I'm glad to hear she's alright."

"Yeah. Bad bruise on her hip, though." I twist a lock of hair around my finger as I remember the ugly purple splotch of it. "Her doctor said it's probably going to keep happening. She's not doing her stretches enough because she's stubborn and infuriating and..."

And even if she did them, it probably wouldn't help that much.

I don't finish the sentence, turning my gaze toward the window. It started raining in the last few minutes, a heavy, spitting kind that hits against the glass as though trying to break through. The storm has officially arrived.

"Can you at least ask about the loan?" I ask. "Or enquire or whatever it is you do."

"Of course. You know I will."

"But you don't think I'll get anything."

"Not a cent," he says, as his phone flashes with a silent alarm. He turns it off, his gaze softening as he takes me in. "I'm sorry about the pub, Katie. I really am."

"Yeah," I sigh. "I know."

"Give me a call if it doesn't work out, okay? I know you're scared to move—"

"I'm not *scared*."

"But us city folk aren't so bad," he finishes. "And a job's a job." He drains the last of his coffee and grabs his coat, looking out the window in dismay. "You get the bus in?"

I nod. "There's one in thirty minutes. I'm good."

"You sure?"

"It'll pass. It's just a shower."

He leans down to hug me and then he's gone, rushing out the door with a newspaper over his head as he tries to escape the deluge. I wait another ten minutes for the rain to ease before resigning myself to the fact that it won't and am barely two steps out of the door before I'm drenched through, my rain jacket doing nothing to keep me dry as the wind whips around me. It only gets worse when I get down the road and see how packed my bus stop is, and I make a snap decision, diving through the door of the nearest restaurant and wishing I had just stayed at the damn café.

The hostess gives me a suspicious look, but I pretend to browse the menu until she's distracted by an actual customer, when I then try to sneakily locate the toilets so I can hide for a few minutes. It's a nice joint. Trendy décor, soft jazz music playing. The kind of place where the menus are small and the wine bottles have corks and not just screwcaps. Feeling distinctly out-of-place, I slip behind a waiter carrying an admittedly delicious-looking cheese plate toward the back of the room only to stop in my tracks when I spot a familiar face.

Callum.

He sits alone at a small table, scrolling through his phone. He doesn't see me. He doesn't look up, or feel me watching, or know I'm there at all. And I know I should turn around and walk out again, but I don't move.

Granny loves signs.

There is no such thing as a coincidence in her mind, only fate and omens and *que sera, sera*s. And while I've never really bought into any of it, it's her I think of now as I squeeze my way between the other diners and drop into the seat opposite him.

He looks up as soon as I do, an expression of relief switching to confusion when he sees who I am. "What are you—"

"Kismet."

"What?"

I let my bag fall to the floor and wipe my damp face with my equally damp sleeve. "This is kismet," I tell him.

His mouth opens and closes before settling into a frown. "You look like you swam here."

"It's raining."

But he has a point. I'm dripping all over the floor and quickly shrug off my coat before tying my hair back as best I can.

Callum looks around like he's the victim of a practical joke, but when no cameramen pop out, he turns back to me. "Did you follow me here?"

"*No.* I told you, kismet."

"Stop saying that."

"Stop threatening to tear down my pub."

He just stares at me. "That's it?" he asks, when I don't continue. "That's your big negotiating tactic?"

"Did it work?"

"No. Not that that matters, though, right? Because of your amazing festival?"

"Oh, so you've heard of it?"

He gives me a look. "I know you don't have one."

"You don't know anything. But I'm not here to argue with you."

"Why are you here at all? *Don't* say kismet."

I press my lips together because I was definitely going to say that. "I think if you can just talk to your boss, you could—"

"I can't do anything," he interrupts. "Traffic flow is where my power ends, and I'm sorry about the pub. I am. But it's just a pub. It's a building with four walls and a sticky floor. There are thousands of them all over this island and yours isn't that special."

"It's special to us," I say sharply. "And our floor is *not* sticky."

"Your whole village has been up in arms ever since we bought the land," he says, sounding just as annoyed as I am now. "It's like you refuse to see a good thing when it's staring right at you. Do you know how many jobs are going to be created because of this hotel? Do you know how much money is going to start coming into the area?"

"And here we go with the money talk."

"Half of your main street is abandoned! Half your houses are too."

"That doesn't mean you can just destroy the other half."

"You know, I don't think you even care about the pub," he says. "I think you're just clinging to the last thing you can because you know you can't stop us."

"And I don't think you care about anything," I retort. "That's what makes it even worse. You don't care about what you're doing or who you're doing it to. The only thing any of you are thinking about is money and profit, and I hate it. I hate Glenmill and I hate people like you."

Callum stiffens at the last bit, and I slam my mouth shut, surprised at myself.

"I didn't mean that," I say, as all my resentment rushes out of me.

He shrugs, his expression carefully blank. "Yeah, you did."

"I didn't. I'm just angry. I say things I don't mean when I'm angry. It's why I don't like arguing."

"Well, you're pretty good at it," he says, as his phone lights up with a text. Whatever it says makes him tense further, and it's only then I notice the empty wine glass beside him and how... how *nice* he looks. He's no longer wearing the practical, weatherworn clothes of a construction site. He's in a long-sleeved navy button-down shirt that fits him perfectly. A silver watch glints on his wrist, and his dark hair is brushed back and swept away from his face. He's dressed up.

I sit back, even more conscious of how I'm dripping all over the place. "Is this, like, a business lunch thing or..."

"It's supposed to be a date."

My eyes bulge at the same time a sharp bolt of jealousy shoots through me, and I do a quick sweep of the restaurant as though a beautiful woman will suddenly appear. "With who?"

"I'm not sure yet. I've sat here for thirty minutes waiting for someone to walk through that door, only for you to show up instead." He swipes a finger across his phone, rereading the text. "Is your name secretly Melissa?"

"No."

"Then I've been waiting here thirty-five minutes."

"You're being stood up?" I whisper-ask. "You're on a blind date, and you're being stood up?"

"Looks like it."

Oh, not cool. Even if he is the enemy. But before I can tell him so, a waiter approaches with a wide smile and places two menus before us.

"Would you like to hear the chef's—"

"No," we say in unison. The man looks a bit miffed but takes the hint and leaves us alone. Or at least he does for a second before he comes back and lights a candle. I mean, read the room, my guy.

Callum doesn't move, and I find my previous determination has vanished as we sit together in stiff silence.

"So do you want company or—"

"No."

I almost wilt in relief. "Right. Okay. So, I should—"

"Yep."

Noted. I stand, the chair screeching as I reach for my coat. Callum doesn't even look at me, he just sits back, tilting his head to the ceiling like he's praying for patience. Or maybe for a sink-hole to swallow him up.

"I don't hate you," I say because I still feel bad about that. "But I think you're on the wrong side and I think you know that. I hope your date shows up."

He drops his head, but I leave before he can reply, striding through the tables and straight out the door, where I come to an abrupt stop as a puff of wind sends icy raindrops into my face.

Jesus.

I shrug on my coat, zipping it up tight as I'm reminded why I ducked into the restaurant in the first place. My bus stop down the road is still crammed with people hiding from the weather, so I decide to stay where I am, figuring it's probably safest for the time being. That is until a minute later when the door opens behind me, letting a second's worth of peaceful background chatter out before it closes again. When no one steps past, I turn around to find Callum standing with his back to it, looking at me like I just spat in his food.

"Hi," I say, when he doesn't.

"It's still raining."

"Yes."

"Why are you standing in the rain?"

"I'm not; I'm sheltering. There's a shelter." I point up at the little eave above the doorway, the one that does nothing to stop the wind from moving the rain in any direction it pleases, but it's the best I have right now. "Why are *you* standing in the rain?"

"Because I can see you from my table, and it's annoying me. Why don't you have an umbrella?"

"It wouldn't last two seconds," I say, as another gust of wind comes hurtling down the street. As if on cue, a woman walks past, angrily shaking her own small umbrella as it flies inside out. God. Summer can't come fast enough. I am not a winter rain girl. I am a summer sunshine girl. A light jacket, short dress, old pair of Converse sunshine girl. "How is it that in the history of mankind, when we've created all of this medical equipment and fancy technology, no one, not a single person, has come up with a better idea than an umbrella?" I pull the ties of my hood tighter under my chin and glare at the clouds. "It's ridiculous that that's what we've settled on. Just think of the money you'd make if you invented something better."

There's no response from Callum, and when I look over, I find him staring at me.

"It's a valid question," I say, defensive.

He looks tired. "Where are you parked?"

"Nowhere. I took the bus."

"You don't drive?"

"I can drive. I just don't like to."

"Then how are you getting home?"

"Also the bus?"

It seems like a pretty obvious thing to me, but Callum appears genuinely irritated now, like I'm being annoying on purpose and not just standing here minding my own business. "There's no bus to Ennisbawn," he says.

"There's one to Rossbridge. I'll walk from there."

"It's raining."

"I *know*. I'll survive. It's just rain."

He mutters something under his breath, something I have a feeling is a not-so-polite comment about me, and goes back inside without even a goodbye. I gape after him, insulted and oddly disappointed, but before I can dwell too much on either of those things, he reappears, stepping back out with a large golf umbrella. At first, I think he's going to give it to me. Then he opens his mouth.

"I'll drop you home."

Um. No. "You don't have to—"

"I'm parked by the church."

"What about your date?" I ask, as he pulls on his coat. "What if she shows up?"

"Then she'll know what it feels like, won't she?"

I step out of the way as he opens the umbrella. "Glenmill Properties" is emblazoned along the side like on all the construction site's boardings. I feel like a traitor just looking at it, but also: rain.

"You coming or what?" he asks, when I just stand there, and I dip underneath the shelter, only for him to immediately swap our places, sidestepping behind me so I'm not standing by the road. I'm grateful for it a second later as a car comes tearing around the corner, driving straight through a puddle and drenching everyone who happens to be too close.

Jackass.

"You really don't have to—"

"This way," Callum says, and takes off without waiting for me, forcing me to jog to keep up with him or get caught in the downpour as he leads me down the street.

CHAPTER EIGHT

It's an awkward few minutes' walk to the church while I try to match my steps with Callum's, while also avoiding puddles. It would be much easier if I could stand closer to him. If he were Nush or Gemma or Harry, I would loop my arm through his and huddle in tight, but with Callum, it's like a game to see how much distance we can keep between each other without getting wet. A game we're both really good at.

When we finally reach the church, he leads me to a dark green van near the entrance. It's chilly inside but dry and clean, and he turns the heater on as soon as we get in.

"Betcha it'll stop raining now," I say, as he strips off his coat. I keep mine on, trying not to be too obvious as I look around. But if I was secretly hoping for some magical bit of insight into Callum's psyche, I'd be disappointed. There's nothing. Naught. Nada. Zilch. Not even an air freshener hanging from the rearview. Maybe it's a rental.

I hit the radio button as a last resort, disappointment filling me when it turns to a generic news station.

Callum gives me a knowing look. "Hoping for something embarrassing?"

"There is no such thing as embarrassing music taste," I say, turning it off again. "But also, yes."

He doesn't answer, pulling out from the tight space and steering us toward home. Or my home, at least.

The traffic is slow with the weather, but we're near the outskirts of the city and, in a matter of minutes, we're back on country roads with dark green fields on either side of us. Callum's wipers work overtime, but I can still barely see through the deluge, only brief glimpses of the tarmac and the lights from the other cars around us. My chest tightens with a familiar clench of anxiety, and I force myself to breathe evenly, in through the nose and out through the mouth.

I'm not great in cars. Never have been. Not since my parents. But it's much worse in bad weather. Especially when I have nothing to distract myself with.

"So," I say. "Do you go on a lot of dates?"

"I'd say a normal amount," he responds dryly, and I nod.

A normal amount is a normal answer. Even if it makes me feel acutely uncharitable to all the anonymous women I imagine sitting opposite him.

"I got stood up once," I continue, aware that I'm babbling but preferring it to silence. "Third date. We were supposed to meet for coffee, but he never showed. I thought he was dead. He wasn't. He just didn't want to see me again and was too chicken to say so. I think he's married now. Last time I checked anyway."

"You checked?"

"Of course I checked."

"You always keep tabs on people you've dated?"

"Not all of them," I say, defensive. "Just the ones I have grudges against. Don't you?"

"No."

"Well, you should. Sometimes, you find out they're doing

badly and it's really satisfying." He doesn't respond and I sit up, fidgeting with my seatbelt. "Your car is very clean."

"My—" He shakes his head. "There are no segues with you, are there? You're just straight in."

"It's a compliment!"

"Not when you sound so surprised."

"I sound surprised because I am surprised."

"Because I work in construction?"

"Well, yeah."

"I spend all day in the dirt. I don't like to bring it home with me." He peers out the windshield before checking his blind spot, and I relax a little with how careful he's being.

"I can't believe you were going to get the bus in this," he says, back to sounding annoyed.

"There is nothing wrong with the bus." When it shows up.

"You know, when the hotel is built, the village will be on a direct route to—"

"I know. I've read your leaflets."

"I'm just saying, it's not all doom and gloom. You're the one who was going to walk forty minutes from Rossbridge."

"I like walking."

"In this?" He gestures out the windshield, and I flinch as he momentarily lets go of the steering wheel. "Did anyone ever tell you that you're stubborn?"

"No," I say primly. "I'm a delight to everyone else."

"Well, I'll try not to take it personally," he mutters, and we fall quiet as other vehicles speed past us, sending surface spray into the air. I grow restless, my knee shaking with each sweep of the wipers, and I reach for the radio again, needing distraction from my thoughts.

I must have hit a different button this time, though, because it doesn't turn to the news station, and a little Bluetooth symbol pops up instead as it connects to his phone. Callum glances at me but makes no move to turn it off as a posh English man starts narrating.

It takes me a few seconds of listening before I figure out what it is. "*Frankenstein*? You're not one of those people who only read books published before 1900, are you?"

"Is that a bad thing?"

"Depends."

"On?"

"On whether you're doing it for enjoyment or because you think it makes you look smart."

"Are you serious?"

"It happens," I tell him, relieved to be talking again. "I had an ex-boyfriend who carried around *Crime and Punishment* the entire time we were dating even though I swear I never saw him open it. He even put it by the bed while we—"

"I'm a slow reader," Callum interrupts with a *TMI* glance. "But I got into audiobooks a few years ago. I'm trying to catch up. Turns out a lot of people have written a lot of stuff."

"So I've heard."

Another eye-dart to me, this one a little unsure. "You read?"

"Not as much as I could." I leave the story on, but Callum doesn't seem to mind that he might be missing a bit, he just turns it down so that it's background noise. "My granny does," I continue. "I live with her, and she has a lot of books, but I'm looking after her when I'm not working, so I don't really get the time."

"You're her carer?"

"I'm her granddaughter."

He frowns at that but doesn't push it. "And how does she feel about the hotel?"

"She hates it," I say automatically. That's kind of a lie, though. "But she didn't like the nuns either. Now she's just apathetic about the whole thing. She says there's no point in her getting annoyed about things changing because she won't be around long enough to see it."

"That's dark."

"It's her answer to everything these days. I asked her last year what kind of funeral she wanted, and she said, 'What do I care? I'll be dead.' Then the next day, she said she wanted to be pushed out to sea on a flaming boat."

"She seems fun."

"She's just Granny."

Though I did spend an entire afternoon looking up the laws for that kind of thing before she told me she was joking.

Callum doesn't respond, slowing down as he lets another car cut in front. I force myself to concentrate on the book.

"You know you've only made it worse for yourself," he says, just as I start to get into it. Some guy called Victor is having a nightmare and it all seems very intense.

"With what?"

"With Jack."

The pleasant little mood lift I had drops immediately. And to think we were being so civil.

"I don't want to talk about him," I say, but Callum doesn't seem to hear me.

"I get it, okay? I get that you're upset about everything that's going on. But it's going to happen. The resort, the pub. All of it. This is the biggest project he's ever taken on and he's got a lot riding on it. His boss is already watching his every move."

"His boss?"

"Gerald Cunningham? He's the chairman of the company." He looks confused. "Don't tell me you haven't heard of him. You've probably already burned his likeness on a pyre or something."

"I'm sure he's on the list," I deadpan, even as I consider his words. "So he's the one I need to convince?"

"Good luck with that. He lives in New York."

"But you're saying Jack's just his gopher."

"Would you—" He breaks off with a dry laugh. "It doesn't matter what Jack is or who he's answering to. Just know this is the biggest opportunity he's had, and he wants to impress. He'll throw as much money as he needs at any problem to make it go away."

"And that's where he'll lose," I tell him. "I don't care about money."

"Everyone cares about money."

"Not me," I say. "Not Adam. He was all set to become some fancy-pants businessman, but gave it all up to take over Kelly's when his dad died. Do you know why?"

"No, but I have the feeling you're about to tell me."

"It's because he couldn't bear the thought of it going to someone else. Because that pub is like another family member to him. Another part of him. And even though he's only breaking even most years, he still gives it his heart and soul."

"Sounds like a great guy," Callum says flatly.

"He is."

Callum's jaw muscles flex. "And what is he, your boyfriend or something?"

"My *what*?" I stare at him in horror. "No. Gross. No."

His glances over at my immediate, admittedly dramatic refusal. "My mistake."

"He's like a brother to me. And sometimes an uncle. And my swim coach. He also helped me with algebra growing up."

"A real saint."

"I never said that. He just cares." Even though he likes to act like he doesn't. I jab the off switch for the book, frustrated all over again. "I know you think it's just a pub. And you're right; to most people, it is. But there's history there. *My* history. Just like there is in every corner of the village. My dad was from Ennis-bawn. And my grandmother and her mother and I'm pretty sure some distant cousin of John F. Kennedy, though we don't have any proof. And it may not look like much when it's gray and gross outside, but it's a lot nicer in the summer. We're usually far enough from the main roads that you can't hear any traffic, and one Christmas we had snow and it looked like a movie, and there's a whole acre of lavender fields ten minutes away that will be bright purple by July and it's just..." I trail off, swallowing at the thought. "It's my favorite place in the whole world. It's my favorite place and you're bulldozing your way through it like it's nothing. And if I can't pull off this festival, I'll think of something else. But I won't stop. I love my home. I can't imagine living anywhere else and I'm not going to see anyone take it away from me just because they want a nice view for their golf course. And I don't even—"

My breath catches, instant panic making me choke on my words as the car jerks to a sudden halt. Lights flash behind the rain-soaked windshield, the world outside obscured from view as my heart slams in my chest, and my brain scrambles to tell the rest of me that we're okay.

Callum just pulls up the handbrake.

"What are you doing?" I ask, outraged as the rain crashes against the roof of the car. It sounds much louder now that we've stopped, but not loud enough that I miss the unmistakable click of the locks opening. "Are you making me get out?"

"Yeah."

"Seriously? Just because I—" I break off, only then recognizing where I am. He's pulled up right beside my lane. "How do you even know where I live?"

"There's only one house on this road. I made an educated guess." He's staring broodily out the windshield but glances my way when I don't move, only then noticing my erratic breathing. "You okay?"

"I'm fine," I mutter, fumbling to free my belt. Adrenaline still courses through me, making my fingers shake with a fine tremor. "Thanks for the ride."

"Hey. Wait a second."

Nope. "I've got to go." I try the handle, but it doesn't budge, which does *not* help things and when I try it again and still nothing happens, my panic creeps upward, tightening my throat. "Is there a trick to this thing or do you make a habit of trapping women in cars because—"

He grabs my elbow, pulling me firmly back into the seat.

"Breathe," he orders, watching me closely. He exaggerates his own breath, his chest rising as his lungs expand, and I follow the movement until I'm managing on my own.

"You're not claustrophobic, are you?"

I shake my head, even though the space in the car does seem to have shrunk in the last few seconds. But I think that's more from the effect of having his full attention on me than anything else. "I'm not great in cars," I admit finally, and he nods.

"I'm sorry. I didn't know."

"I didn't tell you."

I force myself to meet his gaze, a little embarrassed that he's witnessing what I try so hard to keep from everyone else. But he doesn't look judgy, or concerned, or anything that would humiliate me further. He just looks. He looks at me.

The rain cloud above is a dark, swollen gray, dimming the world around us, but that only makes the glow from the temporary traffic lights all the more noticeable. One up the road switches to orange, and I get distracted by the way it falls across him, catching the sharp angle of his face. He obviously shaved for his date, the skin around his jaw smooth and showing off his full lips. I think I prefer the stubble.

And I almost tell him this, my brain so addled that any sense of social preservation has flown out the window. But then his eyes drop to my mouth, and I realize I couldn't speak even if I tried. It's like I've forgotten how to, and when he suddenly moves my way, I think he's going to kiss me, and for one wild moment, I think I'm going to let him, but he just leans across to grab the handle instead, setting me free with a flick of his wrist.

"There's a knack to it," he says, his breath tickling my cheek. He sits back, waiting, and I take the hint, scrambling out before I do something stupid.

"Katie?"

"Yeah?" I turn around so fast my vision spins, not caring that my hood is down, not caring that I'm getting soaked. But Callum does. He stares at the sight of me, abandoning whatever he was going to say as he reaches into the back and grabs the umbrella.

"At least get a better coat," he says, tossing it to me, and then he pulls the door closed with a thump and drives off into the rain.

CHAPTER NINE

Don't get into cars with boys.

My grandmother told me that when I was sixteen, and I am telling it to myself now. Just don't do it. Don't ever do it. Even when it's raining. Even when you trust them. Even when they look at you like they want to do so much more to you than simply drive you home.

Don't get into cars with boys.

You know what you should do instead? You should work on your damn festival, Katie. You should put together the best festival anyone has ever seen. The kind of festival they write legends about. Or at the very least, lengthy blog posts. Or oral histories! Oral histories in *Vanity Fair* about the little festival that could. People love an underdog story. And *you* are an underdog story. You are David versus Goliath, you are Rocky Balboa, you are Reese freaking Witherspoon in *Legally Blonde* and you are going to—

"Would you slow down?" Nush yells behind me. "Some of us have short, if not perfectly proportioned legs."

I whirl around, adjusting my backpack as Gemma and Nush catch up with me.

"I feel like you're in a mood," Nush says.

"I'm not in a mood."

"You look like you're in a mood."

"*I'll* be in a mood if we don't get there before the rain starts." Gemma takes a sip from her flask as she peers distrustfully at the clouds. The storm that swept through the area a few days ago hasn't completely gone, and we've been having frequent showers ever since. I half hoped it would be enough to slow down the construction work, but those guys really mean it when they say they work in all-weather conditions. "This is the start of a horror movie," Gemma adds now. "I just want you both to be aware of that."

I turn on my heel, ignoring them. It's been over two weeks since the village meeting and things are not going well. First, there's the fact that no one wants to invest in my genius idea. No one wants to sponsor or fund or loan me a cent. And turns out you need a lot of cents to host something like this. You need cents for bunting and posters and lights. You need it for food and alcohol. For music and insurance and first aid kits and photo booths and, to be honest, all the things I don't think they necessarily worried about back when they didn't have social media or, like, gluten intolerances. But they're all things we have to worry about now. Especially if we're going to garner the kind of press attention we need to get. And we're going to need a lot of press. We're going to need—

"*Katie!*"

I slow my steps, turning again as the other two emerge around the bend, this time with Nush holding her side like she's got a stitch.

"Remind me never to go hiking with you," she huffs.

"We're here anyway." I gesture up at the big barn before us, nervous about how they both stare at it. Nush confused and Gemma resigned.

"Is this where you're going to murder us?"

"Don't be so dramatic," I say. "It doesn't look that bad."

"It looks pretty bad."

"I forgot this was even here," Nush says, and I grimace. The barn is one of many abandoned buildings around the village, and I'll admit it doesn't look like much. But once we cut back the grass on either side, it won't be so bad.

I think.

Hidden just inside the forest, a few minutes away from the lake, it was the biggest place I could think of to hold something like this.

"I thought the whole point was to have everything at Kelly's?" Gemma asks.

"Kelly's won't be large enough."

"It won't?" She frowns. "Just how many people do you think are going to come?"

"A lot," I insist. "And they need somewhere they can party. Somewhere impressive."

"And you chose here?"

"I think it could work," Nush declares and strides through the door. Or rather, the gap in the wall that serves as a door.

"Please just give it a chance," I say to Gemma, as we follow. "And before you say anything, we're going to work on the smell."

"What sm— oh." Her nose wrinkles as she glances around, and I try and view the space through confident, optimistic eyes, and not hers.

So it needs a little TLC. Who doesn't these days? All we need to do is get rid of all the broken farm equipment, sweep out the cobwebs, and it will look good as new. There's no electricity, but Frank already said we could use his generator, and yes, there are a bunch of gaping holes in the wall letting in the cold air, but that won't matter in the summer.

I spent hours combing through everything I could find

about the festival. I'd seen photographs of it in its heyday before but had never really paid attention to it. And honestly it didn't look that special. It didn't even look that romantic. Just a bunch of people sitting around, talking. We were going to be different. We were going to be festival 2.0. We'd welcome people to Kelly's, they'd make their wish, sign our petition and then they'd travel a few minutes along a beautiful lantern lit path (I still need to figure out that part) and party the night away. It was a simple plan. A good plan. I just need everyone else to get on board with it.

"Do you know what we need?" Nush asks, her neck craned to the ceiling as she rotates on the spot.

"A montage?" Gemma asks. "One that preferably takes us through the next few weeks?"

She shakes her head. "Men."

"What?"

"Big strong men to do all of this for us."

I frown. "It's not going to take that long to—"

"I vote for the men," Gemma interrupts, raising her hand.

"Come on, you guys!" I throw my arms wide, gesturing to all the glorious potential. "Use your imagination."

"I feel like I'm getting ill by standing here," Gemma says. "What does asbestos look like?"

I follow her to the back of the barn, leaving Nush by the entrance, where she pokes at the wall as if expecting it to collapse.

"Okay," I say. "I know being moody is your thing and that life is hard and awful—"

"Excuse me?"

"But you promised me you'd help," I finish. "You promised. So, if you could put a lid on all that negative energy, I'd appreciate it. I guarantee you whatever criticism or concern you have is one I've had a million times myself."

She tsks, clicking her tongue off the roof of her mouth, but she has the grace to look a little guilty. "I'm sorry," she says. "I just don't want to see you sinking all your time into this. It's a lot of work."

"Which is why I need your help," I say. "And hard work doesn't scare me. It just seems like a lot because we haven't properly started yet."

"Is the floor supposed to sink like this?" Nush calls, and Gemma squeezes my arm, her one show of support.

"Alright," she says. "I'll shut up. I promise."

"I'm pretty sure it's not supposed to sink like this," Nush continues.

"Then stop standing on it." I perch on an overturned crate, dropping my backpack to the floor. "I asked Adam if we could host a raffle and he said yes."

"A raffle?" Nush makes a face.

"We need money," I remind her.

"No, we need something cool," she corrects. "Or someone. We should get a celebrity."

"We definitely can't get a celebrity."

"Not *famous*, famous," she says, as Gemma takes a seat next to me. "Someone from the local radio. Or that man from Ross-bridge who got into *The Guinness Book of World Records*."

"He didn't get in; he just tried out for it."

"Yes, but the adjudicator came and everything."

"We're starting with a raffle," I say firmly. "Once we know our budget, we can start thinking about the other stuff."

"Speaking of other stuff," Gemma begins. "We do appear to be missing one key element of the festival. Have you picked a matchmaker yet?"

"A what?"

She stares at me. "A matchmaker," she repeats. "For your matchmaking festival."

"*Our* matchmaking festival."

"Katie—"

"We don't need a matchmaker," I interrupt, reaching into my bag to take out the surveys I printed off this morning. "I found some questionnaires online. We'll pair people up ourselves."

"We need a matchmaker," Gemma insists.

"I'll be the matchmaker!" I wave the paper as proof. "And these are pretty thorough. Fill one in with me now and I'll show you. It's not hard."

"I'm not going to—"

"I'll do it." Nush's hand shoots in the air. "I want to find my soulmate."

"I guarantee you she got those questions from her first Google hit," Gemma says.

"It was the *third* Google hit, for your information. And don't knock it till you try it." I take a pen from my pocket and smooth the paper out on my knee. "Okay," I say, turning to Nush. "What—"

"Anushka Sandar. Thirty-one. I own a salon in Ennisbawn, I have a cat named Chester and I've been single for five months. I dumped him," she adds, and Gemma smirks.

"That's great," I say. "But the question I was *going* to ask is what do you look for in a partner?"

"Oh, easy." She waves a dismissive hand. "Someone who knows how to cook."

"Brilliant. See?" I glance at Gemma. "Easy." *Cook.* I note that down. "And what about—"

"Also, how to bake," Nush says. "Those are two different things."

"Okay, well we can—"

"And they need to care about the environment. But not in an annoying way. Billionaires are taking private jets to their islands on the weekend, I'm allowed to use a plastic straw every now and then."

Gemma swings one leg over the other, looking like she's settling in for the long haul.

"They should be traveled, but not too traveled," Nush continues, as I stare at her. "I don't care about their music taste so long as they don't blare it around the house. But no musicians. Or artists. Or anyone in any kind of creative field. I find artistic types needy. I'd also prefer it if they were an animal lover. That's a hard line, actually. Can you write that down? Good with animals. Financially, it would be nice if they did a little better than me. But not too much. And not too rich. Rich brings its own problems. Religious but not too religious. Just a little bit of faith. In terms of a fashion sense, they'd need—"

"Wait, wait, wait. We have a faith question." I scan the list. "Do you care what that faith is?"

Nush shakes her head. "We're all going to the same place."

"I hope not," Gemma mutters.

"And is the person you're looking for a man or a woman or—"

"I'm not picky," she dismisses. "But I want dark hair. And kind eyes."

I smile at that. "Kind eyes?"

"And dark hair," she repeats, her brow furrowing in fierce concentration before smoothing out completely. "That's it. For now."

Gemma gives her a dry look. "Good to see you being so open to potential partners."

"There's nothing wrong with knowing what you want. Did you get all that?"

"Uh... yes." I scan through the list, trying to tick off everything she said. Nush leans over as I do, peering at the page.

"Can I ask the questions this time?"

"What time?"

"For you."

"Oh." I look up, surprised. "No, I'm not going to do it."

"Just to see."

"But I'm not looking for—"

Nush snatches the paper from my hand, sitting back with a toss of her hair.

"What do you look for in a partner?" she asks.

"It's not hard." Gemma mimics when I just blink. Which, okay, fair.

"No judgment," Nush prompts, taking my pen next. "Safe space. What are your kinks?"

"My— I don't know," I say, bewildered. "Is that one on the list?"

"Now it is. Spill."

"I don't think I have any kinks."

Nush purses her lips and writes something down. "So, would you say you're more vanilla?"

"No."

"There's nothing wrong with boring sex, Katie."

"Just read the actual questions, please."

Nush sighs in disappointment but does as she's asked. "What do you look for in a partner?" she repeats.

"Someone nice?" It comes out like a question, but Nush nods.

"Very important. But let's dig a little deeper. What drew you to your last partners? Did they make you laugh? Have really nice calf muscles? What did they have in common?"

"They were all assholes?" Gemma mutters, and I give her a look.

"They were not all assholes."

"Two of them cheated on you."

"Only one for sure," I say, not knowing why I'm defending them. "Graham—"

"Cheated on you," the girls say in unison.

"Definitely," Nush adds. "He was texting that girl for months before you broke up."

Whatever. "Harry's not an asshole," I tell them. "And neither was Isaac. Isaac was a doctor."

"Who still had his mother do his laundry for him."

"She liked helping!"

"Do the next question," Gemma says, but I shake my head.

"No, wait. Can't I also say kind eyes or something?"

"Put down 'not a dickhead'," Gemma says instead, and Nush does before I can stop her.

"Is their job choice important to you?" she asks.

"No," I say. "Well, yes. I guess I don't want them to be away a lot. I want to spend time with people. Not just see them in the evening for an hour. But if their job's important, that's okay too," I add hastily. "Some people have busy jobs."

Nush murmurs each word as she writes it out. "Does... not... know... anything."

"Hey!"

"What do you do for a living?"

"No, I don't want to do this anymore."

"We're almost at the end," she says pleasantly. "What do you do?"

"You know what I do. I work at a pub."

"And do you like it?"

"Yes," I say, fully sarcastic now. "I get to spend my days with my friends."

"So, community is important to you."

I pause at the seriousness of her tone. "Well, yeah," I say. "Community is important."

"And besides your job, what are your hobbies?"

Hobbies?

Nush goes back through the notes when I don't say anything. "Examples include going to the movies, going to the gym, learning, playing piano—"

"*Learning?*" Gemma scoffs.

"—photography, stand-up comedy—"

"Katie, where the hell did you get this form?"

"—listening to music, volunteering—"

"Volunteering," I say quickly. "I do that. I do lots of that."

Nush makes another tick. "And where do you see yourself in five years?"

"Here."

Both sets of eyes swing my way.

"What?"

"Nothing," Gemma says, as Nush smiles a beat too late before writing it down.

Something squirms in my stomach, and Gemma sits forward like she knows exactly what I'm thinking.

"Katie—"

"Am I boring?" I interrupt.

"Kind of," Nush says, before Gemma can respond.

"You're *busy*," Gemma says, shooting her a look. "Not boring."

"I don't have any hobbies."

"Because you're busy."

"I don't have any ambition."

"It doesn't matter. You don't need ambition. You have everything you need."

Nush nods in agreement. "There is nothing wrong with a simple life."

"I'm not a Hobbit!" I slump down as my existential crisis grows. "I don't even know what I want in a partner. How can I run a matchmaking festival when I don't even know what *I* want? How do you know?" I ask Nush, who shrugs.

"I've always had an excellent sense of self."

"And what about you?" I demand to Gemma. "Do you know?"

"It doesn't matter," she says. "I'm not looking for anyone right now."

"But you still know," I press.

"I mean... *yeah*," she says, still reluctant. "He'd obviously have to be good for Noah. And I guess I'd like someone with a steady job. Financially secure." A pause. "I like brown eyes," she adds on a mumble, and Nush brightens.

"Yes, brown eyes. I love brown eyes. I'm putting that down for me too. Kind brown eyes."

"And I've always had a thing for arms," Gemma says, as I stare at them.

"And backs," Nush says. "Muscly backs."

Gemma nods. "Or when they—"

"Okay, matchmaking over," I announce, getting to my feet. "You're right. It's a bad idea. I'll get someone proper to do it."

"But I thought you—"

"I'll figure it out," I say, only to jump as a sudden bang echoes off the walls, followed by two more even louder ones that occur in such quick succession, it's almost deafening.

"What the hell is that?" Gemma yells, as Nush slaps her hands over her ears. She looks up as if the roof is about to cave in, but after living down the road from a construction site for the past few weeks, I know exactly what it is, and am already moving, following the noise out of the barn and across the field to where the grass meets the forest. The girls follow and we're only a minute or two through the trees before we see them. Two construction vehicles and a dozen men in the near distance, all standing aside as they fell an oak tree while another splinters to pieces in a whirring machine.

"It's the golf club," I say, as the three of us stare at the destruction in front of us. "They're making way for the golf club."

"They're going to end up clearing half the forest at this stage. There won't be anywhere to— *Nush!*" Gemma grabs Anushka, clutching her into a bear hug as she tries to march forward.

"I'm going to kill them," Nush snaps, wriggling violently.

"Don't be such a drama queen," Gemma mutters. "There's nothing we can do. Right now, anyway." Her eyes meet mine over Nush's head, her mouth a thin line. "We're going to need a really big raffle," she says, and I can only nod as they feed another branch into the machine, the noise growing louder until it's all I can hear.

CHAPTER TEN

"Come on, Danny. You know you want to."

"I know no such thing," he says. "In fact, I know the opposite. I've retired."

"You have not retired," I say firmly. "No one retires from music."

"Well, I have," he says gruffly. He's sitting at the table next to me in Kelly's, hunched over a lunchtime pint and is being *thoroughly* uncooperative. It's been days since we started work on the barn and things feel like they're moving at a snail's pace. I want to host the thing in July and it's already the middle of April. But turns out when you don't have money, you can't just get things immediately. You have to borrow. You have to beg. You have to flatter sixty-year-old men with a lifetime of grudges.

"I don't want anyone else to play at the festival," I tell Danny. "You're the best fiddler around."

"Tell that to Maurice Friel."

"Maurice Friel? Is that what this is about?" Seriously? Why are men such children? "You don't want to play anymore because of that... that *thief*?"

His eyes flick up at that, the stubborn look on his face relenting. "A thief, is it?"

"He stole the Jeanie O'Dwyer cup from you, didn't he? I was at the competition, Danny, I saw it. Better yet, I heard it. You deserved to win."

He starts to smile before he catches himself. "Played the best reel of my life."

"You did."

"There's no appreciation for the softer moments these days," he continues, and I nod vigorously. "All about being flashy."

"The worst," I agree. "So why not show that to him? We've already got a group together. But it will mean nothing without you."

"A group? Who do you have?"

"Tadhg Murphy. Jillian O'Mahony. Andy—"

"Jillian?" He perks up at her name, and I try not to smile at the undisguised interest in his voice. Look at me, already matchmaking.

"She owes Granny a favor," I say. "Something about not returning her good spatula."

"I haven't played with Jillian in years," he muses, and I picture the pretty silver-haired accordionist who had reluctantly agreed to travel down for the festival once Granny had strong words with her on the phone.

"She cut her hair short," I tell him.

"Did she?" He considers this for a long, serious moment. "I'd say that would suit her."

"It does. She looks beautiful. Radiant in fact." Okay, too much. "So, what do you say?"

"I guess I could play a few tunes," he says gruffly. "For Adam's sake."

"Thank you," I say, relieved. "That would be amazing."

He's embarrassed now, shifting in his seat from the praise. "How are you getting on with it all anyway?"

"Brilliantly." It's my answer to everyone who asks, mostly because I'm kind of hoping that if I say it enough times, it will turn out to be true.

"Any interest from the press yet?"

"We're reaching out to people," I say, as Noah appears out of Adam's office with Gemma's laptop tucked under his arm.

"Do you really not know how to do this?" he asks, as Danny returns to his drink. He takes a seat beside me and opens the computer to show the website-building site he learned to use at school.

"I mean, I'm sure I could if I tried," I say. "But your mam said you were really good at it, so I thought I should just ask you."

I get a weary sigh for that attempt at a compliment.

"You can pick any of these templates," he says, clicking through a bunch of options. "And we can change the color and the font if you like. Move stuff around." He gives me a look. "A child could do it. It's not hard."

"It looks hard to me."

"Because you're old."

"Of course, sorry."

He presses another button and takes me to the checkout page. "It's one hundred and twenty-five euro for the year."

"I think we can afford that," I say, checking the list. I'm planning to scrimp on a lot of stuff, but not on the important bits. We need a professional-looking website. A professional-looking website put together by an eleven-year-old, but it's not like I know anyone else who can do it.

"I want to help," Noah says, reading my mind. "But I don't work for free."

"That's fair." I blow out a breath, meeting his serious expression with one of my own. "What will it take?"

"Can you convince Mam to get me a dog?"

"No."

"A cat?"

This could go on for a while. "It's your birthday soon, right?"

His gaze narrows, instantly suspicious. "Right."

"Am I still invited to the party?"

"You make the best cakes." He says it like it's obvious and I try not to preen under the praise. He's correct. I do make the best cakes.

"I'll make you two."

"Three."

"No one needs three cakes. I'll make one really big."

"How big?"

"Extremely big."

He watches me for a long moment, weighing up my words before he gives a slow nod. "Deal."

"Thank you, thank you, thank you." I ruffle his hair before he can push me away. "And if any other adult asks what you're doing—"

"I'm working on a school project."

I give him a thumbs-up and leave him to his child labor just as Nush storms into the pub and slams a newspaper onto the table.

"Look at this shit!"

"Anushka!" Adam snaps from the bar, and she purses her lips before turning to Noah.

"Swearing is a conservative social construct. Curse words can't hurt you and only boring people are offended by them."

"Nush," I warn, but she ignores me.

"Live your life, Noah. Be free."

Noah doesn't even look up from the laptop. "Mam says I'm not allowed to swear."

"Because your mother has become *the man*."

"His mother is also at work," Adam calls. "So let's not try and revolutionize her child when she's not around. Noah, forget everything Nush just said to you."

"Okay."

Nush drops down into a chair and jabs a finger at a picture of Jack Doyle's smiling face.

"He's begun."

"Begun what?"

She looks me square in the eye. "The charm offensive."

My stomach knots as I pull the paper toward me. I've been expecting it, I guess. But it still makes me a little nervous to see.

Ennisbawn Hotel Development Breathes New Life into Disadvantaged Community

"Disadvantaged?" I scoff, skimming through the article.

...coming fresh off the redevelopment of the derelict Foxton's Hotel in Waterford, Mr. Doyle is keen to replicate Glenmill's success in their most ambitious project yet. Overseen by the chairman of the company, Gerald Cunningham, the hotel will not only provide much-needed employment opportunities for the area but bring thousands of tourists to a part of the country traditionally left unloved and—

"Have you got to the part about—"

"Still reading," I interrupt, as I skim down.

...like so many rural communities in Ireland, the village has been destroyed by emigration and lack of investment. "It's always a shock to see what was once a thriving town reduced to nothing but empty streets and abandoned homes," Mr. Doyle says. "Our goal at Glenmill is not just to revitalize the

area once the hotel opens, but to give it a new lease of life. A
new beginning. A new Ennisbawn."

It's all I can bear to read.

"There's nothing wrong with the old Ennisbawn!" I snap, flinging the paper down. "And there's not going to be anything for all these tourists to experience if he keeps bulldozing over everything!"

"We're going to have to up our game," Nush says seriously, and I groan.

"Nush, I told you, I'm not setting fire to anything."

"No, not that," she says, exasperated. "I mean that we need to think *smarter*. We should target the Americans."

"I don't think—"

"We can all wear knitwear," she continues. "They love when we wear knitwear. And Adam can put cabbage and stew on the menu, and we can hire a horse and carriage to bring them places. We'll pretend we don't have cars."

"They know we have..." I pause. "Okay, the horse and carriage idea isn't actually a bad shout."

"On it, boss." She slaps her hand on the table, but Noah grabs the paper before she can take it.

"Can I have this?" he asks, and when she nods, he carefully tears out Jack Doyle's picture before asking Adam's permission to replace the old one on the dartboard.

He says yes.

————

Once Noah is well on his way with the website, I head over to the barn, where I spend a few hours clearing out the space before my shift that evening. I accomplish embarrassingly little. It is not a one-person job getting rid of all the old equipment, and, by the time I'm done, I've barely made a dent, but leave the place sweaty and gross and with my lower back at literal pains to inform me I'm not seventeen anymore. It takes me longer than usual to cycle home, but Granny is waiting at the door when I do with a cup of tea in her hand, which I promptly gulp down as I kick off my shoes.

"There's a cobweb in your hair," is all she says at the sight of me.

"It's called fashion. Did you eat lunch?"

"I did."

"And did you get out with Plankton?"

"He wouldn't budge. He's having a sniff in the back."

I nod. The back garden is fenced off, so we let him roam around freely. Everywhere else, the dog needs a leash. He tends to run after anything and everything, and, with the added traffic on the roads because of the site, both Granny and I have gotten a little jumpy.

"I'll take him out later. He can come with me to the barn."

She frowns at that. "You just came from the barn."

"I know. But there's still a lot of work to do."

"So long as you don't tire yourself out," she warns, as I race up the stairs.

"I said I was going to give this everything I've got."

"You also said you were going to learn to make lasagna from scratch," she calls. "But I'm yet to reap the benefits."

I ignore her, tugging my sweater and T-shirt over my head, and stuffing them into the overflowing laundry basket in the bathroom. Between my usual shifts at the bar and all the festival prep, I've been neglecting my chore list. I probably have two days of clean clothes left. So, laundry. I need to do laundry, and go on a food run and get more of that bread Granny likes. Tomorrow, I need to go to the pharmacy and pick up her medicine, and then I need to order a new bulb for her reading lamp, and do some meal prep for the week because it's not like I'm going to have time to cook anytime soon.

But first, laundry.

Or maybe a shower.

I peel down my leggings, kicking them free of my ankles before unclasping my bra. Every bit of skin that was uncovered at the barn now has a fine layer of grime coating it, and my legs are stamped with bruises I don't remember getting.

"Do you have any colors?" I yell to Granny, as I pad barefooted to my bedroom. "I'm going to put a wash on and then I need to—"

I cut off with a screech, clutching the falling bra to my breasts as I come to an abrupt stop in the doorway. I can almost *feel* this new core memory slotting itself into my brain, ready to be analyzed during future sleepless nights as the most embarrassing thing that's ever happened to me. Because, as I stand half-filthy and half-naked in the hallway, Callum Dempsey stands a few paces away, looking right at me.

CHAPTER ELEVEN

He lingers in the middle of the landing, with a toolbox in one hand and an empty mug in the other. A pair of headphones cover his ears, and I can just make out the tinny sound of guitars blaring as we stare at each other in horror. Or at least, I stare at him in horror. Callum looks like someone just whacked him over the head, his gaze darting from my face to my chest and back again like he can't stop himself.

It's only when I back up a step, feeling like my face is on fire, that he seems to snap out of it, scrambling to pull his headphones off as he moves toward me.

"Shit, Katie, I didn't know you were—"

I don't wait to hear the rest of the sentence. I whirl back to the bathroom instead, locking the door shut.

Oh my God. Oh my *God*.

"Katie?" I jerk away as he knocks on the wood, letting my bra fall to the floor as I grab a towel and hastily wrap it around me.

"What are you doing *in my house*?" I shriek through the door.

"Your grandmother asked me to—" He breaks off with a

curse. "I'm sorry. I didn't know you were home. I didn't see anything."

The man's a liar. The girls were definitely free for at least half a second.

"Katie?" He knocks again when I don't answer, and I wince.

"I'm fine!" I lie. "Just going to have a shower now!"

Don't *tell* him that??

Embarrassed pink blotches bloom over my chest as I stay very, very still as if, that way, he'll somehow just forget I'm in here. And honestly, it kind of works because after a long second, he finally leaves, and I listen intently to the unfamiliar sound of his footsteps going down the stairs.

I'm going to kill Granny. I am going to double-check her will and then I am going to kill her.

I drop the towel and take a prolonged rinse in the shower to give Callum ample opportunity to leave. This time, I make sure I'm covered and announce my presence before stepping back into the hall. There's no sign of him, and I can't hear anything other than the faint noise of the construction site, but I still scurry to my room and throw on the first clothes I find before heading downstairs to find Granny sitting in her usual spot at the table.

She doesn't look up when I come in, so I stand there, my hands on my hips, until eventually she deigns to acknowledge my presence.

"What?"

"What do you mean, what?" I snap. "What was Callum doing here?"

"Who?"

Oh, for the love of— "Callum! The man who was just in the house and saw me topless!"

"Is that why you were making such a racket?"

"Why was he *here*?"

"He's clearing out the garden," she explains. "Like you told me to get someone to do."

"I meant some sixteen-year-old looking for pocket money."

"Well, when they knock on the door, I'll be sure to give them a job. I don't see what the big deal is," she adds, when I go to argue again. "You said so yourself: you've been meaning to get someone out to clear it. He stopped by with one of those leaflets and asked if we had any more issues, and I said as a matter of fact, we did."

"The big deal is you should have told me someone was in the house. And he didn't mean issues with the garden. He meant about the traffic and—" I break off with a gasp, ducking behind the table as someone walks past the window.

Granny returns to her newspaper. "Honestly, Katie, you're starting to worry me."

I keep to my crouch as I head to the sink and peek out to see Callum pushing a wheelbarrow toward the far end of the yard, Plankton following him like he's got a hamburger in his pocket.

"He's still here?" I hiss.

"He said he had the afternoon free."

"To do what?"

"*Gardening.* Aren't you listening to a word I say?"

"We can't afford a gardener. How the hell are we going to pay him?"

She gives me a strange look. "Pay him?"

Oh no. "Granny, you didn't."

"Didn't what?" she asks innocently, and I groan.

"There's no need to pay him," she continues. "He's helping an old lady. It's good for the soul."

"Clearing up that mess outside is not good for anybody's soul. We've talked about this."

"At least let him finish!"

I don't bother to respond as I head out the front door. She started doing this in the last few years when we realized we couldn't afford to fix the place up properly. While I didn't mind having the odd person around to help me rewire a plug or move some furniture, Granny started guilt-tripping people into whole days' worth of jobs. I once came home to find Bridget clearing out our gutters after Granny lamented at length about how I was simply too tired at the end of the day. Nush once painted my bedroom ceiling. Badly. Once I cottoned on to what was happening, I quickly put a stop to things, and everyone knew now to check with me before listening to a sob story about how the only thing that would make Granny happy was if someone would regrout the bathroom tiles.

But Callum wouldn't know that.

My sneakers sink into the soft earth as I round the back of the house, throwing open the gate to find him hunched over the hedge bordering our property.

"I'm going to need you to stop whatever she's got you doing," I call, once I'm in earshot. "Because we don't have the money to—"

He whips around at the sound of my voice, and I come to a halt a few paces away, my attention zeroing in on the colorful tattoos wrapped around his left arm. Intricate Celtic knots start at his wrist, covering every inch of skin until they disappear into his T-shirt. It's not like I've never seen a guy with tattoos before, but he was wearing a coat or sleeves the last few times we met and a hoodie in the house, so these are...

These are new.

"Pay me?"

"What?" I drag my attention away from the design and tug my cardigan tighter over my chest. "Yeah."

"I don't mind."

"Well, I do," I say, clearing my throat. "She does this. Granny. If she thinks she can get you to do something for her, she will. And she'll say whatever she needs to get you to do it."

"You mean it's not her dying wish for someone to dig up her weeds?"

"I can't pay you."

"Then I'll be sure to only do a half-assed job. I promise."

"But—"

"I'm not going to fight with you on this."

"We're not having a fight."

"Not yet." He raises a brow. "But you're looking for one, aren't you?"

I open my mouth to retort before snapping it shut again. He's right.

When I don't reply, he turns back to the hedge, picking up a handful of fallen branches and tossing them into the wheelbarrow.

"I'm just assuming this dog is yours, by the way."

"His name is Plankton." And he doesn't seem to even know I'm here, too enamored with the stranger to notice the person who feeds and shelters him standing two paces away. The little traitor.

"Plankton, huh?" Callum reaches forward to scratch the dog's head. "I think he likes me."

"Well, he also likes fox poop, so..." I trail off, watching as he tears a particularly stubborn root from the ground. His arm flexes as he does, and I let myself stare at it for a beat before flicking my gaze away. "Why are you even here?"

"We need to block off your road for a series of deliveries next Wednesday. Had to inform the residents."

"Granny and I are the only residents on this road."

"And you've been informed."

"You couldn't have just sent a letter?"

I catch the edge of his smirk before he ducks his head. "We've seen what happens to our letters," he says, and I know he's referring to Jack's face all over the dartboards. "Anyway, I thought it was supposed to be a five-second job," he adds. "I didn't expect your grandmother to be so persuasive. She also had me put up some shelving over your boiler."

"I was getting to that," I mumble, a little bit of house embarrassment creeping in alongside the whole almost-naked embarrassment. What else did she point out to him? Did he see all the mold along the windowpanes? The peeling paint in the hallway that I still need to do something about? Isn't it enough that the guy got a peek at the goods? Now he has to see how behind on everything I am?

"I don't mind," Callum continues, mistaking my sudden awkwardness. "I like renovating. I try to take on a house a year between site jobs. Buy it cheap, do it up. That kind of thing."

"Sounds time-consuming."

"I enjoy it." He straightens, wiping his forearm across his brow and leaving a smidgen of dirt there in the process. "So, are you going to help me or are you just going to stand there?"

"I'm just going to stand here," I say, as Plankton sniffs around Callum's feet and then wanders off.

I should probably do the same. I mean, I should *definitely* do the same, but my body doesn't seem to be listening to what my brain is telling it to do. And Callum doesn't even seem to mind. He just keeps working, ignoring me as he throws handful after handful of branches and weeds into the wheelbarrow until I crack under the silence.

"So did Melissa text back or what?"

He looks confused for a moment before he realizes who I'm talking about, his blind date who never showed. The fact that he's already forgotten about her makes me feel like the smuggest person in all the land, but he doesn't need to know that.

"She did," he says. "She apologized. Said she had a headache."

"A headache girl." I tsk. "You didn't stand a chance. You should stay away from them in the future."

"You're not a headache girl then?"

"I'm a stomachache girl. Whole different vibe." He bends over, the muscles in his back shifting as he grabs another clump of weeds. "Are you going to ask her out again?"

"Nah." He doesn't even hesitate, and it's kind of dumb how pleased that makes me. Pleased enough that I glance around, looking for something to help him with.

"There's a compost heap around the other side of the house," I begin grudgingly. "If you want me to— Plankton!"

Callum straightens at my sharp tone, following my gaze to where my dog stands with a guilty look by the gate. The gate that I left open.

"*Wait*," I order, taking a tentative step toward him. "Plankton? Wait."

"Is he not allowed out the front?" Callum asks.

"No. Not since you guys started working."

I take another step and Plankton goes unnaturally still. "Don't you dare," I warn him, creeping closer. "Don't you— *Plankton!*"

He's off. With a speed that belies his age, he slips through the gap and heads straight for the driveway, only running faster when I chase after him.

My heart leaps into my throat, and I push my legs harder, following him to the front of the house.

He doesn't usually do this. He's a good dog. A grumpy dog, but a good dog. He isn't a rule-breaker.

He's just not used to his new life.

He had full rein of the place before work on the hotel started. And he *never* ran off. But with the increased traffic, we started locking him inside, and he got antsy. He doesn't like being cooped up and lets us know this every time we don't close the door properly.

A quick glance up and down the road shows it's still empty and I race across it, only vaguely aware of Callum overtaking me as I launch myself into the dense shade of the forest on the other side.

"Plankton!" I yell, as I catch a glimpse of him through the trees. "You get back here right now, or so help me God you aren't getting any more table scraps for the rest of your life. You won't even— don't *move*."

I screech the last two words at Callum, who immediately stops. Unfortunately, the speed he was moving at coupled with the wet earth of the forest floor, coupled with the universe *hating* me, does nothing to help him with this. His arms shoot out as he tries to regain his balance, and I, of course, run straight into him.

We go down.

We go down hard.

My feet slide forward, and my ass hits the ground in a way I know is going to hurt tomorrow. Callum lands half on top of me, twisting at the last second so I don't get crushed, but that just means he pushes himself farther into the sludge until we're both covered in it.

I don't so much as breathe for a long second, staring up at the canopy above me, and wondering what it would be like to simply abandon all my responsibilities and lie here forever, never to be embarrassed again.

"You dead?" Callum asks.

"No." I wince, digging out a small rock from where it's sticking into my back. "You?"

"No. And I don't mean to be rude," he adds. "But what the hell?"

"Sorry." I plant a hand into the ground to push myself up, only for it to slide deeper into the mud instead. "Fairy ring."

"What?"

I point a few feet ahead to where a ring of mushrooms peeks out among the fallen leaves. I forgot it was there until I saw Callum almost go straight through it.

"Oh." He sounds more surprised than annoyed. "They take you or something, don't they? If you step in it?"

"And force you to dance until you perish from exhaustion."

"Well, joke's on them; I'm a terrible dancer." He eases himself into a sitting position, brushing mud from his hands. "Didn't think you'd be the kind of person who'd believe in that stuff."

I shrug as Gemma's words spring to mind. No one believes it. But they don't *not* believe in it either. "Granny kind of drilled it into me when I was younger."

"Better safe than sorry," he agrees. "But we should probably find your... or, you know, never mind."

Plankton appears through the trees and pads our way, his tail wagging as though nothing's amiss. Relief instantly shoots through me, almost overwhelming, and I hold out my arms.

"You can't keep doing that," I tell him, burying my face into his neck. I can feel Callum watching me, but I don't care. Plankton wriggles in my hold to lick the side of my face, and I scratch him behind the ears until he's leaning into my touch. Dumb dog. Dumb perfect dog.

"You're in so much trouble," I tell him, but we both know I don't mean it. Callum smiles as Plankton turns toward him and holds out a hand for him to sniff.

"About earlier," he begins, and I still, knowing exactly what he's referring to.

"So, we're actually never talking about that ever again?" I tell him. "That's the rule of seeing someone naked when you weren't supposed to."

He grimaces. "I don't like listening to music unless I'm severely damaging my eardrums. I swear I didn't hear you come in."

"It's okay."

"It's not. I'm sorry."

He sounds very serious. Serious enough that the lingering

embarrassment I still felt starts to fade.

"It's fine," I sniff. "You just have to return the favor now."

His eyes shoot to mine, and I quickly backpedal at the spark in them. "I'm joking."

"I know," he says. "I like it."

Oh, God.

I grab Plankton's collar, making a show of holding on to him as I get to my feet. "I need to get back to Granny," I say, turning back to the road. "The good news is I was going to do laundry anyway. Though I guess I should—"

"Can I ask you for a favor?"

I glance back at him, brows raised. "No."

He looks surprised. "No?"

"No," I repeat. "No, you cannot ask me for a favor. You work for the enemy."

"Well, see, that's where the favor comes in," he says. "I'm not my boss. I'm not in charge. And I'd like you not to look at me like I'm running the show here. Like this is all my doing. Because it's not and you know it's not, and it would be great if you stopped treating me like it is."

"I don't..." I trail off as he gives me a look. I guess the man has a point. It's the exact kind of thing I used to pester Nush about. When she treated every guy on traffic light duty like they were to blame for what was happening. I know Callum's not. I just needed an outlet. "What?" I ask. "You want a truce or something?"

"A truce sounds good."

It was a joke, but he's still deadly serious, sticking out his hand like we're doing a business deal. I make a face.

"You're covered in mud."

"So are you."

Point taken. We clasp hands briefly as I'm still holding tight to a now restless Plankton, but Callum smiles like I've told him he's just won the lottery.

I show him the way back to the house, bundling Plankton into my arms as we approach the tree line. I'm glad of it a second later as a car speeds past just as we emerge.

"Has no one heard of speed limits?" I mutter, glaring after the shiny black Jeep only for the thing to immediately stop.

Uh-oh.

"Did I accidentally yell that?" I ask, as it starts to reverse. Callum curses under his breath, and I know why a moment later, when the car eases to a halt right next to us and the window slides down.

Jack Doyle sits behind the wheel, dressed in a suit and tie. The three of us stare at each other as he slowly takes in our muddied clothes and then Plankton, who's now squirming in my arms.

"What did you— no," he says, when Callum opens his mouth. "I've changed my mind. I don't want to know." His eyes flick to me, his expression souring.

"Miss Collins."

"Mr. Doyle." I smile sweetly. "Destroy any livelihoods lately?"

"No, but I did create another fifty. There's good news about the proposal," he says to Callum, who's gone *very* quiet beside me. "Get in. I want to catch Andy before he leaves and set up a call with Gerald. Let's go," he adds, when the man doesn't move.

"Yeah, okay," Callum says, sounding terse. "But remember what we talked about? About you being a little less you?"

I blink, surprised he'd talk to his boss like that. Though I guess I talk to Adam like that. But still.

Jack, however, doesn't seem fazed by his tone. "I'll take it under consideration," he says. "Get moving."

"Wait, what proposal?" I ask, and Jack reaches through the window, brandishing a piece of paper at me.

"Did you know there's only one road in and out of the village?" he asks. "Not exactly great town planning."

Plankton growls at the man as I step closer, and Jack eyes him warily as I examine the page.

It's a map of Ennisbawn. I recognize it immediately, the curving street, the forest up ahead. Only in this one, one side of the village has been drawn over in red pen, drawing a completely new entry intersecting the original one.

Confusion clashes with horror as I realize what I'm looking at. "This will cut through the main street."

"And connect you straight to the motorway."

"But you're going through at least three buildings!"

"Yeah. Empty ones," he says, snatching the paper away when I go to take it. "Do you always have to look for the worst in everything?"

"Just because they're empty now doesn't mean they'll always be." The road was going to come in straight by Nush's salon and looked like it was going to cut through John Joe's garden entirely. "It completely changes the west side of the village."

"I prefer the term improve."

"But—"

"It's just a proposal," Callum says to me. "You'll have plenty of time to launch an objection."

"Callum." Jack taps his watch. "Haste. Make it."

Callum's jaw tenses, and I almost think he's about to snap at the man, when he turns to me instead. "Tell Maeve I'll pop around again," he says. "And sorry." The last two words are low enough that only I can hear them, and he gives Plankton a rub on the head before rounding the car to the passenger side.

"Nice dog," Jack says, before turning to Callum as he shuts the door with a little more force than necessary. "What?"

"You know what," Callum snaps, and that's all I hear as Jack closes the window and drives off.

CHAPTER TWELVE

"You ready?"

"No."

"On the count of three."

"I'm not ready," Nush says loudly from above me. Her legs are wrapped around my shoulders, and she's squeezing me like she wants to snap my head off.

"One."

"I take back what I said. I don't agree to this."

"Two."

"Katie, seriously don't—"

"Three."

She yelps as I rise from my crouch, hitting me in the face with the feather duster in one hand, while her other grips my hair like a rein, holding on for dear life.

"You're going to pull my hair out," I snap.

"Well, you're going to drop me."

"I'll only drop you if you keep pulling my hair! Just— *ow*. Nush!"

"Katie?" I blink rapidly as the feathers sting my eye and

glance to my right to see John Joe at my elbow. "Can I have a word?"

"I'm a little busy right now," I tell him, and his gaze goes up. "Oh, hi, Anushka."

"Gross," Nush complains, ignoring him as she swats at a cobweb. "Gross, gross, gross."

"It won't take a second," he says to me. "I heard a rumor you were looking for some fireworks."

"It's not really a rumor," I say, as Nush wobbles dangerously, trying to reach up into a corner. "I'm going to close the festival with them."

"Right. Well, I wanted to let you know that I know a guy who might be able to help with that." He lowers his voice for the last bit, and I frown.

"Fireworks isn't a code word for some new drug, is it? Because I don't really—"

"It's my cousin," he explains. "Colin. He could use the job. Between Paddy's Day and Halloween, it's a little barren, gigs-wise."

"I don't know," I say slowly. It's not that I don't like John Joe, but I definitely don't trust anyone who tells me they *know a guy*. "The last thing we need is to have the guards on our case. Glenmill would have a field day if something went wrong."

"It's all perfectly legal," he assures me. "He's got a license and everything, but he's up against the big event people, and it's a struggle. Really, he's a bit like us if you think about it."

"Uh-huh." I wince as I clutch Nush's ankles tighter.

"He could also get you a discount," he says, as my attention goes back to Nush. "Thirty percent off the market rate."

Thirty percent? I pause, thinking it over. I really want fireworks. People love fireworks. *I* love fireworks. But fireworks are expensive. "And it's definitely legal?"

"He can show you all the paperwork."

"And he can organize them in time?"

"He's already sent over some ideas," John Joe says quickly, knowing he has me. "He can do hearts and everything. Big bursting hearts in the sky. You know, because of the romance."

Because of the romance. I sigh, wincing as Nush grabs my hair again. "Alright," I say, and he beams. "But I'm trusting you not to screw me over on this, okay?"

"You've got it, Katie. He'll be thrilled. Really. You won't regret this."

"I want to see his license before we agree to anything," I call after him, as he walks off, bringing his phone to his ear. "And make sure he's— *ow.*"

"Stop wobbling," Nush huffs.

"I'm not wobbling. You're wobbling."

"Because you keep shifting around. I need to get higher. Stabilize your core."

"My what?"

But she's already moving, planting both hands on my head as she slowly climbs until she's standing on my shoulders.

"*Nush.*"

"We've got insurance, right?"

"Not for this!" I exclaim, shuffling closer to the wall. She uses one hand to balance herself against it and reaches up to bat at a particularly large cobweb in the corner, only for me to almost drop her on the first go.

"I said stabilize!"

"I don't know what that means!"

"What the hell are you two doing?" I jump as Adam's furious voice thunders behind me, and the predictable happens.

Nush's sneakers dig painfully into my shoulders as she teeters back and forth before hurtling to the ground, only for her screams to cut off as Adam catches her. Meanwhile, I go tumbling to the hard concrete as she knocks me to the floor on her way down.

"Do you want to get yourselves killed?" he snaps, as he sets her on her feet.

"I almost had it," Nush grumbles, dusting off her hands before helping me up.

It's all hands on deck day, a new holiday I made up last week, where I get everyone in the village to give up their Sunday morning and help me finish the barn so we can start mapping out how we want to decorate it. A surprising amount of people showed up, and we'd gotten the final few things cleared out and brought to the dump. We were almost there.

Nush steps back, sizing Adam up. "Maybe if I stand on *your* shoulders," she begins, but before he can respond, Gemma approaches, her coffee in one hand and her phone in the other. The latter she passes to me.

"The Laketon Hotel got back," she says. "They've agreed to set aside some rooms."

"They have?" I skim through the email, only to frown. "This says they're only setting aside ten."

"How many did you want them to set aside?"

"I don't know. A hundred?"

"You'll need to sell some tickets first, Katie."

Nush's eyes widen. "We haven't sold any tickets?"

"We will," I say confidently. "We haven't even begun our press blitz."

Gemma's brows raise. "It's a blitz now, is it?"

"*Gemma.*"

"Sorry, sorry. I'm positive. Did you get a matchmaker yet?"

"Not yet," I say, ignoring her groan. "Don't worry. I won't just use the list. I'll figure something out."

Adam frowns. "What list?"

"Katie tried to cut corners," Nush says.

"I did not!"

"She found this big list of questions online to find our ideal partners. Gemma wants brown eyes," she adds, looking up into his blue ones. "Tough luck."

"I'll try to survive," he says, and Gemma scowls at him. "Why don't you ask Maeve to matchmake?" he asks me. "Didn't she meet your grandad at the festival?"

"No," I say, still brushing the dirt from my clothes. "She met Grandad when he was cleaning the windows of her house and she opened the curtains naked, and he fell off the ladder."

Gemma starts coughing into her flask.

"It was romantic!" I insist. "She nursed him back to health. He had a concussion."

"You should still ask her," Adam says, as Nush slaps Gemma between the shoulders. "I'm pretty sure she's introduced a few people over the years. Could be a nice selling point. And you've got your parents too."

My eyes snap to his. "My parents are not a selling point."

"I know," he says gently. "But it's a connection. People might like that."

"I guess," I say, as my attention catches on a couple of the guys carrying the last crates out of the barn.

"We can repurpose those," I call, as Adam and Nush go over to help. "Don't just dump them."

"Repurpose into what?" Gemma asks.

"I don't know. We'll figure it out." I glance around the barn, wondering what to start on next. "Okay, I need to—"

"No," Gemma interrupts. "You don't need to do anything right now. Take a break."

"I'm fine."

"You're not. You've been here for hours, and you've got work tonight. You can't do full shifts at the pub *and* keep doing all of this. You're going to burn out."

"Yes, like a phoenix."

"Like a cigarette butt," she says. "Just take a walk or something. Five minutes. I promise we won't burn the place down in your absence."

"Why would you even joke about—"

"Goodbye."

She pushes me toward the entrance, and I know she'll just be on my case if I don't go, so I announce my break and take off blindly through the trees. I'm not worried about getting lost. I spent whole summers in this forest when I was younger and know it as well as anyone. Glenmill have made a decent dent in the area on the other side of the barn, but this direction remains largely untouched.

For now, anyway.

I walk for a few minutes before stopping, not so much taking a break and becoming one with nature as counting down the minutes until I can get back to work.

I never really thought of myself as impatient, but it's all I've felt in the last few weeks. There's just too much to do and too little time to do it, and I'm almost growing used to the constant churn of anxiety that I wake with each morning.

Maybe I should take up yoga.

I close my eyes, inhaling until my lungs hurt, and open them again, only to freeze as I spy a flash of color between the trees. A second later, Callum emerges, unaware of me as he heads in the direction of the lake.

I am immediately suspicious. We called our truce last week, but then Jack revealed his plans for a new road, and Callum didn't come around again. I don't really know where we stand, but I do know it's a Sunday, which means the site is closed. Which means he shouldn't be anywhere near here. They all disappear on the weekends. Like they can't wait to get out of here fast enough. It's why I brought everyone to the barn today. So they wouldn't know what we're doing.

Without giving myself a chance to think about it, I take off after him, following the trail as it veers left toward the water. I usually wouldn't be so paranoid, but with Jack clearly going after other parts of the village, I've been on high alert, wondering what they'll come for next. There's no reason for Callum to be in these woods.

Unless this is a reconnaissance mission. A little *hey, why don't we drain the lake to build an apartment block* groundwork that they intend to blindside us with next month.

The more I think about it, the more I'm scared of it, and I pick up my pace, bursting through the trees, and— okay, I've lost him.

I huff as I glance around the empty lake, weirdly disappointed.

Maybe I hallucinated him. That would be fun. A fun little thing to add to my list of things to tell my doctor. Give her something new to discuss with me instead of just period pain and low iron levels.

With no hint of another soul around, I start to head back to the barn, only for my gaze to snag on a small pile of stones by the water's edge. They're all the same size and shape, flat, smooth, and perfect for throwing, and I pause as the childish part of me begs me to throw one. So I do, rubbing one clean before launching it into the lake. It skips a respectable three times before vanishing into the water, and I crouch back down to get another.

"Watcha doing?"

"Jesus!" I jump, straightening from my crouch to see Callum standing directly behind me. "Don't sneak up on people!"

"Don't follow people through the woods," he counters, and I say nothing because that's exactly what I was doing. I just didn't know *he* knew that's what I was doing. I turn back to the shore instead of answering, watching him from the corner of my eye when he joins me.

He's in his jeans again, as well as a dark green jacket that he's zipped up tight. His headphones loop around his neck, but I can hear no guitars coming from them.

"No music today?" I ask, and he shakes his head.

"Audiobook."

Huh. "Which one?"

"*Crime and Punishment*," he says, only to laugh at my unimpressed look. "It's a thriller. The murdery kind."

"Wow. What a great choice to listen to while walking alone through the woods," I say dryly, and he grins, his gaze flicking between me and the lake.

"You need to twist your wrist better."

"What?"

"You're twisting at the beginning of your throw," he explains, nodding at the stone in my hand. "You need to twist at the end."

"You're critiquing my *stone skipping* technique?"

"Yep." He crouches down, examining the pile before plucking out a few chosen ones. "Want to make a bet on how many jumps I can get?"

"No."

"Why not?"

"Because you look really confident," I admit, and he smirks, tossing a stone into the air.

"I'm going to say... twelve."

"*Twelve?*" Twelve skips? Now he's just cocky. The best I've ever managed is eight. "Fine. Bet made."

"Yeah?" His eyes light up. "What do I get if I win?"

"Your pride."

"Deal." He doesn't even hesitate. He catches the stone one final time, and then flicks it in. It grazes the water in swift, elegant bursts, and my mouth falls open as it moves so far away that I can't even count them anymore.

"What the hell? How did you do that?"

"Incredible skill," he says, and sends another in. It goes even farther.

I grab one of my own, not to be outdone, but only manage two skips this time before it slips into the lake.

"You're turning too much," he says. "Here." He tosses me another from the pile, and I'm so preoccupied with catching it that I don't realize he's moved closer until his hand wraps around mine. I still instantly as he opens my palm, revealing the flat stone inside.

"Hold it like this," he says, placing my thumb on the top and my middle finger on the bottom. His index finger trails a path along my own, straightening it out to wrap against the edge, until I'm clasping it in a loose grip.

His touch is warm and rough, hinting to the callouses he's earned from years on the job. I become hyperaware of the pleasant scrape of them as he moves me about until he's satisfied, and then he steps behind me, not breaking his hold as his hand slips to my wrist, encircling it easily.

"Bend your knees a little," he says, drawing my arm back. "Palm up. Elbow by your side." He brings it forward again, almost like he's showing me a golf swing, and I catch a hint of his scent, earthy, and warm, and oddly familiar.

"Twist at the end. Not at the beginning."

"'Kay," I say, only to hate myself at how high my voice sounds.

Callum doesn't seem to notice, though, stepping away so I can do it myself, and I stare at the water, trying to remember what he told me while also what hands are and how to use them.

In the end, I give up thinking altogether, throwing the stone in, and flicking like he showed me. It skips seven times before it drops, almost matching my glorious record.

Well.

"Okay, so you're an incredible teacher," I say, and he cuts a bow. "They're yours?" I add, looking back at the depleted pile of stones beside us.

"Yeah."

"You come here a lot?"

His lips twitch at the suspicion in my voice. "I do. There's not much else to do around here. And I got to thinking about what you said in the car. About the lake. The forest. You were right. It's beautiful out here. I stop by nearly every day now."

"You do?" I ask, confused. "Where do you even live?" I'd assumed he was in the city like the rest of the workers, but he just nods back to the village.

"In that farmhouse near the lavender fields."

"Mr. Rankin's old place?" I frown. "No one's lived there for years."

"Is this where you tell me it's haunted?"

"It's where I tell you I wouldn't be surprised."

"He's letting me stay there for cheap if I do it up," Callum explains, and I remember what he said to me in the garden the other day about renovating. "And what are *you* doing out here?" he asks before I can press for more. "Shouldn't you be match-making or something?"

I open my mouth with an excuse when a crash sounds from the direction of the barn, and Callum looks behind me with interest.

"What's over there?"

"Nothing," I say, suddenly panicked. I don't want Glenmill knowing anything about what we're planning, but he's already walking away. "Callum, wait."

"Why? What is it?"

"It's for the festival," I blurt out. "And it's top secret, so you can't see it."

"Top secret?"

"Yes."

He wants to laugh. I can see it on his face, but he stops at the flustered expression on mine. "Okay," he says, holding up his hands. "I won't snoop. But it sounds like you're building a rollercoaster."

"And if that's the rumor you want to spread, then by all means, go for it. But I'm—"

"Katie!" I freeze as Nush calls from nearby, her voice echoing through the trees.

Shit.

"You have to go," I tell him, and his eyes widen.

"Seriously?" he asks. "What? Are you ashamed to be seen with me?"

"You want to know who the first person to put Jack's face on the dartboard was? It was that girl. She does not like Glenmill."

"She doesn't even know who I am."

"She'll know you're not from Ennisbawn, and she's a smart cookie. She'll put two and two together. It's for your own safety."

"Now that sounds a little dramatic. Just introduce— okay, okay."

Nush calls again, even closer this time, and I push him up against a large oak tree, hiding him from view.

"I've never been a dirty secret before," he says, laughing, and as Nush emerges through the tree line a little way up, I slap my hand over his mouth to keep him quiet.

Big mistake.

His laughter stops immediately, his attention zeroing in on me in a way that makes me feel like I'm the prey in this situation, and not the person who just manhandled him against a tree.

"Katie!" Nush calls. "Marco!"

She pauses by the lake, waiting for me to answer before giving up and heading back to the trail. I turn my head to the side, ignoring the feel of Callum's gaze on my cheek and try to listen in case anyone else has come looking.

"Okay," I say. "I think we're—"

My eyes dart back to his as his lips part, his warm breath hitting my skin for half a second before I drop it.

"Don't do that," I tell him.

"Why not?"

"Because."

He nods like I've made a compelling argument, but before I can step away, he hooks a finger through one of the belt loops on my jeans. It's a small movement, and an easily breakable hold, but the gentle tug of it sends a bolt of heat straight between my legs, locking me in place.

"Can I do that?" he asks, when I don't move.

I don't trust myself to answer.

Standing together like this, we're as close as two people can be without touching. And I suddenly, desperately want us to be touching.

Whether these thoughts are clear on my face or Callum can read minds, I don't know, but he brings his other hand to my hip, and when I don't move away, he pulls me in a step until our stomachs brush.

We stay like that for the longest time, and I know he's giving me the opportunity to say no. To back out. To march dramatically away. But I don't. I don't do any of those things. I just stand there with my dry mouth and my little crush, and his head dips down, so close to me that I can count his eyelashes and—

"I have to get back to work."

His grip tightens against my waist as he pauses, his lips a hair's breadth from mine. And then his fingers slip from my waist and his hand drops from my hip, and he straightens, resting the back of his head against the tree as he puts distance between us again.

"Guess I'll see you around then."

It takes a second to get my legs to move. When they do, they're stiff and not my own, and I have to force myself away, mumbling a goodbye as I head back into the trees. I don't look back until I reach the barn, where Nush is literally tapping her foot as she waits.

"Didn't you hear me calling?" she asks, when she sees me.

"That was you? I thought it was a ghost."

"Just come on," she grumbles, towing me back inside. I don't know whether her urgency is a good thing or a bad thing, but I'm too relieved she didn't catch me with Callum to care.

"You found her," Gemma calls from where she sits with Adam on some folding chairs.

"She was skulking."

"I was *walking*," I say. "Like I was told to, and I..."

I stop just inside the entrance, all muddled thoughts of Callum vanishing as Nush lets me go, spreading her arms wide in a big ta-da motion. Sometime in the last few minutes, the guys have removed the last of the debris from the far corner and swept away the dirt in the sides and...

"It's ready?"

"It's ready," Gemma confirms, as I step further inside. "It still needs electricity and furnishing and a hundred other things. But the hard part's done."

The hard part *is* done.

I mean, the barn is still empty, yes. But it's clean. Clean and big and bright and full of possibility. Now, all we need to do is dress it up. The hard part's done.

It's *done*.

"I've been researching Jacuzzis," Nush says seriously. "There's a spot outside that would be perfect for one, and I know it might be a little out of budget, but I was thinking if we set up a VIP package, we could—" She cuts off with a laugh as I squeeze her to my side and even Gemma's smiling when I spin her around.

"Is that a yes to the Jacuzzi?"

"It's a no," I say. "It's a firm no."

"But—"

"One thing at a time, Nush." I bring us to a stop in the center of the room, dizzy from the movement. "One thing at a time."

CHAPTER THIRTEEN

"And the *winner* of the signed 1997 intercounty division B second runner-up championship football team jersey *is...*" Frank takes a dramatic pause as I hold the prize aloft. Two hundred pairs of eyes stare at me, rapt in anticipation like I'm offering up a priceless relic, and not a shirt Danny found in the back of his closet.

"Jenny Monaghan!"

The crowd cheers. Like, they literally cheer. Some even burst into applause and wolf whistle as Bridget's wife, Jenny, hurries up to us with a wide smile.

They might be drunk.

I mean, they're definitely drunk.

But that means they're buying an awful lot of raffle tickets.

"Next winner will be announced in thirty minutes," Frank calls. "This one's for the blender, folks. Used only once, according to Paudie."

"We're up five hundred euro already," Jenny says, as I hand over her prize. "This was a great idea, Katie."

It was, wasn't it?

The pub is packed. More packed than I've ever seen it.

Outside of the Christmas season anyway. With only a month to go until the festival was supposed to start, we'd not only managed to get the whole village out to support, but also what felt like half of Rossbridge as well. We had a few decent items for the raffle, signed GAA jerseys, some books, the blender. But people are also chipping in with their own prizes. Someone already bagged a free carpet cleaning service from Danny, and Bridget is offering a week's worth of coffee. She's also the winner of Nush's free color consultation and haircut, while Nush herself won my prize, which is the chance to make any drink she wants, on the house. To my delight, she's chosen one of my cocktails, and it's her I return to now, slipping back behind the bar to find her putting the finishing touches on her glass.

"Perfect timing," she says. "I hope you don't mind, but I adapted your recipe. I don't like pineapple. Or lime. Or orange juice."

I frown. "Then why did you choose to make a Caribbean rum?"

"I don't know; it sounded cool."

"Katie!" Noah calls over from where he stands with Adam in front of the dartboard. "Are you watching?"

"Yes!" I say, turning to him.

"Mam, don't look."

"What?" Gemma glares at him from her seat by the bar. "Why can't I look?"

"Because you do it weird."

"How is it weird? I'm just looking."

"*Mam.*"

"Oh, for the love of—" She spins around to face me, doing as she's told. "Why do you get to look?"

"Because he thinks I'm cool," I tell her, and she scoffs, reaching for Nush's cocktail only to almost spit it out at the first sip.

"What the hell is in that?" she coughs.

Nush looks affronted. "Rum."

"How much rum?"

"Well, it's a *rum* cocktail, Gemma. I don't want to be stingy."

I tune them out, slumping over the bar to watch Noah line up behind the throw line, his tongue peeking out between his teeth as he concentrates.

"Just like I showed you," Adam says, adjusting his arm. "Remember your stance."

Noah shuffles at Adam's words, planting his feet on the ground before he takes a breath and throws. Those of us allowed to, watch as the dart bounces harmlessly off Jack Doyle's left nostril and falls to the floor.

"Not too shabby," Adam says, but Noah's shoulders slump.

"I'm bad at it."

"You're not bad at it," Adam says. "Katie's bad at it."

My mouth falls open. "It's *hard*."

"Very bad at it," Adam mock whispers and Noah smiles a little. "You're just moving too fast," he says, shaking the kid's shoulders until he loosens. "Take your time and let yourself go still. Then throw."

"That's what I did."

"It was. But go even stiller this time. You'll get there."

Gemma has another sip of Nush's cocktail, makes a face, and then takes a gulp. "Who's that?" she asks me.

"Who's who?"

"The guy who keeps staring at you."

I frown, turning to face the crowd. "What are you—"

Callum.

He's standing on the other side of the room, just inside the door, with a slightly lost expression, like he's completely out of his element. Gemma didn't exaggerate the staring thing. Our eyes meet as soon as I turn around, and I quickly spin back to the bar, my heart flipping over in my chest.

"Do you know him?" Gemma asks, watching me curiously.

Nush snatches her drink back and pokes at the ice. "Does she know who?"

"Mr. Handsome by the door."

"You mean Frank?"

Gemma blinks at her. "*Frank?*"

"Frank's handsome."

"He's thirty years older than you!"

"And he's still got it," Nush says, stung. "A girl can appreciate."

"What's Callum doing here?" Adam's joined us now because sure, why not?

"*Callum?*" Gemma's gaze narrows. "You know him too?"

"He works for Glenmill. One of Jack Doyle's guys."

Nush's smile drops. "Glenmill? He's a spy?"

"He's not a spy," I say, which is dumb because everyone's attention swings back to me. "He's not! He just works on the site. A lot of people work on the site."

"But a lot of people don't hang around with Jack Doyle," Adam says. "Did you invite him here?"

"No," I say. "And they don't hang around. They just work together. It's not a big deal," I add because all three of them have the exact same frown on their faces, which would be funny if it wasn't directed at me. "He's the one who helped me with my traffic problem. And he gave me a ride home from the city when it was raining. *And* he helped Granny out with the garden. He got a whole corner cleared."

"Sounds like your new best friend," Gemma says flatly. "You don't think it's weird that he's just around all the time?"

"I think it's a small place and he works nearby, so no. I bump into you all the time too."

"Yes, that's exactly the same thing."

"Katie?" Frank appears at the bar, gesturing to Adam for another drink. "It's almost time for the next prize."

"I'll be right there," I promise, as Nush gives Gemma an exasperated look.

"How do you not see it?" she asks. "That is big silver fox energy."

"Oh my God."

I hand out the prize. And then I hand out another. And in between, I work the room, encouraging people to donate, explaining the festival, and ignoring Callum Dempsey. For two whole hours, I ignore him. Or I pretend to, at least. Because I find the man impossible to ignore. I'm aware of when he buys a raffle ticket from a beaming Bridget. I'm aware when he gets a drink from a stony-faced Adam and finds a spot along the wall. I'm aware when he starts talking to two men from Rossbridge, and I'm aware when he's chatted up by a pretty redhead who keeps putting her hand on his arm before he politely excuses himself. I'm aware when he goes to the freaking *bathroom*. And I'm aware when he finally leaves. Slipping out around thirty minutes before closing time, with only a brief glance in my direction.

I try not to read too much into it. Especially when the other three are still watching me like hawks. I throw myself into my work instead. Eventually we run out of prizes, Adam calls last orders, and the pub begins to empty as, one by one, the designated drivers patiently take their friends and families home. A few of us stay to clean up and count the cash. I'm so busy that he's almost gone from my mind when I grab the last trash bag of the night and push open the door to the back.

There were some smokers out here earlier, but now the patio is deserted. Empty except for Callum, who's leaning back against the wishing well, facing the lake.

He doesn't hear me step out, probably lost in thought, because it's only when I toss the bulging trash bag to the side that he glances over his shoulder, straightening when he sees me.

"Hey."

"I thought you left."

"No."

No. I take a step closer, pulling the sleeves of my fleece down over my wrists. "It's weird that you came here."

"Is it?"

"Yes. You've been labeled a spy."

"Must be a pretty bad one if I've been found out."

"Well, if you're not, then why are you here?"

He looks surprised by the question. "I figured this is where you'd be."

Voices call to each other from around the front of the pub as more people leave, but no one comes out back and I don't move from my spot, except to swing on the balls of my feet. I feel restless. Like I'm waiting for something, but I don't know what.

He picks up on it, of course. I'm not exactly being subtle about it. "You okay?"

"You make me nervous," I admit, and he nods like he knew that already.

"Good nervous or bad nervous?"

"I haven't decided yet."

"Still got a chance then," he says, and I have no idea what to say to that, so I don't say anything at all. "Or maybe not." His expression grows thoughtful. "Do you want me to leave?"

"No," I say quickly. I'm aware I'm being confusing, but that's because I'm confused, and being this close to him isn't helping matters.

More noises. More voices. Still, we're left alone.

"Do you know how many projects like these I've been on?" he asks, when I just stand there. "Dozens. This is the biggest one, but I've worked on office blocks and housing estates. Hotels. Shopping centers. You always have to knock down to build up these days. Always. And I've never thought about it before. We've demolished houses and shops that were sometimes a hundred years old, and I've never cared about them. It was always just a job. And I always just got on with it. But with you..." He trails off, his brow furrowing like he's figuring out his own thoughts as he says them. "He's nervous about this. Jack. He won't say it, but I know he thought you'd fold after a couple of days. The fact that you didn't has him on edge. You're getting to him. And you should keep going. If you want to save your pub, you should keep going."

I stare at him, confused. "You *work* for him."

"Yes."

"So why are you telling me this?"

"I don't know. Maybe I don't like what we're doing here. Or maybe I'm just bored and want to stir the pot." Callum's gaze snags on mine, and the feel of it is so intense that I almost look away. "Or maybe," he continues. "It's because I don't know how I'm going to tear down your favorite place in the world when I can barely stand the thought of you getting caught in the rain."

There's a strange pang in my chest, one that hurts in the best kind of way.

Green eyes, I decide. I like men with green eyes and men who look at me like that.

Like I'm the only person in the world.

He takes another step, closing the distance between us, and I force myself to keep still as he slowly, *finally* brushes a kiss to the corner of my mouth.

His lips are soft.

I don't know why I'm so surprised by this. Maybe because the rest of him feels so tough, but his lips are very, very soft, and it's all I can think about as he tilts his face, his nose skimming mine as my eyes flutter closed.

I hadn't planned on getting kissed tonight.

I would have put on some Chapstick if I knew. Maybe

double-checked that chin zit I'd been diligently applying tooth-paste to. But as colossal as those worries were a second ago, they fly out the window as soon as he captures my bottom lip between his, giving it a gentle tug that I feel all the way down to my belly. He does it again, and I shuffle closer, slipping a tentative hand between the folds of his open jacket. His body feels hard beneath his T-shirt, hard and warm and perfect, and I curl my fingers into the material as his own hand burrows into the hair behind my ear, sending prickles of pleasure down my spine.

Oh man, I could do this all night. All night and tomorrow night and the night after that and the night after—

"Ahem."

The pointed cough breaks through the haze I'd slipped under, and I break away so fast I almost get whiplash.

Gemma stands in the doorway, her arms folded across her chest. I have no idea how long she's been watching us. But I know it's too long. And even with her scarily neutral expression I know she's not happy.

"Adam's looking for you," she says, when neither of us moves. "And I'm going to head if you want to say goodbye to Noah."

"Right." I duck my head, not looking at Callum as I grab the trash bag from where I left it and hurry to the shed. "Just give me a second," I call back.

My heart is thumping for all the wrong reasons now, and when I return to the pub, Callum has vanished, and Gemma is looking at me with that stern Mam expression that usually sends Noah running in the opposite direction. And now I understand why.

"Katie—"

"I know."

"Do you?"

"Yes. And way to be a creeper, by the way."

"You were standing right outside the door. Apologies for using it. Look, I'm not Nush," she says, when I try to move past. "I don't think everyone who works there is the devil. But just think. He still works for them, and I don't want to see you getting hurt."

"It was just a kiss. I've been very stressed and he's very handsome and I just wanted a little kiss in the moonlight, okay? Drop it."

"Fine," Gemma mutters, and though I know she's not finished with the conversation, she obviously takes pity on me because she turns back to the pub. "But at least do it in a shadowy corner like normal people," she adds, and nudges me inside.

CHAPTER FOURTEEN

"How are these things still the most delicious food in the world?"

One afternoon the next week, I drag my gaze from the stock list to where Harry sits at the bar, polishing off a cheese toastie.

"We use extra butter," I explain. "And local cheese. Not crappy cheese."

"I don't know. I think it's how you cut the sandwich diagonally instead of horizontal." He pushes the plate away and sets a hand against his stomach. "I'm going to regret that in about thirty seconds, and it will be all your— wait, no. Ten seconds. I'm getting old."

I abandon my work to slump on the bar next to him. He texted me this morning asking if I had time to see him, and I immediately said yes, but asked him to swing by the barn first so he could see it and then come and admire me and my brilliance. Despite this very clear task, he hasn't even mentioned it. And as each moment passes, I'm getting more and more impatient. A girl needs praise.

"So?" I ask now, as he checks his phone.

"So what?"

"What do you think?"

"Best toastie ever."

"Of the barn," I groan, and he grins.

"It looks great. I'm very impressed. I thought that place was good for nothing other than underage smoking and maybe a location for a horror movie, but you've proved me wrong."

"And we haven't even put the decorations in yet," I say. "I don't know why we didn't do something like this before. We could rent it out in the future. Host some traveling theater troupes or something."

"How many traveling theater troupes do you know of?"

"Ask me that question in six months and the answer will blow your mind."

"It looks great," he says again. "And the festival will be great. You just need to dress the place up a bit more and it will be incredible."

"Dress what up? The barn?"

"The village."

"What's wrong with the village?"

He gives me a look.

"What? The village is fine."

"The village is depressing," he says. "You expect all these people to come and just not notice the state of the main street? It looks as gloomy as it did when I left."

"That's a horrible thing to say," I chide. "It's not gloomy."

"It's gloomy. It's dystopian gloomy. And you know you need to water those hanging baskets, right? You can't just put them up and hope for the best. You've also got a litter problem."

"We do not have a litter problem. We have foxes. That's different."

"You've got to clean it up, or no one's going to come here and think, yes, that girl is right. This sad little place I've never heard of deserves my time and energy to save it. Here's ten thousand euro."

I pout, seeing his point. "Well, what do you suggest we do?"

"As I said, dress it up. Sweep the streets, water the plants, put some fake displays in the empty shop windows and a *gone fishing* sign on the door."

"That's lying."

"That's life. Better yet, that's business." He leans back on the stool, rolling his shoulders back. "Speaking of business. Will you be partaking in any of this matchmaking yourself, or will you just be standing in the back with your clipboard and headset? Because a new guy started at the office who I think would be great for you."

"My ex-boyfriend wants to set me up?"

"Only weird if you make it weird."

"I'm not looking for anyone right now," I say, and he hums.

"That's what they all say."

I shrug, returning to my stock list while keeping my eyes round and innocent and—

"Alright," he says flatly. "What happened?"

"What do you mean?"

"You're really bad at secrets, Katie Collins. You're a bad liar and a bad secret keeper and you're doing that thing where you obviously want to tell me something, but you want to pretend that I forced it out of you."

"No, I'm not."

"Bad at lying," he reminds me. "Tell me. I'll be gone in an hour anyway. Did you kill someone?"

"No."

"Are you pregnant?"

"No! Harry! I met someone. That's all."

"Who?"

"Nobody."

"Katie—"

"We also kissed."

"Is he local?"

"He works for Glenmill."

Harry snorts. "Of course he does. Always have to make thing difficult for yourself, don't you?"

"He's an on-site project coordinator. Doesn't that sound impressive?"

"Not really," he says, before his eyes narrow. "Are you blushing?"

"I don't blush. I'm warm."

"You're blushing. You're blushing because you have a crush on an on-site project coordinator? What are you? Fourteen? What's his name?"

"I'm not telling you. Callum Dempsey." I lean back over the bar as the office door opens and Adam emerges. "What are you doing?"

Harry takes out his phone. "I'm googling him."

"Googling who?" Adam asks. He rubs his eyes in his *I've been looking at numbers for the past hour* way and snatches one of the orange slices I cut earlier.

"Nobody," I say, as Harry looks up.

"Katie kissed a boy."

"Harry!" I whack his arm with a dishcloth. "Snitch move."

"You kissed *this* guy?" Harry makes a show of peering at the screen, and I glimpse a picture of Callum on it. "Well done you."

"Okay, I don't need to be around for this conversation." Adam grabs his keys, looking distinctly uncomfortable. "It's like hearing about my baby sister."

"Where are you going?" I ask. "We could have a whole busload of people show up here in the next hour and I'll be all by myself."

"I'll have to take my chances. I said I'd take Noah to the pool."

"You did? That's nice of you." The nearest public swimming pool is at least an hour's drive away.

"Yeah, well, he deserves it. He said Gemma was supposed to bring him because he got an A on his French test, but she had to work today."

I bite back a smile. "An A, huh?"

"Yeah. Great, isn't it?"

"The greatest," I agree. "Except Noah's school doesn't have tests. And he doesn't do French. He does Spanish."

Adam pauses in the middle of putting on his jacket. "Well, then I guess I've been played."

I can only grin as his expression settles into his usual scowl.

Adam's been in a noticeably better mood the past few weeks. Maybe not noticeable to *everyone*, but definitely to me, the person professionally obliged to spend a lot of time with him. He'd never admit it because he's a perpetual pessimist who still expects the world to come crashing down around him, but I know he has his hopes up that the festival will work.

"Just go," I say. "He should be rewarded for his shamelessness."

"I said I'd take him for a burger as well," Adam mutters, and I laugh. "You're good here?"

"We'll be fine."

"I'll be back by five. And Harry pays for everything he orders," he adds, pushing open the door. "No freebies."

I give him a two-fingered salute and turn to Harry. "Do you want a mocktail? It doesn't have any alcohol in it, but it does have a year's worth of sugar."

"Hmmm," he says, not looking up from his phone, and I pause at the carefully blank expression on his face.

"What's wrong?"

"Nothing. But what's Callum's second name again?"

"Dempsey."

"Are you sure?"

"Yes. That's what Jack said it was."

"Jack Doyle?" His eyes snap up. "The director guy at Glenmill? The one writing all the articles?"

"Yeah," I say slowly. "Why?"

"When did he say that?"

I pause, confused by the suspicion in his voice. "The first time they all came to the pub. When I found out what was happening."

"Why was Callum there?"

"I don't know," I say, growing annoyed when he just continues to scroll. "If you're going to say something rude like he's out of my league or—"

"I wasn't going to say that," he interrupts. "I just want to know what you're doing kissing the boss's brother."

I stare at him, waiting for the punchline. "What are you talking about?"

"You really don't know?"

"Know what?" I snap.

He turns his phone around to show me the screen, but I don't even glance at it. "Katie, Jack Doyle is Callum's brother."

More staring. More waiting. No punchlines. "No, he's not."

"According to all these articles he is," Harry says. "Though most are from a few years ago when Jack got the job. *Following Mr. O'Hara's retirement, executive Jack Doyle will be stepping into the role. Glenmill Properties has become something of a family business for Mr. Doyle, whose younger brother Callum also works in the firm. Together they—*"

"Wait, wait, wait." I lean over the bar, plucking the phone from his hands. "That's... no. It's a mistake. They're not brothers. They look nothing alike."

"It's not a rule. And they kind of do."

I'm already pulling up an image of Jack in another tab and, after a second, I type in both their names together. A picture of them immediately comes up. They both look younger and the date on the article is more than five years old, but there they are side by side, standing in front of some construction site in Belfast.

"Nu-uh." It's all I can say. It's all I can think, even as a little bit of doubt creeps in. A little bit of doubt followed swiftly by a whole lot of hurt. *You don't think it's weird that he's just around all the time?* That's what Gemma asked when he showed up here. That's what I dismissed without even considering it.

"Okay," Harry says, sensing my growing unease. "This doesn't have to be a big deal."

"What if he's a spy?"

"He's not a spy."

"How do you know?"

"Because this isn't the Cold War. This is rural Ireland, and you are hosting a matchmaking festival. Let's just calm down."

"Why didn't he tell me?"

Harry's mouth opens and closes. "I don't know," he says.

"Right. So he just happens to show a massive interest in me. The girl who's trying to halt his boss's plans. His *brother's* plans." His *brother.* Christ. "What if he's not even a site guy? What if he's a boardroom guy? What if he was just pretending to be Mr. Normal and he's actually—"

"Okay," Harry interrupts. "Now we're just spiraling."

"What if he's playing me?" I finish. "What if I have a crush on someone who's playing me?"

To that, Harry doesn't respond.

Oh my God.

"Am I jumping to conclusions?" I ask, and his face screws up. "Harry, tell me I'm jumping to conclusions."

"You're... assessing the full picture," he says, and I drop my head to the bar, ignoring the toastie crumbs as they stick to my forehead. "I'm sorry, Katie."

I grunt and he pats the top of my head.

"You know what?" he says. "Maybe I will have one of those mocktails."

CHAPTER FIFTEEN

"I'm going out," I call, taking one final look in the mirror before grabbing my purse. "Granny? I'm leaving now. I'm—" I jump as she appears in the doorway, dressed all in black. "Entering your crone years, I see."

"Susan's here to pick me up. I'm going to a funeral."

I pause, instantly guilty. "I'm sorry. Who died?"

"Mary Boyd," she says, and smiles like it's the best news she's heard all week. "I used to play bridge with her."

"And we're..." I wait for her to stop smiling. She doesn't. "We're sad about this?"

"God, no. She was a horrible woman."

"Then why are you going to her funeral?"

"To gloat," she says, like it's obvious. "I outlived her."

"That is such an unhealthy way of thinking about it."

She shrugs, taking in my outfit before her eyes narrow on my face. "Are you wearing lipstick?"

"No." Yes. I fight the urge to scrub it off, squirming under her gaze.

She stays right where she is, watching me for a long, uncomfortable moment.

"Your hair looks lovely," she says eventually, and heads down the stairs. "But you need a better bra if you want to wear that top."

I scoff, turning back to the mirror as I wait for the front door to close. Then I do exactly as she suggested.

Five minutes later, I'm marching down the road toward the site, my heeled boots clacking against the tarmac as I try not to let my nerves take over. I spent all day yesterday mulling over my new revelation, and woke up this morning determined to learn the truth. Because that is what adults do. They talk to each other. They speak plainly and clearly and give each other ample opportunity to explain why they withheld such important information. Important information, like the fact that the other person has a brother whose sole purpose in life seems to be tearing down mine. Information that the other person just casually forgot to mention, even when said person looked at me with those bright green eyes, and touched me with those strong broad hands, and kissed me with those soft full—

"Stop right there."

I halt, spinning to see a curly-haired man standing by a hut just inside the entrance. It looks like they tightened their security since the last time I was here.

"Katie Collins," I say, before the man can ask. "I'm here to see Callum Dempsey."

"You're not on the list."

He didn't even check the list. Not that I'd be on it, if he did, but still. "I should be," I say. "Could you call him and check?"

The man doesn't call him. He just stands there instead. "You look familiar."

"I live down the road."

"Yeah? Is this you?" He jerks his head to the wall beside him, and I look over to see a grainy black and white photograph taped to it.

It is me.

It's me in my duck pajamas the day I stormed down here and jabbed a finger in Jack Doyle's face.

"I don't think so," I say, making a show of peering at it.

He still looks suspicious, but I nod to the phone, knowing he has no other choice but to check.

He stares at me the whole time in a *I take my job very seriously* way. Callum must give him the okay, though, because it only takes a few seconds before his scowl deepens, and he grabs a visitor's pass from the table.

"You can wait in his office," he says, only a smidgen friendlier. "It's the third one on the right." He hands me a hard hat and a hi-vis jacket, waiting for me to put them on before getting me to sign in.

I find the door with Callum's name on it, knock once, and let myself in when there's no answer. Inside the space is sparse, the kind of office that tells you its owner rarely uses it. There's only a desk with a laptop on it and two chairs on either side. Paper is stacked in neat piles around it and the corkboard attached to the wall is filled with calendars and order forms.

I ditch my safety gear, prepared to wait a while, but barely a few seconds pass before Callum strides through the door, scanning me from top to toe with a worried pinch to his brow.

"Are you okay?" he asks. "Is it Maeve?"

"I'm fine," I say, thrown by the concern in his voice. "And she's fine. But your security is mean."

"Yeah, well, I had to chew them out over some woman wandering in off the street a few weeks ago, so I'm glad to hear it."

"Did you know they've got my picture on the wall? And not in a good way?"

"Jack put it there." His gaze snags on my face. "Are you wearing lipstick?"

Mother of— "No," I lie. Again.

His phone rings at his side and he checks it briefly before canceling it.

"I was hoping we could talk," I say, but he doesn't seem to be listening to me.

"You *are* wearing lipstick." As soon as he says it, his gaze drops down to the rest of my outfit. I was trying for mature and professional, but I suppose the one nice pair of jeans I own coupled with the silk blouse I'm wearing is the most dressed up he's ever seen me. And from the look on Callum's face, he likes it. He likes it a lot.

"What did you want to talk about?" he asks, with a small smile. When I don't answer, he takes a step toward me like I'm here for a very different reason. My mind goes blank when he does, but whether that's from nerves or something else, I don't know. I tell myself it's nerves. Nerves for my impending accusation, and definitely not because he's staring at my mouth like he wants to kiss the lipstick off it.

One of his hands find mine, and he smiles outright when I clench it, holding on tight. Okay, this is not going to plan.

"I can't talk," he says, oblivious to my inner crisis. "I've got a million and one things to do. But I can stop by the pub tonight?"

"The pub?"

"Or the house. I think your grandmother likes me."

"She doesn't like anyone."

"I don't know," he says. "I can be pretty charming." His phone rings again, and he silences it again, an apologetic look on his face. "I have to get back to work."

He doesn't though, he doesn't even move. And when I don't either, he leans in, his intention clear, and all my grand plans go flying out the window.

"Is Jack Doyle your brother?"

I blurt out the words so fast, I think I spit on him a little. For a moment, Callum goes rigid, like his body has been frozen in ice before he pulls back, his expression guarded.

My stomach drops.

"Oh my God, he is." I don't know what I'd been hoping. That it was some kind of elaborate prank? That this was one of those doppelgänger situations that always freaked me out so much?

I spin away from him, ending up in the corner of the room, beside the door. "Since when? Don't answer that," I interrupt myself. "Obviously since you were born. Duh."

He doesn't move from his spot at the desk, looking at me like I'm some sort of wild animal that's been released in his office. "You're freaking out."

"Yes," I tell him, abandoning all my adult plans. "Yes, I'm freaking out. Because the other day you kissed me right outside the pub that your brother wants to tear down. The brother that you conveniently forgot to tell me about." Dumb. I am so dumb. "Are you spying on me?"

"Spying?"

"Digging up dirt? Finding something that could bring me down? Well, you're not going to find anything. Do you know what I've done? Nothing. That's the great thing about being boring. I've done *nothing*. I mean, yes, one time at the self-checkout I paid for one banana instead of two, but I just wanted to see what would happen. I was testing the system and the system failed."

"Katie—"

"It's because you shouldn't trust people. You shouldn't trust people with their bananas, and you shouldn't trust people with their kisses."

His phone goes again, and I glare at him.

"Do you need to get that?"

"No."

"Why didn't you tell me he was your brother?"

He sighs. "Because you've made it perfectly clear how you feel about him, and I wanted to know how you felt about *me* first. And before that, I didn't tell you because I don't tell anyone. Neither of us do. I've worked with some of these guys for years and they still don't know."

"Why not?"

"Because he's their boss? Because I'd like to do my job and be friendly with the guys and not have them be on edge around me the whole time? We don't make a thing of it. I use my mother's surname whenever we're working on the same project. I always have."

"Sure," I scoff, and his jaw tightens.

"Whatever nefarious plan you think I'm involved in, Katie, it's not happening. I swear to you. I wasn't spying. I wasn't scheming. I came to the pub the other night because I wanted to see you. Because that's all I've wanted to do since I met you. And I—" He breaks off with a curse as his phone rings for the fourth time.

"Just answer the damn call."

"No," he says. "You wanted to talk so let's talk." But almost as soon as he's said the words, footsteps stomp up the metal steps outside, and a second later, Jack bursts through the door, almost whacking me in the face with it.

"Why aren't you answering me?"

Alarm flashes across Callum's features. "Jack—"

"And why I am getting petitions from a man who calls himself a *druid* about the goddamn road proposal? Two months! We're going to be behind two months because of this farce. Do you know how much this is going to cost us?"

"Jack—"

"I'm already going to lose half of Malone's crew in September. What the hell are we going to do now? Gerald isn't going to allow any more delays and—"

"*Jack.*"

"What?" he snaps, spinning around when Callum gestures to where I stand.

His eyes widen when he sees me, but any surprise he shows is quickly replaced by annoyance. "Christ, Callum, when I said you should seduce her, I didn't mean on company time."

"*Woah.*" Callum holds up his hands as the blood drains from my face. "Hold on a second."

"Did you do this?" Jack asks me, waving a newspaper in my face. "Send the druids after me?"

The who now?

"Can you please calm down," Callum begins, but his brother ignores him.

"This has gone on long enough," he says. "You've had your fun. But we've got work to do. I'm buying your pub. I'm building my road. And we're completing this hotel on time."

"Over my dead body," I snap, just as furious as he is. "I am going to make your life a living hell. And *you.*" I round on Callum, who looks like he has a migraine. "You can forget about ever kissing me again. No more truce."

Callum's brows draw together, looking like he's about to argue, but I march out of there before he can. Just as the door bangs shut behind me, I hear Jack's furious voice as he turns on his brother.

"What does she mean *again*?"

CHAPTER SIXTEEN

Okay, so I'm moving to France.

I'm going to learn French, and I am going to move to France.

Or maybe I'll move to Japan. I think Japanese would be much harder to learn as a beginner, sure, but it's a lot farther away than France.

A lot farther away from Callum Dempsey.

Callum Dempsey, whom I can certainly never see again.

I mean, what was that?

What the *hell* was that?

What was I *thinking*?

I stare at the cobweb in the corner of my kitchen. The same cobweb that's been there for a few months now. The same one I've been staring at all morning.

I can never see him again. That's the only answer.

Because way to think with your vagina, and not your head, Katie.

Way to be a complete *idiot*.

"You alright?"

"I'm fine." The words are clipped and a lie, but Gemma

doesn't call me out on it. She came over after her shift at the nursing home to help me with some admin, and I've been nothing short of rude to her all afternoon. She knows something's up. I'm just too embarrassed to tell her.

I click through my email, scrolling through my unanswered pleas to local journalists, begging for scraps of attention. I'd been bullish about it before, so concerned with getting the venue ready that I didn't think about the fact we weren't even selling tickets. But now it's all I can think about. Especially after what Jack said yesterday. The whole point of this was to get attention and we weren't getting any of it.

Every small town in the country had some sob story about something closing down. Nush was right. We should have gone flashier. "Do you know any famous people?"

"Do you?" Gemma asks dryly, and I look up to see her licking one of the dozens of envelopes she's been stuffing to mail out to local businesses. As I watch her reach for the next one, she starts to blur before me, and I blink, rubbing my eyes. They're sore and slightly stinging from staring at a laptop screen for the past few hours. And of course, by my lack of sleep.

"My internet is slow," I say.

"Frank said they're doing some work in the area today."

Of course they are.

"We can go to mine," she offers. "But I don't think it will be any better. Or maybe Bridget has some—" She breaks off with a curse as a horn suddenly blares outside. "What the hell is that?"

Jack's revenge. "The traffic started again this morning."

"But I thought you said Callum—"

"I know." I doubt it was him, though. All my money was on the brother. "Looks like they changed their mind."

"That's just petty," she says.

And that's who we're dealing with.

"You'll get used to it." My phone lights up, a local number flashing on the screen. I grab it, and head into the hallway.

Granny took Plankton with her to a friend's house for tea, so I have the front room to myself.

"Miss Collins?" The man on the other end introduces himself as someone from guest services at the Laketon Hotel. "I just wanted to check in and see how the festival was coming along?"

"Brilliantly," I say. "We're getting great interest."

"That's wonderful." A polite pause. "It's just we haven't had any bookings."

"Oh?" It's an appropriately surprised noise, even though I'm not surprised at all.

"I'm afraid not," he continues. "And for that reason, we'll need to release the rooms we have for you."

"What do you mean release them?"

"Well, when we set them aside for bookings, we do so expecting there to *be* bookings," he explains. "If none come in in the next day or two, we'll need to put them back on general sale. It's a busy season for us."

"But where will people go if they need to stay? We had a deal."

"We had an email," he says, not unkindly. "But tell you what. You come to me when you have someone, and I promise we'll give them a good rate."

We chat back and forth for another minute as I try in vain to keep him on the line, to give me time to think of a way out of this, but this is a man used to working in customer services and he smoothly, and a little impressively it must be said, cuts me off, politely putting the phone down.

"Who was that?" Gemma asks, when I drag my feet back into the kitchen.

"The hotel just wanted to check in."

Her brows lower, but before she can say whatever's on her mind there's a sudden tapping of rain against the window, hinting at an approaching downpour.

"Noah's at after-school football," Gemma says with a curse. "I'd better go collect him, or I'll be the worst mother in the world again. You okay here?"

"I'm fine."

"I'll swing by later and we can make a plan for tomorrow. I switched shifts, so I don't need to go in until the weekend."

"You don't need to do that."

"I want to do it. Hey." She waits for me to look at her. "Chin up."

I nod, mustering a smile as she leaves, and return to my work.

The room grows progressively darker as the rain continues, and eventually I have to switch on a light, one that flickers once as the electricity cuts out and comes back again, but it's a warning sign I don't like. I know why when, two minutes later, I try to log on to my email and the inbox won't load.

The internet is down.

Is this my test? This feels like my test. One of those times when I have to prove what I'm made of. Stand up to the challenge.

But I am not up for the challenge.

In fact, I would like the challenge to stop.

Because surely, *surely* it shouldn't be this hard. I deserve a bit of luck, right? A bit of divine intervention. A little, *hey, that girl needs a break.*

The rain falls harder, and I go to the window to look out at it. As I do, I catch sight of the hawthorn tree at the back of the garden. The one I still need to deal with if I can get past Granny first.

Maybe I should give them an offering. Do fairies like offerings? Besides, like, human children? Maybe I could...

I rest my forehead against the glass, watching the world blur.

Something feels wrong.

It's a deep, heavy kind of wrong, like a rock is weighing down my stomach. Like you know danger is coming, but you don't know when.

Another truck passes by, making the window frame vibrate, and knowing I can do nothing with the internet gone, I grab my rain jacket and leave the house, heading down the road toward the village.

Usually, the more I move away from the hotel site, the quieter the noises from it gets, but this time I hear different sounds, coming not from behind me, but from somewhere in the distance, and I make a sharp turn, heading through a field that will lead me to the western side of the forest.

It should be a fifteen-minute walk to the barn, but I do it in ten, running through the downpour, as the bad feeling gets worse and worse and worse. I'm soaked through by the time I get there, and I start sprinting when I see the large tire tracks drawing a dirty path from the road and down the trail, where a crashing noise sounds.

I feel like someone just punched me in the chest.

The barn is half-gone. One side of it has been demolished into nothing but rubble and dust. The ground around it is no better, muddy piles and haphazard holes where green grass once stood. A large machine lumbers about, moving slowly over the ruins, *creating* the ruins, and I move faster, almost through the clearing before I'm spotted.

"You can't come in here," a man yells, holding up a hand as if to physically stop me. "This is an active building site."

"It's not, it's... you don't own this land. I'm working in there."

He frowns at that. "We cleared out all objects we found inside. You can pick them up down the road, but it's been marked as abandoned and, from the looks of it, has been for a while." He smiles then, like we're joking. "Unless I'm about to be fired."

He clears his throat when I just stare at him and starts flipping through his clipboard before showing me a map. One that shows this part of the forest. This property. Now owned by Glenmill.

"Well..." the man continues, when I just stand there. "If you just keep a good bit away there, you're grand to stay for a bit." He nods as if I've responded and heads back to what's left of the barn, his boots squelching in the mud his team has created.

This is what Jack meant when he said I'd had my fun. Adam was right. He really was just playing with me before. He really was just...

"Katie."

Callum stands a few feet behind me. He has his big orange construction jacket on, but it's open, and doesn't have a hood, so does little to protect him against the rain.

"Did you know?" I ask.

"No." His expression is tight, almost furious. "I came down here as soon as I heard."

"Bullshit."

"I swear. Jack didn't tell me he was doing this. He knows I would have stopped him. It's because I— *Katie*." He follows me as I stride past him, heading to the road. I need to get back to the village. I need to call everyone I know and get them down here.

"We had an argument when you left the other day," Callum continues. "We've had to push back delivery by a couple of months and he's panicking. That's all this is. He's lashing out and—"

"You knew what we were doing to the barn," I interrupt, barely listening to him. "You said so yourself, you go through these woods every day. You were at the raffle. You knew what we were doing, and you told him."

"I didn't."

"You did!" I tear my hand away when he goes to grab it and turn right, just as another excavator comes trundling around the corner. The driver flashes his lights when he sees me, but I hold my ground, clinging to my impromptu protest until Callum yanks me back, giving the machine plenty of space to get past me.

"What the hell are you doing?" he snaps.

"I am obviously having a *meltdown*." I push the wet hair from my face, watching the digger disappear into the woods.

The rain is easing now, but I'm so drenched through it doesn't matter.

"It's just a barn," Callum says, as if I'm about to chase after it or something. "That's all it is. Just a barn. You can host the festival somewhere else."

"There's nowhere else with any space. That was the perfect spot. We spent weeks on it. We were ready."

He steps toward me, hesitating when I send him a warning glance. "I already told—"

"I know what you told me," I interrupt. That he didn't have anything to do with it. That he didn't know anything. But that doesn't matter. It doesn't matter because Gemma was right. She was right from the start. I should have waited a year and done it right. I mean, the hotel is still a giant hole in the ground. I had time. I had time, but I rushed into it. I rushed into it because I was upset, and I didn't *think*. And now I was hurt just like she warned me I would be.

"You want to know why it doesn't matter if you want to see me?" I ask, repeating his words from yesterday. "Why it doesn't matter if you knew about this or not? It's because of your brother. Because he's building a hotel down the road from my house, and I'm terrified my dog will be run over every time we go for a walk. Because he's taken away half the land that used to be open to us. Because he's knocked down my barn and he's going to knock down my pub and then I'm going to hate you."

"You don't know that he's going to—"

"I do," I say. "I know it. Because I can't do this. I give up.

We have nowhere to host the festival, but that doesn't matter because no one's coming. We've barely sold a handful of tickets, and no one is picking up their phone or answering their emails or paying any attention to us at all. Because we don't matter to them."

My throat starts to burn, and I swallow, trying to force down the ball of pressure that feels like it's trapped there.

"No one's coming," I say, my voice rising with each word. "No one's booked in and no one's coming, and I don't know what to do. Because I really thought people would care. I thought if they knew what was happening, they'd come out and support. Because we're *trying*. We're really trying. We were going to have fireworks and music and dancing. We were going to have so much dancing. And it wasn't just going to be about the pub or about attention. It was about us. About the village and showing the world who we are. It was going to be about people falling in *love*. They were going to fall in love and meet their soulmate here and years from now, when people asked them how they met, they could say Kelly's. They could say Ennisbawn. And no one would want to get rid of us then. No one would think we were unimportant. But we're not going to have any of that because everyone who thought I couldn't do this was right. I can't."

The rain has stopped completely now. A hint of blue sky appearing between the clouds.

A little too late. Just like everything else in my life.

"It doesn't matter what you know or don't know," I tell him. "Kelly's is my home. And if you think I'm going to be able to forget that you're one of the people playing a part in destroying it, even if you don't want to, then you haven't been listening to me. You haven't been listening at all."

Callum stares at me, his jaw set, and his eyes intense. His clothes are plastered to his skin, his hair to his head, and I know I don't look much better. But I don't have the energy to care.

"I'm going home now," I tell him. "And then I'm going to have a very large glass of wine and do some stress baking. Tell your brother I give up. He can do what he likes."

"Katie—"

I don't wait for him to continue, turning back to the road and spying his green van parked up ahead. Behind that, flashing her lights, sits Gemma. I'd been so focused on the excavator, I didn't even see her before, but from the look on her face, I know she's been sitting there a while.

"You want to come to mine?" she asks, and I nod, wiping the curls from my forehead.

She already has a towel in the passenger seat for me, and I grab it as I climb inside, pressing it to my face.

"Hi, Noah."

"Hi." He doesn't look up from where he sits in the back, his thumbs flying across his phone screen.

I sniff, wiping my nose for good measure as Gemma pulls out onto the road. I don't look at Callum, who's still standing at the entrance to the lane, watching us go.

"The barn," she begins, but I just shake my head.

"I don't want to talk about it," I say, and Gemma, bless her heart, leaves it at that.

CHAPTER SEVENTEEN

Adam takes one look at me when I walk into work that evening and sends me home again. I'm miserable. I've never given up on anything before. Mainly because I haven't *tried* anything before. And that realization just sends me spiraling even more. I go straight to bed with a bottle of wine and one of Granny's books and fall into an exhausted sleep somewhere between glass three and chapter nine.

The next thing I know, the sun is shining, and my phone is vibrating somewhere nearby.

I'm a little hungover, and it takes me a few seconds to figure out where it is, slapping blindly around the blankets before I find it.

"Hello?" My voice is groggy, and I check the time to see it's a little after eight.

"I had nothing to do with it."

"Gemma?" It is Gemma. But this Gemma doesn't sound like Gemma. She sounds nervous and hesitant and thoroughly *not* Gemma. "Nothing to do with what?"

"The video."

"What video?"

There's silence on the end of the line and, as the last vestiges of sleep finally leave my brain, I sit up, propping myself against the headboard. "What video?" I repeat.

"You haven't seen it?"

"Seen what? What are you talking about?"

Our doorbell chimes through the house before she can reply. That's a first. We're knocking people around here. Peer-through-the-window-and-wave people. I didn't even know the bell still worked.

"Someone's at the door," I say, kicking the covers off my legs.

"Katie, wait—"

"I'll call you back. They're going to wake Granny."

I hang up, yawning widely as I shove my feet into my slippers and head down the stairs. The bell goes again just as I reach the hallway and I don't bother to hide my frown as I nudge an equally confused Plankton out of the way and answer it.

A young woman stands on the other side, smiling radiantly. She's wearing a blue trench coat and her dreadlocks are dyed silver and piled high on her head. Her lipstick is bright pink and so perfectly applied that I can only stare at it in envy.

"Katie Collins?"

"Yeah?"

"My name is Michelle Kayode from *The Irish Weekly News*. I was hoping I could—"

"As in the paper?" I interrupt, and her smile widens.

"That's right. I was wondering if you'd be available for a quick chat?"

"Katie?" I glance over my shoulder as Granny yells from her bedroom. "Who's that?"

"I'd really love to talk to you about the video," Michelle says. "If you've got time?"

The...

Okay. Hold on.

"Can you give me one second?" I ask.

"Of course."

"I just have to check something."

"I'll wait right out here," she says. "There's no rush."

"Cool... I— okay. One second. Don't leave. Stay right there."
I close the door to keep Plankton in, and retreat to the kitchen to
call Gemma back. She answers on the first ring.

"What video?"

The words come out in a rush. "Noah filmed you and
Callum arguing yesterday. And then he put it online."

"He did *what*?" I hiss, as Granny shuffles into the room, a
cigarette half-hidden in her hand.

"Who was at the door?"

"Nobody. Go back to bed."

She gives me a look that lets me know I'm going to be
paying for *that* comment for the rest of my life and disappears
down the hallway.

"What do you mean, online?" I ask, as I hurry after her,
making sure she does indeed go to her bedroom before taking
the stairs two at a time to mine. "How online?"

"He put it up on one of his social media accounts yesterday.
It was picked up by someone else overnight and it ballooned
from there."

"But how big is the balloon?"

"I'm sending you the link," Gemma says. "I can't apologize
enough, Katie. And Noah feels awful too. I don't think he realized what he was doing, but he definitely will when I ground
him until he's eighteen. He wants to say sorry if you can stand
to face him."

"Okay," I say, distracted as I peek out the window. The
reporter is still there, standing by a small red car. "Just let me
deal with this first. You've sent the link to me?"

She confirms she has, and I hang up, opening my phone to

see a whole host of notifications that I missed when she first rang. At the top of them is a text with a link to a video app.

The clip takes a few seconds to load, the spinning circle taunting and teasing, and then suddenly I appear, soaked to the skin and gesturing wildly at someone I know to be Callum even though he remains just out of shot. I climb back into the bed, horrified and yet unable to drag my eyes away. I look like... I don't even know what I look like, but it's not good. It is very *not* good.

It's a gross invasion of privacy that someone would not only film this but put it online. And the fact that it was Noah... I suddenly understand Gemma's terse tone on the phone, and though I'm obviously furious with him, I know she'll take it seriously and I don't envy whatever punishment that kid is about to receive.

The video stops halfway through my feverish plea and loops back, starting over, and I know I should just put the phone down. I know I shouldn't do what I'm about to do next. It's the number one rule of the internet and yet I can't help myself. I can't stop.

I read the comments.

There are hundreds of them, maybe even thousands. Crude jokes about my body, laughing emojis, *get a room*s. My heart beats rapidly until I feel like I'm going to throw up, but my thumb keeps scrolling, my eyes keep reading, and, after a while, the laughing emojis start to blur into one and I read the actual words between all the spam.

The ones that... aren't so bad.

this sounds cute I wanna go

Glenmill destroyed our neighborhood. I, for one, applaud this young woman for standing up to them.

And on and on and on. People tagging their friends and their friends responding. People sharing the link to our website.

I dare you to come with me @LisaHigg92!!! We were just talking about something like this!!

I drop the phone onto the bed and reach for my laptop. It takes a minute to turn on and another minute to connect to the Wi-Fi, but when it does, I log on to my email and see... well, emails. My festival inbox doesn't really get emails. But now I have three pages of them. All of them booking requests.

Requests because the booking system on our website has crashed.

I jump as my phone rings again, the Laketon Hotel's number flashing up, but I ignore it as a car door slams outside.

The reporter.

I scramble off the bed, throwing on the first clothes I find before running back down the stairs, where Michelle is waiting as promised. I careen to a halt at the front door and give her my most professional smile.

"Would you like to come in?"

———

An hour later, after I've told our story, the reporter goes off in her car, and I cycle into the village. I had to turn my phone off since I was getting so many calls and when I arrive at Gemma's house, it's to find her standing in the doorway, waiting for me.

"I'm so sorry," she says. "I don't think I've ever been so mad at him in my life, but I take full responsibility for—"

"It's okay," I interrupt, propping my bike against the wall. "Really."

"It's not okay. I can't even begin to imagine what—"

I slip past her into the house, pulling off my jacket as I glance around. "Noah?"

"Noah!" Gemma's shout is a lot more forceful than mine was and, a second later, I hear the floorboard creak above me.

"I've already told him he'll be running errands for you and Maeve every weekend for the rest of his life," Gemma tells me, as he appears on the upstairs landing.

Noah creeps down the stairs, stopping halfway as if I'm going to attack him. "I'm sorry, Katie."

And he sounds it. It might be because of the raft of punishments he's about to receive, but by the miserable tone of his voice, I can tell he knows he did the wrong thing.

"I'll never do it again," he continues.

"Because you're never allowed on the internet again," Gemma mutters.

"Apology accepted," I tell him. "But what you did was bad, Noah. You shouldn't film people without their permission, even if you think they won't mind. Things like that can't be undone."

"I know. I'm sorry."

"I forgive you. But please think about it before you do something like that again, okay?"

He nods, looking serious, and Gemma steps in to free him, jerking her head in the direction of the stairs. "Homework only," she reminds him, as he disappears up them again.

"I took away his PlayStation," she says to me. "At least until his birthday. And we've had a stern talk about consent and social media." She sighs, her frown lines so deep they look permanently etched into her forehead. "I can't believe he did that."

"It's not your fault."

"I'm his mother, which means it is. He's never done anything like that before. At least not that I know of anyway."

"It was a shitty thing to do, Gem, but he'll learn from it. I know he will. And this might be just what we need. Have you checked our emails this morning?"

"I've been a little busy yelling at my child."

I pull my laptop out of the bag as we enter the kitchen. "Our ticket sales shot up overnight. We have a *waiting list.*"

"What do you mean?" She's distracted, busy putting the kettle on and checking the time on the washing machine and putting the milk back into the fridge. I wait until she's dropped the teabags in the mugs before trying to explain.

"I think, as wrong as what he did was, Noah might have just inadvertently given us the best promotion we could have hoped for. We're sold out."

Still, she looks confused, as though the obvious is inconceivable to her. "Of what?"

I spin my laptop around as she sits at the table. Our inbox fills the screen, crammed with another hundred messages in the twenty minutes since I last looked at it. Gemma frowns in concentration, her eyes growing wider and wider as she realizes what she's looking at.

"What the hell?"

"We're *sold out*," I say. "Every ticket. These are all people asking if there's any space left. Two hotels called me this morning. All the rooms they set aside are full and I've got businesses contacting me from every nearby town asking if we need sponsors. People are coming. We just have to run the freaking thing now."

"Oh my God."

"I know."

"Oh my *God*." She stares at it. "We should put the prices up," she says suddenly. "And we're going to need more food. And more buses."

"We're not putting the prices up."

"But—"

"It's the publicity we need," I remind her as my phone rings.

"Not their money." I glance at the screen, expecting to see another unknown number, but it's Nush.

"Where are you?" she asks, three words that put me immediately on edge.

"Gemma's house. Is everything okay?"

"Yeah, it's just... I think you should come down to the barn."

"The barn?" I ask, and Gemma looks up. "Why?"

"I don't know really know," she says, and sounds confused enough that I believe her. In the pause I hear raised voices in the background, and the familiar sound of construction vehicles working away. "Just come down here," she says.

I don't need any more convincing.

CHAPTER EIGHTEEN

The rough trail that leads to the barn is jammed with cars and people. At first, I think Nush has organized another one of her protests, but she's standing off to the side when I arrive, a small frown on her face as she takes in the scene. The men who were here yesterday are here again today but, instead of going about their job, they're standing in clumps along with the locals, laughing and joking among themselves.

"He's been here for hours," Nush says, when I approach with Gemma and Noah.

"Who?"

"Callum."

"Callum's here?" I look back to the barn and suddenly see him and another man carrying a large piece concrete out of the ruins. "What are they doing?"

"They're putting it back together," she says, a grudging note of respect in her voice. "I think he roped in a few of the guys from the site to help."

"But... why?" I ask, bewildered. "They can't put it back together. They half knocked it down."

"I know. I think he's making a point."

A point? I glance back as Callum directs a digger forward, filling up one of the giant holes that they created yesterday.

"Surely he's going to get into trouble for that?"

"I think that's part of the point."

"But why is he..." I trail off as Callum turns around, catching sight of me.

"Oh boy," Gemma mutters, as he starts toward us. A traitorous lick of heat swipes through me at the sight of him. Nush says he's been out here for hours and at the sight of him, I believe it. He's filthy. And sweaty. He discarded his jacket at some point and his T-shirt sticks to his skin in a way that—

"Hey!"

My visual appreciation is cut off as he grabs my hand, tugging me into the woods.

"Callum!"

He doesn't answer, and Gemma just shrugs when I glance back at her. Nush is already directing the others to keep working, leaving me on my own.

He doesn't go far, just deep enough that no one can see us when he lets me go, rounding on me with a determined look that I should *not* find as attractive as I do in this moment.

"I should have told you about Jack," he says, before I can snap at him. "That's on me, and I'm sorry. It was a mistake. And yeah, I can pretend it's because that's how it is with everyone, but really, it's because I knew once you found out, you'd probably never speak to me again. And I didn't want that, so I didn't tell you. And you were right. What you said yesterday about how it doesn't matter if I want to see you? You were right. It doesn't matter if my actions don't back it up. So I made a decision. And my decision is you. I choose you."

I blink at him, my brain trying to grapple with everything that's happening today. "You chose me?"

He nods, his eyes bright with purpose and possibly an energy drink or two. "I quit my job."

"You can't do that!"

"Why not?"

"Because it's your *job*."

"I've been thinking about doing it for a while," he says, using his arm to wipe the sweat from his brow. "A long while actually. I don't like these big projects. I was doing it for Jack. Because it's always been easier to say yes to him. Because it's what I've always done. But I wasn't happy."

"But what about money?"

"I've got savings."

"But what about—"

"It might not have been the best timing, but it was the right decision, Katie. Believe me."

I do believe him. How can I not when he's practically vibrating just from making it. Like a weight has been lifted from his chest. Like he's never been surer of anything in his life.

All the despair I felt yesterday has vanished after this morning, and all the anger before that has faded into a childish sulkiness, one that eases the longer he looks at me.

"You really weren't trying to seduce me?"

"Only for my own gains," he says, and I almost smile. Almost.

"You and Jack have more in common than you realize," he continues. "You both say things in the heat of the moment. And you both regret it."

I don't answer that. I can't picture Jack regretting anything.

"He did ask me to find out what I could about the festival, *and* I told him no," he adds at my narrowed eyes. "He wanted me to keep an ear out in case you guys were planning some giant march and we had to delay some work. That was it. And again, I told him no. Said I had better things to do."

"And the barn?" I ask.

"His version of nipping this in the bud. I didn't know what you guys were doing out here. If I did, I would have told you it was on the list to be demolished. But we weren't supposed to start work out here for weeks. And this morning..." He grimaces a little. "It was supposed to be a grand gesture. To prove myself. Or to apologize or something. But we've been working for hours, and I don't think it's salvageable. Seemed like a great idea last night."

"Some men buy flowers," I say weakly, and he nods like that was his backup plan.

"Look, this doesn't have to be..." He trails off, and I can almost *see* him searching for the right word. "I'll admit, I wasn't really thinking when I first met you. There was a lot of 'she's over there, so now I want to be over there' going on. But the more time I spent here, the more I liked it here. I like the people. I like your pub. I like you. I like you a lot. And I don't want you to hate me. I don't want you to be sad or disappointed or angry because of me. So I chose you." He blows out a breath. "And now my brother will probably kill me."

I can't tell if he's being dramatic or not.

"You didn't have to quit," I tell him, but he just smiles at me.

"Solves a lot of problems, though."

It does.

"So what now?"

"Well, I'd really like to kiss you again," he says. "If you want me to, that is."

That's not what I meant, and he knows it. But I don't think he cares. I don't think I do either.

There's a faint ringing in my ears like I've been thrown underwater, and when I step forward, closing the gap between us, the forest around us fades, leaving just him and me, and that look in eyes like he's been waiting for me his whole life.

He raises a hand to my face, fingers skimming my jaw before they curl around the back of my neck, drawing me closer.

I was expecting something soft, like what we shared outside Kelly's, but there's a possessiveness to his touch that I've never felt before, a sureness to his hold that sends a feeling like hot wax pooling through me.

It's a gentle kiss, at first, but there's nothing gentle about the way he's holding me, his hand flexing as he massages my neck in a firm grip, the other landing on my hip, making me gasp. His tongue meets mine in a confident sweep when I do, moving as surely as if we've done this a thousand times before, and it's this strange dichotomy of new and familiar that sends my mind spinning.

He smells like clean sweat and fresh air, and I can't get enough of it, my hands sliding up the honed muscles of his arms, pulling him down toward me, as all the emotions of the last few days finally release. I'm probably a little too eager, but it only seems to spur him on as he wraps an arm around my waist, and draws me into him until the full length of our bodies are pressed together.

And then he takes complete control.

My back arches as he crowds me in the best possible way until I'm positive the only reason I'm still standing is that he's keeping me upright, his hands confident and sure as they caress me, tugging my shirt up so he can feel the skin of my stomach, the curve of my waist. His lips press harder, tongue delving deeper, and I try and keep up with him, matching him stroke for stroke, determined not to be left behind as I come alive.

It's the only way to describe it. I mean, I've been kissed before. I've felt wanted before. But this? This skin-humming, blood-heating, heart-thrashing sensation sweeping through my body? It's like a whole new world. A whole new me.

We stay like that for a long minute, our kisses dragging and deep until I have no thoughts in my head except for thoughts of him. Of Callum. Callum and his hands on my skin and his mouth on mine, until eventually I even forget how to breathe and have to pull away, even as I keep my death grip on him.

He doesn't seem to mind, sounds just as breathless as he presses his forehead against mine.

"Where'd you learn to kiss like that?" he asks, and I huff.

"Where did you?" I ask haughtily, but only because I'm trying to hide the fact that my heart is still racing. Though the way his finger rubs along my pulse point makes me think he's well aware.

"Are you okay?" he asks quietly. "About the video?"

"The one that made me a roaring success?"

"The one I'm guessing was posted without your consent?" He's back to serious Callum now, and the concern I see in his gaze sobers me up pretty quickly. "It must have been a shock for everyone to see you like that," he continues.

Some of the nastier comments I saw flash through my mind, but I take a breath, trying not to dwell on them.

"It was," I admit. "It's a lot. But I'm okay. If that's what works, then that's what works. The festival is more important than a few anonymous idiots on the internet."

"Are you sure?"

"Yes," I say, and he smiles. It's a gorgeous smile. A handsome, lights-up-his-face smile that has me reaching for him again before I realize we're no longer alone.

"As romantic as this all is," Gemma says from where she stands a few feet away. (Seriously, *such* a creeper.) "We still can't use the barn."

Callum pulls away from me, but doesn't go far, grabbing my hand as though challenging her to say something about it. Gemma doesn't even blink.

"Is it completely unusable?" I ask him.

"They stopped before it was gone completely, but it would be a lot of work to get something built in time."

"Well, maybe if we see what the damage is, we can—"

"Katie." Gemma looks pained. "Come on. There's dilapidated chic, and then there's just a half-demolished building. There's no way we can hold anything there."

I wince, knowing she's right. It's the thing my brain didn't want to grapple with yesterday, choosing instead to moan and sulk and feel miserable.

"We're a month out," Gemma continues. "And now we're sold out. You've promised these people a lot of things, and you've got half the village back there waiting to see you."

"They are?"

"*Yes*. You disappeared yesterday. They don't even know if we're still going ahead. I didn't know until this morning when you came over. You've got to tell them something."

"But I don't—"

"It has to come from you."

"But I don't know what to do," I say dumbly, and she frowns at me. Callum shifts at my side, but he doesn't come to my rescue. Doesn't offer a magical solution. He just waits. Waits for me.

Because I'm in charge.

The realization doesn't so much scare me as it does surprise me. Mainly at how I've never thought about it before. I always viewed this as an all-village thing. And it still is. But Gemma's right.

This is my idea. My thing.

Which means I need to make a decision.

Or I could just give up. It would be much easier to give up.

I gaze through the trees, away from the barn toward where I know the lake sits, and, on the other side of that, Kelly's.

"We'll go back to the pub," I say, and the two of them stare at me.

"They're not going to fit," Gemma says. "That's why we were going to host it here in the first place. And that was before we had five hundred people sign up. They're definitely not going to fit there now."

"We don't have another choice." I'm surprised at how calm I am. Maybe because I know it's the right decision. Maybe because it should have been my decision all along. "Kelly's isn't just four walls and a roof. We have the patio. We have the lake. We'll spread out. Use all of it."

"And if it rains?" Gemma asks.

"Then it rains. But what are we going to do? Give up? Like you said, we've got people coming. We've got attention, which is what we wanted from the start. So let's go."

I start forward, tugging Callum with me all the way back to the barn.

"Help me up," I tell him, and he lifts me onto a large slab of concrete that was once a part of the wall. Two dozen or so people mill about inspecting the damage, but no one notices when I wave, even as I tower over them.

Nush tugs on my sweatpants, while Gemma and Noah watch on. "Do you want me to get the bell?"

"We don't have time for that."

"Do you want me to—"

"I've got this, Nush."

She smiles at me in surprise, and steps back to join the others. I take one look at the group, cup my hands over my mouth, and shout as loud as I can.

"Everyone, shut up!"

They immediately fall quiet.

"I know this is a setback," I say. "A big one. But we can't let it stop us. We can't let them win. We're going to move the festival to Kelly's. I'll make it work," I add, as a few people start to mumble. "*We'll* make it work. But this will put us behind. So whatever spare time you have, whatever you can contribute, please let me know. Because in a few weeks' time, we've got hundreds of people coming to see us. Hundreds of people who want us to succeed. Glenmill did this because they're scared. Well, we're not. We know what we're fighting for, and that makes all the difference. We can still do this, but only if we work together. So let's go!"

I start to raise my hands at the last bit, but get embarrassed halfway through, and stop.

Okay, I won't lie. I thought there might be *some* cheering. Just a little a bit of cheering. A whoop. But there's nothing. There are, however, several smiles, along with some firm nods, and as the talking starts up again, it's with a new air of determination that wasn't there before.

God, this leadership thing feels great. Maybe I should keep going. Really rev them up. Maybe I should—

"Quit while you're ahead," Nush says, reading my mind. "But good job."

Callum holds his arm out, helping me down, and she lingers by his side, gazing up at him in an appraising, thoroughly Nush way.

"I like men with conviction," she tells him, and he pauses.

"Thanks."

"And men with tattoos."

"Okay," I say. "Thank you, Nush. He's taken."

"Will you add tattoos to my—"

"Yes," I interrupt. "I will add them to your form."

Her gaze flicks to his arm with an almost wistful expression, and then she moves away, ushering people back to the pub.

Callum turns to me. "Taken, huh?"

"You got a problem with that, dramatic gesture boy?"

"I'm just not really ready to put a label on—" He laughs as I jab him in the ribs, and quickly pulls me into his side. "No problem at all," he says, and I lean into him as everyone else starts to leave.

"Do you think this is the right decision?" I ask quietly.

"Do you?"

I glance up at him, searching my heart for any shred of doubt. For any part of me that whispers *this is a mistake*. But there's nothing. Only a warm hum of conviction, stronger than I've felt in weeks.

"Yes," I say. "I do."

"Well, then," he smiles. "Where do you want me?"

CHAPTER NINETEEN

There's a lot of work to do. So much work that I try not to think about it too much. Breaking it down and delegating as best I can. We need to call every hotel and B&B in the area to get what rooms we can. There's transport to be organized, revised food and drink orders. A clean-up of the village was already underway, but now we had to get Kelly's organized too. But before any of that, there was one crucial part to get sorted. Because now that we have guests coming to our matchmaking festival, it means we really need a matchmaker.

"I don't want to just be a tick in the diversity box now," Granny warns, as I sort the forms into piles. Everyone who bought a ticket filled out the questionnaire online, and while it wasn't like they'd be tied to their matches all weekend, it was part of the fun of coming. "I'm not going to be the token old person."

"You're not the token old person," I say. "Frank's the token old person."

"Frank's not even that old," she snaps, and I shrug.

"Adam said you've introduced people before, right?"

"I may have," she sniffs. "It's well known that I introduced

Bridget to Jenny. And Danny's second wife, of course. I don't like to make a big deal about it, but I do have a sixth sense for these things. *This*, however," she says, eyeing my orderly piles. "Is new."

"We're streamlining," I say. "We have a lot of people to get through, and this will help speed up the process."

"Well, I'm positively swooning from the romance of it all," she says, and I give her a look.

"We don't have time to sit down with everyone. These will help us know what people want."

"First rule of matchmaking, Katie. No one knows what they want. Not even about themselves. You can have the perfect pairing on paper only to meet them and feel nothing at all."

"Alright, but see, that's not going to work here because we only have paper to go by. What else do you suggest?"

"Instinct," she says. "Feeling. We give people the best opportunity they can have and leave the rest down to chemistry."

"Okay," I say slowly, still not feeling overly confident with her "trust the chaos" mentality. I know my questions weren't exactly popular with Nush and Gemma, but they did help weed out obvious dislikes and lifestyle differences. "Sometimes the questions can work, though. Nush was pretty clear about what she likes in a—"

"Nush has no idea what she likes," Granny dismisses. "Overly picky people never do until it's right in front of them."

"But what about this guy?" I ask, sliding a form her way. "Ryan Harrison. He's a teacher. He matches all her physical descriptions. He has a hamster. He—"

"*Just* a hamster?" Granny stares at me. "No grown man should own just a hamster."

"Well, Ryan does," I insist. "That means he's an animal lover. He ticks all her boxes."

Granny stares at the form for a long moment, and then gently pushes the paper back toward me.

"Tell you what," she says. "Why don't you take Plankton for a walk and leave me to get on with this."

I hesitate, gripping my pen.

The last few weeks has drawn out the control freak in me. I'd always suspected she was there, but now she rears her ugly head, making me cringe at the thought of giving up even one bit of my festival.

"*Or,*" I say. "How about you pair these people." I push half the forms toward her. "And I'll pair these ones. It can be like an experiment. I'll do it my way and you can do it your way and then all our bases are covered."

"You're the boss," she says, uncapping her special crossword pen. She takes the first one from her pile, scanning it only briefly before she frowns.

"I didn't know Gemma signed up."

I smile, thinking she's joking, but her expression remains serious.

"What?" I snatch the form from her, glancing at the details. Gemma's name is at the top. "Maybe it's just a practice one," I say, confused.

"Or maybe not," Granny says, holding out her hand.

"No, I want to do it."

Granny raises a brow. "She was in my pile."

"But she's my friend," I say, suddenly feeling protective over her. Sure, Nush is the picky one, but Gemma's a lot softer than she lets on. She can't just have anyone. She rarely dates as it is these days, and she deserves someone who'll... who'll...

Okay, that's way too much pressure.

I quickly hand the form back to her, getting nervous just thinking about it. "Gemma likes brown eyes," I tell her, and she nods sagely.

"Duly noted. And what about you?" she asks, as she slots it

into the middle of her pile. "Any practice forms for you? Or are you still dallying with the gardener?"

"I'm not—" I scowl at her. "Why do you have to make it sound like one of your books? And he's not even our gardener!"

"He should be," she remarks. "He did a good job. You should get him to come around again."

"So he can work for free?"

"We can always make him dinner this time if you insist."

It doesn't take a genius to read between the lines. "Are you inviting Callum around for dinner?"

"I think I deserve to properly meet the man you're sleeping with," she remarks, and I groan.

"Why can't you be a normal grandmother who says normal things?"

"Because it's too much fun to watch you squirm," she says, and reaches down to pet Plankton as he lays his head in her lap.

———

"The hedgerows in this country provide a vital wildlife habitat," states Vinnie O'Ceallaigh. "The proposal to cut down such an important shelter for the sake of another road that no one needs is a worrying sign for all of us." When asked if the redevelopment of Ennisbawn was going too far, he was firm in his response. "As a nation, we must do what we can to protect our countryside. That's why we've launched our objection. We are throwing our full support behind the community in Ennisbawn and the steps they're taking to preserve Ireland's cultural and natural heritage."

The door to the pub swings open, interrupting my third reading of the article, and I don't even look up as I start again.

"We're closed, Danny."

"I'll come back tomorrow so."

My head snaps up to see Callum standing in the doorway. The days have been getting warmer, and he's only in jeans and a T-shirt tonight, one that shows off his arms in all their glory, and yes, I am an arm girl now. I get it.

"Looking for me?" I ask.

"And a drink, if it's going." He steps inside, letting the door close behind him.

"Well, you've come to the right place. On both accounts."

I gesture to the stool in front of me, and he takes a seat.

"Guess I'm a little late," he says, glancing about the empty pub.

"That doesn't matter."

"It doesn't? You ever hear about liquor licensing hours?"

"That's only if I sell to you. The wonderful thing about living in the middle of nowhere? Nobody cares."

"Wild west, huh?" His eyes drop to the paper I was reading, and I spin it around to show him the article.

"The druids really are involved now," I explain, and he lets out a low whistle.

"Stuff's getting serious. Because of the well?"

I shake my head. "The road. Glenmill aren't only cutting through buildings, but they'll be cutting through hedges to build it. Turns out, druids don't like when you cut through hedges. Lots of nature in hedges."

"And druids love nature."

"They do." I grab a pair of scissors and start cutting out the article to add to our wall. "I'm going to need another corkboard," I say. "That's how famous I am now. I am someone who needs two corkboards."

"What you guys need is a pool table," he says. "And a television."

"We are not a television pub. We are a talking pub. And we don't need pool, we have darts."

I say the last bit without thinking, and immediately regret it when his eyes latch onto his brother's face tacked to the boards.

"Sorry," I say, and he gives me a small smile.

"It's fine."

"It's not. It kind of feels incredibly violent when I look at it now." I put the article down, avoiding his gaze. "How is he? Jack"

"I don't know," he says simply. "I haven't talked to him."

"You haven't?" I frown. "I don't know how I feel about that."

"You don't have to feel anything. It's not on you. This is between us."

"I don't want you to not talk to him," I say carefully. It's not as if I like the guy, but he's still Callum's brother.

"We'll talk eventually," he says. "He just needs to get over himself first."

"You guys had a fight, huh?"

"I told him I didn't agree with what he was doing here," Callum says. "With the barn, with the roads, with any of it. And I told him the truth. That with the way he was going we'd be over budget within a month. That we'd need to push delivery back by three or four at least. That he's working the guys too hard, and we'll lose them if we're not careful. That you were picking up steam and people were starting to pay attention." He gives me a humorless smile. "He didn't like that."

"I can imagine."

"The whole thing has just gotten out of control," he says. "We didn't think we'd get as much land off the church as we did, but they wanted the money, and we had plenty of it. Then it was like the floodgates opened, and they started adding in all this extra stuff. It's not even about the hotel anymore. And Jack wants to impress his boss, and his boss wants to be impressed, so here we are."

"He could just stop," I point out.

"He could," he says. "But he won't. It's not in his nature. Never has been."

"A real go-getter," I mutter.

"We didn't have a lot of money growing up," he says, and I still. "Mam was a shop assistant, Dad worked in construction. Jack wanted more. Even as a kid. You know he started a black market at school? He used to steal the multipacks of mini chocolate bars our parents bought us and sell them off at twice the price during Lent. Every year he did it until Dad found out and made him give all the money to charity. I think he was actually pretty impressed with it all, but he couldn't tell Jack that. He always wanted more. And he wanted it for me too."

"That's why you work together?" I guess, and he nods.

"We both started in construction. Dad took us along on jobs when we were still teenagers. And I loved it, I did, but it wasn't enough for Jack. He went on to college, got his degrees, talked his way into internships and moved his way up from there. He wants to run the company someday. Or start his own. He used to always talk about the two of us starting new somewhere in a few years. Building our own thing from the ground up."

"But that's not what you want."

"No." He looks close to laughing. "No, I want... I don't know. Money would be nice, sure. The security that comes with that. But I'm happiest working on my own projects. Smaller ones. That's my plan. Get a couple of guys together, keep it small. My own hours, my own time." He smiles then, like it makes him happy just thinking about it. "I think the last few weeks was the push I needed to make me see that."

"Well," I say, crossing my arms against the bar. "I think that deserves a toast. Or at the very least, a shot."

"A shot?"

"Why not? It's a Saturday night."

"It's Wednesday."

"Is it?" I ask innocently, and he laughs.

"Alright then." He says it like he's humoring me. "What you got?"

I gesture grandly to the series of bottles on the shelf behind me. He points to the vodka.

"Excellent choice."

"You're having one too?" he asks, as I set out two glasses.

"We closed thirty minutes ago," I tell him. "I'm off the clock." I pour our drinks, and slide Callum's toward him before toasting it with mine.

"Cheers," he mutters, and we knock them back.

I keep my eyes open and on him the entire time, enjoying the sight of him, the way his throat moves when he swallows, the sound of the empty glass when he sets it down, the swipe of his tongue when he licks his lips.

"Another?" I ask, and he laughs again.

"I feel like you're trying to get me drunk."

"I'm just really good at my job." I hold up the bottle, and he shakes his head.

"You sure?"

"I'm sure. You go ahead though. You deserve it."

I do, don't I?

And though I'd have much preferred to watch him again, I still enjoy the warmth of the liquid moving through me as I set the bottle back on the shelf. When I turn back, it's to find Callum watching me,

"Yes?" I ask, and he grins.

"I forgot. I'm not allowed to look at you."

"You can look at me now," I tease. "Men who make grand gestures can look at me all they want."

"Good to know," he murmurs, as I join him back at the bar. "You really love this place," he says. "Don't you?"

"Yeah," I say. "I mean, it's hard work. Weird hours. But I don't want to do anything else. I rarely want to be anywhere else. Even when I'm not on the clock, I'm here." I tense a bit as soon as I say the words, remembering the conversation I had with Gemma and Nush that first day at the barn. Although, it felt more like an interrogation at the time. "I guess that makes me kind of boring, huh?"

He gives me a strange look. "Why would that make you boring?"

"I don't know." I shrug, feigning nonchalance, even as self-consciousness chips away at me. "Small town girl. Small town dreams. It's not a lot, I know."

"Being passionate about something doesn't make you boring," he says. "It makes you the complete opposite."

He holds my gaze far too seriously for me not to believe him, and I fight the urge to squirm under his attention.

"What if I was passionate about laundry," I hedge.

"Is this a 'would you still love me if I was a worm' conversation?" he asks, and before I can even *begin* to react to the casual L word drop, he continues on. "Katie, you could tell me that your sole interest in life is snail migration, and I'd listen to every word you say so long as your eyes light up like that."

Okay, well, that's weirdly sweet. "What are you passionate about?" I ask.

He doesn't even think about it. "Concrete."

"*Concrete*? As in the gray stuff?"

"The gray stuff that built the modern world? That was born in the bowels of volcanoes? Forged by the eruptions of earth? Used for thousands of years by—"

"Okay," I interrupt, but I'm smiling as I say it. "You're a concrete guy."

"The biggest," he says solemnly. "We exist and we matter."

My smile widens, and his eyes drop to it, and all I can think about is how I basically mauled the guy in the forest the other day. And how much I want to do it again.

Danny was my last customer, and he left over an hour ago. Adam left soon after that when I told him I'd close up. And I need to close up. I need to mop and take the trash out and go home to my bed. I need to. But I don't want to. Not yet.

"You done?" I ask, nodding to his empty glass.

"Yes."

"Then come on." I step back, feeling a little giddy as I gesture to the back door. "I want to show you something."

CHAPTER TWENTY

The moon is out tonight. Not a full one, but an almost full one, and strong enough that it casts a white glow over the lake, illuminating the space just enough that we don't need any other light to see.

"We tried to figure out a way to put the dance floor inside," I say. "But Adam called it a fire hazard, so we're putting it by the lake. And we're going to put flowers all along this wall," I add, pointing to the bricks. "And a bar over there. More benches. A small stage for the band."

"And the fireworks?"

"I've earmarked a field a five-minute walk away. We'll get everyone to meet back here and then we're going to light up the trail with little torches by the west side of the forest. Have them walk around. Set up some blankets. And then boom." I waggle my fingers in the air. "Beautiful and impressive fireworks exploding across the sky. The only thing is the path and field might get a little muddy if it rains."

"But it's not going to rain."

"No, it will not," I say firmly, leading him to the well. "Give me your hand."

He does so immediately, and I bring his fingers to the stones, running them across the uneven surface until they reach the engraving.

"My dad did that," I say, when he glances at me. "It's their initials."

Callum smiles. It's a warm smile. An almost sweet one. "They met at the festival, right?"

"Yeah," I say. "He was completely in love with my mam. Like dumb, teenage, head-over-heels in love. I swear, in every single picture I have of them, he's just staring at her like an idiot. Like he can't believe his luck." I trace over the letters again before dropping our hands. "Granny said that he came home after their second date and told her he couldn't get her out of his head. He even tried to write her poetry, which apparently if you knew my dad, was the funniest thing in the world, and... anyway." I look up at him, not wanting to be sad tonight. "That's how they met. How did your parents meet?"

"I don't know. I'll have to ask."

"Are you close with them?"

"Yeah," he nods. "They're good people. You'd like them. I'll bring them in for a drink if they're ever around."

I make a face, and he smiles. "Too soon to meet the folks, huh?"

"It's not that," I say. "I'd love to meet them. I just don't always make the best first impression. I get nervous and—"

"Say things you don't mean," he finishes.

"Worse. It's like my brain just latches onto one thing and won't let it go. My last boyfriend took me into the city to meet his mother for dinner and I kept complimenting her on her dentures. Even when she told me she didn't wear them, I insisted that she did and that my grandmother loved hers and she didn't like that comparison, let me tell you. And then the boyfriend before *that* took me to his parents' house for lunch, and I started speaking in an accent? Out of nowhere. His dad opened the door and I put on an accent. And then I just had to go with it for the entire meal, and my ex thought I was doing this weird joke and then he got upset and then I got upset and then— I'm just going to stop talking." I clamp my lips shut at the strangled look on Callum's face.

"What kind of accent?"

"I want to say vaguely Scottish," I say, and he laughs. "I think I'm just not used to new people," I admit. "Granny used to say it's why I never wanted to leave here."

"I doubt she'd want you to even if you did."

I give him a dry look. "She's been trying to get me to go for years."

"Really?"

I nod. "I think she's given up now. She thought I'd move away to college and never look back. She still sends me the odd job she comes across, even though she knows I never apply for any of them."

"Jobs where?"

I shrug. "Dublin. London. Timbuktu. Anywhere but here."

Callum grows thoughtful. "And you've never gone for one?"

"Nah. Too old. Plus all my friends are here," I say. "Do you know how hard it is to make new friends as an adult? Extremely hard. I don't want to move to a new place and be all by myself."

"You wouldn't be by yourself."

"At the start, I would."

"Not if I went with you."

I keep my expression neutral, even as my heart skitters in my chest. "You'd go with me?"

"Why not?" he asks, as if that's not a big deal.

"Where?"

"Anywhere."

"To Timbuktu?"

He smiles faintly. "If you asked nicely."

"I always ask nicely. I'm very nice."

"And that's why you won't have any problem making friends. Even as a wizened, geriatric twenty-eight-year-old."

"I'm twenty-nine."

"Ah, well, then you might have a problem."

"Granny's lived in this village her whole life," I muse. "But I guess she never had the chance to leave. She met my grandad when she was only a teenager, and they had my dad pretty young. And then she had to look after me and..." I trail off, realizing I'm heading into new territory, but when I don't change subject, Callum picks it up.

"That first day here," he says. "When you found out about Jack's plans, you said your parents were gone, but I didn't know if that was just..."

"The heat of the moment?" I ask, and he shrugs. "It wasn't. They were in a car accident when I was kid."

"I'm sorry."

"Yeah."

"And the car accident," he continues carefully. "That's why you got nervous in the car that time?"

I nod, and he drops his head back.

"And now I feel like an asshole."

"You didn't know," I remind him. "And I'm not usually that bad. It's better if I'm talking or distracted, but if I let myself think about it too much, I get..."

"Anxious."

"Yeah." I give him a weak smile. "Still want to go to Timbuktu with me?"

"I don't mind walking."

I look up at him, my heart doing that rapid thumpity-thump that it seems to do more and more when he's around.

"I'm going to kiss you now," I tell him, and then do just that.

A low, gravelly noise rumbles through him, and he starts moving, backing us toward the picnic bench, where he picks me up as if I weigh nothing at all and sits me on the table.

He doesn't stop kissing me, and I inch forward, pressing myself against him and running my hands over the waistband of his jeans, just above where I can feel his growing desire for me. He allows it for a few minutes until my fingers slip underneath his T-shirt and follow the trail of fine hair I find below his navel, going down down down to—

"Alright." He pulls my hands away from his body, pinning them gently by my side. "Slow down."

"Why?" I breathe, kissing his neck.

"Because you're buzzed."

"I'm not."

"You downed two shots," he says, and I grin against his skin. Bless his little heart.

"It's going to take more than that to get me tipsy."

"Seriously?"

I can hear the reluctance in his voice, so I pull back, letting him see my honest, sober self. "Seriously."

He peers into my eyes, his expression clearing when he sees I'm telling the truth. "You'd tell me if you were?"

I nod, and reach for him, only to be blocked again.

"Stop *doing* that," I groan, but he ignores me, kissing me again before he puts a hand to my chest, urging me down until I'm lying along the picnic table. My legs dangle off the side and I take a breath, staring up at the stars as he slowly pushes them apart so he can stand comfortably in between them.

Oh.

The skirt of my dress rides up until it's caressing my thighs and I'm pretty sure I stop breathing for a second as his hands roam upward, going all the way until gently, almost reverently, he slips his fingers underneath my underwear and slides them down my legs.

I tilt my head, chin to my chest, as I watch him pocket the pale blue cotton like that's a completely normal thing to do and not the hottest thing that's ever happened to me.

Oh, God. Oh God oh God oh God.

Callum smiles like he knows the exact effect he's having on me right now and leans back over, pressing a kiss to my lips. He palms my thigh, massaging gently before inching up, and though I'm expecting it, I still jolt at the first touch of his fingers against me.

He pauses instantly. "You good?"

"Mm-hm." It comes out like a high-pitched squeak, and I press my lips together in embarrassment as I try to relax. But I can't do that. Not when I have Callum Dempsey standing between my legs.

"I'm not too bad with bodies, but I can't read minds," he says, his other hand finding mine where it's clenched at my side. "So, you've gotta talk to me."

I nod and then, when he doesn't move, "I will."

"You swear?"

"I swear. I don't want to stop. I don't want to—" I break off as he kisses me again, the pad of his thumb rubbing a slow circle into my palm. With each sweep, the muscles in my body relax, melting bit by bit, and when he moves his other hand again, stroking down my center, I know he can feel how much I want him. I know because he presses harder, his touch firm and sure in a way that makes my hips lift, chasing it instinctively.

The man is annoyingly good at this.

Our kisses grow increasingly uncoordinated until he pulls back, looking down at me as he rotates his wrist, applying pressure right where I need him to. His brow furrows as he takes in my reaction, concentrating so intensely on each hitched breath I take, that it's almost like he's learning me, and the mere thought of that is enough to send me over the edge.

It builds slowly, an unfurling coil that then unleashes so suddenly I cry out. Callum doesn't stop touching me the entire time, even when I try and push him away, he stays right where he is, seeing me through it and murmuring words I can barely take in, that he's there for me, that I'm doing so well, that I look perfect, feel perfect, am perfect.

When I finally come down, when I can open my eyes and catch my breath, it's to find him grinning at me, his hair a complete mess from where I must have been pulling at it, and his eyes sparkling like he's the one who just had his world rocked and not me.

"Katie?"

"Yeah?"

He leans down to peck my cheek and then my nose, before finally my lips. "Anywhere in the world," he murmurs.

"What?" I ask, still a little breathless.

He eases back to sit beside me, his thigh pressed against mine as he laces our fingers together. "Anywhere you want to go. If you want me to, I'll follow."

CHAPTER TWENTY-ONE

I throw myself into work the next week. I spend my days working on the festival, and my nights at the pub. We start a waitlist for tickets, and then a waitlist for the waitlist, and everyone from climate change activists to local politicians all get in touch asking if they can help. It becomes Gemma's entire job just responding to them.

It's not all smooth sailing though. The website keeps crashing the first few days, and Adam eventually ropes a friend into setting us up somewhere that can handle the traffic. I meet John Joe's cousin about the fireworks, only to find out he's eighteen and that it's "really more of a hobby" for him than anything else. But John Joe looks so proud of him, and I am a pushover so agree to take him on. Then of course, there's figuring out the logistics of how to host five hundred plus people in a pub with capacity for just over half that amount.

But even with all the chaos, we never forget the real reason we're doing it. Glenmill go quiet, and all the positive articles about their work that used to pop up vanish. Nush puts a *Save Ennisbawn* petition online that quickly gains thousands of signatures, and the news stories keep coming. But no one gets in touch. No sharp suited lawyer comes striding through the door, no grand gesture is made. Even as public opinion turns our way, they don't respond. And, though I don't tell anyone, I get more and more nervous every day that they never will.

So it's with some relief when the Saturday before the festival, I cycle over to Gemma's house with two cakes (one extra-large) packed carefully away in my basket, with no other plans than to spend the afternoon celebrating Noah's twelfth birthday.

Or at least that's my intention when I ring her doorbell a little before one p.m. and greet the man of the hour.

"Happy birthday!"

Noah looks up at me, his smile fading into abject horror. "What are you wearing?"

"Clothes," I answer, confused, as I glance down at the simple sweater and dungarees combo I put on this morning. Wait. "It's not a dress-up party, is it?"

"No," he says hotly. "I'm not *six*."

"Then what's wrong with—"

"Why are you wearing *that*?" he interrupts, pointing to the top of my head.

Ah. I reach up to adjust the bright blue cone fitted tightly over my hair.

"It's a birthday hat. Are birthday hats uncool?"

He gives me a look as if to say *yes* and I wince.

"You have to take it off before my friends get here," he warns.

"Understood." I lift up my boxes in apology. "One extra-large cake. One normally large cake."

This time he smiles, a little embarrassed as he lets me inside. "Thanks, Katie."

Gemma steps into the hallway just as Noah makes a beeline for the living room, the niceties done.

"You didn't need to do that."

"Technically it's payment," I say, as she takes the top box. "Anyway, I don't mind spoiling him. He's twelve now. That's a big age. One more year before he's a teenager."

I swear her face pales. "Can we just get through today please?" she asks. "I'm not ready to be a mother of a teenager. No matter how big my eye bags are."

"You don't have eye bags," I lie, and she huffs, leading me into the kitchen.

"It looks like Willy Wonka threw up in here," I say, taking in the mess of snacks and sugary drinks scattered everywhere.

Gemma shrugs, stacking a bunch of plates together and dumping them in the sink.

"You really didn't have to come," she says. "Not that he doesn't want you here. But I know you're busy."

"Of course I had to come. I've never missed his birthday."

"But the festival—"

"I think I can take a few hours off."

Unlike Gemma, who moves around her kitchen like she has a grudge against it, slamming cabinets and pulling open drawers so forcefully, I'm surprised they don't fall out.

"Need some help?" I ask mildly.

"I'm fine. I'm just running behind. I told everyone to arrive after two and thought I'd have the place cleared by now. I still have to heat the sausage rolls and get the food out of the freezer."

"What are we eating?"

"Noah wanted to order— I'm still using that," she adds, as I go to clean up a bowl. I promptly leave it be. "Noah wanted to order pizza," she continues. "But the prices are ridiculous. So, I got frozen ones. If we time that with the cake, they should be done by four. Sugar comedown by bedtime. Bed by nine."

"Sounds perfect," I say, but my enthusiasm does not seem to calm her down. For a moment, I think it's just stress. A house that's about to be filled with a bunch of pre-teen boys is not fun, but she's managed before, and Noah seems happy, so there's no reason for her to be glaring at a plate of cupcakes like they just insulted her mother.

"Gemma?"

"Pass me those M&Ms, would you?"

I hand her the packet, and then another when she motions for that too. "What happened?"

"What do you mean?"

"I mean, you look like you're one spilled drink away from screaming into some poor child's face."

"It's nothing," she mutters, pouring the chocolates into a bowl.

"Gem—"

"It's just Darren."

I try to fight my scowl at the mention of her ex-husband. Try and fail.

"What did he do?"

"It's what he didn't do." She sets the bowl onto the table, avoiding my eye. "He didn't even send a card. His kid's twelfth birthday and not even a card."

"Did Noah notice?"

"Yep," she bites out, and I wince. "He's asked twice already today."

"What did you say?"

"What else could I say? I told him it was on its way. That it takes a while for stuff to come these days. That no, his father didn't forget his freaking birthday."

Her voice breaks at the last word and she heads to the sink, filling it with running water as she starts dunking cutlery and mixing bowls into the basin. I frown as she stays like that, her hands moving mechanically before she raises her arm, using her wrist to do a quick wipe of her cheeks.

And that's when it hits me.

She's crying.

I'm immediately horrified. I've never seen Gemma cry. I've never even seen Gemma emotional unless you count being pissed off with everyone.

"Gem..."

She doesn't respond, her body rounding in on itself as though she's trying to make herself as small as possible. Like she's trying to hide herself from the world.

The doorbell goes as I reach over and turn the water off before pulling her into my side. She's not a hugger. Not really a toucher. And this is the most affection she's ever allowed from me, so it's a little awkward, me holding her like she's some fragile bird, but she leans into my touch as the tears stream silently down her face, letting me be there for her, even though it must kill her to do so.

"Shit," she mutters. "*Shit.*"

"It's okay."

"It's not. This is your fault."

"It is."

"You shouldn't have talked to me."

"I shouldn't have," I agree, as Noah's excited voice sounds from the hall. "I'm sorry."

She grows flustered as soon as she hears it. "I can't let him see me like this."

"He won't notice. Just pretend you got dish soap in your eye and go upstairs. I'll put out some plates and—"

"I brought doughnuts!"

Gemma breaks away from me, blinking rapidly as Adam appears in the doorway. Adam who takes one look at us, spins around, and promptly bumps into Noah. "You got the PlayStation set up?"

"Mam says I'm not allowed to turn it on until my friends get here."

"Are you or are you not the birthday boy? I'm pretty sure you can do what you like."

"But Mam—"

"Show me that new game you were telling me about. The one with the aliens." Adam's voice fades as he ushers him back into the front room and the television soon starts blaring.

Gemma grabs a piece of paper cloth and blows her nose. "Sorry," she says thickly. "I didn't get much sleep last night."

"It's not that, Gem, and you know it. Why didn't you say anything?"

"Because I'm fine. Honestly. This was just the final straw." She throws the tissue away and reaches for a stack of disposable plates, stripping off the plastic wrapping. "I'm just annoyed that even when Darren's gone, he's getting to me. I don't know why I keep letting him get away with this."

"You're not letting him do anything. He's just a dick."

"Yeah, but I don't want Noah to know that." She drops the plates on the table, her eyes already dry again. "He's getting to the age where he's starting to compare himself to his friends, and I know he thinks he's coming up short. And it's question after question after question. Why don't we go abroad like other families? Why don't I have time to chauffeur him around all the sports camps? Why can't I afford to send him to the camps in the first place?" She shakes her head. "He's starting to resent me."

"He's not."

"He is. When he was younger, I could pretend it was a game. But he's too smart for that now. He's too..." She tips her head back, her hands going to her hips as the doorbell rings again. "Am I wearing mascara?"

"No."

"Thank God."

I'm about to tell her again to go upstairs and take a break, but before I can, Adam slips back into the kitchen, shutting the door behind him.

"What the hell did he do now?" he asks, furious.

"Who?"

"Your shithole of an ex-husband. Don't even pretend this isn't because of him," he warns. "What did he do?"

"Why?" she asks sarcastically. "Going to beat him up? Just leave it. It's not a big deal."

"Not a big— you're *crying*."

"And it's none of your business!" she exclaims.

The two of them glare at each other from opposite sides of the kitchen until a quiet knock sounds on the door. A moment later, it creaks open, and Callum sticks his head in.

"Hope it's still an open invite," he says, stepping fully inside. "I got him a... uh..." He trails off, his attention bouncing off the three of us as he detects the charged energy in the room. "New football?"

I may or may not have forgotten that I'd invited Callum. With Gemma's reluctant permission and Noah's apathetic one, I'd hoped to *integrate* him a little more with my friends.

Seemed like a great idea at the time.

"Come on in," I say, pushing away from the counter. The act seems to break the spell and Gemma turns to the sink. "That's great," I continue. "He loves football."

"Yeah, you mentioned. I don't plan on sticking around or anything," he adds, handing me the present. "Don't worry."

Adam watches the exchange stonily, but Gemma turns around, giving him a rare smile.

"Don't be silly," she says. "Stay. There's plenty of food and I need all the help I can get."

Loud laughter from the hall punctuates her words, and she takes a breath, grabbing a packet of Doritos from the table.

"Wish me luck," she says and slips past Callum without another word. Adam waits a beat before snatching the nearest soda bottle and following her.

"I'll go," Callum offers, but I shake my head.

"That had nothing to do with you," I say, staring after them. "It's her ex. He's a dick."

"Adam? Really?"

"Huh?" I glance over to see a matching look of confusion on his face. "Adam's not her ex."

"Oh. Sorry, I thought..." He shrugs. "Never mind. My mistake."

"Darren's her ex-husband," I explain. "And Noah's dad. By blood anyway. Or sperm, I guess. He shows up every now and then but never for long and never when it counts."

"Jesus."

"Yeah." I grab some more dirty bowls and dump them in the sink. "To be honest, we all thought she was having a breakdown when she moved back here. But she was right to. She needed a new start and that just happened to be in her old home."

"It's nice she was able to come back."

"Yeah."

More excitement sounds from the next room, but neither of us move.

"I like your hat," he says after a moment.

"Oh *shit*."

He grins as I take it off. I'd forgotten I was wearing it.

"I promised Noah I'd get rid of it when his friends came," I explain.

"I think you look cute."

"Well, he didn't and he's the birthday boy," I say, smoothing my hair back into place.

"Does that mean when I'm the birthday boy, you'll wear it for me?"

"If you ask nicely," I quip.

He eyes me for a moment before he picks up the discarded hat, stretching the elastic band to fit it gently under my chin, and back over my head.

"I'm about to be proclaimed desperately uncool," I remind him.

"You'll survive." He dips his finger into the leftover frosting, ignoring my warning look as he dabs it on my nose.

"Are you five?"

"No," he says, and I think he's leaning in for a kiss before he licks it off with a quick flick of his tongue. I inhale sharply, but he doesn't try anything more, grinning cockily while I just stand there, until he nudges me out of the way.

"Now what are you doing?"

"Trying to make a good impression on your friends," he says, pulling on the washing-up gloves hanging over the side of the sink. "One of whom was just in here crying and is now in there trying to hold it together in front of a bunch of kids. You think the first thing she wants to do tonight is wash dishes for an hour?"

"You're going to clean?"

"Only if that's something you find endearing," he says, and I smile.

"Very endearing."

"Then yes, Katie. I'm going to clean. And you're going to help me."

And help I do, far more happy than I should be about dishes, as I grab a towel and dry the first plate.

———

The last of Noah's friends leave a little after eight, but it might as well be two a.m. with how exhausted I am. Once the plates have been cleared and the bin bags firmly trussed and taken outside, I sit with Gemma in the kitchen, watching her pick moodily at a cupcake while Callum and Adam play a video game with Noah in the front room.

"Well," I say, as she dabs her finger on the table to pick up crumbs. "I think that was a roaring success."

"Sometimes, I want him to stay a child forever," she says absently. "And then sometimes I can't wait for him to be sixteen and sneaking out to drink with his friends. At least then all I have to do is sit at home and wait to yell at him." She slumps back in her chair, eyes flicking to me. "Sorry for freaking out earlier."

"Never be sorry for that."

"Still. Thank you."

"Of course," I say firmly. "You're my best friend."

She smirks. "Does Nush know that?"

"She's my best friend too," I say. "I'll make us bracelets."

She laughs, and she's so tired that her eyes grow a little watery as she does.

"I'd actually really like that," she says, as Noah appears in the doorway. Adam hovers behind him, looking like a proud uncle.

"Your son just beat me fourteen–nil in the championship final," he says. "Which we both agree deserves another round of cake."

"For the winner or the loser?" Gemma asks, stretching across the table to get the knife.

"I think..." Adam looks at Noah. "Both? Both."

"Did you have a good party?" I ask Noah, as they take a seat at the table. He nods as Callum trails in from the hallway, taking up position against the counter. He looks a lot more comfortable than he did when he first showed up and watching him spend an afternoon making an effort with my friends fills me with such warm, gooey feelings that I have to stop myself from going over to him.

"Billy only had one cake at his party," Noah announces as he accepts another slice from his mam. "Did Dad call?"

We fall silent, even though Gemma doesn't bat an eyelid as

she passes around more plates before cutting some cake for herself. I know that despite her calm mask, she's thinking hard about how to answer him. On whether or not to lie to him, and I look down at my food, what little appetite I had left gone.

"No, honey," she says eventually. "He hasn't yet. Maybe tomorrow."

Noah just nods, his expression unchanging, like that was the answer he expected, and he ducks his head, thoroughly focused on his icing as he shovels it into his mouth.

Gemma's jaw tenses and I can tell she's trying to keep calm when Callum suddenly points a plastic fork at me, his eyes narrowed in a mock challenge.

"Right. You and me, Katie. Best out of five."

"I have no idea how to play that game."

"So, we'll play for money."

"Yes, a thing I famously have lots of."

He smirks. "Fine. I'll play Gemma."

"Mam can't play," Noah says dismissively.

"Woah now," Adam says, as Gemma bites her lip. "Who told you that?"

Noah looks confused. "She never plays."

"Does she not?" Adam asks, grinning from ear to ear at my now... *blushing* friend? Is Gemma blushing?

"Don't look at me," I say, when Noah sends a questioning glance my way. "I'm as lost as you."

"Let me tell you a secret about your mother," Adam says, as Gemma blatantly kicks him under the table. "She's a ruthless bi—"

"Adam!"

"Person," he corrects. "And one hell of a gamer. We used to play when we were younger all the time."

"You did?" Noah sounds suspicious, looking like he's trying to figure out if we're teasing him or not. "You never play with me."

"Because she knows if she so much as picks up a controller, she'll be lost for eight hours. And then who's going to cook your dinner, huh?"

Noah's eyes slide to his mother curiously. Gemma just shrugs.

"I played to relax."

"There is nothing relaxing about watching you play." Adam sits back. "Winner out of five games," he says. "Ten quid. Except that gambling's bad," he adds, flinching when Gemma kicks him again. "So no money. Winner plays you for the trophy and loser of that has to clean up."

"Mam says I don't have to clean up because it's my birthday."

"So it's a win-win for you. Gemma, get your butt in here. Show the birthday boy what you're made of."

"I'm not—"

"Yeah, you are," Adam says, pushing a now grinning Noah back into the front room. Gemma, for all her show of reluctance, follows them quickly, smiling to herself.

"Bring the rest of the icing, Katie," Adam adds. "Birthdays don't end until midnight."

"No one is staying up till midnight," Gemma calls, and Adam responds with something I can't make out. Whatever it is, it makes Noah laugh.

Callum and I watch each other from across the kitchen, and I know the contented glint in his eyes is reflected in mine.

"I like your friends," he says, and I smile, grabbing the bowl of leftover icing, and taking him by the hand before going in to join them.

CHAPTER TWENTY-TWO

You might think that with all the interview requests I get after the video, I'd get used to answering the same questions over and over again. That the words might come easier to me, or that my voice would stop wavering. But you would be wrong. I am not good at public speaking. I am not good at being on radio or television or any form of attention on me at any stage. And no matter how many tips or tricks or times Nush mouths at me to *enunciate*, I can never fully hide how nervous I am. I agree to do them only because I know we need as much attention as possible, but they drain me, and it's agreed by everyone that I should stop.

That is until the day before the festival when we get a call from a major television show in Ireland, who want to record one final chat to go out that evening. It's a show I've watched with Granny a few times, one where they go around the country interviewing "normal" people about local achievements. It's the exact audience we need to find people to support us, but that only puts more pressure on me to get it right.

Which is why when most of my friends and neighbors are

out putting the final touches on everything; I am in the ladies' room at Kelly's with Gemma and Nush as they argue over which blush I should use.

"Maybe I should change," I say, as Nush pulls my hair back with a small army of clips.

"You don't have time to change. And you don't need to change. You look beautiful."

"You're grand, Katie," Gemma pipes up. "You look lovely. Really."

I guess. I'm wearing a black jumpsuit that I thought made me look very chic and sophisticated when I first put it on, but now I just feel overdressed and have the urge to pee all the time because I know I can't do so easily.

"Just remember to smile," Nush says. "And if you laugh, try not to do it so loud."

"What?"

"Nush," Gemma warns, as she powders my face.

"Do I have a loud laugh?"

"No."

"Sometimes," Nush says soothingly.

"Okay. We're done now." Gemma bats her away and pulls me into the lounge. "You'll be fine," she says. "Just think of it like a chat."

Kind of hard to do with two cameras and a bunch of strangers all staring at you. Not to mention all the non-strangers here as well.

"Do all of you really need to be here?" I complain, as Callum comes up to me. Adam is frowning at everyone from behind the bar and Granny sits in the corner, sipping on a tonic. "Scatter. Hide. No one look at me. That includes you," I add, as Callum lingers beside me. "What?"

"Nothing." He trails a finger along the side of the jumpsuit. "This is nice."

"If you're trying to calm me down, you're not helping," I say, and he grins, kissing me on the cheek.

"Katie! We all set?" The presenter of the program is Mandy Brennan, an enthusiastic, middle-aged woman with very shiny, dyed red hair and a constant smile on her face. I am all set, but no one else is. And it's another few minutes of adjusting lights and doing checks before we finally begin.

I feel better once we do. She starts with the usual questions, the ones I can almost predict before she asks, and I go through my spiel about the village and Glenmill, about what we were trying to do here and what we had planned for the guests visiting. It's all going fine, and I'm just beginning to properly relax, when her gaze softens, her smile turning so sympathetic, it's almost pitying.

"And tell me," she says, in a hushed voice. "What's this I hear about your parents meeting at the festival?"

"My parents?"

The room, which had been quiet before, goes deathly silent. I don't dare look at any of my friends.

"It's one of the reasons you feel so strongly about this pub, isn't it? Why you want to keep the tradition going?"

"It is," I say, clearing my throat. "They met at the festival when they were teenagers. It was still going back then, but not as big. Not like it's going to be this year."

"Yes, it all looks very impressive." Her expression doesn't change, and I know exactly the route she's going down. I don't know where she got her information, but I suppose it doesn't matter. No one in the village would have told her, but a quick internet search is all she'll need to bring up the funeral notices from that time. To put two and two together.

"They died when you were very young," Mandy continues. "That must have been hard."

"It was a long time ago."

"And your grandmother raised you."

"She did," I say stiffly, my answers growing shorter by the second.

"This must be a lovely way to honor them." She nods as she speaks, so I nod too, though, behind her, Adam is frowning like he's two seconds away from barging in front of the camera and calling cut, so I muster up a smile as well.

She beams at me in response. "And will you be taking part in any matchmaking yourself?"

I don't know why I say the next part. I really, truly don't. Because the answer is a simple no, a cheerful, *I'll be far too busy for that!* And then a friendly laugh. But I'm thrown by the questions about my parents, and I'm too hot in this stupid jumpsuit and everyone is looking at me, and the lights are too bright and I'm on autopilot when I open my mouth and state loudly and clearly.

"I will be, yes."

From the corner of my eye, I see both Callum and Gemma stiffen, the movement so identical that it would have been funny if I wasn't, you know, majorly panicking.

"That's exciting!" She trills like we're two friends gossiping. "And what kind of partner are you hoping to find? Give the lads coming some clues."

No way does my smile look real. I can't see what I look like, but I can *feel* it straining.

"Someone nice," I say eventually, and Gemma coughs. A bead of sweat trickles down the small of my back, and Mandy *keeps going*. Most likely because I don't stop her. It's another five minutes of probing questions about just *how single I am* and my ideal date (apparently, I really like coffees and chats) before she finally wraps it up. As soon as she does and people can move freely again, Callum is up and out the door.

"You're in trouble," Gemma sings under her breath, and I give her a look.

"Excuse me," I mutter, extracting myself from the group, as

I race after Callum. I don't have to go far. I'm barely two steps out of the building before he catches my hand, pulling me to the side by the flower wall we'd put up.

"Someone nice?"

"I panicked, okay?"

"You sure? Or are you trying to make me jealous?"

"No!" I say, even as my heart skips proudly. Jealous? I'm making him jealous? "I'm trying to do my job. It's like when you're in a boyband and you have to pretend you're single. It doesn't mean anything."

"It means something to me. But good to know where you stand."

"That's not what I— Callum!" I screech in surprise, not quick enough to stop the noise as he grabs me by the waist, lifting me easily against the wall.

"There are like twenty people right—"

He kisses me. Hard and brief and toe-curling good. The rough edge of the brick scrapes my back while flowers tickle the side of my arm. A bolt of heat shoots through me at the sensation, and I tighten my legs around him, as though trying to keep him there.

"I feel like I must not have been clear before," he says against my lips. "So let me be clear now. You want to do this with me?"

"*Yes.*"

"Then no matches. No dates. No open for business, even if it's just for the cameras. Or I'll kiss you just like that in front of them too. Got it?"

"Callum—"

"Got it," I mutter, dazed.

"Good." He lowers me to the ground, and I clutch at his arms, my legs still a little wobbly. "By the way?" he adds. "I'm officially mad at you."

"What?"

"Yeah, this is our first couple fight."

"But..." I gape at him. "I said I wasn't going to—"

"Still mad," he says, and kisses me again, his hands tightening against my waist before he abruptly lets go, leaving me gasping by the flowers.

CHAPTER TWENTY-THREE

"I will give you twenty euro if you let me put it up."

I glance up at the mirror to see Nush standing behind me, a determined expression on her face. It's late afternoon and the first guests are due to arrive in a few hours. She insisted we get ready at her salon beforehand, which means I've been sitting in this chair for forty-minutes while she tries to get me to put on bronzer.

"You always want me to wear my hair up."

"Because you always wear it down."

"I don't like wearing it up," I tell her, as she drags a brush through the strands. "There's too much of it to wear up, it will just fall down."

"But you have such a pretty neck," she pouts, but before I can respond to *that* compliment, Gemma appears out of the back room, stealing both our attention.

"What?" she asks, and then glances down at her very bright, very red dress that can only be described as terrible. "Oh. Right."

"Is that a joke dress?" Nush asks. "Are you playing a prank on me?"

"I was just seeing if it fit," she mutters, tugging at the bodice. "I'm not going to wear it."

"Then why do you still have it on?"

"Because I can't reach the damn zipper, Anushka! What do you want from me?"

Nush abandons me in my chair as she goes to help Gemma, giving the zip a firm tug to free her.

"You should wear the blue dress," Nush says. "It's your best color."

"It also shows off half my boobs," she grumbles.

"Is Noah coming tonight?" I ask, as she pushes the thing down to her ankles.

"He's staying at a friend's house," she says. "But he'll be at the picnic tomorrow. What now?" she adds, when Nush and I share a look.

"Why's he staying at a friend's house?" I ask.

"In case I'm back late," she says, and Nush starts to smile.

"Late because of your date?"

Gemma shoots her a warning look before turning her accusing gaze toward me. "You could tell me his name, you know."

"Of your match?" I shrug. "I don't know who it is," I say truthfully. "Granny matched you. Plus, you're not supposed to find out until everyone arrives so no one looks each other up."

Nush scoffs. "I looked mine up."

"What? How?"

"I may have had a sneak peek at the list," she says innocently. "Perks of the position."

"What position?"

"Executive Assistant. Put on the blue dress," she adds to Gemma, who's striding back to bathroom in her underwear.

"I'm going with the green one."

"The blue one's better," Nush sings, but her attention is back on me, as she stabs me in the head with another pin. "He's very handsome," she says to me, and the smile on her face wipes away my annoyance.

"I'm glad you approve," I say, but whatever excitement I might have felt for her is lost in the usual bout of nerves I get when I think about the festival.

Nush notices immediately. "What's wrong?"

"Nothing. I just thought I would have heard from Glenmill by now. Do you think that it's bad that we haven't?"

Nush doesn't answer at first. She doesn't answer for so long that I think she never will. And then she picks up a comb, and starts dividing my hair into sections, her expression thoughtful as she focuses on her work.

"Did you know you were the first person I met in Ennisbawn?"

"I was?"

She nods. "I was searching for somewhere outside the city to open a salon and had it narrowed down to here and Rossbridge. It was a no-brainer on paper. Rossbridge was prettier. It was also bigger. I'd have more clients, more space. But the moment I stepped out of my car that first day, I felt like I belonged here. It was just one of things, you know? Like it suddenly became easier to breathe. But I made my decision when I met you. I went into Kelly's, and I think we spoke for a total of thirty seconds before you offered to give up your break and show me around. In any other village this size, I'd be forever known as a blow-in, but I've never been made to feel anything less than welcome here." She twists a clip into place, and parts my hair. "This is my home," she says. "I made it my home, and that's why I fight for it like I do. I want to save the street, and the pub, and everything I can. But at the end of the day, I know they can take a sledgehammer to the whole area, and it wouldn't matter. Not really. Because Ennisbawn is more than some boundary map. It's people. It's you and it's me and everyone else. And they can't take that from us. So, screw Glenmill.

Screw Jack Doyle and screw that hotel. Tonight isn't about them. It's about us. So promise me you won't think about petitions or interviews or whether or not this is working. Promise me you'll have some fun tonight."

"Nush—"

"Promise."

"I promise," I say, and she squeezes my shoulders just as Gemma steps into the room in the black dress, takes one look at our unenthusiastic reaction to it, and turns back around.

———

The village looks incredible. Bridget, who usually manages our Tidy Towns committee, took charge of getting the main street into shape. We painted the old buildings, we set up Harry's fake window displays. We plucked wildflowers from the roadside and arranged them in bright, mismatched bunches every few steps. It all reminds me of the Ennisbawn in some of Granny's old pictures, and not that I didn't expect us to pull it off, but as I walked from Nush's salon down to Kelly's, a route I had taken so many times before, it was still a shock to the system.

What I really didn't expect was so many people. It's dumb, I know. It's what I wanted. What I hoped and planned for. But when I envisioned the pub and the village teeming with guests, they were always just a faceless blur of color and movement. An abstract impression of *activity*, but with no actual realness to it.

These people are real. They are real and there are a lot of them, all dressed up for the party as they stroll around taking pictures and line up outside the pub, signing in to get their hand stamped, and find the name of their match.

Inside is even busier, something a few guys on the door were keeping track of, while others tried to keep everyone moving, flowing them through and out to the other side where the dance floor was ready by the lake and Danny and the rest of the musicians would soon take to the stage. We are going to have an outside bar too, but not for a while, and as a result, the queue for the inside one is several people deep. Adam just waves me on when he catches my eye though, telling me silently that he has it under control.

The patio is my favorite bit. The sun shines like it's been doing all afternoon, and people were already taking pictures by the well, just as I'd hoped. Frank stands nearby with Nush's petition, explaining in his teacher voice about what we're trying to do.

"There's the star of the show."

I turn to see Harry walking toward me, his partner Richie at his side. Harry's husband is a devastatingly handsome, soft-spoken librarian, and I'm still not sure how Harry got him to marry him. A few people are already ogling the man, and Harry, instead of appearing jealous, only seems smug.

I give them both a hug, my eyes straying to the drink in Harry's hand. "I thought you only drank on special occasions."

"Is this not a special occasion?" He gestures wildly as he says it, the liquid (a whiskey sour by the looks of things), sloshing dangerously.

"How many of those have you had?"

"I don't know; it's an open bar."

"No, it's not," I say sharply, but he's already grinning, enjoying teasing me.

"That's his first," Richie assures me. "He's just excited. I think he's had too much fresh air."

"Just reconnecting with my true village self," Harry says. "How are you doing? No stress hives, at least."

"That you can see," I retort. "And I feel awful. I hate being in charge. Never let me be in charge of anything again."

"It all looks great," Richie assures me, and I nod, needing every bit of reassurance I can get.

"Did you see the village?" I ask. "How long have you guys been here?"

"About an hour or so?" Harry turns to Richie, who nods. "We've been taking in the atmosphere. Trying to find a third person to join us in the bedroom."

"He's joking," Richie says pleasantly, but Harry's still glancing about the crowd.

"Am I?"

"I'm afraid we didn't have that option on the forms."

"Maybe next year," he says with a wink. "But what about him." He points to a well-dressed older man talking animatedly a few people away.

"Too good-looking," Richie dismisses. "You'll get nervous."

"I'll get *what*?"

"No propositioning the guests," I say firmly. "Jokingly or not."

"Well, that's no fun."

"Do you know what would be fun?" I say. "Helping us out. I need someone out here to collect empty glasses before we open the outside bar. And then you can..." I trail off as a beautiful blonde-haired woman in a short, sparkling silver dress steps outside the pub, a glass of white wine in her hand. I swear to God, everyone within a few meters of her immediately turns her way. She must be used to the attention because she barely notices as she glances about with vague interest before joining the line for the wishing well.

"Is she famous?" I ask, growing excited. "She looks famous."

Harry scoffs. "You think every person with good posture is famous."

True, but she has *great* posture.

"Maybe she's a model or something? I bet she has a massive following. Do you think she'll post about us?" I glance back at the flower wall, wondering if I can subtly drag her over to it, when Harry makes an amused, slightly strangled noise in the back of his throat.

"What? What's—" My mouth clamps shut as I turn around to see the woman still waiting in line, only now with Callum standing right beside her. I haven't seen him since yesterday when he kissed me not two feet from where we're standing now, and while I know it's because we've both been busy, a small, immature part of me can't help but think that this is also some kind of punishment.

"I'd take him," Richie says casually, and Harry grins at me. "Unless that's her match."

"That's not her match," I say sharply.

"Does she know that?" Harry asks, as she puts a hand on Callum's forearm. He laughs at something she said, and I stare at them.

"Your neck has gone all pink," Harry adds gleefully. Richie just looks confused.

But before I can do anything like stomp over there and make a scene, Callum glances up, his eyes immediately finding mine. As he does, the woman's hand drops away and she turns back to the well, and Callum gives me a look that says he knows exactly what I'm thinking, and heads inside the pub.

"Do you need to cool down?" Richie asks politely, and I leave Harry to explain what's going on as I follow Callum back inside. There are so many people inside that I lose track of him immediately, and I'm so focused on finding him that I don't even notice someone slip out from behind the bar until Adam almost walks into me.

"And where do you think you're going?" I ask, spying the gym bag clenched in his hand.

"I just need to head out for a second."

"You what?" I spin around as he sidesteps me. "We're starting in twenty minutes! Who's minding the bar?"

"I got Nush to fill in."

"You put *Anushka* behind the bar?"

"She wanted to help. I gave her your punch recipe."

"Adam—"

"I'll be back in a bit, I promise. Everything's under control."

Everything is *not* under control, and he can't just leave me here alone, but before I can correct him, he slips off around the back of the pub and disappears.

Well, that's just su*perb*.

I slip inside, trying to keep smiling because everyone is smiling. They're smiling and excited, and I need them to stay that way because I refuse to let everything go wrong.

"Nush."

"Hi!" Anushka beams at me from behind the bar, looking like she's having the time of her life as she adds decorative sugar around the rim of the punch bowl. "It's going well, isn't it? There are so many people. Has Gemma met her match yet?"

"I don't know. I don't know if he's even here yet. Actually, I don't think *she's* even here yet. And what about you?" I ask. "Did you meet Ryan?"

"Yeah."

"*And*," I prompt, when she doesn't continue.

"Oh." She makes a face. "I didn't really like him."

"What do you mean, you didn't like him?"

She shrugs, setting out more wine glasses. "When you know, you know, right? He didn't seem too upset about it."

"You *told* him you didn't like him?"

She looks up as though finally realizing how horrified I am. "What was I supposed to do? Ghost him? He was fine with it."

"Nush, you're supposed to give him a chance! You're supposed to talk for a few hours and get to know each other."

"We talked," she says defensively. "I showed him a picture of Chester. He told me about his trip to Thailand. We had zero chemistry and his phone kept going off. He had the volume *on*, Katie. I haven't taken my phone off silent in twelve years, and his was just dinging away with every news alert and weather report in the world. You expect me to spend an evening with someone like that? I'm too pretty. I refuse."

"But..." I'm oddly stung by her rejection of him. "He ticked all your boxes."

"Yeah, but it's more about the spark, isn't it? It's fine," she adds at the look on my face. "I already found someone else."

"What? Who?"

She nods across the room, and I'm startled to see the woman from outside, the one who'd been chatting with Callum, has wandered back in, tapping her fingers against her now empty glass.

"Her name's Monica. Did you see how straight her shoulders are?"

"You can't have her! That's someone else's match. And how do you even know her name?"

"I've already talked to her. She didn't get on with her match either. Your grandmother really needs to up her game."

"That doesn't matter," I say, deciding not to point out that I was the one who matched her. "You're not allowed to steal matches. And she's blonde," I point out. "You said you didn't want a blonde."

"I didn't say that. I just said I'd prefer dark hair." Her attention strays back to the woman. "And kind eyes."

"And she has kind eyes, does she?"

Nush nods. "And great legs."

"Oh my God, *Nush*."

"It's not a rule!" she exclaims. "I'm allowed to flirt. I can't help that I'm good at it."

I fight back a groan as both of us turn Monica's way, only to find her staring at us. She turns around immediately when we do, pretending to be fascinated by one of our posters.

Fine.

"You can flirt," I say, reaching under the bar for the ice bucket. "Nothing more."

"Aye, aye, captain."

"But first, could you grab me some... I didn't mean flirt with her *now*, Nush. I need you to—" *Annnd* she's gone. I glare at her back as she weaves through the crowd and turn back to the impatient-looking man in front of me. "Hi. What can I get you?"

I spend the next ten minutes pouring drink after drink with no sign of Adam returning. It's busy and for every person I greet, three more are there trying to make eye contact with me. I haven't even made a dent in the crowd by the time Granny finds me.

"What are you doing in here?" I ask, as I pour a glass of Prosecco for a woman who looks like she's already had three. "You're supposed to be outside checking in on the matches."

"And you're supposed to be basking in your glory, not running around like a headless chicken." She's dressed up in a red velvet dress, and matching purse, one which she slams down beside me, making two men next to her jump.

"We've got no one on the bar," I mutter, grabbing a pint glass.

"I'll be on the bar."

Funny. "It's fine. Adam will be back any minute now. I just need to—"

"You think I don't know how to make a gin and tonic?" she barks, shooing me aside. "I've been pouring drinks long before your father was a twinkle in my eye. I think I'll manage."

She grabs the glass from my hand, and a bottle of wine with the other.

"You can be off duty for one night," she says to me when I linger.

"I've got to go find Gemma."

"Then find her. Find her and come back here and get your-self on the dance floor. Everything's under control."

"Granny—"

"*Go*," she says, shooing me away as I kiss her on the cheek. Ignoring the gathering crowd, I push my way through the now very packed pub and back outside.

There's only a small trickle of people still signing in and I hurry over to the reception desk, the sweat I got from working at the bar cooling uncomfortably on my skin.

"Is Gemma here yet?"

Bridget hesitates, not even looking at the long list of names before her.

"What?" I ask. "What's wrong?"

"Nothing," she hedges. "She's probably still getting ready."

"She should have been here an hour ago! Has her match signed in?"

"Yes, but you should probably know that— Katie!"

"I'll go get her," I say already striding away. "She can have cold feet tomorrow."

"But she's—"

"Just stall him if he comes looking!" I call, and hurry up toward the village.

CHAPTER TWENTY-FOUR

The evening sky is a faint pink color, and the air is warm and dry. We couldn't have hoped for better weather, but I barely have time to take it in as I make my way back to Nush's salon. The blinds are closed, but the door is unlocked when I try it and I let myself in, spying Gemma's purse where she left it on the counter.

"Gem?" I head toward the back, taking in the scattered makeup and curling tongs before knocking on the bathroom door. A thin strip of light is visible underneath. "Gemma?"

"I'm peeing," she calls.

"You're late."

"Doesn't stop me from peeing."

I roll my eyes, moving away to give her some privacy. But when a few more minutes pass and she still hasn't come out, I start to get antsy.

"Are you doing more than peeing?"

"Don't ask me that!"

"It's only me out here," I remind her. "You can tell me. Girl code."

"I'm fine."

"Then come out, will you? You're giving me stress hives."

"You're so dramatic," she huffs, but I finally hear some movement and, a second later, the door flies open.

My mood instantly changes.

"You look so beautiful," I coo, but she just pushes past me to the makeup chair. She really does look stunning. She chose the blue dress, the one that Nush likes, and black strappy heels that I definitely wouldn't be able to pull off, but she walks in like she wears them every day. Her jewelry is gold and understated and whatever she's done to her skin has made it shimmer with each step.

"What's with the face?" I ask, as she starts to pack away the lipsticks and brushes that clutter the table. "Are you nervous?"

"I'm not nervous."

"It's okay to be nervous."

"But I'm not." She zips up the makeup bag. "I've decided not to do it."

"Do what?"

The skirt of her dress balloons around her when she sits, and she smacks it back down as she reaches for her heels, undoing the straps with quick, jerky movements. "Tonight," she explains. "I'm not going to do tonight. I'm not meeting my match."

"Very funny," I say. "But we've got to go. You're late and I have, like, three tasks to do. Maybe four."

"I'm not going, Katie."

"Again, so funny. Chop chop."

She removes her shoes and stands, blowing a strand of hair from her eyes. "I'm not going," she repeats, and I hesitate.

"You have to go," I say slowly. "Your match is waiting. You can't stand him up."

"I'm sure he'll be fine."

"You don't know that."

"I do. Believe me, I do."

"Gemma—"

"It's not like he's going to want me anyway," she mutters, and my mouth drops open.

"Ex*cuse* me?"

"Oh, don't do that. Don't pretend you don't know what I mean. It's insulting."

"I'm not pretending. What are you even talking about it?"

"I'm talking about the fact that I'm way too old for something like this."

"You're forty-*two*."

"Exactly!" she exclaims. "Forty-two. Not twenty-two. Not thirty-two. Not any of the fun ages. And I can barely fit into this *stupid* dress, and I've made a mess of my hair and—"

"Gemma! Chill!"

She shuts up as I take her by the shoulders, holding her steady as she starts to hyperventilate.

It freaks me out seeing her like this. She's not the freakout one. Nush and I are the freakout ones. Gemma is the sarcastic one. The tough one. She's had to be for Noah.

"Where's this coming from?" I ask, and she pulls out of my grip, smoothing down the front of her dress before doing it again. And again and again and again until I bat her hands away. "Stop it. Sit down."

"Just go back to the—"

"Sit. Down," I say, and she pauses at the warning in my tone. She takes a seat, watching me warily, but I don't care. I've never heard Gemma speak about herself like this. Not once. And screw her if she thinks I'm just going to let her do so now. "I'm only going to ask one more time," I say. "What the hell are you talking about?"

She scowls, unable to hold eye contact. "It was a mistake signing up for this. I don't know what I was thinking putting that form in. All this talk of romance and soulmates and finding the one... I just got caught up in it."

"We all did," I say. "And that's okay. But this sounds like something else, and it feels like it's from out of nowhere."

"It's not from out of nowhere, it's from experience. From a lot of experience." She sighs, rubbing her forehead for precisely one second before seeming to remember she has a faceful of makeup on. "I went on lots of dates after Darren left," she says. "And I didn't lie about Noah. I was upfront that I was a single parent and that's what they were getting. And for the most part, no one had a problem with it. No one but me. Because it was always in the back of my mind. What if I let myself fall for someone and he and Noah didn't get along? Or what if they did get along, and it didn't work out between us? I don't want to put him through something like that again. I don't want him to get attached to someone who's just going to disappoint him. Noah has to come first, Katie. He will always come first."

"I get that," I say. "You know I do. But that doesn't mean you have to put yourself last. Not every time. And definitely not tonight."

But she's not listening to me. "Darren called," she says, and I tense, getting that instant reaction I always get when I hear his name. "The day after Noah's birthday. He rang up with some half-ass excuse and Noah refused to talk to him. It's the first time he's ever said no to his dad. Darren was furious. You should have heard him, Katie. He said I've been poisoning his own son against him."

"That's ridiculous."

"I know."

"You lie for that man every single day."

"I know! I know I do. But the whole thing threw me. Maybe I've been slipping lately. Or maybe Noah's getting to the age when he's picking up on that stuff."

"So what if he is? He's not an idiot, Gemma."

"I know he's not, but I never wanted him to think he

couldn't have a relationship with him. He deserves to have a dad."

"Agreed, but just not that one."

"Then who? Who's to say if I'll ever find someone for both of us?"

"You can't keep thinking like that," I groan. "If you do, you're going to shut down every opportunity before you even recognize it. And it's not like you're marrying the guy tonight. If you don't like the guy, you can always swap. That's what Nush is doing."

She snorts, staring down at her lap. "I don't even know his name."

"Well, I can call Bridget and see," I say. "But he's only a five-minute walk away."

"Ten in these heels," she mutters.

"Beauty is pain. And you look beautiful tonight, Gem."

"My highlighter cost thirty quid, I better look beautiful." She swallows, indecision playing over her features.

"One drink," I say. "One drink. One dance. See what happens. That's all you've got to do tonight."

She sighs, fiddling with her bracelet. "Okay."

"Okay?" I repeat to make sure there is no confusion here. "You sure?"

"Yeah."

"Fanfreakingtastic." I pull her to her feet, trying not to show how relieved I am. "Now put your damn shoes on."

Despite my subtle rushing, it's another fifteen minutes before we're out the door. She insists on fixing her makeup and her hair even though there is nothing to fix because my friend is a flawless annoying angel, and I'm at a loss as to how anyone could think differently. By the time we're walking down to Kelly's, we are past fashionably late. We are dramatically late. Horribly late. And I admit to hurrying her up a little bit, ignoring her grumbles about her toes pinching when I see everyone else has gone inside.

Everyone that is but Bridget who's still manning the reception desk and is obviously waiting for us. She visibly exhales when we round the bend and points to the one other person left waiting by the doors.

Over there, she mouths, as if it isn't obvious, and though she tenses beside me, I pull Gemma along before she can run away again.

"Just be your usual charming self," I say. "Remember, there's no pressure here. Have a drink, get to know the guy and then maybe you can— oh, for feck's sake. Adam!"

I huff in annoyance as Adam steps out of the doorway. He's changed his clothes, swapping his usual uniform for a handsome black suit that I know for a fact the man must have rented because the man only has, like, three outfits. He scrubs up well, though. I'll give him that.

"I hope you're happy," I say, dropping Gemma's hand as I go to the desk. Bridget shuffles beside me as I flip through the clipboard, looking for the name of Gemma's match. If he's pulled a runner after my great, *you can do this* speech, I'm going to be furious. "I had to leave Granny on bar duty, so God knows what's going on in there. Everyone will get a triple measure of gin and it will be all your fault."

Adam doesn't answer, too busy staring at Gemma, who hasn't moved from where I left her. She seems frozen to the spot, staring at the man like she's never seen him before.

"What?" he asks, when she doesn't say anything. "You don't like the tux?"

She shakes her head and then, as if realizing what she's doing, starts to nod. Great. She's officially going back into panic mode.

"Where's her match?" I ask Bridget, keeping my voice low. "Is he inside?"

"What?"

"Gemma's match. You said he signed in."

"He did."

"Then where is he?"

Bridget just stares at me. "I can't tell if you're joking or not," she says eventually. "You know I'm bad at jokes."

"What are you—"

She jabs a finger at the list, right under Gemma's name, before sliding it across to...

Shit.

"You're kidding me," I say, glaring at Adam's name. "I'm going to kill Granny. I'm actually going to do it this time. It's not like we had a shortage of sign-ups."

"Sssh," Bridget says, nodding toward the other two.

"You knew it was me?" Gemma asks.

"I looked at the list," Adam admits. "I assumed you did as well. Thought you were going to leave me hanging."

"Yeah, well. I'm still considering it." She smooths out her dress again, a move I'm beginning to realize is a nervous tic. "This is weird, right?"

"It doesn't have to be," he says. "We can pretend we're two strangers, just like everyone else."

"We can't do that."

"Why not?"

"Because I've known you my whole life?" She shakes her head. "Don't you want a real match?" she asks eventually, and he huffs like she said something funny.

"Come on, Gem. It's you." And then, so quietly I almost miss it, "It's always been you."

I watch in confusion as he holds out his hand, closing the distance between them. Gemma doesn't do anything at first and then slowly, like he might snatch it away, she takes it in hers.

"Look at us," he says. "We're already good at it."

That gets a smile from her, though it's more of her usual

smirk, and at the sight of it, Adam grins so wide it's all I can do not to stare at him. Who is this man and what did he do with my grumpy boss?

Bridget watches the whole thing with barely disguised glee. "I knew it."

"What do you mean, you knew it?" I whisper.

"They like each other."

"No, they don't. I mean, they do, but not like that. They fight like cats and dogs half the time they're together. They're not going to last five minutes."

"Oh, honey."

"What?"

"Nothing," she says, patting my shoulder as Adam leads Gemma inside the pub. "Nothing at all."

CHAPTER TWENTY-FIVE

"Point your right foot out. That's... no, the right one. The... there you go. And hold hands now, don't be shy." Jenny stands on a little box at the edge of the dance floor, a huge grin on her face as she gets everyone into position. "Just like we went over before. Row one make an arch, and row two go under. And one, two, three!"

Everyone bursts into laughter as the band starts playing, most people immediately going the wrong way and not caring a bit.

The céilí was a good move. Even if most of those taking part don't know what to do. But they don't seem too worried about getting it right. In fact, they're happier when they get it wrong, falling over themselves with laughter, sometimes straight into each other's arms.

I should be thrilled with the sight. But I'm finding it hard to concentrate. Not when I just want to watch Adam and Gemma all night. I have a perfect view of them from my perch by the outside bar. They haven't moved from their little spot by the picnic benches. Talking. That's all they've been doing. Talking all night. No kissing, no dancing, no selfies by the wall. Just talking like they've only just met. It's the first time I've ever really seen them get along and I mean that. They've known each other for more or less their whole lives and, while I have no doubt deep down they love each other, I had assumed that love was platonic like it was for the rest of us. I mean, half the time, they can barely go five minutes without fighting.

It's only now that I'm starting to think that maybe they were fighting something else.

"You know you're just staring at them, right?"

I jump as Callum pops up behind the bar, appearing as if out of nowhere.

"Where have you been?" I ask, as he starts clearing away empty glasses.

"Kitchen. Why the long face?"

"I'm busy," I say. "This is my busy face."

"Okay," he says calmly, barely even paying me attention.

"You have bar experience?"

"None at all."

I tap my fingers against the bar, annoyed that he won't look at me. "Everyone's switching their matches."

"So?"

"So I matched them."

"Are people complaining?"

"No."

"Then what's the big deal?"

"You don't get it," I mutter. I sound as childish as I feel right now, and I don't know why. Everything was going fine the other day, but between the interview and Gemma and that woman's hand on his arm...

"Look around, Katie," Callum says. "Everyone's having a good time."

He's right. In fact, everyone's having a great time. Nothing but smiles and laughter and even a few captivated looks. Especially from Nush, who's watching Monica talk with rapt attention like she wants to squish her up and put her in her sequined purse. I turn my back on them, too stubborn to let this go, only to see Callum attempting to open some champagne.

"You're doing that wrong," I tell him. "Twist the bottle, not the cork. And you need to hold it at an angle."

He sighs. "Katie—"

"Whatever." I slap a hand on the bar and push myself off the stool. "Be mad at me. I don't care. I know I messed up and I'm sorry, but at least I'm taking this seriously."

Callum's barely listening to me as he finally pops the cork, and I catch his pleasant surprise for a second before turning away.

"Where are you going?"

"To dance," I call back, as another guest immediately takes my place.

Despite my intention, my steps slow as I head down to the makeshift dance floor, lingering awkwardly by the edge until suddenly my hand is snatched up and I'm tugged forward.

But it's not Callum who's leading me onto the floor, it's Harry.

"Um, hi?"

"Hello," he answers cheerfully, spinning around to face me. "You seem tense."

"I'm working."

"You don't look like you're working," he says, leading us through the crowd. "You're kind of just walking around glaring at everyone. You used to be fun, you know that? Remember when you drank too much at my wedding and fell asleep talking to my Great-Aunt Sophie?"

"That was you."

"Was it?" His hand goes to my waist, his other raising my hand into the air. "I don't remember." A push and I go reluctantly spinning.

"What are you doing, Harry?"

"Making your boyfriend jealous."

"I don't want to make him jealous."

Harry gives me a disbelieving look. "Have you ever made anyone jealous before?" he asks. "It's really fun. Plus, you've been going around with a pout all evening, and it's turning off the guests."

"I don't pout."

"You're pouting right now," he says. "Trust me, Katie. I know what I'm doing."

"He's not even looking."

Harry grins. "He's definitely looking."

"But he's— hey." I scowl as Harry tugs me close, gripping my waist as we spin around the floor.

"Hands, much?"

"Humor me, would you? Oh, look. That didn't take long."

Harry comes to a halt, spinning me around as I come face to face with Callum.

"Mind if I cut in?" he says, his eyes on Harry, whose response is to push me so hard that I stumble straight into Callum's arms. I look over my shoulder to glare at him, but he only smiles in response and goes off to join Richie. Callum snatches my hand before I can curse him out and then we're moving again.

"What are you doing?"

"Dancing," he says, moving me farther into the middle of the floor.

"You said you're a terrible dancer," I remind him.

"I've decided that I go where you go." He gives me a gentle nudge, encouraging me to spin out, and as I do, his eyes drop to my dress, taking me in. "You look beautiful tonight." And he says the words so simply, so matter of factly, that I blush.

I turn back into his arms, and he pulls me closer, much closer than Harry and I stood.

I notice the difference immediately. The way my skin heats

wherever his hands are, the way my body automatically wants to move with his. The way the rest of the room seems to fade into the background. Until it's just him and me. Until I can't look away.

"I'm sorry about the interview." I must have said it a million times already, but something in my voice now makes him pause. "I just panicked," I continue. "I want this to work, and I'm scared that it won't, and I panicked. I'm sorry."

I can feel him looking at me, but I can't meet his eye, taking the coward's way out, the better way out, and watch the other couples move around. He doesn't say anything for the rest of the song, but when it comes to an end, he squeezes my hip before another can start. "You want to sit down?"

I nod, and he leads me into the pub, but instead of heading to the lounge, brings me straight to Adam's office where he sits in his chair and, before I can stop him, pulls me into his lap.

"What?" he asks, when I give him a look.

"I meant sit in the main room."

"Did you?" he asks innocently.

"And in my own chair."

"Well, that's nowhere near as fun." He rubs a slow circle into my back while the other hand toys with my dress. I don't really mind, though. His lap is oddly comfortable. And the way my feet dangle off the ground comes as a huge relief. I relax into him even as his fingers trail up my leg, slipping through the folds of my skirt to caress the bare skin he finds there. "I really like your dress."

Goosebumps follow the trail of his touch, but I keep my expression stern.

"Callum," I warn, though I don't move away.

"You need a distraction."

"What?"

"You're not enjoying yourself," he says. "The one thing

everyone wanted you to do tonight, and you can't do it. So you need a distraction."

"What kind of distraction?" I ask, even though I can guess where his mind's gone as he gently grips my thigh. A smile pulls unwillingly at my lips and I'm just about to say to hell with it and stay back here with him when the door opens.

I scramble off his lap so fast, I almost fall to the floor, and turn to see Harry standing in the doorway. He doesn't seem fazed to catch us like this, and I'm stopped from feeling my usual embarrassment, when I see his worried look.

"What is it? What's wrong?"

"I'm not sure," he says. "I thought I'd better come find you and see what you think."

Callum and I share a look before hurrying back into the pub.

I have no idea what he's talking about at first, the lounge is busy with people dancing and talking and...

Hmmm.

Callum checks the time on my phone as I seek out the clock on the wall for the same reason. It's still early, not even ten p.m., and yet the dancing on the floor, the volume of conversation...

"They're just a little drunk," I say.

"More than a little," Harry mutters, his eyes on two people making out nearby.

I shake my head, looking toward the bar. "The guys know to keep an eye on people. It's Adam, he wouldn't serve anyone who he thought was too far gone."

"Then maybe it's not that," Callum says, frowning as he looks around the room. He takes off suddenly and I follow, slipping through the packed crowd as he makes his way to the buffet table, straight to Nush's punch.

One bowl is already empty, and the other is quickly on its way to being so as Callum politely cuts through the people gathered around it and pours himself a cup.

He grimaces as he sniffs it but takes a sip anyway. "Okay, yeah. Try that."

"Why? What's wrong with— oh my God." I start coughing on the first sip. I've never been a big drinker, but I don't consider myself a lightweight either. But that's... I mean, that is...

"I'm going to kill her," I say, setting it down. I head to the kitchens and then to the storeroom until I eventually find Nush standing outside the ladies' bathroom, scrolling through her phone.

"Monica's fixing her makeup," she tells me, when she sees me. "And then we're going back to dancing. She has two cats, Katie. Two."

"Great," I say. "What did you put in the punch?"

"Huh?"

"The punch, Nush. You said you were going to make it earlier."

"Oh yeah. Adam gave me your recipe, but I found a better one online. I added some pineapple juice to... it's too sweet, isn't it?" She groans dramatically before I can respond. "I knew it would be too sweet. Everyone always tells me I have a sweet tooth, but I couldn't taste it because of the alcohol and then—"

"You put alcohol in it?" I interrupt.

"Of course."

"What do you mean, of course?"

"Because punch has alcohol in it," she says like it's obvious. "I used vodka."

"How *much* vodka?"

"I dunno. A bottle?"

Callum shifts beside me as I stare at her. "You put a bottle of vodka in that bowl of punch?"

She hesitates, eyes flickering between the two of us. "Is that not enough?"

Oh my God.

"Tell them to take the punch away," I say, whirling to Callum. "And to stop serving at the bar. Only non-alcoholic drinks for the rest of the night."

"On it," he says, as Nush's eyes widen.

"Is that not good?" she asks, trailing me as I follow him back to the main room.

It all seems much more obvious now I know what the problem is, the noise that bit louder than it should be, the movements a little looser.

They are more than a little drunk. Half the room is completely smashed.

There are even a few protests when Callum wheels the serving bowl away, but he thankfully ignores them, disappearing into the kitchens.

I'm starting to feel a little lightheaded. "We didn't mark it as non-alcoholic or anything, did we?"

"I don't think anyone could take a sip of that stuff and think there wasn't any alcohol in it," Harry says diplomatically. "It was free, and a lot of people were nervous. They probably used it to settle their stomachs. Which," he adds. "Is pretty ironic when you consider how *unsettled* they'll be in the—"

"Yes, okay. Thank you."

"Relax," Harry says, slapping me on the shoulder. "If this is the bad thing that happens, then you can do a lot worse than people losing some of their inhibitions." He pauses as a couple go giggling past, tripping over in their heels. "But ibuprofen might be handy," he adds, and I sigh.

CHAPTER TWENTY-SIX

"I just think I'd be better suited to an Aquarius."

I force down a sigh, my smile plastered to my face as one of the guests pleads her case. She's my third one this morning and I am starting to take it personally.

"And one of the other girls said the matches were more like suggestions anyway and I—"

"What are you asking?" I interrupt, even though I already know what's coming.

"Can I swap? My friend Amy already did, and she said it's cool so long as—"

"No problem. Knock yourself out."

She beams at me, delighted, and runs off to join her friends by the lake. We couldn't have wished for better weather. It's like we had the wettest spring since records began all so we could have the warmest summer. The sun is beating down on the lake, showing off the pub in all its glory, and as predicted, a few people have waded into the water as a way to cool down and are taking pictures of each other. It's perfect. Or it would have been if more than half our guests had bothered to drag themselves out of bed.

"It could have been worse," Nush says to me now like she's reading my mind.

"How could it have been worse?"

"A hangover is not that bad," she says. "There could have been food poisoning. Or a murder."

"A mur— Nush!"

"No, like a fun one," she insists. "Like in Clue."

"Oh my God. Stop talking."

And it's not just one hangover judging by the line outside the pharmacy this morning. Nush fell over herself apologizing to me and is being extra attentive, but all that means is she's been following me around for the last hour.

Then there's Gemma and Adam who are as far away as two people can be while still being in the same space, with Adam doling out ice creams cones and Gemma staying firmly several picnic tables away, pretending not to notice him. Something must have happened last night, but between making up with Callum and making sure all the drunk people got home, I'd missed whatever it was.

"Any word from Glenmill yet?"

I shake my head at Nush's question, stomach tightening with that familiar worry. I'd been expecting *something* by now.

"Well. I'm going to do another loop with the petition," Nush says decidedly.

"Don't annoy people, okay? Especially if they're hungover."

"It hurts me when you doubt my charms," she says, completely serious, and wanders off to get her clipboard.

I turn my focus to Gemma, who's peering out at the water with an absent expression, her iced coffee untouched beside her. She's so in her own head that it's only when my shadow falls over her that she even notices my approach.

"Hey," she says, peering up at me.

"Hi. Did you sleep with Adam?"

"*What*? Katie!"

"Well, I don't know," I say, as she huffs, drawing her dress down her legs like she's all prim and proper all of a sudden. "It's not like you don't know the guy."

"We had a nice night," is all she says.

"And?" I prompt, flopping down next to her.

"And nothing. I'm just happy my boob tape stayed in place." But even as she speaks, her eyes flit to Adam by the cart and promptly away again.

"Did you fight?"

"No."

"And you didn't sleep together and wake up regretting it?"

"No and stop talking so loud," she hisses.

"Then why are you ignoring each other?" I ask.

"We're not," she says. "But Noah's here."

"So? He's seen you speak with Adam before."

"This is different."

"No, it's not! This isn't the big thing you're making it out to be. You know Adam. Noah knows Adam. It's kind of the ideal situation, if you think about it." I scowl when she doesn't move, my frustration spilling over. "Fine. If you won't talk to him, then I will."

She latches onto my wrist so hard I yelp. "Don't you dare," she warns, but I just shake her off. "Katie? *Katie.*" Gemma scrambles to follow me as I stride up to the cart.

Adam glances up when I approach, looking confused before he spies Gemma behind me. Then he just looks awkward.

"No," I say. "I'm telling you right now, that this can't happen. You two either need to just kiss or—"

"Noah!" Adam says suddenly, and I shut my mouth. "It's Noah! Hey, buddy!"

Gemma and I turn to indeed see a startled-looking Noah standing by the cart. And I can understand why. I don't think Adam has ever said the word "buddy" in his life.

"What can I get you?"

"I just want some ice cream."

"Sure thing," he says in an enthusiastic, very not Adam voice. Gemma looks like she wants the earth to swallow her up, but she manages to smile at her son when he turns his questioning gaze toward her. "Here you go!"

It's kind of creepy, actually. I decide I don't like happy Adam.

Noah doesn't either, judging by the long, wary look he gives him. "Thanks," he says finally, and goes off with his cone.

Gemma shakes her head. "I promised Nush I'd help her with the petitions," she says before either of us can say anything, and spins around, her dress fluttering around her knees as she strides off.

I turn back to Adam just in time to see him gazing after her. Men.

"What did you do to her?" I snap, and he startles.

"I didn't do anything."

"Then why are you both acting like that?"

"It's not me," he says. "It's her. I'm just following her lead."

"What if she's following *your* lead? How long have you been into her? Wait." I hold up a hand as he opens his mouth. "No, don't tell me. I don't want to know."

He grimaces, scratching the back of his neck as he glances over my shoulder, to where I know Gemma is. "Do you think it's weird?"

"No," I say truthfully. "If anything, it's only weird how not weird it is."

"That doesn't make sense."

"It does," I say. "If you really think about it."

"Look, I don't know," he says quietly, as another couple comes up looking for ice cream. "She's barely said two words to me all day, and if she doesn't want this, then I'm not going to pressure her."

"But—"

"Drop it, Katie, yeah? Let's just get through the weekend. What can I get for you?" He says the last bit to the people waiting and I step aside, smiling warmly at them even as I'm frowning on the inside. What's the point of hosting a goddamn matchmaking festival if you can't even matchmake?

I'm starting to make my way inside to check in on those hiding from the sun when I spot Noah sitting in the exact same place Gemma had been moments before, gazing out at the same lake with the exact same expression.

The genes in that family are *strong*.

"Hey."

Noah glances over at me, eyebrows rising in greeting.

"Having the best time ever?" I ask, and he smirks, turning his attention back to the lake.

"It's not so bad," he says, as I take a seat beside him.

"Enjoying the ice cream?"

"It's okay."

I watch him watch the crowd, his gaze skating over the couples without really seeing them. "Your mam said your dad rang the other day," I say carefully. "But that you didn't want to speak with him."

Noah doesn't respond at first, he doesn't even acknowledge the question, and I'm about to abandon ship and swiftly move on when he shrugs.

"My dad's a dick."

Oh boy. I hesitate, trying to think of what Gemma would want me to say in this situation. Darren is a dick. We hate Darren. But we don't want Noah to hate Darren, that's what Gemma's always maintained. She's never said a bad word about that man in front of him, and I've seen the lengths she goes to to protect Noah from the continuous disappointment that is his biological father.

"He's not a dick," I begin. "He's just..." I trail off, as Noah finally turns his head to look at me, pinning me with such a bored, *don't-even-try-it* stare that I immediately give up. "Yeah. He's a dick."

Noah nods and his attention returns to the water. "That's why I didn't want to talk with him. Plus, it's worse when he tries."

"What?"

"Sometimes, he'll send me a card," Noah says absently. "Or he'll give me money. He got me a guitar last year."

"He sent you a guitar?"

"Two months after my birthday."

I frown, not remembering one in their house, but before I can ask more, he explains.

"Mam had to throw it out because it broke," he tells me. And then, "I broke it."

"On purpose?"

Another nod. "I said I dropped it by mistake, but I didn't. Mam went to the shops, and I threw it down the stairs. Twice."

"Noah..."

"He didn't send it for me," he says defensively. "He never sends anything for me. He sent it to hurt her. Because he knows she doesn't like it when he gets in touch with me. Not really. And I don't like it either. Because he lies. He always lies. He says he's coming to visit, but he never does. He says he'll bring me on holiday, but he doesn't. He doesn't give a shit."

"Noah! Language!"

But he ignores me, his features settling into a familiar scowl. One his mother was wearing not ten minutes ago.

"Adam takes me places," he says. "He takes me to the pool all the time. And the beach and the cinema. And when we go, he never acts like he doesn't want to be there. You've been to every one of my birthday parties and Frank goes to all my football games, even when it's raining. Bridget helped me finish painting my room when Mam had to go work and Nush taught me how to pick a lock. And—"

"What do you mean, Nush taught you how to pick a lock?"

"My dad's a dick," he finishes. "And I want everyone to stop treating me like I don't know it. I'm not five. And just because we're related doesn't mean I have to like him."

I can only stare at him, watching the red angry flush of his cheeks begin to fade as he glowers unseeing at the lake. Alright, so maybe he's a lot more observant than Gemma gives him credit for. Than any of us give him credit for, and I'm just about to tell him so when a distant rumbling draws my attention to the main road.

It's a sound I know all too well, and I give Noah's worried look a reassuring wink and, keeping the smile plastered to my face, hurry around to the front of the pub.

The noise grows louder as soon as I do, and I soon see why as a procession of trucks and Jeeps go rumbling past, making enough noise to drown out any music or conversation down by the lake.

"Do you think they're here to protest?" Nush asks quietly, her eyes narrowing on the shiny black Jeep parked across the road as she joins me out front.

"They're not going to knock down the pub, Nush. There are people inside."

"They might wait until we're at the fireworks tonight." I feel her looking at me. "We could always—"

"You're not chaining yourself to the doors," I interrupt.

"I was going to suggest sleeping overnight."

"They can't just knock it down. That's all kinds of illegal."

"Then what are they doing?" she asks, as another truck passes by.

"I don't know. Intimidation?" And it's working. I hate to admit it, but it is. The last of the vehicles rumble past, leaving only the Jeep still loitering across the road and a dirty gray van bringing up the rear. The van actually pulls up to the pub, though, and a bearded man in mud-stained overalls pops out with an almost sheepish expression.

"Can I help you?" I ask, instantly suspicious as he makes his way toward us.

"You the wishing well lady?"

I swear to God Nush gets into a fighting stance next to me. "Yes," I say, giving her a look in case she plans to attack him with her clipboard.

"I'm working on the hotel right now, and my sister saw you guys on the news. She was wondering if I could take a picture of the well. For my nieces. They asked me to make a wish for them."

I shut my mouth as soon as I realize it's open. "Sure," I say. "Yeah. Of course. It's right through there."

"Cool." He lingers awkwardly. "And the festival is, uh... are you still selling tickets for that or is that a done deal now?"

"We're all sold out."

"You doing it next year?"

"If we're still here," I say slowly, but he doesn't seem fazed by that.

"Great, yeah. Getting harder to meet people online these days, you know."

"Sure," I say, and he nods before following my wordless gesture around the pub.

"Is that a good sign?" Nush asks, as he goes off.

"I don't know," I say helplessly, but my attention goes back to the shiny Jeep. There have been lots of new cars around the village lately, and, even though it's too far away for me to see inside, I suddenly know in my heart exactly who this one belongs to, and so I lift my hand in a mocking wave, greeting Jack Doyle, until the engine starts again and he drives off, out of the village.

CHAPTER TWENTY-SEVEN

The rest of the day passes by without incident and, by dinner, most of the guests who slept in to *recover* from the night before have re-emerged. It feels like in the blink of an eye all the activities we'd planned are done, and we have nothing left to do, but tilt our heads and look up at the night sky.

When the sun finally sets, we gather all the guests and the press back at Kelly's to lead them over to the fireworks, and I know I just have to get through the next few hours before I can go home to my bed and sleep for an eternity. But of course, nothing is ever that easy. I've just finished welcoming the last group of people off their hotel shuttle when I step back into the pub and see Jack Doyle standing by the bar.

I freeze at the sight of him, every muscle locking down as I watch him look about the room with vague disinterest.

"What are you doing here?" I ask, just as Callum reaches my side.

"Jack," he says, sounding disappointed. "Come on. What are you doing?"

"I'm just trying to order a drink."

"It's the final night," he says grimly. "Just let it go."

"Believe me," Jack says. "I'd much rather be spending my time somewhere else. But I was asked to be here."

"By who?"

His eyes flick over my shoulder in response, victory flickering in his gaze, and I spin around to see a man entering the pub.

He must be in his mid-sixties. A small man, with a head of white hair and large brown eyes, he looks kind but looks can be deceiving and I watch warily as he strides toward us, the crowd on either side parting like the Red Sea.

"Jack?" Callum's voice is low and angry, but his brother doesn't seem to care. "What's he doing here?"

Jack doesn't answer, and a moment later, the man stops before me, beaming like we're old friends. "You're the young lady I've been seeing on all my television screens," he says. "It's a pleasure to meet you." He shakes my hand, his grip strong and sure. "Gerald Cunningham. I'm sorry I haven't stopped by before."

Those closest to me immediately go quiet, and Callum meets my questioning gaze with a small nod.

Jack's boss.

"I hear you've been causing my protégé a bit of trouble," he says, slapping Jack on the back. "What's the delay now, Doyle? Three? Four months?"

"Five," Jack says, clearing his throat.

Gerald just thumps him again. "No matter, no matter. These things happen. It's a beautiful place you have here," he adds, as Adam steps out from behind the bar. "A beautiful village."

"Is there something we can help you with, Mr. Cunningham?" I ask, and Callum's hand goes to the small of my back in a reassuring touch.

"I'm afraid it's more a question of what we can offer you," he says, and the smile that had been pulling at Jack's mouth drops in confusion. He glances at his boss, while Gerald looks right at me.

"I'll admit we've had to do some soul searching," he says. He's speaking just to me, and yet his voice carries over the room, as if he wants everyone to hear what he has to say. "And that my team here may have gone overboard." At this Jack goes rigid, a dawning look of horror on his face.

"We just care so deeply about our work." Gerald continues. "That we sometimes overlook the important things. I'm incredibly impressed with what you've done here, and I'd like to apologize on behalf of the company for not listening to you sooner." His hand goes to Jack's shoulder, and he smiles like he's Father Christmas and not a tax-avoiding multimillionaire. "As of right now, Glenmill will be stepping back from its acquisition of Kelly's," he says loudly, as cameras start to flash and phone screens record. "You've won."

The room erupts.

Granted that may be the free Prosecco we've been passing around for the last thirty minutes, but I don't really care. All the press and all the interviews have paid off. Everyone knows our story now, and for them the story has come to an end. And it was good one. At least for us.

For Jack, not so much. He stares at his boss for a beat before turning and pushing his way through the now overexcited crowd. Callum gives my arm a brief squeeze before he follows him. Gerald smiles widely at me and then moves too, but only so he can go deeper into the fray as journalists fight to shuffle as close as they can to him.

"He's stealing your spotlight," Gemma remarks, as the man starts shaking hands in the crowd, beaming at the praise.

"I don't care." And I don't. Let him take it.

Because I won. I stand there, hoping for the words to sink in, but they don't. They still don't feel real, hovering above me just out of reach. I still have my job. I still have my home. I still have my village.

"Okay. Oh... Katie?" Gemma's voice sounds very distant as she touches my arm. "You alright?"

"I think I'm freaking out."

"That's allowed. But you still have to breathe, okay? Do you want some water?"

No, I don't want some water. I want a glass of champagne and possibly a shot of whiskey.

But before I have time to ask for either of those things, Adam grabs me from behind, spinning me in the air like I'm five years old, and I give a startled yelp, one that quickly dissolves into laughter.

"Thank you," he says, setting me down only to grasp me by the shoulders. "Thank you."

I grin at him. "Anytime, boss."

"Congratulations," Gemma says, smiling at the two of us, and I barely have time to blink before Adam lets me go, takes her face in his hands, and kisses her soundly on the lips.

My mouth drops open as wolf whistles sound around us. Cheers from guests who have no idea what they're really looking at as, just as quickly as it happened, Adam lets her go. Gemma stumbles back with a dazed look and a blush on her cheeks.

"See!" I exclaim. "That's all you had to do."

But neither of them is looking at me, both turned to Noah who's standing nearby.

Gemma looks horrified. "I didn't—"

"Can you do that in private from now on?" he interrupts. "My mind is still developing, and I probably shouldn't see that."

They both just stare at him.

"Sure," she says after a moment.

"Will you take me to the pool next week?" he asks Adam.

"Okay," Adam says, still looking a little shell-shocked.

"Katie?" My name is a singsong as Nush hurries over with an unusually pleasant smile that immediately puts me on edge. "You're needed outside. Your boyfriend's about to throw down."

My eyes go wide as she turns her attention to Gemma.

"What happened to your lipstick?"

I hurry outside before anyone can answer her. The parking lot is empty of people and dark except for the lights streaming out from the pub, and for a moment I'm confused before I see the two men standing over by Jack's Jeep.

"Go back inside, Katie," Callum says, when he spots me. "I've got this."

"You come too," I say, eyeing Jack warily. He looks frazzled, pulling at his hair, and while I don't think he's been drinking, I've been around enough drunk people in my life to know what it looks like when someone wants to throw up. "Do you want to sit down?" I ask him.

"No," he snaps, and Callum's gaze narrows.

"Don't speak to her like that," he warns, but Jack only scoffs.

"Do you know how much of an idiot I look right now? For weeks I've been doing his bidding on this. For months. And the whole time he's telling me to push and to push and that this is his decision and that this is what he wants and then he does this!" He lets out a little laugh, like he's telling himself a joke. "I'm the one who's been doing all the interviews. I'm the one who's been pushing back. He's made me look ridiculous."

"Think you managed that all by yourself," Callum says, but Jack's not paying attention to him. His gaze is on the pub, and I know he's thinking of Gerald inside schmoozing and basking and doing all the things he threw Jack under the bus to do. And while we might have saved the pub, I still have a festival to pull off.

"No," I say quickly, stepping in front of Jack. He looks down at me like he'd forgotten I was even here. "You're not welcome here right now. Cool off and if you want to kill the man, do it at your own place of business."

He just scoffs at me and steps forward again.

"*Hey*," Callum says sharply, and even I freeze at the tone of his voice. It's not one I've ever heard from him before. "She said back up."

He doesn't, he keeps coming. Stubbornly I stand my ground and Jack crowds me for one second as he attempts to move past and then suddenly Callum is there, slipping into the small space between us, and pushing me behind him as he rears a hand back and hits his brother square in the jaw.

I always thought I knew what hitting someone looks like. I've seen movies. I've watched clips online. But in real life it's very different. Surprising for one thing. I'm not expecting either the action or the sound it makes. Not a *bam!* like how it's described in comic books, but a dull thump, kind of underwhelming, especially when Jack doesn't stagger back or go sprawling to the ground. He just kind of jerks back, putting a hand to his cheek and staring at his brother like he doesn't know who he is.

The two men stare at each other and, though I'm nervous one of them is going to try something again, I don't intervene. This isn't about me.

Jack's mouth opens and closes wordlessly, but I can't tell whether he's just testing nothing's broken or is trying to say something. Nothing happens in the end; he just gives his brother a steely look and turns back to his car. A few seconds later, he's gone.

The excited chatter of the party continues behind us, but neither of us move. Callum flexes his fingers almost absently, his thoughtful expression morphing into one of confusion when he sees me staring at him.

"What?"

"What do you mean, *what*?" I snap. "You just punched him in the face!"

"Barely."

"No, not barely. That was a punch. In the face. How's your hand? Did you break it?"

"Did I... no." He sounds amused now, like I'm the ridiculous person here, when he's the one fighting like he's in an action movie. I take his wrist as gently as I can, making sure no fingers are sticking out at weird angles.

"I can't believe you hit him," I say, as the rest of our merry group hurry over following the commotion.

"He'll get over it."

"What happened?" Gemma asks. "We heard yelling."

"Callum punched Jack."

"*Nice,*" Nush says, and I glare at her.

"Not nice. No to violence, Nush."

But now Noah is staring up at Callum with something akin to awe. "In the face or the stomach?"

"The fa—"

"Okay." Gemma slaps her hands over his ears. "Come on, we'll miss the show."

"But—"

"No."

She takes him by the shoulders and pushes him back toward the pub. Nush lingers.

"Did he cry?"

"I'll see you inside, Anushka," I say, and she looks disappointed, but takes the hint.

"I'm getting the feeling the macho thing doesn't really work for you," Callum says, when I turn back to him.

"I didn't say *that*," I mutter, and he grins. "I just don't want you to hurt yourself. Or your brother."

"He had it coming," he says calmly. "And when he wants to apologize to you, we can talk about it. But not until then."

"Well." I finish my inspection of his hand, satisfied he hasn't damaged it, but not exactly sure what it would look like if he did. "Thank you for protecting my honor."

"Anytime, Katie Collins."

"We ready to go?" Nush makes a show of pointing to an imaginary watch and gestures toward the pub. Right. Procession. Fireworks.

"I'm going to have champagne," I say decidedly, and Callum nods like that is a great idea (which it is) and leads me back inside. Thankfully, not many people noticed our absence. Another viral argument probably wouldn't go my way this time and I slip through the crowd as Bridget starts checking off people on the list. But no sooner have the first people left the pub than the lights flicker above us, sending us briefly into darkness.

Confusion reigns for an instant and then the crowd gasps as one (some of the more overdramatic among us let out a little scream) as the music cuts out and the lights flicker off for good.

Blackout.

A goddamn *blackout*.

I freeze as nervous laughter gives way to panicked murmurings. I hadn't prepared for this. A resident of Ennisbawn all of my life and I hadn't prepared for a blackout.

I suppose we've been lucky really to have escaped them for so long and I glance around, waiting for someone to say something and tell us what to do, only to belatedly realize that *I'm* the person that's meant to do it.

"Get up there," Gemma hisses, her phone to her ear, hopefully on the line to the electricity company, and I turn with a gulp toward the stage, climbing the steps before I can lose my nerve.

"Um... excuse me? Hello?" My voice grows surer as more people than I'd expected turn to me, seeking guidance.

Project, Nush mouths to me, and I straighten my shoulders like she's always told me to, calling to be heard with no microphone.

"My name is Katie Collins, and I'm the organizer of this festival. We get these. I'd love to say that this was planned or that we should think of it as romantic, but it's not. It's annoying and also a health and safety risk to have people stumble around in the dark. I'm sure you can understand why we have to cut short this evening's festivities for these reasons." I pause, using the disappointed grumbles to take a breath. "If everyone could just stay here for the time being, I'd like to do a headcount and then we'll make sure to get you back to your hotels and accommodation safely. Thank you for bearing with us."

I quickly climb down while the going is good. I thought I'd be swarmed with people asking questions, but I must have been pretty clear because everyone just kind of lingers in clumps. A few of them even seem to be enjoying themselves, but I can't shake my worry. The last thing we need is for someone to trip and break their ankle in the dark and sue us for all it's worth.

"I read a thriller about this happening," one woman near me mutters, which does not help things.

I jump when someone touches my elbow, but it's only Callum.

"You okay?"

"I'm fine. Just..." I gesture around me, and he nods.

"We need to make sure everyone gets home safe," I say. "Let's contact the hotels and a taxi service and explain what's going on. Get them to send any cars they have to collect people. We need staff out in hi-vis jackets on the roads and we need to cordon off the paths so we don't have anyone wandering off and getting lost. Shut the bar and food service down unless anyone needs water. And then we'll see where we go from there."

"On it," he says.

We get to work.

It takes an hour before we manage to get everyone where they need to go. The hotels are quick to react and, in no time at all, we're out on the street directing cars and minibuses and trying to keep track of everyone as best we can so we know who's getting home okay.

I thought people would be mad, but, for the most part, they're pretty understanding and know that it's out of our control. A few even ask if we can put on the fireworks for tomorrow, treating this as just part of the experience, and I go along with it.

I'm exhausted by the time we're done clearing up the pub with the few others who stayed behind so we're not walking into a giant mess in the morning. I offer to lock up the pub while Adam walks Gemma and a hyper Noah home and am halfway across the parking lot before I spot Callum lingering by his van.

"Where are you going?" he calls.

"Home."

"I'm not letting you walk home in the pitch-black."

"I've walked home a million zillion times before."

"In those heels?"

Well. No. I glance down at my stupid stilettos and scowl. Why do things so pretty have to hurt so much?

"Give me a ride then. Is Granny still here?"

"She's already left with Susan," he says, and I pause. Susan lives by herself at the other end of the village and hates the blackouts. She sometimes comes to stay with us during them if they go on long enough. Which means I'll be on the couch tonight.

"Just come home with me," Callum says, not even waiting for a response as he strides toward his van. "I'll make you French toast in the morning."

I huff a laugh, sorely tempted. Our couch is *not* a sleeping couch. Does Callum even have a sleeping couch? Would he take the couch? Would neither of us take the couch? Would he—

"Stop thinking and get in the van, Katie."

"Says the *murderer*." But I do as I'm told, climbing into the pristine vehicle, and putting my seatbelt on.

CHAPTER TWENTY-EIGHT

"I'm still not sure this isn't my brother," Callum says, as he turns left onto a side road and pulls up beside a small house.

"Are you imagining him climbing an electricity pole with a pair of wire cutters?"

"I wouldn't put it past him."

I smirk, climbing out onto the gravel. I don't know how, but I know this isn't on Jack. He's an asshole, yes, but I don't think he'd put people in danger just to be extra petty.

"You know, we might have escaped it," Callum says hopefully, as he unlocks the door. He reaches inside to flick on a light switch, only for his face to fall when the house remains in darkness. "Or not."

"Welcome to Ennisbawn."

"I've got this. Wait here."

"I can help."

"No. Don't move or you'll walk into something."

I roll my eyes, but the man isn't wrong. It's pitch-black inside and, in this dress, I'd like to keep my knees unbruised, thank you very much. I wait by the door as he disappears into the house and emerges a second later with a flashlight to illuminate the space.

"Look at you, all prepared," I tease, and he grins.

"And they try and tell me I'm not a local."

He leads me down the hallway to the kitchen, where he goes straight for the kettle before stopping. "Right. No electricity. I guess we could..." He stands in the middle of the room for one long second before turning back to me. "I literally can't do anything, can I?"

I laugh. It's one of those times when you don't realize how much you need electricity until it goes away. It's not like when you're camping when you don't expect there to be any. You come prepared. It's part of the fun. It's different in a house where you expect it in every room, in every corner. Where you realize you can't boil the kettle or even open the fridge because you need to try and preserve whatever cold air is in there.

"I don't need anything," I assure him.

"Well, neither did I, but now I can't have it, I desperately want it. Plus, it goes against everything in my being not to offer a guest something to eat and drink." He scratches his jaw, looking genuinely perturbed he can't entertain me appropriately. "I've got some movies on my laptop if you want to watch something," he begins, but I shake my head.

"You should preserve your battery in case there's still nothing in the morning."

He is immediately alarmed. "It might not be back in the morning?"

"One time we didn't have it for three days."

"Well, that's just great."

"But usually, it's a couple hours at most," I reassure him and reach down to unstrap my heels. "Is there somewhere I can change?"

He looks confused. "Do you have other clothes?"

"No?"

He grins. "Upstairs. There are only two rooms so you're not going to get lost. Take whatever you need."

"Dangerous words," I tell him, and use my phone light to show me the way.

The bathroom is tiny, one of those new additions to a house that once didn't have any indoor plumbing. With the toilet, shower, and sink squished together, I can just about fit inside, and I wonder how he copes with it. His bedroom is just as tidy as I'm coming to expect from him. The bed neatly made; his clothes put away. There are a few coins on the dresser, a framed photo of an older couple I presume to be his parents, and the same headphones I saw him wearing the day he first came to my house.

I call Granny first, who grumpily assures me she's fine and that, as assumed, Susan will be staying the night in my room. I then return to the bathroom, where I carefully extract all the pins and clips I hid in my hair, letting it not so much tumble down my shoulders as fall in clumps, the copious amount of hairspray I used making it difficult to tame. I probably look ridiculous, but my scalp, which had been aching for the past few hours, thanks me, so I leave it as it is.

With my phone lit up in one hand and my other trailing along the wall, I stride back into the bedroom like I know exactly where I'm going only to immediately walk into the edge of a dresser.

"*Ow.* Shit."

"Katie? You okay?" Callum runs up the stairs, taking them two at a time before coming to a stop in the doorway. "What? What is it?"

"Nothing," I mutter. "I stubbed my toe." I hobble over to the bed, muttering a stream of curses that would make even Granny blush.

Callum turns on the flashlight, sweeping it over me as though I'm lying and maybe stabbed myself instead.

"Don't look at my gross toe."

"It's not gross."

"All toes are gross," I inform him, but he ignores me, kneeling by my side. He grabs my foot before I can stop him, inspecting it briefly before running a finger along the arch.

I squirm immediately, fighting the tickling sensation with a scowl.

"Callum," I warn.

"I think you'll live," he says solemnly.

"You playing Doctor now?"

"We can play Doctors." He sweeps his palm up my calf, his touch warm and rough and perfect, and I can't help but smile as he looks up, meeting my gaze in the dim light.

Slowly, without looking away, he presses his lips to the top of my foot, as though to kiss it better. Meanwhile his hand doesn't stop moving slowly up and down my leg, inching higher each time it reaches my thighs. His mouth follows the movement, gentle, tickling brushes that make my chest grow tight, my breathing shallow as he works his way up. He nuzzles into my lap and then my stomach, roving upward until he's kneeling before me, capturing my mouth.

I loop my arms around his neck, holding on to him loosely as he deepens the kiss until we're both panting. It's only when his hands travel down the front of my dress, caressing my breasts through the material, that I break away.

"You good?" he murmurs, and I nod, lifting my knee between us and extending my leg until I'm pointing my foot at his chest. He gets the hint and backs away, rising to his feet.

With a steeling breath, I follow him, standing from the bed and reaching for the hidden zipper of my dress. I hesitate for only a heartbeat, searching for an inner reluctance that never comes, and then pull it down.

The noise seems ridiculously loud in the quiet space, but before I can get nervous, I free my arms from the sleeves and let the material pool at my ankles before nudging it aside to stand before him in nothing but my underwear. I'm about to remove those too, in for a penny and all that, but then I catch the look on Callum's face and freeze.

It's a look I've never had directed at me before. An intense, hungry expression that should make me feel like one of those powerful women in Granny's books, but instead just sends a sprinkle of nerves through me. Like, if he looks any closer, he'll see all the little things that I'm told not to worry about, but I still always do. Cellulite! Stretchmarks! The bulge in my tummy that I sometimes try to suck in even though I know I shouldn't, but I can't help it. I can't. And the nerves just increase, and I reach for the dress again and Callum looks so adorably confused before he realizes what's happening and shoots forward, tossing it into the corner of the room.

"Don't you dare," he says, and I laugh a little at how choked the words sound. "You've been wearing those the whole time?"

"Nush made me buy them last year."

"I've always liked that girl," he says seriously, and I grin.

I'd never thought of underwear as sexy before. I mean, obviously, I knew they could be, but all my life they've just been practical daily things. Definitely not seductive. But the way he's gazing at the little bow in the middle of my cups at the front has me pressing my thighs together, and the way he swallows tells me he notices the movement immediately, but he doesn't move, waiting for something, waiting, I realize, for me.

I'm still a little nervous. It's a good kind of nervous, but one that makes me linger where I am before I make myself take a hesitant step to him.

Only to burst out laughing as he grabs my hand and pulls me forward the final steps, straight into his arms.

———

Callum Dempsey has been holding out on me.

I think I'd be forgiven for not realizing it before. After all, he'd never been shy about letting me know how much he wanted me. We'd only shared a handful of kisses, but each time we did, it brought out a side of me I never knew was there and left me wanting more until I was almost breathless with it.

But this? This is more than lust. More than smooth moves in the shadows and butterflies in the stomach. It's all-consuming and overwhelming, and even a little frightening, the depth of what I feel for him, but I wouldn't stop it for the world. I don't think I could if I tried.

There's just suddenly so *much* of him. So much heat, so much skin. His hands are everywhere, his touch is everywhere, and I still can't get enough, clinging to him as he somehow pulls me into him and walks me backward at the same time. He lowers me onto the bed, his knees digging into the mattress on either side of my thighs as he hovers over me, never once breaking our connection.

His mouth is blazing and insistent against mine, and relief fills me that he's as eager for this as I am, that he's not holding back or trying to play it cool. He lets me know just how much he wants me with every drag of his tongue, every sweep of his hand. We're kissing so hard that I'm struggling to catch my breath, but I can't stop, I don't want to stop, and honestly, if this is how it ends for me, then I can think of worse ways to go.

He falls to the bed, rolling me above him, a position I take full advantage of as I plant my hands on his chest for balance and grind down, moving my hips against his until he groans.

"This okay?" I ask, not really sure what I'm asking. *This* as in this cheap teenage move I'm doing, or *this* as in where I want to take this. Where I think we both want to take it.

"More than okay." But even as he says the words, his hands find my waist, gently stilling me. "But just... just give me a second."

"What's wrong?" I ask, and he gives a strangled-sounding laugh.

"My libido, that's what's wrong. And I'm man enough to tell you."

I grin down at him, and he appears captivated by the sight, reaching up to brush the hair from my face.

"I like you like this," he says, and I raise a brow.

"Half-naked?"

"That," he agrees and his stomach muscles flex beneath my fingertips as he moves, standing from the bed in one fluid movement and bringing me with him. "And happy."

Happy. My legs wrap around him instinctively, a warm glow spreading through my chest at his words.

"You know what would make me even happier?" I tease.

His smile is slow and playful and very, very sexy. "I think I've got an idea."

He holds me up with no effort at all, a thing I have just decided I like very much, but I like it even more when he sits on the edge of the bed, lowering us until I'm straddling him. I grasp the hem of his shirt and he helps me pull it over his head. The material ruffles his hair as it goes and, I swear to God, I'm almost jealous of the fabric. It's my fingers that ruffle that hair and nothing else.

As soon as he's free of it, Callum's attention zeroes in on the little blue bow again. He gives it a flick, looking at it like it's the most fascinating thing he's ever seen, and I make a mental note to thank Nush as soon as I get over the embarrassment of telling her about my sex life.

"Off," he finally says, the word ragged, and I do as I'm told, undoing the clasp and dropping the bra to the floor as he encourages me to lean back. When I do, my chest rises as though I'm offering myself up to him, and he wastes no time in dipping his head, sweeping his tongue along the underside of my breast before dragging it across my nipple. A bolt shoots through me and I stiffen in his arms as his lips close around the bud, sucking with just enough pressure that I cry out, cupping the back of his head to hold him to me. He gets my very subtle hint, lavishing it with attention and stopping only to show the same due deference to the other one until I'm panting in his arms.

Only then does he twist, laying me back on the bed so that my head rests on the pillows. My belly tightens as he drags a hand down my chest and my stomach, catching the lacy hem of my underwear around my hips. Just like he did before, he slides them down my legs, and just like he did before, he slips the material into his pocket. Only this time, he stays right where he is, running his broad palms up my thighs before parting them gently.

I prop myself up on my elbows, bending my knees as I gaze down at the man between my legs, and he doesn't move until I do, keeping his eyes trained on me as he nips the soft skin of my thigh before turning his face an inch to the right.

The elbow thing doesn't last long. I collapse back at the first kiss, crumpling to the bed and closing my eyes against the onslaught of sensations. Callum doesn't seem to mind, content to torture me at his leisure until I'm digging my heels into the mattress, twisting the sheets between my fingers.

It does not take long.

Like... at all.

I can feel the smugness radiating from him as he waits for me to return to earth, but I've become nothing but a boneless mass on the bed, so I couldn't care less right now.

It's only when he begins to kiss his way back up my body that I register the coarse sensation of his jeans against my legs, reminding me how very naked I am and how very much he is not. And that just won't do.

That won't do at all.

The promise of bare skin against skin gives me a second wind and I sit up, almost bumping heads as I take him by surprise. I press a hand against his chest, pushing him until we're both kneeling, and then I reach for his belt, undoing it with impatient fingers. The rough slide of the leather sounds very loud as I pull it free, as does the clatter of the buckle as I throw it to the ground with zero finesse, but Callum doesn't seem to mind, standing to shuck off his jeans before reaching for the black boxers underneath. The sight of them sends my pulse racing, and he groans when I touch him, allowing me only a few seconds before gently brushing me away.

"Condom," he whispers and leaves me briefly to grab a packet from the dresser. I rise up on the bed as he rolls it on and he pauses at the sight, staring like he's trying to commit me to memory.

"I think you're the most beautiful person I've ever seen," he says, and I still at the simple truth in his words. The utter sincerity of it.

"Callum?"

"Yeah?"

"Get back on the damn bed."

He doesn't need to be told twice.

I yelp as he grabs me by the waist with one hand and throws back the sheet with the other, making it billow around us. My head hits the pillow, my hair flying everywhere, but he doesn't wait for me to catch my bearings as he gathers me in his arms, his erection rocking against me until I feel like I'm about to snap.

"You've gone quiet," he murmurs, dragging his teeth across my bottom lip. "You going to talk to me?"

"I'm fine. I'm just..." Trying not to implode.

"You want to slow down?"

"No," I say quickly, and he laughs.

"Keep going," I tell him, drawing his face back down to mine. "Please keep going."

And he does, dipping his head to kiss me again and again and again, deep, drugging, endless kisses that leave me squirming beneath him, desperate for the release that remains just out of reach. A part of me almost wants to keep it there so I can carry on feeling like this forever. I'm pretty sure I never want him to stop touching me. Like ninety-nine percent positive that I would simply cease to exist if he did, like he's the only thing tethering my soul to this body.

But the pressure grows more insistent, the ache too much. I've never wanted anyone like I've wanted him, and I try to hurry him along, but he remains just out of reach, seemingly content in the cradle of my thighs even though I feel how ready he is for me, can sense it in the growing desperation of his movements, less skillful than before.

Eventually, I stop fighting it, letting him touch and tease until the nerves in my belly start to melt away and my body relaxes against his, and it must be what he's been waiting for because it's only then that he lines himself up, kissing the whispered yes from my lips as he eases himself inside.

The noise I make doesn't sound human and his expression heats at the sound of it, his jaw clenching as he moves inch by inch, working his way into me. My nails dig little crescents into his arms, fighting the pleasure at the same time as I chase it, and all the while, Callum takes me in, his gaze roaming from my hair to my mouth to my lips like he's determining that this is real, that I'm not a mirage, that I'm right here, *we're* right here.

And though he dips his head down to kiss me, though I slide my hands around his back, kneading the firm muscles I find there, it's still not enough.

He drops his forehead to mine, his face creased in concentration, and I know he's holding back, I know he's keeping himself in check because this is still new and we're still learning each other, but I don't want him to. I want him, I want all of him and all he has to give me.

And I want it now.

"I can take it," I tell him, urging him closer. "I'm good. I feel good."

"Good?" He chokes on a laugh. "You feel perfect, Katie. You feel... *God*."

I raise my hips, drawing him into me, and then we're moving together, finding our rhythm, finding ourselves.

Every part of me feels sensitive and hot to the touch. I am aware of every point where our bodies meet, and as bit by glorious bit I open up to him, he starts to move faster, thrusting harder until I'm mindless with sensation, until I really hope he doesn't ask me to talk again because I don't think I'll be able to.

He wraps a hand around my hip, each finger searing into me as he holds me steady, and when he drags my thigh up so he can go even deeper, I'm pretty sure I see stars. He stays right there, hitting that perfect spot over and over until I'm wrapping myself around him, tightening my muscles until he curses.

Any sense of rhythm flies out the window. I can't touch enough of him or feel enough of him, even though I try, my hands grasping at slick skin as I plant messy kisses on his lips, cheeks, wherever I can reach. His breathing grows ragged in my ear, and I urge him closer, meeting each drive of his hips with one of my own and though I want to watch him, want to see him come apart, the man has other plans. Lips meet my temple as he slides his fingers between our bodies, caressing the most sensitive part of me until I'm hurtling toward the edge. I almost sob from the pleasure of it, pleasure made all the sweeter when I bring him shuddering along with me, and when he speaks again it's my name I hear, repeated like a prayer as he brushes the hair from my face and presses a kiss to my lips before collapsing on the bed next to me.

He pulls me into him as though even that inch of space between us is intolerable and as he tugs my exhausted, sated body to sprawl over his, I rest my cheek against his chest, listening to his heart as I give him my own.

CHAPTER TWENTY-NINE

The electricity comes back on at some point during the night. I know this because when I open my eyes, blinking at the rising summer sun, the beaten-up digital clock on Callum's nightstand tells me it's sometime after three a.m. Now, I might not have been great at maths in school, but even I know that doesn't add up.

I reach automatically for my phone and then for my charger when I see it's completely out of juice, but I'm prevented from moving farther by a warm, heavy arm draping itself across my stomach.

"Don't move," Callum murmurs behind me. "You'll wake me up."

I smile, settling back into the bed. "Wake you up, huh? Did anyone ever tell you you talk in your sleep?"

He pulls me closer in response, and I shift carefully around to face him. He looks like he's dead to the world.

"Callum."

"It's still dark."

"It's not still dark, your eyes are closed." I peck his lips when he doesn't answer, and when he still doesn't move, I free one of my hands and push, turning him over onto his back so I can kiss my way across his chest.

"You know, I'm pretty sure I've had dreams where you did this," he mumbles.

"Oh yeah? And do you always just lie there doing nothing?"

"I'm usually more awake in them," he admits. "And you're wearing clothes."

"Clothes?"

"Lacy clothes."

"Well, now I know what I'm getting you for your birthday," I say, and lean up to gently bite his earlobe.

"Did you sleep at all?" he asks.

"A little."

"And yet you're wide awake."

I pause at the accusation in his voice and pull back to find him peering up at me. "You're not a morning person," I say, delighted with this new fact.

"Whatever gave you that idea?"

"How are you not a morning person? Didn't you usually get up at, like, five a.m.?"

"Just because I had to doesn't mean I liked to," he mutters. "And we're going to have to rethink this whole relationship thing if you're someone who doesn't have lie-ins."

"Why sleep when I can do this?" I whisper, finally doing what I've wanted to do since the moment I saw him in my garden. I settle back over him and, with frankly stunning attention to detail, trace his swirling tattoos with my fingers and my tongue, tasting every inch of inked skin.

"Do they have a story?" I ask, as I return to a beautiful interlocking Celtic pattern on his right bicep.

"Yeah. I thought they looked cool."

I jab him in the ribs, and he grunts.

"You really are awake."

"Uh-huh."

"The first time I met you, you yelled at me because you weren't getting enough sleep and now you're wide awake."

"I'm unpredictable like that."

He sighs, but his gaze is warm when he opens his eyes. Warm if not still very sleepy. "Is the electricity back?"

"I think so."

"Then I need coffee," he rasps. "Lots and lots of coffee."

"Anything else?"

A smug smile pulls at his lips even as he closes his eyes once more. "Thought I said I'd be the one making *you* breakfast."

"You did, didn't you? Then I want French toast."

"I've got no bread. How about eggs?"

"Eggs are gross."

"Eggs are not gross. What the hell?" He peers up at me, pushing my hair back to see my face. "What other wrong opinions do you have?"

"They are slimy and gross," I tell him. "Like mushrooms."

He rolls his eyes, but he's smiling. "Alright, what about pancakes? No visible eggs. Only hidden ones."

"I like pancakes."

"Hallelujah," he mutters and then kisses me in a way that makes my toes curl, slow and lazy and deep. I melt against his chest, practically falling over him as he drags the moment out.

"I should get dressed," I say, pulling away. "I need to check on things in the village."

He frowns in disagreement, dragging a finger down my forehead and my nose before tracing my lips. "Or you can stay here."

"You said we'd have pancakes."

"Or we could stay— oh, come on." He groans as I wriggle off him, bringing the sheet with me. I drop it to the floor as I grab my dress instead and head to the bathroom to freshen up. It feels silly to wear it again, but I figure I'll change properly when I'm home.

When I return to the bedroom, Callum looks like he's still in the middle of a ten-stage process of getting out of bed, something I find incredibly endearing, so I leave him to it and head downstairs to give him some peace. My stomach rumbles as I do, and I decide to make myself at home, putting plates on the table and searching through his cabinets to find the necessities to start on breakfast.

Eventually, I hear the floorboard creak and the shower turn on, and I'm figuring out how his stove works when he finally enters the kitchen, shirtless in a pair of loose navy jogging pants and looking so delectable that I immediately regret leaving his bed. I think he's thinking the same thing too, heat filling his gaze as he takes in my dress and bare legs. But then he sees the spatula in my hand.

"What are you doing? Sit down."

"I can make—"

"You're not making me breakfast," he says. "I will make you breakfast. What did you want? Pancakes, right?"

"You know how to make pancakes?"

"Do I know how to beat eggs, milk, and flour together? Yes."

I bite my lip, enjoying this way too much. "You're grumpy in the mornings."

He just presses a button on the coffee machine and gives me a look. A whirring noise fills the kitchen along with a delicious smell and, when I don't move, he pushes me toward a chair, kissing me soundly before taking up my position by the stove.

He is not a good cook.

And he does not know how to make pancakes.

But I indulge him, content to sit with my coffee and watch him move about half-naked as he googles recipes and burns the butter, and accidentally makes double the amount of batter because he added in too much flour and then too much milk trying to balance it out.

He doesn't have maple syrup, but he does have a lemon and

sugar and he even grudgingly lets me set the table when he's distracted trying to make the perfect circle.

When he turns around with the first stack, he gives me an unhappy look and grabs the chair I'd placed opposite mine, dropping it with a bang right next to me. The plate and orange juice I'd set out for him are next, and when he finally sits down, we're so close that our arms are touching.

"What?" he asks, when I just stare at him.

I somehow, against all odds, keep my smile to myself. "Nothing."

I like grumpy morning Callum.

In fact, I think I could start every day with grumpy morning Callum.

"What's the plan for today then?" he asks, gulping back his coffee.

I blow out a breath. "Damage control, I guess. Though hopefully not too much." It had seemed like the worst thing in the world last night, but Callum's right. The festival was mostly over, and we might be able to move the fireworks to tonight.

"Maybe we should..." Callum trails off, as he pops a forkful of pancake into his mouth. "Oh, God. Oh, this is not good. This is..." He swallows, grabbing both our plates. "Don't eat that. We'll have cereal."

"I'm sure it's fine!" I say, laughing as I try and take my food back.

"I'd like you to maintain any attraction you have toward me for a little while longer," he says, dumping everything in the sink. "And whatever the hell I put in front of you is not going to help with that." He opens a cabinet, scratching his abdomen with an absent hand. "I've got granola? And some fruit. Correction. I have *a* fruit." He starts taking things out of the cupboards, narrating as he goes, but I've stopped listening, too distracted by the sight of him moving around the kitchen.

The thought of spending more mornings like this makes me

unusually giddy. The thought of being domestic with him. Of knowing where he keeps his dishes and where he keeps his cups. Of what milk he likes to buy and how he takes his coffee or how burned he likes his toast.

I feel like I've spent the last few weeks snatching moments with him, each one exciting, maybe even a little confusing as we test and learn each other. But it's only now that I realize we're entering the next stage of what we have between us. The boring stage of chores and schedules and routine. Of meaningless texts and shared jokes and touching him whenever I want to.

And I can't wait for it.

I rise, padding over to him on quick, silent feet, and wrap my arms around his stomach. His hands drop to mine, gripping me tightly as though I'll pull away.

"Hey," he says, amused, and I rest my forehead in the space between his shoulder blades, inhaling deeply. He smells like coffee and cotton and minty shower gel, and I want to bottle it up and spray it everywhere.

When I don't move away, he turns to face me, careful not to break contact as he bundles me into a giant man hug that I now want to spend the rest of my life getting.

"You good?" he asks, pressing a kiss to the top of my head.

I nod into his chest, not able to answer otherwise because I don't know how to explain just how *good* I am right now. How it's the most good I've felt in a long time and how even better I feel that he seems to get it, not questioning me any further, and just holding me for as long as it takes for my stomach to rumble again and ruin the moment.

———

It takes more effort than it should to leave him. After I make another round of pancakes, Callum decides to make up for his lack of cooking skills with his many other talents and insists on showing me in detail how the shower works. He offers me his clothes when we're done, but I decide to get back into my dress, and head straight home to change properly before dealing with everything else. I can already tell it's going to be a long day, which means a sports bra and another cup of coffee. Maybe two.

He drives me to the top of my lane before kissing me long and deep. My face is flushed when I pull away and he gives the smuggest grin, to which I give him the rudest finger and let myself out, waiting for him to round the bend before I head up the driveway.

Susan's car isn't here, which is a relief. She's a nice woman but a huge busybody, and I know showing up in a dress from the night before will fuel her for weeks. Though I suppose it wouldn't be the *worst* gossip in the world. I always thought my reputation around here could use a little spicing up. And maybe...

I pause in front of the door, frowning as the noise from inside reaches me.

Plankton is barking. Plankton never barks. I mean, he *does*. If he's startled or cornered or something. He gives an alerting *woof* to a fox or a bird he doesn't like the look of. But not this constant racket. Not like he's...

I fit the key into the lock, feeling strangely calm as I let myself in. The barking gets louder as soon I do, but he doesn't come running to see who it is.

There have always been moments when I know something's wrong. A beat of time when I'm aware that my life might be about to change and there's nothing I can do to stop it. I remember as a child seeing the shadow of my grandmother's footsteps in the crack between my bedroom door and the floor. Knowing she was about to come in. Knowing it wasn't good.

"Granny?"

I almost expect her to call out sarcastically like she usually does, but there's no answer, only barking, and so I follow the noise down the hallway to the kitchen where I've found her so many times and where, for one brief hopeful second, I imagine her sitting in her usual spot with a crossword in front of her.

But she's not at the table. She's not at the sink or the stove or rummaging through the cabinets.

She's lying on the floor.

She's still dressed for bed, her nightdress bunched around her legs, her slippers still on her feet. There's an empty water-glass nearby, the spilled liquid wetting her sleeve where she dropped it. She must have gotten up this morning to get it. She must have been lying there for hours. She must have—

"Plankton," I snap, as my dog continues barking, frantic now I'm here. He's hiding under the table, his panic only making me panic as I try and keep my wits about me. I kneel beside her, trying to look for any obvious injuries and seeing none. Did she have a stroke? I hold on to her hand as I reach for my phone, calling everyone I can think of, but no one picks up.

Either their electricity hasn't come back, or they just haven't charged their phones, but no one answers, and I know there's no point in calling for an ambulance. We're too far away and they won't be quick enough.

"Katie..."

My eyes snap back to Granny as she takes a ragged breath.

"You're okay," I say. "It's going to be okay. Do you know what happened?"

"Fell..."

"What?"

"Wasn't... looking... fell."

Fell. No stroke then.

"Did you hit anything?"

She doesn't answer, but she's breathing louder and seems to be aware of her surroundings. I pat gently around her head in case she hit it, but I feel no blood or abrasions, not that that means anything.

"Alright," I say, more to myself than to her. "We're going to get you to the hospital."

"Katie..."

"I'm going to get the car. I'll be right back."

I grab the keys from the bowl in the kitchen, praying the thing has enough petrol in it. Neither of us use the car that much. Granny used to all the time, but she lost confidence a few years ago and stopped leaving the house so much. We considered selling it altogether before eventually deciding to keep it for emergencies.

An emergency like this.

It seems to be working okay and I rush back inside to get her, pleading with Plankton to stay where he is because it's not like I can bring him with us. For once, he does as he's told, still cowering under the table.

It takes a very long time to get her to the car. I make her as comfortable as possible in the back seat and then slide behind the steering wheel.

I wasn't scared of being in cars after my parents died. It wasn't until I learned how to drive that I started getting nervous about it, the unease creeping up on me with each lesson. I don't know what triggered it. Maybe it was learning about all the things that could go wrong. Maybe it was because I knew that no matter how safely I went or how much care I took, it didn't matter if the other driver didn't do so as well. All I know is it didn't get better. And while I could just about manage being in the passenger seat, being the one driving is a whole different experience, one that makes my fingers tremble now as I turn the key in the ignition, and pull off down the lane.

I try not to think about it, even though my anxiety demands that I do. I try instead to keep my mind focused on my goal. On Granny. On getting her to people who can help her and make sure she's alright. And I do okay. For more than five minutes, I do okay, and then it all goes to shit.

I hear the engine before I see it, the exaggerated revving of it like my worst nightmare come through. And then the car speeds around the bend so fast I nearly don't see it in time. In a split second, my heart rate soars and the panic I'd been trying so hard to keep at bay crashes through me. I freak out, hitting the brakes as I swerve to avoid it. The boy racer or whoever it is behind the other wheel zooms straight past, dodging me easily as he vanishes down the road, while I screech to a halt in a small ditch at the side, my seatbelt cutting into my chest as I strain against it.

"Katie?"

"It's okay," I call, as Granny stirs behind me. "I'm sorry. It's okay."

It is not okay. *I* am not okay.

My heart slams against my rib cage, the blood moving around my body too fast, making my vision blur and my chest tighten. I can't do this. *Why* did I think I could do this?

"Just give me one second," I say to Granny, even though I'm not sure I'm speaking out loud. I can't even take my hands off the steering wheel. I can't even move. And if Granny responds, I don't hear it, I don't hear anything but a faint banging sound that pulls at the corners of my panic.

Eventually, I realize it's someone knocking on my window, and my head feels like it's rusted to my neck as I force myself to turn only to see Jack Doyle scowling at me.

At least, I think it's Jack.

He doesn't really look like Jack. He looks like a before photo of Jack. Clothes rumpled, hair uncombed. There are patches of stubble on his jaw and bags under his eyes.

He knocks again, his expression impatient as he gestures for me to open the door.

"Are you okay?" he asks. Behind him, I can see his sleek

black Jeep parked on the other side of the road. It's not the one that came at me, but it wasn't here before either, meaning he drove up without me even realizing, which only terrifies me further. How long have I been sitting here? "Katie."

My name snaps me back to the present. "Granny fell," I say, and, for the first time, he glances into the back, his eyes widening when he sees her. "I'm taking her to the hospital, but I'm not... I'm not good at driving and they were speeding and..."

He stares at me for a long moment, his expression unreadable, before he turns and goes back to his own car. He returns in a matter of seconds, locking the Jeep behind him and throwing a smart leather bag into my passenger seat.

I can only sit there as he slams the door shut and moves around the front to my side.

"Move over."

"What?"

"Move." He flaps a hand at me, almost hitting my arm as he forces me to scramble over the gearshift. "Mrs. Collins? You alright back there?"

Granny doesn't answer, but when I twist around, she's breathing normally. I tell myself she's just resting.

"I'll drive you to the hospital," he says, and I just nod because I figured that was happening.

"Thank you," I say woodenly, and he adjusts the seat and the mirrors, frowning when the engine makes the noise it usually makes (probably not a healthy one).

"You should call ahead," he says. "Let them know we're coming."

I do. They're not happy that I moved her and that makes me feel more guilty, but I know waiting for an ambulance might have taken hours, especially if there were more accidents with the electricity down.

We talk through what I need to do before I arrive, and I've barely hung up the call when Nush rings me back. It's only then I realize a lot of people will have had a lot of missed calls from me and be thinking the worst, but Nush sounds incredibly calm when I tell her what happened, as though knowing any other reaction would just set me off. I decide to leave out the part about Jack, who keeps his gaze studiously to the front while pretending not to listen, and Nush agrees to let everyone else know, so I won't have to.

There is one person I should tell about Jack, though. One person who might not be too happy about the turn of events, but when I go to call Callum, my fingers freeze over the screen. I don't even know where to begin.

"There's a charger in the console," Jack tells me, mistaking my hesitation.

"Thanks," I say, plugging it in.

He grunts in response. "This happen a lot?"

"No. I don't..." I clear my throat. "My parents—"

"You don't have to explain yourself." I can't tell if he means *you don't have to talk about it* or *I don't care*, but I'm grateful not to have to do so anyway. So grateful that my throat gets tight with it.

"I feel useless," I admit.

"You're not." His tone is dismissive, even if his words are not. "If I hadn't stopped, you would have gotten over it. You would have kept going."

But he did stop. And though I want to ask why, I'm too exhausted for that kind of conversation now, so instead twist in my seat and hold Granny's hand, trusting this man not as Jack Doyle but as Callum's brother to get us safely where we need to go.

CHAPTER THIRTY

I think I get it now.

I don't want to, but I do.

I get why Callum followed this man around for so long. I get the look in his eye whenever he talks about him, a begrudging kind of respect for the man, even if he disagrees with his actions.

Jack Doyle is good in an emergency. That stoicism and *I know what I'm doing* attitude that I wanted to rip apart before is now what's keeping me from having a panic attack right there in the passenger seat. He doesn't bother with small talk or any talk for that matter for the rest of the ride, breaking the silence only to check in with Granny and make sure she's lucid.

He switches on the radio at some point, and I can only sit there as they talk about traffic jams and politics in between pop songs. It baffles me how the world can keep turning. How other people can keep continuing as normal when my world has been brought to a sudden, terrifying halt.

By the time we get to the hospital, I'm a wreck. Exhausted and emotional. I don't know whether I'm hungry or thirsty or both. But I'm too stressed out to figure it out as I sit in one of the hard plastic chairs and fill out all the details, my hands moving automatically across the page with all the information I've memorized over the years. Because despite my panic, I've prepared for this moment. I know all her security information, I know her medical history, I know her GP and her medical team, and I know which medications she is taking and the dosage of each. I know the side effects, even the ones she tries to hide from me.

It takes a very long time to answer all their questions, but it feels even longer once they leave me alone in the waiting room. Jack disappears, which I'm not surprised by, and I think I must zone out because the next time I'm aware of my surroundings, a nurse is standing in front of me and showing me the way to the ward.

It's quieter than I expected, even though it's visiting hours. Many of the beds have curtains drawn around them for privacy, but I can hear people talking on the other side, and I find myself absurdly grateful that she's not in a room by herself. I know she'd prefer to be alone, but I'm desperate for her to be around people. To know that if I can't always have eyes on her, other people do.

I'm led to the last bed in the room, one underneath a small window where my grandmother sits, propped up by a mound of pillows, waiting for me.

Despite my concern for her, I've never thought of Granny as frail before. Not once. She made up for her diminishing strength with sharp eyes and a sharper tongue, and had always seemed larger than life to me.

But she looks frail now. Frail and tired and very, very small.

"Nice to see you've made an effort for once."

I glance down at myself, almost surprised to see the pink skirts billowing over my knees. I'd forgotten I was still wearing the dress.

"You should have changed," Granny continues, sounding disapproving. "You've probably torn it."

"That's what you're... I was in a rush to get here," I protest. "Because I was saving your life."

She just huffs. "I wasn't going to die."

"You fell! You could have hit your head!"

"But I didn't." She's still looking askance at the dress. "You'll need to get that dry cleaned, you know."

"I know," I mutter, suddenly horribly aware of the thing. I must look like I stepped out of *Carrie* or something. I adjust the straps and take a seat in the chair beside the bed, placing the jumbo crossword book I got her in the gift shop on the nightstand.

Granny doesn't even spare it a glance. "Are you alright?"

"Am *I* alright? You're literally lying in a hospital bed." I scoot closer, feeling less worried and more annoyed as each second passes. "What happened?"

"Nothing," she says, but she looks a little embarrassed. "It was my own fault. Susan left and I was getting Plankton his breakfast. I was only wearing my slippers and I slipped and fell. It happens."

"It shouldn't happen." The last time it *did* happen, Granny hurt her hip so badly that she almost needed to get it replaced. "I should have been there."

"Don't be ridiculous."

"I should have," I say. "Blackouts are dangerous."

"It happened in the morning," she huffs. "It was broad daylight, and I slipped on the kitchen floor. I'm an old woman. It *happens*. I'm alright now, aren't I?"

She is. But what would have happened if I hadn't swung by the house first? What would have happened if Callum and I had gone straight to Kelly's or decided to stay longer at his? She could have been lying there for hours with no one to help her.

Just the thought of it makes my eyes sting and Granny sighs at the sight, reaching for my hand.

"You can't look after me twenty-four hours of the day," she says, her voice softening. "In fact, I don't want you to. We'd kill each other."

"We've managed so far," I say. "And we could always—"

"*Katie.*" She squeezes my fingers, looking exasperated. "You know this isn't your fault, don't you?"

"Yes."

But I must sound as unsure as I feel, because she just looks at me for a long moment before shaking her head. "Sometimes, I think I should have encouraged you to leave more when you were younger," she says. "Kicked you out of the house and packed you off to college whether you wanted to or not."

"You don't want me living with you?"

"Of course I do. Don't be ridiculous. But I know how much you've had to take on in the last few years. And I know how much I've let you. I don't intend to leave this life anytime soon, but the last thing I want for you is to spend the best years of yours worrying about me every moment."

"I don't do that."

"Don't you?"

I fall silent.

She's been there for me since my parents died and she's supposed to stay forever. And every time something like this happens, every time a task that once came easy to her becomes too difficult, every time we get instructions for new medication and new ways to live, it kills me a little inside. I didn't realize how long I've been waiting for something like this to happen. And how unprepared I still was for it.

"It's not your job to look after everyone," she says, when I don't respond. "Between me and the pub and your friends it's a miracle you're still standing most days."

"You sound like Gemma now."

"Well, a word of advice, Katie. If a single working mother says you're doing too much, you should probably listen."

"You're not too much," I chastise. "I like looking after you. I *want* to look after you. I love you."

"I know you do," she says, squeezing my hand again. "And I love you more than you can possibly imagine."

"So stop talking like you're—"

"Just let me get this out," she says with the same *you're giving me a headache* look I remember from my childhood. Even now, it shuts me up.

"I never expected to raise another child," she says finally. "And I'm still not sure how I didn't mess this up. How I didn't mess *you* up. Even when you were a teenager you were as good as gold. To the point where I almost wanted you to rebel, just to see what you'd do. I know how lucky I am to have you. I'm grateful every day for it, and I'm so proud of you. So proud. But..." She pauses then, her eyes growing damp. "But I know," she continues, a little more slowly. "That that pride would pale in comparison to how your parents would feel if they could see you now."

"Granny," I begin, and she shushes me, putting her other hand on top of our clasped ones.

"They loved you very much," she says. "So much it terrified them at the start. And I wish they could have seen how you've grown. I wish they got a chance to meet the exceptional young woman you turned out to be. You are hardworking, and generous, and you care deeply. I know you do. But life moves faster than you think. One day you might have a family of your own and you'll have to put them first. So right now, I want you to make time for you. I want you to make choices for you. For what *you* want. No matter if that's staying right where you are or traveling the world. I want you to be selfish because I know you can do that without being cruel. I want you to be happy. That's all I want in the whole world,

Katie. For you to look me in the eye and tell me you're happy."

"I am."

"But do you mean it?"

"*Yes*," I say. "I promise you. I promise that I'm happy. I promise I'm right where I need to be. Where I want to be."

She relaxes as I say the words, knowing I'm telling the truth. "Good," she says. "That's good."

"You sounded like you were saying goodbye," I accuse, and she scoffs.

"I have a few years left me in yet," she says. "You're not getting rid of me that easy."

She lets go of my hand, sniffing dramatically as she nods her head to the crossword book. "Well, pass me that. Might as well do something to pass the time here."

"As if you wouldn't be doing the exact same thing at home," I tell her and spend the next while dutifully reading out the clues and filling in the answers as she gets every single one right.

———

The nurse tells me it will be a while before I get an update and Granny grows tired, so I leave her to rest and head back to the waiting room, only to stop dead in the entrance.

Jack Doyle sits on the far side, his elbows propped on his knees, his head in his hands as he slowly rubs his face as though trying to wake himself up.

I am more than surprised to see him there. As grateful as I am for what he did, I thought when he disappeared earlier that he had left, having fulfilled his Good Samaritan duty. But instead, here he sits, waiting for me.

Before I can think twice about it, I fill two cups with water from the fountain and walk right over to him.

"Hi."

He jerks as if he's been electrocuted and sits up straight, looking embarrassed to have been caught slumping. "Is your grandmother okay?"

"I think so. I'll know more in a few hours." I offer him one of the cups, and he knocks it back like a shot of tequila as I take the seat next to him. "Why are you still here?"

"Someone has to drive you back."

"I'll get the bus."

He gives me a look like that's the most ridiculous thing he's ever heard. "There's no bus to Ennisbawn," he says, and I burst out laughing. It's a tired laugh, a slightly hysterical one. But I feel better at the end of it.

Jack, however, looks annoyed, like it's at his expense. "What?" he asks. "There's not."

"I know," I say, with a small hiccup. "You just reminded me of your brother."

Jack doesn't respond, eyeing his cup as though it contains a hundred different diseases.

"You know," I say. "Some people might think you *like* being the bad guy."

"They're right," he says flatly. "I love being hated for doing my job."

"You're not hated for doing your job. You're hated for how you do it."

"Successfully, you mean?"

"You didn't care," I say simply. "We knew we weren't going to stop the hotel. But it would have been easy enough to win us over. You just didn't care about us enough to do it. The leaflets weren't for us. The emails weren't. The boards and the promises. They were all for show. All for your boss, and so you had something to fall back on when we did push back. You were never going to listen, and you were never going to compromise."

"No."

"Why not?"

"Because you don't *matter*," he says, exasperated. "That's what's so irritating about this whole thing. Ennisbawn is nothing but a bunch of land. It's economically deprived and too small to even be on a map. I've never met people who had it so bad and yet were so keen on denying millions being pumped into your pockets."

"There's a difference between revitalizing an area and bulldozing it over to start again. We might not have been anything special, but we were happy as we were."

"It would have happened sooner or later," he dismisses. "And according to your own accounts, that pub had four, maybe five years, left before it went under and that's being generous."

"We would have found a way. We would have kept going."

"Why on earth would you want to if you're not making anything?"

"Because we don't have to!" I exclaim. "It's a small pub in a small village. We don't have to turn it into some money-making success. It doesn't have to bring in tourists or make us all rich. It can just be. And I'm sure there'll come a day when it's not needed. I'm sure one day it will close and that will be that. But not now."

I sit back, watching him watch me with a baffled expression.

"You still don't get it, do you?"

"*No*," he says, and he says it so forcefully, so *truthfully*, that I give up trying to convince him otherwise.

"Maybe you're right," I say, and I remember what Nush had said to me the other day. "Maybe Kelly's isn't special. Maybe it really is just four walls and a roof. But its people are special. We make it special. And we'll fight for it. Always."

"Well, I suppose you need something to do living out there," he mutters, and I almost smile.

"You're really not a small-town guy, are you?"

He shakes his head, looking bleak. "I never thought Callum was either. I should have known when he decided to rent out that damn farmhouse instead of getting somewhere in the city. He said he just wanted a shorter commute. But he actually seems to *like* that place." He says the last bit like the thought is unfathomable. "Or maybe he just likes you enough not to care."

"I think there's a compliment in there somewhere."

"We've just signed on for another project next year," he says, ignoring me. "A multi-block office development in Canary Wharf. It will be a good change of pace. They want a swimming pool on the roof of a skyscraper."

"That sounds dumb," I tell him. "And windy."

"It's big money. Great money. I'm going to offer Callum his job back."

I try not to show my unease at that. "And if he doesn't take it?"

"He will," he says decidedly. "It's a good opportunity. Good money. It'll be good for him."

Good for him.

The simple confidence in his voice has me feeling a sliver of doubt for the first time in days. They might not be talking to each other, but Jack's still his brother and he knows Callum a lot better than I do.

Jack vibrates next to me, or at least his pocket does, and when he takes out his phone, I realize how long it's been since I've checked my own.

It is, predictably, not good. My screen is filled with missed calls and texts from everyone I tried to call earlier. But most of them are from Callum, who's left me a string of messages on top of his missed calls. Concerned ones at first, turning sympathetic once Nush must have spoken with him. And then back to concern when I remained unresponsive throughout the day.

Shit.

Sorry, I start to text back before glancing at Jack, who's now wiping his hand with a wet wipe he must just carry around with him because, of course, he does. I know Callum's not going to like what I tell him next, but I don't want to lie to him. *Granny's doing okay. The nurse said she should be out by tomorrow at the latest. I tried to drive her to the hospital, but I couldn't do it, and Jack gave me a lift.*

I press send and drop the phone on my lap.

A second later, it starts to ring.

Jack looks down at it, his face settling into a scowl when he sees the Caller ID. "Someone doesn't trust me," he says, and then: "Aren't you going to pick it up?"

I should. I know I should. I know he's worried, but I cancel the call and text him instead.

It's okay. It was really nice of him.

Call me. NOW.

"Better do as he says before I get punched again."

"Stop reading my texts," I snap. Jack just rolls his eyes, settling back in his chair like I'm not even there. Not wanting him to eavesdrop on our conversation, I go out into the busy corridor and find a corner to call Callum.

He picks up immediately. "Are you okay?"

I feel instantly guilty at how relieved he sounds.

"I'm fine," I assure him. "We're waiting to see if they want to keep her in overnight. How's everything back home? Were people mad?"

"No, of course not. A lot of people were staying another night anyway. We're going to do the fireworks tonight."

"Thank God," I say, relieved. Granny's fall had put everything into perspective, but it was still my festival. "Are you alright to help Adam with the bar again?"

"He'll get someone else," he says. "I'm coming to you. Where are you? St. Mary's?"

"No, don't. I have no idea how long we're going to be. I'd prefer if you were in Ennisbawn."

"And I'd prefer to be with you. How are you going to get home?"

"Jack said he'll drive me."

Callum goes quiet. "He's still there?"

"Yeah. We're... well, we're not bonding exactly, but we're talking."

"Talking?"

"I'm as surprised as you are. He's a lot less of a dick when he loses."

"Katie—"

"I'm okay," I assure him. "Honestly. The nurse said they'll know more in a few hours, and I'll feel so much better if I don't have to worry about things back home. Please, Callum. To make up for the pancakes."

He huffs, but he sounds less worried now I'm making jokes. "Okay," he says. "If that's what you want me to do. But I want updates from you. Tell Jack to text me if you can't. I'll unblock his number."

"You blocked his—" I cut myself off, shaking my head. Brothers. "I'll text you," I say. "I promise. I—" *love you*. The two words are on the tip of my tongue, about to spill out of me so naturally it's almost frightening.

"Katie?"

"I'll see you tonight," I say, clearing my throat.

"Okay." He sounds confused, but I hang up before I make my life even messier and return to the waiting room to find Jack where I left him.

"You really don't have to stay here," I tell him, but he ignores me, scrolling through his emails until I sit beside him again.

"You should see someone," he says, when I do. "About your car thing."

I frown, thinking back to the noise the engine made. "It's a little old," I say defensively. "But it works fine. And we don't use it enough to—"

"Not a *mechanic*," he interrupts, like I'm an idiot. Which, yes, fine. "I mean a therapist."

"A therapist?"

"For your anxiety," he clarifies. "Have you seen one before?"

Not since I was a child. I did the usual "answering questions while I filled in a coloring book" thing and I'm pretty sure Granny took me to a grief counsellor, but no one since. "I don't really like to talk about it."

"You should," he says. "It would help. I can give you the name of someone, if you want."

His tone is offhand, his attention still on his phone, but I recognize an olive branch when I hear one.

"Thanks," I say, settling back in the chair. "That would be great."

And that's how I start my truce with Jack Doyle.

CHAPTER THIRTY-ONE

The doctors decide to keep Granny in overnight, a development neither of us is pleased about, but we don't really have a choice.

Jack insists that he should drop me straight home, that I need to rest, but a whole day has passed since the blackout, and I want to make sure everything is okay. So, despite his oddly well-meaning protests, I direct him through the village to the fireworks field, and he pulls up just as the first one is released into the sky. A loud cheer from the gathered crowd sounds as soon as it does, and for a moment, the two of us just sit there, before I twist in my seat to face him. "Do you want to join us?"

I have a sudden vision of welcoming Jack into the village fold. Of him and Callum embracing, of Jack maybe making a little speech, eating some popcorn, and undoing the top button of his shirt to show how he's a changed man. Instead, he just looks at me like I've grown two heads.

"Why would I want to do that?" he asks.

"I don't know. It just seems like something that should happen."

"Well, it's not going to," he says, unlocking the doors so I can get out. "I need a shower and a firm mattress. Out you get."

"But—"

"Out."

I do as I'm told, scrambling out onto the path as Jack drives off, disappearing into the night. Okay. One step at a time, I guess.

Taking a breath, I make my way over to the field. I spy Adam and Gemma standing side by side, close but not touching. Bridget is directing people to the best viewing spots, while Nush is doling out buckets of popcorn like it's the most important task in the world. I feel a rush of affection as soon as I see them, and I know they're waiting for me. I know I need to talk with them, but the thought of having to go over what happened, to deal with their concern, however well-meaning, sends a wave of exhaustion over me so strong I stop where I am.

And that's when I spot him.

Callum stands at the edge of the crowd, wearing a pair of jeans and a plain black T-shirt, a plastic pint glass in his hand as he nods at something Frank is saying.

He looks comfortable. He looks like he belongs, and my heart pangs at the thought. It's a new feeling, one I'm not sure what to make of yet.

The music grows louder, blaring a pop song everyone seems to know as the fireworks go off loosely in time with the beat. One particularly large one draws everyone's attention upward and, when it goes back down again, Callum's eyes land straight on mine, his smile fading as his easy expression morphs into one of concern.

And it's all suddenly too much. The emotions hit me one after the other. The stress of this morning, the anxious wait at the hospital, the relief that threatens to overwhelm me as soon as our eyes lock. It has been a bad day. A bad, long day and I have never felt more vulnerable.

I choke on a breath and turn, slipping through the crowd as I leave the crowded field behind and head back up the road to the village. Jack was right. I need sleep. I need a shower and a change of clothes and a few minutes to be alone. I need—

"Katie!"

I keep walking even as I glance over my shoulder, watching Callum weave between the villagers and the remaining guests, following me.

"I know you can hear me," he calls, when I start moving faster.

I hear him curse as I take off, running back up the path and onto the road that leads to home. Turns out, if you don't think about it too much, you can run pretty well in heels. The thing is not to second-guess yourself. To just keep going and barely touch the ground.

It almost feels nice. Stretching my legs like this. Maybe Plankton's onto something. Maybe I should run more often. Maybe I should be that kind of person. Maybe—

"Ow! Mother— ow!" I stumble to a stop, almost tripping as a sharp pain spikes up my calf.

Callum's on me in a second, grabbing me by my waist, so I don't fall. "What's wrong?" he asks, alarmed. "What is it?"

"Cramp."

"What?"

"Cramp," I hiss, not caring that I'm being ridiculous. "Ow, ow, freaking ow."

"You shouldn't have run in these shoes."

"I wouldn't have run if you hadn't chased me."

"I'm supposed to chase you."

"Says who!"

"Says everyone!" he snaps and leads me off the path into a small field.

"What do I do?" I moan, the pain not abating.

He guides me to the earth, first so that I'm sitting, and then presses my shoulders until I get the hint and lie down, the grass cool but dry as it cushions my body.

"What are you doing?"

"Helping you, you idiot. Which leg?"

I point to my right one, and he grabs it and slowly stretches it upward.

"Is that better?"

"No."

His frown deepens and he grabs the heel of my shoe, tossing it to the side. The skirt of my dress parts, giving him a clear view of my underwear, but his focus is on my foot as he covers my arch with a warm hand, pressing on it firmly as he pushes my leg higher. Immediately the pain abates.

"Okay," I gasp. "Keep doing that."

The music still blares from the party, but we're so far away that all I can hear is the muffled beat of it. The fireworks, however, might as well be right beside us the way they light up the sky directly overhead. It's completely dark out here otherwise, but they illuminate us every few seconds in blues, reds, and greens before fading again.

"What about now?" Callum asks after another minute.

I flex my leg experimentally, finding none of the discomfort I'd felt earlier. And though a part of me doesn't want him to stop touching me, I nod and he lets me go, gently lowering my foot to the ground.

"Are you going to start running again?"

"No," I mutter. "Emotional outburst done." I'm embarrassed, but he just nods, collapsing to the grass next to me.

"You'll stain your—"

"I don't care," he says, pressing his fingers to the bridge of his nose. "How's Maeve?"

"Scared," I say. "But she's okay. The doctor said she can come home tomorrow."

"Then why are you upset?"

"I don't know," I say, and I know the answer's not good enough for him even though it's true.

"Did Jack say something to you?"

"No. Yes. I don't know."

"You're freaking me out, you know that?"

"Sorry." I blink up at the sky, trying to control my thoughts and my fears and my wants as they scatter in a million directions, clashing with each other until I can't tell which is which. "I've had a long day."

Some of the tension leaves his body at my words, and his hand finds mine by my side.

"Jack said he's going to offer you your job back," I say, keeping my gaze trained up. "For that big office development in London. It sounds pretty cool, actually. They're going to have a swimming pool on the roof of a skyscraper."

"Sounds like a dumb idea to me," he says, echoing my own words.

"Yeah." I wet my lips. "Exciting though."

I can feel him staring at me, but he waits until I look at him before he speaks.

"What's happening right now?"

"I don't want to leave here." I say the words slow and clear, leaving no room for doubt. "I have never wanted to leave here. This place has been the one constant in my life and, even if it changes, even if it no longer stays the Ennisbawn I grew up in, I can't imagine living anywhere else. I don't want to."

"I know that."

"Right." I clear my throat. "But I also know that's not for everyone."

There's a long moment of silence as he understands what I'm trying to say. "You mean, not for me," he says flatly.

"No."

"Why not?"

"Because you'll get bored." I press my lips together as soon as I say the words, mortified as my biggest self-conscious thought comes tumbling out.

Callum looks shocked. "You think I'll get bored of you?"

"Maybe not of *me*," I say. "But of this life, yeah. It's not for everyone. And you said you wanted to travel, start your business. That you wanted to find something more. You're not going to find that here. This is it. Believe me."

"Katie—"

"And I mean, sure, it's all fun and games now," I say, starting to babble. "There's a lot to do with the festival and it's sunny and nice and the lavender is out. But it gets cold in the winter. It gets cold and it rains, and there's nothing to do and nothing ever really changes. And I'm okay with that. I like that because I like it here. And yet, for my entire adult life, people have looked at me like I'm the wrong one for feeling like that. Like I'm some poor, confused child who doesn't know any better. You asked me yourself why I never left, and I get it, I do, and you... you might need more than this. So eventually, yeah. You'll get bored. You'll leave."

Callum doesn't say anything for a long moment, his expression unreadable in the darkness, and then, seriously, so seriously he almost sounds mad, he asks, "When have I ever suggested you leave this place? When have I ever suggested you need to change your life? That you need to go somewhere new and be someone new?"

"You—"

"Never," he interrupts. "I've never wanted you to be anything more than who you are. Katie, I am in *awe* of you. I've spent my life trying to figure out what made me happy, what I wanted to do with my days if I was brave enough to try. I never found it. Not until I came here. I came here, and there you were, putting everything on the line because you knew what you had and refused to let it go." He pushes himself up with one arm so he can look down at me. "I thought you were just being stubborn, but I get it now. I told you already that I made my choice, and my choice is you. What part of that didn't you understand?"

"It's only been a few months," I say weakly.

"So?" he retorts. "You think I don't know my own heart? You think I don't know when I've found a good thing? How can I get bored of this place if it's where you are? How can I get tired of it when all you need to do is stand there breathing and you have my full attention? Katie, for the first time in my life, I feel like I've found a place I can call home. And I'm not saying I know what's going to happen. No one does. And if you don't want me to stick around because you don't see a future with me, because you never intended for this to get serious, then I'll respect that, of course I will. But if you don't want me because you're scared of something bigger? Because you can't handle the fact that I'm falling in love with you? Then that's a whole different conversation we need to have. And if you think I'm going to just let you run away from that, then you don't know me at all."

He falls back down to the grass, scowling at the sky. "You told me once that Kelly's was your favorite place in the world. Well, you're mine. You're mine and I'll go where you go. For as long as you want me to, I'll be right there with you."

I watch him for a moment, a little speechless but unable to ignore the one very important thing he just told me. "You're falling in love with me?"

"Understatement of the century," he mutters, rubbing his face like he wants to wake himself up.

"Since when?"

"I don't know. Forever?" He sounds pissed off and he must realize it because he takes an audible breath, forcing himself to calm. "Or maybe from the moment you stomped across the construction site in your pajamas and jabbed a finger in my brother's face. You think the guys were happy with me rerouting our entire traffic route? I wanted an excuse to see you again. Wanted you to think I was a good guy. I couldn't get you out of my head and I didn't want to. I still don't want to."

A particularly loud firework explodes above us, but I keep my attention on him, watching his eyes trace the bursts of light.

"So maybe I'm not falling in love with you," he murmurs. "Maybe I'm already there." He tilts his head to face me and we're so close now I can feel his breath on my lips. "I'm in love with you, Katie Collins. And I'll choose you every time."

We stay like that, watching each other until his expression softens into one of faint amusement.

"Not that you have to say it back, but—"

"Crap. Sorry. No, I do. I love you too."

He laughs as my face heats in embarrassment.

"Sorry," I repeat. "It's because I was listening to your big proclamation."

"Is that what that was?"

I nod. "About how you're so devoted to me."

He smirks but doesn't deny it as I close the space between us and press my lips to his.

"I love you," I whisper. "I love you, I love you, I love you. And I want you here. I want you with me."

"Well, that's good," he murmurs. "Makes my life a lot easier."

He kisses me until a faint cheer rises from the field, and I break away at the sound, looking behind us as gold ribbons spiral upward.

"You want to go back?" he asks, starting to sit up, but I shake my head. "You sure? It's your moment of glory."

"I'm good."

He lies back down, and I nestle into him, resting my head on his chest as he wraps an arm around me. His body is completely relaxed beneath mine, but I can feel his heart thumping in a way that belies his outer calmness, the beat perfectly matched with the frantic pounding of my own.

As we watch, the promised hearts finally appear in the sky, and I swear I can hear the oohs and ahhs coming from the crowd. But I don't move. I don't want to move. I'm exactly where I need to be.

"Callum?"

"Yeah?" He kisses the crown of my head, and I burrow into his side.

"You're my favorite place too."

CHAPTER THIRTY-TWO

They keep Granny in for another day, just to be sure, before finally letting her go home. She's shaken, but otherwise uninjured, and when Callum drives the two of us back, we find a brand-new ramp installed by the front door, courtesy of Jack, according to the men who installed it. Plankton is also beside himself. The two days might as well have been two decades with how he acts when he sees her again and he doesn't leave her side, not even to go to the bathroom. I'll admit I'm equally as cautious for the first twenty-four hours, watching the woman like a hawk, even though I know it annoys her. But eventually I'm pulled back to my other responsibilities and resume the rest of my neglected life.

It's a little strange how quickly the village empties, and even stranger how odd it feels once they do. Even though it's normal and is how it always is, I can't help but feel like Ennisbawn is a little like a ghost town over the next few days. A small part of me even starts to look forward to the hotel opening, to people walking around. But right now, I have to deal with more pressing matters.

The cleanup.

"Have you figured out where we're going to store all this stuff?" Gemma asks, as Nush lays another bag of bunting by my feet.

"That's a problem for tomorrow."

"That's what you said yesterday."

"And it still stands," I say, as Adam sticks his head through the back door of the pub. He and Noah have been clearing out the wishing well all morning and his face is already a little sunburned.

"Is Callum here yet? I need his help lifting something."

"He went back to his to get some packing tape," I say, checking the time on my phone. "But he should be back any minute."

"I can lift things," Nush says.

"You weigh a hundred pounds."

"Yeah, of muscle."

He turns back to me. "Send him out when he's here, yeah?"

"You've got it."

"Half of lifting is *how* you lift," Nush argues, following him out to the patio. I head out front, wondering where Callum got to.

I don't have to wonder for long.

I spot the Jeep first, gleaming in the sunlight. And then I spy the brothers next to it. I immediately tense, watching the two of them talk. The body language is... not great. They both stand rigidly, several feet apart. I know Callum still hasn't spoken with Jack since their argument and every time I've tried to bring it up (which has been *frequently* the last few days), he either ignores me or kisses me to shut me up.

But he obviously got tired of waiting and it's Jack who spots me first, nodding over Callum's shoulder to where I linger. I relax a little at the grin Callum sends me and don't hesitate when he beckons me to them.

"Everything alright?" I ask, trying to sound more blasé than hopeful.

"Everything's great," Callum says. He draws me into his side, that grin still plastered across his face. "Jack has something he'd like to say."

Jack gives him a look. "Seriously?"

"Oh, extremely. After you."

I shoot Callum a confused look as Jack turns stiffly to me. "Katie, I wanted to apologize for the last few months. Both regarding my handling of Kelly's and your relationship with my brother. I hope you can forgive me."

"He's been doing a lot of soul searching," Callum whispers, earning himself a sharp look.

"I have *not*," Jack says. "You're just—"

"Apology accepted," I interrupt, not wanting another fight on my hands. Brothers. "Thanks, Jack."

"And thanks for looking after her and Maeve," Callum says, turning serious. "I'll never forget it." He starts forward, only to stop when Jack grimaces.

"What?" Callum grins. "Afraid I'll wrinkle your suit?"

"Yes, actually I— okay." Jack stiffens as his brother draws him in for a hug. "Alright, thank you."

Callum takes pity on him, slapping him on the back before releasing him.

"We don't have to hug," I tell Jack, when his eyes go to me. He looks relieved.

"You're good here?" he asks in a careful tone, and Callum nods.

"I am," he says. The two words so simple yet meaning so much.

The brothers stare at each other for a moment and then Jack clears his throat. "I'll see you in two weeks," he says with a businesslike nod before turning to me. "You'll be fine."

I'm a little confused by that last comment, but I wait until he returns to his car before I nudge Callum.

"What's in two weeks?"

"Family dinner," he says pleasantly, and I go rigid.

"What?"

"My parents are visiting the area. They invited you."

"They... what?"

"They found a nice restaurant in the city. I hope you like seafood."

"I'm meeting your *parents*?"

"You don't want to?"

"Of course I want to!" I exclaim. "But didn't you hear my accent story?"

"I'll warn them in advance." His eyes slide to mine, his expression softening when he sees how nervous I look. "Seriously, Katie. Relax. They'll love you."

"You can't know that. How do you know that?"

"Because I love you. And I'm the favorite child."

That doesn't make me feel any better, but he grabs my hand before I can worry further and leads me around the pub to where the others have joined Adam and Noah by the well.

When we stopped being able to hear splashes of water at the bottom of it, we figured we'd better bring all the contents up. Adam's getting a professional to come out and look at it next week, but, for now, we're having fun with an old-fashioned rope and bucket situation to dig up our treasure. So far, as well as the expected coins, we found a fifty-dollar note sealed in a ziplock bag, a *wedding ring* that we've already posted online, hoping to reunite with its owner, and a number of trinkets, charms, and thingamabobs that make me think most people don't know how wishing wells work. Then again, it's not like there's a rule book. Shoot your shot, I guess.

"We're putting up a sign next year," Adam says, when he spots me. "Only coins allowed."

He plucks a stuffed animal from the bucket to prove his point and tosses it to Nush, who adds it to her collection.

"I found another ten euro," Noah says, rifling through his own pile. He stares at the plastic bag for a long second before handing it over. "What are we going to do with all of it?"

Gemma makes another note on her spreadsheet. "We're giving it to a children's charity."

"*I'm* a child," he points out, and she ducks her head to hide her smile.

Callum meets my eye and nods toward the back door, which Adam just disappeared through. My good mood vanishes, replaced by nerves and a distinct feeling of *I don't wanna*, but he just gives me a look, ignoring my pout until I force myself to head inside.

The door to his office is open, but I knock on it anyway, swinging inside to see Adam working on his laptop.

"Hey, boss."

"Hi there." He does a double glance, pausing when he sees the look on my face. "You seem chirpy."

"I'm always chirpy."

"You're right. I guess the word I'm looking for is smug."

"And I'm always smug. I just hide it well." I close the door, ignoring the urge to put myself back on the other side. "Do you have a minute?"

"Sure."

"Really? Because I can come back."

He gives me a patient smile. "What do you need, Katie?"

I take a seat by his desk, immediately forgetting the entire speech I'd planned. And I mean all of it. Every word. Gone. And Adam lets me sit there and stare at him for approximately ten seconds before he realizes it. "What's up?"

"I want a raise." The words spill out of me, each one tripping over the other to the point where I'm not sure they're actually decipherable, but Adam's expression doesn't change.

"A raise?"

"Yes," I say. "I think I deserve a promotion."

"A promotion or a raise?"

"...both."

"Okay." He settles back, lacing his hands across his stomach as he nods for me to continue.

"I know margins are tight," I begin. "And I know with the new pub at the hotel, they're going to be even tighter. But I think I've more than proven my loyalty to this place. I work hard. I never miss a shift except when I'm sick. My theme nights have gone down a treat, and I am always looking for ways to improve how we do business. I've also helped you with finances the last two years and, therefore, I know we have some wriggle room in the budget, and with everything I've done the last few months, I think I more than deserve to take the next step in my career and—"

"I agree."

"—help you run this place on a more..." I trail off, blinking at him. "You do?"

"Yes."

"With what?"

"All of it."

"Oh. I mean, good," I add hastily, trying not to sound too surprised. "Great."

"I've been thinking about it for a while," he continues, while I just sit there, buzzing. "Before everything happened with Glenmill. But I was waiting to see if you wanted to spread your wings a bit first. The last thing I wanted to do was tie you down here."

"Very considerate," I agree. "So, what are you thinking? Because I'm thinking head bartender."

"I was thinking business partner."

"I know the title is a bit of leap, but I think it will... come again?"

"You got a hundred quid?"

"On me?"

He grins and I freak inwardly. Adam doesn't grin. I don't think I've ever seen him grin in my life, but he's looking at me now like he's got some big secret and is waiting for me to catch up.

It takes me a second. A very long one.

"Nu-uh."

"You said you wanted a promotion."

"Yeah, but I meant like a normal one. I can't own a pub."

"Co-own."

"I mean, surely, I need a business degree or something," I say, ignoring him.

He just shrugs. "I have one and I barely use it."

"Yeah but—"

"You have more than a decade's worth of experience, which is more than I had when I took over. You worked your way up and you've never complained once. You've mopped floors and cleaned toilets and you're right; your theme nights do go down a treat. You know every one of our regulars. You know every drink on our menu. You push me to go further and stand your ground when I push back. There's a reason this place was left standing when all the others closed. When my dad owned it, it was nothing but a couple of grumpy men drinking the same sad pints every night. Now, it's a place to be proud of. It's a place for everyone and the only reason it's not a pile of bricks is because you showed everyone how much you love it. And for all of those reasons and a dozen more, I'd like you to be my partner in it."

Voices sound on the other side of the door, laughing and joking with each other, but they barely register as I stare at the man before me, the man who's been my boss for the past ten years. Who's been my teacher and my friend and as close to family as you can get without being related. Who's just offered me my dream job.

"Holy freaking shit, Adam."

Thankfully, he's spent enough time around me to know

what I mean. "Is that a yes?"

"*Yes*. I don't know what to say. I... and just to confirm, this comes with more money?"

"It comes with more money."

"And can we get business cards?"

"No."

"Can we take a photo for the bar?"

"Sure."

"And can we—"

"Knock, knock."

I spin around as the door opens and Gemma sticks her head inside. "I'm taking Noah to football," she says, before her gaze lands on me. "What's up with you, little Miss Smiley Face?"

"I think I just bought a pub," I say, and she smirks, not looking even a little bit surprised. "You *knew*?" I ask.

"He told me the other day. Congratulations."

I glance between them, annoyed. "So that's how it's going to be? You two talking about us behind our backs and swapping secrets?"

"We've been doing that for years," she says dryly, before turning to Adam. "I'll stop by later?"

He nods, *painfully* casually, and she leaves without another word.

"Don't," Adam says, when I twist back to him with a knowing smile.

"Don't what?"

"We're taking things slow. And we're keeping it quiet."

"But that's not fun for me."

"We've got to think about Noah."

"Oh, please, Noah's looked up to you since he moved here."

Adam's expression wipes clean even as the tips of his ears turn pink. I take pity on the man, too happy for him to tease him and too scared that he'll renege on his offer if I piss him off too much.

"I'd better get back to work," I say. "At the pub I own."

"Co-own. I'll get my solicitor to draw up some... Okay, we can hug."

He doesn't really have a choice, seeing as how I've lurched forward and wrapped my arms around him already. Callum was onto something here. I mean, sure it's a more awkward angle than he had with Jack, but Adam and I make the best of it.

"What's this for?" he asks, when I hold on to him a little longer than is probably professionally appropriate.

"For being like a dad to me," I tell him, my voice muffled in his shoulder. "For letting me do my homework here because I didn't want to be alone. For giving me a job even when you didn't have to. For looking after me my whole life."

"What was I supposed to do, lock you outside? You were very persistent as a nine-year-old. And you're very persistent now. I've always admired that."

I give him one last squeeze and sit back, wiping my eyes.

"No," he says immediately. "No crying in the office. You've got to leave now."

"I'm going to look up karaoke machines," I tell him, and leave before he can say otherwise.

The lounge is quiet, with everyone outside enjoying the sun. But it's not empty. Callum stands alone at the bar, drumming his fingers against the wood and waiting for me. My heart squeezes a little at the mere sight of him, even as he raises a brow and makes a show of checking his watch.

"Service is terrible around here."

I smirk, slipping into my usual spot behind the counter. "Sorry about that, sir. What can I get you?"

"I'll try one of those cocktails I keep hearing so much about."

I drop all pretense of being cool. "Really?" The word comes out like an excited squeak, and he grins. Oh my God. *Finally.* "What do you want?"

"Something that makes me look cool."

"*Or* something with strawberry lemonade and edible glitter."

"Or that," he says seriously, and I fly around getting what I need. It takes around five minutes, but Callum waits patiently as I mix everything together before presenting him with a tall, colorful drink that honestly looks amazing, if I say so myself.

It's ruined only slightly by me shoving a Christmas napkin under it, but we really do need to use them up. "It's on the house."

"No, it's not," Adam yells from the back room. "Not with how much those ingredients cost me."

That reminds me. "Hey," I call back to him. "If I'm half in charge now, does that mean I get to put my drinks on the menu?"

"If your boyfriend keeps buying them, it does," he says, and swings the door shut in a clear Adam signal of *I have work to do.*

"Did you say half in charge?" Callum asks. "I'm guessing your talk went well then."

"You could say that," I tell him. "You're looking at the new co-owner of Kelly's. Either he thinks I'll be an excellent business partner, or he's secretly saddling me with a load of debt."

"That does sound like the kind of thing he'd do," he says, leaning over the bar to kiss me. "Congratulations."

"Thank you. Do that again."

He does. Only this time, when he pulls back, I'm ready, grabbing the front of his shirt and holding him to me, tasting the sugar on his lips.

"Guys?"

And promptly letting him go again.

I huff as I break away, settling back on my side of the bar as Nush barges into the pub, dangling something from her fingers.

"I think someone dropped their keys down the well?"

EPILOGUE

ONE YEAR LATER

They're calling it a heatwave. Last week it was a warm spell. But now it's a heatwave. More than one sunburned body is walking around the village, and I've already had to redo my makeup twice today because it keeps melting away. I'm pretty sure it's only the battered fan in the corner that's stopping it from doing so now.

I reach for my powder just in case, only to hesitate as a burst of laughter sounds from close by.

The noise outside the tent has grown louder in the last thirty minutes. The good weather pushed people through Kelly's quicker than we planned, and it sounds like nearly all of them have now made their way outside, waiting for the show to begin. Waiting for me. Abandoning my makeup, I peek through the flaps, even though I know it will just make me more nervous. I can't see much from where I am, just the edge of the crowd, but everyone I *can* see is dressed to perfection, clinking champagne flutes as they gather in small groups. News of the festival spread far and wide last summer, and we sold out within minutes of this year's announcement. We were the hottest ticket in town, and everyone was excited.

Everyone except me, who feels like throwing up.

I turn back to the mirror, adjusting the straps of my dress and checking for sweat patches as Gemma slips into the tent, wearing a simple black dress and looking like she just came off the runway.

"Are you ready?"

My answering smile fools neither of us.

"It will be over before you know it," she says, grabbing my powder brush and dabbing my upper lip.

I'd prefer it if it was over now. "Is Callum here yet?"

"He's finding a seat for Maeve," she says, and I nod. Granny recovered well after her fall last year. I thought it might have scared her a little bit, but if anything, it's made her more active, like she's trying to prove a point both to the doctors and to herself. She's stronger than ever, and I was grateful for it. Not only because I loved her and wanted her well, but also because it meant she was able to take full control of the matchmaking this year, which meant I was able to steer clear of it. Really, it was a win for all of us.

"Just take deep breaths," Gemma continues. "But remember the news crew is in the corner by the benches, and they have a second camera by the dance floor, so if you need to—"

"You're not helping."

"Right. Sorry." She presses her lips together as Nush steps inside, holding her long glittery skirt out of the way.

"Okay, the last bus is here so we need to... oh." Nush tilts her head, taking in my outfit with a frown. "You went with the yellow?"

"Ignore her," Gemma says firmly. "You look beautiful."

"I didn't say she didn't look beautiful," Nush protests. "I just thought we'd decided on the teal suit."

"I'll be too hot in that," I say.

"But—"

"She's just afraid you're going to upstage her," Gemma says dryly, and Nush bristles.

"Well, it's rude to upstage the bride."

"You're not a bride! And Monica hasn't even said yes yet. You haven't even asked her."

Nush ignores her, striding forward to unclip my hair, which barely starts to fall before she twists it into an effortless braid that would take me forty minutes to accomplish and her two.

"She's obviously going to say yes," she mutters. "Have you seen the ring?"

We have. And it's beautiful.

Nush and Monica have been inseparable since they met, and it was only a few months after the festival that they started living together, with Monica moving into her apartment above the salon.

She's been planning to propose for weeks but can't decide on how to do it, her plans growing more and more elaborate with each passing day. She wanted to do it at the festival. Then in Paris. Then New York. But I have a sneaking suspicion that nothing will be good enough, and she'll end up blurting out the question one random evening when they're both wearing sweatpants and eating takeout. Either that or Monica will ask first.

"The last bus is here," she says to me now, a small line between her brows as she finishes off my hair. "The driver said the last drop back to the hotel is one a.m., and anyone who misses it will just have to walk. I liked him."

The hotel. Or to use its full name, The Ennisbawn Hotel & Golf Club, the thorn in our side which opened to great fanfare two months ago, just in time for the tourist season. They had a red carpet featuring high-heeled influencers and famous golfers, and the man who reads the news when the usual people are on their day off. And all of Ennisbawn, of course.

Everyone accepted their invitations, too curious not to, and we descended en masse on the party, with a stubborn few of us determined to hate everything in sight.

And while Nush was still emailing the hotel management about some issue or another every other week, the rest of us grudgingly admitted that it wasn't that bad.

It was kind of nice, actually. They built a beautiful space. Big and bright with views over the forest. Once the higher-ups changed their tune about how to deal with us, it became easier to wrangle back access to old walking routes and get included in planning decisions before they were passed and not afterward. But it was still different.

We didn't get everything we asked for, and it would never be the village that we once knew, but we were adapting to it, we were making the best of it, and we were learning to work together.

Only right now, I really wish that I could work alone. At least for a little bit.

Nush sniffs. "Are you okay? You smell nervous."

"How do I *smell* nervous?"

"You just do," she says as my mouth drops open.

Gemma glares at her. "You're fine. Don't listen to her."

"I am not fine. Nush is right. I am nervous, and you are making me more nervous, and I just need a moment to— oh, for the love of God."

"What did I do?" Adam asks, appearing through the flaps.

"This is supposed to be my freakout tent," I remind them, as Nush sprays perfume over my head. "Mine. My therapist said I needed space to prepare. *Alone.* Nush, tell them I'll be right out. Gemma, check with Bridget if we've got any no-shows. Adam... *Adam.*"

My business partner drags his gaze away from Gemma's dress. "What?"

I manage to hold back my smile.

Unlike Nush, who's thrown herself headfirst into all that

love has to offer, Gemma and Adam have taken things slow. Snail pace slow. It was months before they made it official and, even then, they were so quiet about it I got scared they'd secretly called it off. And then, early one morning I passed Gemma's house on my way to the pharmacy and caught Adam creeping out, looking like he had just woken up. I almost screamed in his face I was so happy, even though he acted like it was the worst thing that had ever happened to him.

Even now, they're still very much *dating*. Game nights, dinners, trips to the cinema. They still live apart and act the same as they always did whenever they're in public.

But maybe that's less because they're trying to be low-key and more because that's just the way it's always been. Adam has always been a part of Gemma's life. A part of Noah's. So from the outside, it's like they're carrying on as normal. It's only if you're looking that you notice (and I am always looking because I'm someone who's happy for her friends but also a big giant creep). But it's sweet, the shared glances and the small touches, the way she heads straight over to him now as though it's inconceivable she'd be anywhere else.

"We're ready to go," he says to me, as she adjusts the collar of his shirt.

"So everyone keeps telling me. Go away. I'll be out in a minute."

"But we need to—"

"I'm not listening," I tell them. "I'm doing my breathing exercises and I'm not listening."

They indulge me, one by one trickling out until I'm left alone. But my solitude barely lasts ten seconds before the tent opens again.

"I *said* go awa— oh. Hi."

Callum lets the flap fall behind him, watching me with amusement. "The freakout tent is living up to its name, huh?"

"I thought you were Nush."

"We do look alike," he deadpans, before his eyes drop to my dress. "And you look beautiful."

"So do you," I say, taking in the simple black suit. I've never known anyone who can look as comfortable in mud-stained overalls and tailored formal wear as he does. Or pull it off as well.

"You got your notecards just in case?" he asks, and I nod. I was giving the opening speech. I still hated public speaking though I was trying to get better at it, and while once I started talking things went okay, it was the waiting beforehand that made me spiral. "A missive from my brother," Callum adds, handing me his phone.

Best of luck. Jack.

"How sweet," I say dryly, passing it back to him. But I kind of mean it. I've learned a lot about Jack in the past year, and while I wouldn't say we were firm friends, we weren't exactly enemies either. He'd left Glenmill a few months after Gerald threw him under the bus, took precisely one week off, and then started work at an equally impressive company at an equally high position. He's now working on some luxury apartment development in Dublin, but comes down to visit surprisingly often, sometimes going so far as to sleep on Callum's couch when he ends up staying too late to drive back.

Coming downstairs to him snoring away is something I don't think I'll ever get used to, but it's kind of nice to know he's as human as the rest of us.

I moved into Callum's farmhouse six months ago. He wanted it to happen a lot sooner, but he was patient with me, knowing it was a big step for me to leave Granny and the house I grew up in. But when the time finally did come, it felt easy. It felt right. I fit into his space as effortlessly as he fit into mine and it wasn't until I had it that I realized how much I craved waking up to him at the start of the day, how much I wanted to kiss him goodnight at the end of it. Being with him was as easy as breathing and I wouldn't change it for the world.

He was a huge support when I took on the extra responsibilities at the pub, and in return I got to be there for him when he did exactly what he said he was going to, taking a few guys he trusted from Glenmill, and starting a business of his own. I don't think a day goes by when he's not excitedly updating me about some new deal he's struck or an abandoned building he's found. It makes my heart sing that's he happy, and even more so that I get to be a part of it.

"Katie?"

"Yeah?"

"You keep looking at me like that and you're definitely going to be late," he says, and I blush, turning back to the mirror for one final check.

"Are you ready?"

"Yes." A lie.

"Will I ruin your makeup if I kiss you?"

"No." Another lie, but I don't care, meeting his lips with my own and taking comfort in the familiar.

"You've got this," he whispers, and takes my hand, pulling me outside to where Nush is waiting.

She hands me a microphone with a beaming smile and Callum gives my hand one final squeeze before I climb the few steps to the makeshift stage where Danny's band waits to start playing.

It's one of those perfect summer evenings, the heat of the day finally fading as the sun sets and twilight takes over. Swaths of pink and purple streak across the sky and the lanterns which Adam and Noah had spent a whole day putting up glow with warm yellow light.

Hundreds of pairs of eyes gaze up at me, and among them I

pick out my friends and neighbors among them. My family. My people.

Callum takes position at the front, winking when our gazes meet, but the moment is ruined a second later when Nush joins him and gestures to her chest. *Boobs out*, she mouths, and I smile as I turn my gaze to the crowd and turn on the microphone.

"My name is Katie Collins," I say, holding my head high. "And on behalf of the people of this village, I'd like to welcome you all to the annual Ennisbawn Matchmaking Festival."

A LETTER FROM CATHERINE

Dear Reader,

Thank you so much for reading *The Matchmaker*! I hope you enjoyed Katie and Callum's story.

If you want to keep up to date with my latest releases, you can sign up for my newsletter at the following link. Your email address will never be shared and you can unsubscribe at any time.

www.bookouture.com/catherine-walsh

If you liked *The Matchmaker*, and I really hope you did, I would be so grateful if you could spare the time to write a review. It makes such a difference in helping new readers to discover one of my books for the first time. I also love hearing from my readers—you can get in touch on my Twitter page, through Instagram, or my website.

All my best,

Catherine xx

catherinewalshbooks.com

 twitter.com/CatWalshWriter
instagram.com/catwalshwriter

ACKNOWLEDGMENTS

My apologies in advance to everyone I will again forget to put in here. I always have to write these in the middle of weeks of edits and my brain is nothing but commas and slush right now. But I am, as always, going to do my best.

Rachel, this book is dedicated to you, but I hope you know that *all* my books are secretly dedicated to you because I truly don't know where I would be if I hadn't had your support over the years. Thank you for always being my first reader, editor, and champion as well as my personal book recommendation service. I love you lots and I'm so thankful for your friendship.

Áine, thank you for putting up with constant daily updates about everything in my life and, most importantly, for letting me use your Canva account. Tilda, I'm amazed you're still speaking to me. Truly amazed. What an idiot you are for being my friend. I'm grateful every day for it and hope you never realize what a mistake you've made or else I'm screwed. Bex, thank you for all the book photoshoots, and for making a Big Deal out of things because you know I secretly want people to.

Isobel, thank you so much for all your support and editorial expertise. However, I can't believe you left me for an exciting and totally deserved career move. I will never forgive you. Susannah, I feel like you took me on at peak dramatic author stage. I promise I am usually very normal and chill. Thank you for all the pep talks, wonderful guidance, and book recommendations.

To my agent, Hannah Schofield, who I signed with in the

middle of writing this draft. Thank you for all your enthusiasm and support these past few months. I can't wait for all the books to come! To my incredible cover designer Beth, who always gives me the most beautiful covers in the world. To all my author friends (yeah, I know people), especially Danielle, Kristen, and Jo for letting me moan and complain and celebrate at all hours of the day. This job can be isolating and maddening, so thank you for keeping me sane. This also extends to all my family and friends who reached out with words of encouragement even though they're getting really tired of the whole "she keeps writing books" thing. Sorry.

Special thanks to my parents for this one. To my dad for giving me a detailed rundown of planning laws in Ireland and the idea of a golf course. To Mam for being a constant rock for me these past few years and for always picking up the phone.

Finally, a big thank you to all the bloggers, reviewers, readers, and all cool girls online who have said hi to me these past few months. I'm so grateful to have gotten to know so many of you and am so thankful for all your support. Unfortunately, you can never stop supporting me now. There is no escape.

Printed in Great Britain
by Amazon

30979913R00196